My Reckless Heart

My Reckless Heart

Jo Goodman

Five Star
Unity, Maine

Published in 2001 by arrangement with Zebra Books,
an imprint of Kensington Publishing Corporation.

Set in 11 pt. Plantin by Al Chase.

Printed in the United States on permanent paper.

Library of Congress Cataloging-in-Publication Data

Goodman, Jo, 1953–
   My reckless heart / Jo Goodman.
     p.   cm. — (Thorne brothers trilogy ; #2)
   ISBN 0-7862-2947-0 (hc : alk. paper)
   1. Ship captains — Fiction. 2. Boston (Mass.) — Fiction.
   3. Seafaring life — Fiction. 4. Brothers — Fiction.
   I. Title.
   PS3557.O58374 M89 2001
   813'.54—dc21   00-064630

For Donna Doo-dah . . .
This is small thanks.

Prologue

London, October 1820

It started with a handkerchief. Edged with lace, monogrammed with the letter *R* and hinting of the scent of musk and roses, Decker would never have difficulty calling it to mind. It was the first thing he learned to steal.

"Here, boy. Keep your wits about you and take it out of my pocket." The trick, of course, was to do so without being detected. A difficult maneuver at best, what with two pairs of very interested eyes following his every move. An impossible maneuver, perhaps, given the fact Decker Thorne was only four.

"He's nervous, *cher.*" This observation was offered in a lightly accented, melodious voice. The owner of the voice was a woman whose kind and concerned expression softened her sky blue eyes. "And the carriage is bouncing. How can he do it?"

The badly sprung carriage was indeed bouncing. Decker toppled forward as the driver veered around a milk wagon. He was caught between the man and woman and set back in his place only to have a collision with a rut almost unseat him again. His small, sturdy legs churned to keep him from being ejected from the padded leather seat to the floor. The movement twisted him around, and he caught a last glimpse of Cunnington's Workhouse for Foundlings and Orphans just before the carriage turned the corner.

Decker couldn't read the name of London's venerable

children's institution on the iron gate, but he understood it was the place he had been living these past four months, ever since the death of his parents. He righted himself in his seat and regarded the couple across from him with the deliberately frank and curious look that was peculiar to four-year-olds.

"Shall you be my parents now?" he asked forthrightly.

The question startled them. The woman blinked, and the man cleared his throat. For the time being, the handkerchief was forgotten. They exchanged uncertain glances. It was rather more than they had expected when they had approached Mr. Cunnington about taking one of his wards from the workhouse. Posing as missionaries, they had quite purposefully deceived the headmaster. Not, as they realized now, that their occupation would have made a whit of difference to the man. He had been cooperative, perhaps eager, to find a boy that would suit their needs as they described them. Cunnington would have been an even happier man if they had agreed to take Decker's older brother as well.

It wasn't possible. They had concurred privately before going to the workhouse that one child, properly trained, could be an asset. A second mouth to support posed a liability. What they had not considered was that rescuing a child from Cunnington's Workhouse—and surely a rescue was what it was—gave them certain responsibilities, if not in their own minds, then at least in the mind of this child.

He was still regarding them with that maddeningly candid and expectant expression. His gaze didn't waver, but seemed to encompass them both. His small mouth was slightly pursed, and the effect would have been cherubic if it had not been for those very wise blue eyes.

The woman spoke first. "Not parents exactly," she said. "But family."

"Yes," said the man. "Most assuredly family."

Decker considered that. The distinction they made was not entirely understood, but neither was it missed. He nodded, filing this information away. "That's all right, then," he said solemnly.

That air of gravity in one so young was the woman's undoing. Tears made her clear eyes luminous. She tried to blink them back.

Seeing the tears, the man reached for his handkerchief. The lace-edged corner was no longer peeking out from his pocket. He thrust his hand inside to dig deeper and was genuinely puzzled when it came away empty.

It was then the couple witnessed Decker Thorne's incorrigible grin and heard his bubbling laughter. Resistance wasn't possible. Jimmy Grooms and Marie Thibodeaux, for all that they were hardened to life's inequities, were not proof against the purity of a child's joy. Decker Thorne hooked their hearts as easily as he had snared Jimmy's handkerchief. That article of linen and lace now dangled from his chubby fingers as he offered it up to Marie.

"He's a charmer," Marie said as she took the handkerchief.

Jimmy was thinking much the same thing. Their choice had been a good one. He patted Marie's knee as she sniffed elegantly and dabbed at her eyes. "That was quite something, boy," he said. From Jimmy Grooms, who had been practicing light-fingered feats since he was eight, it was high praise. "When did you—" He broke off as the carriage slowed suddenly and Decker was catapulted out of his seat. Jimmy caught him easily and set him on his lap. "So that's the way of it, is it?" he said approvingly. "When you were tossed from your seat before. Good boy. Diversion is everything in the trade. And you are a diverting sort of fellow, aren't you?"

Jimmy chuckled at his own play on words. "Ain't he a diverting sort, Marie?"

Marie tucked the handkerchief into her cuff, then held out her hands to Decker. He went into her arms willingly, and she cuddled him close. "He's beautiful," she said against the crown of his head. Her breath fluttered strands of his dark hair, and the silky threads tickled her lips. "Beautiful. That's what he is."

Marie Thibodeaux had never given any thought to her maternal nature or, until this moment, the lack of it. The urge to protect and nurture was strong in her now, almost overwhelming. As the oldest of five children she had mostly raised her siblings, yet she had never experienced this tug on her emotions. She'd cared for her brothers and sisters while her mother and father managed their tavern, and when she'd become more valuable on the Paris back streets than she was as a surrogate parent, she'd been sold as matter-of-factly as a skin of wine, and perhaps with less regret.

It was Jimmy Grooms who eventually rescued her from that life. While he was in Calais to ply his trade during a summer festival, she caught his eye. He stole a pair of ivory combs and used them as barter with her pimp. They left France that very evening in typical Jimmy Grooms style, stealing aboard a merchant ship scheduled to make a channel crossing. Marie had not known where she was going with the young Englishman, but she knew where she had been. Throwing her lot in with Jimmy Grooms was not a difficult decision. In the eleven years they had been together, he had never made a misstep or caused her to regret her decision. Marie's trust in him was absolute.

And now he had given her this child. If Jimmy had any sense he'd make another proposal of marriage. This time Marie Thibodeaux was of a mind to accept.

"What shall I call you?" Decker asked, raising his head from against Marie's breast. He saw them exchange glances again. Clearly they had not given this much thought. Jimmy Grooms rubbed the underside of his chin, his mouth screwed comically to one side. "Well, there's a poser," he said. "Uncle Jimmy sets nicely now that I say it out loud. What do you think, dear? Uncle Jimmy . . . Aunt Marie? We did say the boy was family."

"Uncle Jimmy," she repeated softly. "Yes, that's fine." There was a small hesitation, then she added in a rush, "But I want him to call me Mère."

Jimmy's brows lifted. He stopped rubbing his chin and studied her face. Marie was a handsome woman, not an especially pretty one, but she had a calming smile and a quiet way about her that transcended the notion of physical beauty. "Mère," he said in his deep, rich baritone. "Mother. I suppose the boy and others would think it was short for Marie. Who would know it means mother?"

"*I* would know."

He saw that it was important to her, and it was not in his nature to deny Marie. "Then Mère it is." Jimmy tapped Decker lightly on the tip of his nose. "Do you hear that, boy? It's to be Uncle Jimmy and Mère from now on."

The moment was not as auspicious to Decker as it was to the two adults. He nodded absently, his thoughts having taken flight in another direction. "Are we going to the ship?" He pushed slightly at Marie, restless now. She let him go, and with remarkable self-sufficiency, Decker climbed back onto the opposite seat and knelt at the open window. "Where is the ship?"

Jimmy looked to Marie for an explanation. "What's he saying, dear?"

"He's asking about the ship," she explained patiently.

11

"I got the gist of that. But what ship?"

"It's clear his memory is better than yours, *cher*. Do you not recall you told Mr. Cunnington we were prepared to make a voyage? We went to great pains to convince the headmaster that we would be long gone from London on the Lord's work."

"Oh *that*." Jimmy chuckled. "You might as well know it now, boy, we were lying. It's a sad fact, but there you have it. Lying through our teeth."

That got Decker's attention. "My mother says I shouldn't lie. I think Papa said it, too. I'm not sure." His brows furrowed in adultlike consternation as he tried to recall an admonishment from his father on the subject of lying. "Yes, when I said Grey sat on Papa's hat and crushed it. That wasn't right."

"Is that so?" Jimmy remarked.

"Yes, sir. I should have said it was Colin."

Marie raised a hand to hide her smile. When she could ask the question with the import it deserved, she said, "And why should you have done that?"

Decker looked at her as if she had cotton wool between her ears; the answer was so patently obvious to him. "Because Grey's a baby and Colin's big."

"I see," Marie said. She looked sideways at Jimmy. "Apparently he has it in his mind that lying isn't wrong, but to do it badly *is*."

"A remarkably bright boy. I was much older when I learned the truth about lying." He chuckled deeply, amused. "The truth about lying. That's got a ring to it, damn me if it don't."

"Don't be vulgar, *cher*." Marie ignored Jimmy's surprised look and leaned forward in her seat. When she was at eye level with Decker she said, "We're not going aboard a ship. Perhaps one day we will. Uncle Jimmy thinks he'd like to see

America." She gave her partner another sidelong glance. "That is if Van Diemen's Land doesn't get him first."

"Now see here," Jimmy interjected quickly, "there's to be no talking about Van Diemen's. Are you of a mind to scare the boy?" But when he looked at Decker he saw Marie's reference to the Australian penal colony was not understood. The child was simply raptly attentive to Marie's sweet voice.

"Is Grey your brother?" asked Marie.

Decker nodded.

"And Colin?"

Decker nodded again. He glanced out the window as if he might glimpse his brother among the passersby. His mouth puckered; then the corners turned down when he didn't spy the familiar face in the crowd.

Marie sat back. "I don't think he realizes he won't see his brothers again," she whispered. "I wish . . ." She let her thought go unfinished. It had been cruel of the headmaster to march out Decker *and* his older brother for a look-over. Jimmy had been quite clear they could take only one child. Apparently Mr. Cunnington was eager to be rid of the older boy. Marie could understand why. Colin had looked sickly, even consumptive. She doubted the child, who couldn't have been more than eight or nine, would live out the year. No, it would have been impossible for her and Jimmy to have taken him, too. Still, for a moment back at the workhouse she had been powerfully tempted. "What about the baby?" she asked softly. "Did Mr. Cunnington tell you anything about the other child?"

"Only that he was first to be taken. Greydon, I think he called him." Jimmy saw Decker's head swivel in their direction as he recognized the name. When Jimmy remained silent for a few moments Decker's attention went back to the window. "I must have remembered it right," he said. "A

13

couple from America took him. Apparently they had it in their minds to pass him off as their own. That's why they refused this little fellow and his half-starved brother."

"Half-starved?" Marie's insides knotted, and her eyes grew troubled. She looked over Decker from head to toe. Here was a sturdy little boy with strong legs and arms and a bit of baby fat on his belly. This child hadn't lacked for food. Why had the other? "I thought Colin was consumptive."

Jimmy Grooms shook his head. "He was hungry," he said quietly. "I know that look. I've *felt* that look. So hungry he was ready to eat his own insides."

"*Mon Dieu,*" Marie said. "I didn't know."

Jimmy was suddenly sorry he had told her. It would deepen her regret at not taking the boy. "Of course you didn't. Starvation like that is as bad as consumption. Just as deadly." He put an arm around her. "Listen to me, Marie. We did the best thing by the boy, taking this one away."

Marie's look was uncertain. "What do you mean?"

"How do you think this child stayed so round and rosy? Did you see any others in that damnable workhouse that looked as healthy? I can't be wide of the mark when I tell you that his brother was giving up his own food for this one. Now that we have him, the brother can go about the business of eating for himself."

Decker stared out the window. With a wisdom that owed nothing to his age and everything to his upbringing, he remained quiet. More than that, he pretended not to have heard. He pressed one hand to the pocket in his black coat. Through the wool he could feel the outline of Colin's last-minute gift. Decker didn't even know what it was. He had been too excited and frightened to look at it when Colin thrust it into his pocket. If he had had to make a guess, he would have said it was food. Colin had always been giving him scraps and spoonfuls from his own plate. Now he could tell that the object was not something to eat. For the first time ever he was fiercely glad of that. He blinked rapidly, shielding tears. His chin trembled slightly. He hadn't cried when his parents died or any time since. That Colin hadn't let him had only been part of the reason. Mostly he had been too scared. Fear, it seemed, could give one a stiff upper lip as easily as an older brother's severe but silent glance.

"What have you got there, boy?" Jimmy Grooms asked. Decker stopped rubbing his pocket and let his hand fall away quickly. The expression he faced Jimmy with was a composed one, if shaded with guilt. "Nothing."

"A poor lie if ever there was one," Jimmy told him. His shrug was philosophical. "No matter. One has to start somewhere." He held out his hand. "Show me what you have in your pocket."

"Leave him be," Marie said gently. "And you may as well start calling him by his name. He can't be 'boy' forever."

Jimmy conceded one point but not the other. To his way of thinking, life was full of compromises. "All right, Decker. Let's see what you have in your pocket." Instead of holding out his hand, Jimmy picked Decker up and tickled him until the child was helpless with laughter. The musical giggles were like a melody above the clatter of carriage wheels and the deeper rumble of voices on the street. The tempo was stamped by the staccato clip of horses' hooves. By the time Decker was set, breathless, back in his seat, Jimmy was smiling widely and Marie's eyes were brimming with happy tears.

Jimmy Grooms held up the object that Decker had been so carefully guarding minutes earlier. Decker made a swipe at it, but Jimmy retracted his hand. "Made my own diversion," he said with a touch of pride.

15

"Really, *cher,*" Marie scolded lightly, "you shouldn't be so full of yourself for besting a boy. It's not becoming."

Jimmy sobered. "Right you are."

"Mine!" Decker declared loudly, surprising both adults. "Mine!"

Jimmy closed the object in his fist and eyed Decker steadily. "Yes, it's yours. In a moment." When Decker pushed backward into one corner of the carriage, his expression mutinously sullen rather than cowed, Jimmy unfolded his fingers to examine his prize.

"An earring," Marie exclaimed somewhat breathlessly.

"It is indeed," said Jimmy. And what an earring. Here was an exquisite piece of jewelry, a pearl stud with a raindrop of pure gold dangling from it. The letters *ER* were engraved in script on the drop, and the pearl was set in a gold crown. Jimmy whistled under his breath. "Do you realize what this is, Marie? This is our passage to anywhere we want to go."

"To Van Diemen's Land more likely," she said quellingly. "Where did you get this, Decker?"

Decker shrugged.

Marie tried to mask her own anxiety. "You mustn't be afraid. I'm certain you haven't done anything wrong, but Uncle Jimmy and I need to know where you got this."

Jimmy Grooms wasn't sure he liked being referred to as Uncle Jimmy by Marie. Before he had a chance to comment on this, Marie was posing the question again to Decker.

"Colin gave it to me," he said. The truth was offered reluctantly and because of that he was believed.

"Colin? Your brother gave this to you?" Marie said just to be certain.

Decker nodded.

"Where did he get it?"

Decker shrugged.

"That's no answer, boy," said Jimmy. "Did he steal it?"

"No." Decker was confident in his answer. He recognized the earring, knew he had seen it before. He was less clear about the circumstances.

Marie's voice was more gentle. "Do you suppose he found it somewhere? Perhaps at the workhouse?"

Decker didn't respond at all this time. He stared straight ahead, his mouth flat as if a secret pressed his lips closed and it could not be released.

After more than a minute of silence, Marie sighed. "Give him back the earring, *cher.*"

"What if it belonged to the Cunningtons?" Jimmy asked. He knew that had been Marie's first concern when she saw it. It certainly had been his. The last thing they needed was for the headmaster or his wife to set the authorities on their trail.

Marie took the earring from Jimmy and held it out to Decker. It was taken from her quickly and pocketed with speed and deftness. "Do you really think the Cunningtons would have an exquisite piece like that in their possession? They'd do what we would do."

Jimmy cocked one cinnamon-colored brow. "And that would be?"

"Sell it, *cher.*" She held up one finger to silence him when she saw the hope in his eyes. "That's what we would do *if* the piece were ours. It's not. It belongs to Decker. I'm quite clear on that even if your thinking is a little muddled."

Marie Thibodeaux snuggled next to Jimmy. "If that is his good-luck piece, then he's ours. Good things are going to happen to us, *cher.* You'll see."

Jimmy had to be satisfied with that. He doubted the boy would ever give up the earring again willingly, and Marie would never forgive Jimmy for taking it with cunning. Decker was on his knees again, looking out the window. As far as Jimmy could tell, he and Marie were out of the child's mind.

"Who do you suppose he's looking for?" Jimmy asked.

Marie didn't answer immediately. She couldn't say with any certainty. "His brothers, *peut-être*. His family. Who is to say what he knows about them?"

"Cunnington told me there was a search for more family, but that none could be found. I suppose he thought there might be money in it for him if he could have located a relative to take the children." The earring in Decker's possession seemed to bear that out, but Jimmy was just as certain that the headmaster hadn't seen it. Cunnington would have confiscated it as payment for boarding the children. No matter that the heirloom piece would have paid the room and board of an army of children for a score of years. Cunnington was lacking in more scruples than Jimmy Grooms. Jimmy, at least, had Marie to rein him in when greed got the better of his common sense. Mr. Cunnington had only Mrs. Cunnington. Jimmy's meeting with the headmistress had been brief, but it was long enough to learn there was no conscience in that quarter.

"What do you think he knows about the night his parents were killed?" Jimmy asked under his breath. "He was there, Cunnington said. All the children were."

Marie shook her head. "Don't talk about it. It would be God's blessing if it were all forgotten."

Decker chose that moment to slump sideways in the corner of the carriage seat. His eyelids fluttered once then closed. The long thick lashes lay darkly against his cheeks. His sweet mouth was slightly parted and a bubble of dew swelled on his bottom lip as he expelled an exhausted breath.

"God's blessing," Marie said again, giving thanks that

sleep had at last caught up with the child.

But he hadn't forgotten. For Decker the difference was more subtle. He chose not to remember.

One

Her life had become a cliché.

Jonna Remington was standing on the fog-shrouded docks of Boston Harbor waiting for her ship to come in. It hardly mattered that she was waiting for the ship in a very real way. When she heard the words roll through her own mind, when the truth of her position on the wharf became known to her, she could find no humor in either.

She was only twenty-four years old, and suddenly she was very weary.

An icy burst of wind shot over the water. White caps hurled the chilled air onto the dock, and Jonna had to grip her cape to keep it about her shoulders. She hugged the dark gray wool closer to her body, but the hem still beat a tattoo against her legs. Her skirt and underskirt and all four of her petticoats were pressed flatly to her slender frame until the wind subsided. At one point the wide brim of her bonnet lifted and curled back. It remained on her head only because of the large, tightly drawn bow under her chin, and for one humiliating moment, Jonna thought she would be choked by it.

Hanged by her own hat. It only got worse.

In anticipation of another blast of arctic wind, Jonna removed one hand from her cape and placed it firmly on her head. She was painfully aware of the sight she presented, but she was also aware that no one would comment—at least not so they could be overheard. She was, after all, Jonna

20

Remington. And she was waiting for her ship to come in.

Decker Thorne, master of *Remington Huntress*, the new flagship of the Remington trading empire, called out orders to his second in command. His voice was calm and clear, as if he had been issuing such orders all of his twenty-eight years rather than only in the last twenty-eight days. He didn't show it by so much as a raised brow, but he was still a little surprised when the words coming from him were translated into action by all the men under him.

Standing at Decker's side, Jack Quincy nodded approvingly. "You've got the way of it," he said quietly. "Damn if you don't." He shifted his weight to loosen one of the crutches under his arms and pound it sharply on the deck to punctuate his point.

"Careful, Jack. You'll slip and break your other leg."

Jack shrugged awkwardly. "These sticks aren't what's keeping me up, boyo. It's the wind at my back and saltwater spray in my face that does the trick."

There was a surfeit of both this morning. And fog as thick as any Decker had experienced. Of course Jack said it could be worse, and Decker took him at his word. His own three years on the world's oceans were of little account against Jack's two score. Decker relayed another order to his second. Out of the corner of his eye he saw Jack nod with satisfaction.

Decker grinned. "There's no danger that I'll run her aground," he said.

That had never been in Jack's mind. Jack Quincy's approval was for the way Decker had taken to this command. It had been thrust on him soon after they left Charleston for London on the second leg of their voyage. When Jack's ignominious fall down the gangway stairs injured his leg and made him bedfast, it was Decker he gave command of the ship. And *Remington Huntress* was not just any ship. She was designed to exacting specifications to be the swiftest clipper plying any of the world's trade routes. This voyage was meant to break a record, not a leg. Now it was left to Decker Thorne to prove it could be done.

Setting out to make a record run was a risky proposition at best. Rarely was that the purpose of any voyage. There was money to be made from the effort and certainly there was notoriety for the captain of the clipper and his crew, but it was only a short-term gain for the owner of the line. Steady and reliable transportation was important over the long haul. If the China or Liverpool run was made a few days or even a few hours faster than the last time, it was a feather in someone's cap, but not as critical as delivering the goods to their destination ahead of the competition.

There was the key to market success. It was not that every clipper run had to break a record, it was that each clipper had to outrun others carrying the same cargo. The real money was in being the first to bring the trade goods to port. That was when tradesmen were willing to pay the highest prices and would put up the least haggling.

Huntress had been two hours too late arriving in London from Charleston to capture that record, but the record for the complete voyage back to Boston was still in her grasp. Every man aboard her knew it, most especially the one who was now charged with her command.

Watching Decker as he went through the orders that would bring the clipper about to fill her sails, Jack Quincy was again struck by the rightness of his choice. Decker's easy smile, his loose and relaxed bearing, could be mistaken for carelessness or lack of purpose. Jack had never seen him in quite that light, though he was aware that others had and continued to do so. The fact that Decker knew and never appeared bothered by it was a mark to the good in Jack's log.

Jack's broad face split in a crooked, dryly amused grin as Decker walked away. Had he ever been as trim and agile as this young man? he wondered. Decker Thorne was light on his feet, like a cat, with a rolling stride that was beautifully synchronized with the rhythms of the clipper and the sea. "Youth," Jack muttered to himself. He was surprised by the surge of envy he felt. It was best not to dwell on things that couldn't be changed. Jack's age and his growing list of infirmities were two of those things. You lived with them or died from them. There wasn't any in-between.

Jack Quincy knew this was his last voyage. It had been two years since he had taken out a clipper except on a trial run. He had agreed to master *Huntress* at Jonna's request, even though he had pressed hard for her to accept Decker Thorne as captain. It was one of the few times in his long association with Jonna Remington that she did not embrace his advice. *Huntress* was too valuable, her mission too important, for her to be given into the command of an untried captain. If Jack wouldn't do it, then she had other masters she could entrust, but she was adamant *Remington Huntress* would not have Decker Thorne at the helm.

Jack Quincy grimaced as the clipper lurched when the sails were strained by the wind. His weight settled uncomfortably for a moment on the crutches, and they dug in under his arms. He gripped the braces in his large hands and raised himself up. The splints chafed his calf. He had been too long standing topside already, but he wanted to see Decker bring *Huntress* into Boston Harbor.

More than that, he wanted to see Jonna Remington's face when she realized who was in full command of her clipper. He was thinking that breaking the record was not going to be enough. He was still going to feel the sharp edge of her tongue. "Hell to pay," he said to himself. "Damn if there won't be hell to pay."

But it would be worth it just to see her face.

A crowd had begun to gather on the dock behind Jonna. As word spread that she was on the waterfront, and as the reason for her early morning outing became common knowledge, work in the busy harbor slowed. Wagons moving from ships to warehouses crawled along the dock now as the drivers, taking advantage of their high perches, looked out over the water for a first glimpse of *Huntress*.

It said something about Jonna Remington's reputation that men found their eyes trying to pierce the thick wall of fog for the curve of the horizon. There was no way the owner of the Remington line could be certain her ship would appear in the next hour or the next day, but the fact that she was waiting told others she expected it to be sooner than later. The timetable, they knew, was one Jonna kept in her head, along with a plethora of other facts and figures, of debits and credits, of manifests and maritime laws. Not a man working the harbor that morning doubted that Jonna Remington had plotted her flagship's course and anticipated the vessel's arrival within the accuracy of a heartbeat. In a business that was fraught with risk, things that could be plotted and planned were never left to chance.

Jonna turned only once to survey the gathering at her back. They were careful to keep their distance, a sign of their respect but also an acknowledgment of Jonna's natural aloofness. She was not unapproachable but neither was she casually available. Her mien was sober and steady, even dispassionate, and her manner was straightforward. She worked hard and she expected others to do the same. She never said as much; it was there by example. Men in her employ who did not understand that were quickly given their leave. Jonna Remington did not suffer fools in any fashion.

Her brief study of the crowd had laid a blanket of silence over it. To a man they felt they were shirking their duty by waiting for *Huntress*. This guilt didn't move them to go back to their work, but they were aware of their discomfort now where they hadn't been a moment before. A few of them, in a paltry show of defiance, stared back hard at her. If she knew they were doing it, she remained unmoved.

Another biting breeze swept over the dock. Jonna felt her bonnet lift again, and the purple satin bow caught her under the neck. This time she unfastened the ribbon rather than hold the hat to her head. The wind tore at the bonnet as soon as it was loosened, and Jonna barely managed to keep it in hand. She held it in front of her, letting the salt spray sting her unprotected face and whip at her hair.

She had had no patience with having her hair dressed that morning. Instead of fashionable ringlets, she'd told the maid to simply tie it back and tuck it into a bun. The wind made short work of the maid's efforts. The anchoring pins lost their moorings as glossy black tendrils slipped free. Jonna's hair unfurled and was beaten back. In moments it came to define the invisible currents of air that lifted it behind her.

Jonna had an urge to glance over her shoulder. Had anyone noticed, or were the men still watching for the ship? With an uncharacteristic consideration of feminine vanity she wondered which of the two possibilities would be more insulting. She quelled the impulse to look around and clutched her bonnet tighter.

It wasn't that she was unused to being stared at. She was. But it had been her experience that it was for reasons not to be regarded as truly flattering. The first thing that usually struck people was her height. At just three inches under six feet she was taller than all the women of her acquaintance and stood eye to eye with most men. If her height went unremarked—and truly, she thought, why did people think they had the right to make some comment on it, or more to the point, think that she should accept their observations graciously—then something was said about her eyes.

Why, they're purple, my dear. How very unusual. Actually they were violet, but when someone was visibly caught off guard by the odd coloring, "purple" was the word that came quickly to mind and was voiced. To make it more maddening, her eyes seemed too large for her face and did not remain a constant hue but captured shades of blue and gray depending on the predominant colors of her costume. Until she had removed her bonnet and its purple ribbon, Jonna had been assured her eyes would remain violet. Not that it was a matter of great importance to her. She only had to look out of her eyes, not into them. For that she was grateful.

Jonna raised one arm to shield them now. Behind the fog the sun was burning brightly. The light was diffused throughout the gray mist, the effect almost blinding. She waited for the sun to break through. She was selfish enough to want the sighting of her flagship to be unfettered by the low-lying clouds.

Soon, she thought, let it be soon.

Huntress rolled through a bank of fog and into a clearing. She rode the crest of each wave smoothly as the wind swelled her sails. Like an albatross with great white wings spread, *Huntress* seemed to take flight just above the surface of the water, moving forward in defiance of the laws of nature that commanded friction and gravity. Her swift progress brought a rush of pride to the men who labored in her yardarms and on her decks.

"Land Ho!"

It was the cry they had all been waiting for. Twenty pairs of eyes, all of them unaided by a telescope, strained to see what the one man with a spyglass could. It was two long minutes before they saw the same New England shoreline. The cheer that went up was deafening, and in that moment the swell of voices seemed to add substance to the burgeoning sails.

The spyglass was passed to Decker, but he handed it to Jack before he looked himself. He ran a hand through his dark, wind-ruffled hair. His mouth was set in a quirky, yet somehow rueful grin. "Tell me if you can see her," he told Jack.

Jack Quincy raised the telescope. He knew Decker wasn't talking about the coastline in general. His reference, in spite of its lack of specificity, was to Jonna Remington. The older man gave a bark of laughter as he pressed the 'scope to his eye. Another chuckle rumbled in his barrel chest. "You're not afraid of her, are you?" he asked.

"Down to my toes," Decker admitted easily. His loose and relaxed posture didn't change, and there was nothing about his quietly amused expression to suggest he was telling the truth.

Jack dropped the spyglass a fraction, looked sharply at Decker, then raised it again. "Damn liar," he said. "Had me going there, just for a moment, mind you. Can't imagine why anyone would be afraid of Jonna. Just the same, I know it's true. She just doesn't warm up to people the way she did when she was a young'un. I never figured out whether she puts them off or t'other way around."

Decker didn't comment. He had his own thoughts on the

matter and he was determined they would remain just that—his own.

"She'll be as mad as my great-aunt Lottie," Jack said.

"Mad crazy?" asked Decker. "Or mad angry?"

"Lottie was both." Jack looked up, interested as Decker groaned softly. "Didn't I ever tell you about her?"

Decker took the spyglass. "No. And I'm not listening to one of your tales now."

Unperturbed, Jack went on. "Lottie would raise her fist at the sun if it got too hot to suit her, then strip down to her skin to get the better of it."

Decker raised a single dark brow and spared Jack a sideways glance.

Jack Quincy leaned his large frame on one crutch and crossed himself awkwardly. "I swear."

Raising the telescope, Decker said dryly, "No chance of that happening here." He had never seen Jonna Remington truly angry. He had seen her frustrated and flustered, aggravated and annoyed, but she invariably had some brake on her emotions that kept her anger in check. When he thought of it, he imagined she was more likely to go cold than hot. As for tearing off her clothes . . . he didn't think in that direction at all. The owner of the Remington line probably bathed in her shift.

Through the spyglass the coastline was rising in sharp relief on the horizon. Decker knew that with the last dregs of fog burned off by the sun, *Huntress*'s sails would reflect light like mirrors. If Jonna was waiting for them she would be sighting them soon.

Jonna raised herself on tiptoe. Nothing moved on the wharf now except men who craned their necks for a better view than they had had before. Wagons stopped. Cargoes were left unattended. The warehouses had emptied of their last workers minutes earlier. If the glimpse of gleaming white sail in the distance was indeed *Remington Huntress*, then history was being made.

She knew it was her ship before anyone else. Jonna had put down the design on paper, supervised the building, and toured every one of the decks. She had hired the men who worked on the ship from her inception to the day the vessel left the Remington shipyard north of Boston. From the coast road Jonna had followed the progress to the harbor on her short maiden outing, but it was in Boston Harbor that she had christened *Huntress* and set her free for her first true test.

Jonna Remington had done everything but sail on her. She never spoke of her regret in that regard. For years she had been a private person, but in this case it was less a desire to keep her thoughts to herself than it was that she had no one to tell. Her most trusted confidant, Jack Quincy, would not have understood her regret, not when the choice to stay on land was hers. Grant Sheridan, the man who was pressing his marriage proposal, would not have understood why she had felt a need to board her vessel. Privacy came with a price, she realized, because now there was no one who understood her.

Jonna pushed back this thought as she squinted against the sunlight. Yes, it was her ship. *Huntress.* She had given as much thought to the name as she had to the design of the cant frames and keel. This would be the last great clipper of the Remington line, and Jonna had wanted a swift and beautiful ship that would make its mark. She had thought of Diana, goddess of the hunt, as under her watchful eye the graceful curve of timber took shape.

Iron ships would follow soon. Jonna was sure of it. They were lumbering floaters of iron and wood, hybrid hulks that burned coal and used sails only when the wind was high.

They had no style or elegance of form, and worse, rather than working in concert with nature, they strove to overpower it.

Jonna's sound business sense meant that all of the Remington line would someday be powered by steam, but business did not dictate her passion. And her passion was the tall ships.

Aboard *Remington Huntress* the activity came about with such precision it appeared to be choreographed. Captain Thorne's orders were relayed quickly and sharply and carried out in much the same manner. Men climbed into the rigging to hoist the sails and make the wind's power ineffective. The great sharp-lined ship shuddered as her crew strove to take in the spread of canvas. It was as if she could not bear to be stripped of her finest adornments.

The shudder brought Decker shoulder to shoulder with Jack Quincy. Quincy had never seen the younger man lose his footing before, even in stormy conditions, and it was nothing like that today. There was a lightness in Decker's step, in his very *being*, that made Jack think his new captain couldn't stumble. In the next moment, when Decker was holding the telescope again, having stolen it away from Jack's belt, the old salt knew he'd been right. Decker Thorne didn't make a misstep unless it was intentional.

"How do you do that?" Jack growled. "Should I check my pockets for change?"

"Oh? Did you have any?" asked Decker. "I counted two bills but no coin."

Jack's laughter was like a cannon shot, explosive and loud. "I'll bet you did, too." He sobered momentarily. "Is it true you can remove a lady's corset while she's wearing her dress?"

Decker raised the spyglass. "What's the point in that? I'd

still have to get the dress off. I've never been one for tossing up a woman's skirts. You shouldn't believe everything you hear about me, Jack. What isn't an outright lie isn't likely to be the whole truth."

Jack nodded. "Fair enough. But tell me how you got the scope without me feeling a thing."

Decker continued to scan the harbor. He could make out a crowd standing on the wharf but not the individuals in it. He shrugged. "Magic, Jack."

Not satisfied with that answer, Jack grunted.

"Some people call it sleight of hand," Decker said.

This time Jack snorted.

"Judges mostly call it stealing."

"That's the word I heard for it, too," said Jack. "Now give me back the 'scope."

"In a moment." They were close enough now that the spyglass brought Jonna Remington into focus. Decker smiled wryly to himself. Even though the arrival of her flagship was cause for celebration the chiseled face of an iceberg would have offered a warmer reception than this woman.

Her posture on the lip of the dock was the only thing that betrayed her eagerness, and that was an optimistic interpretation of her position. "I'll be damned," he said softly.

"What?" Jack demanded, sidling closer. "Give me that thing. What do you see?"

"She's not wearing a bonnet." He handed the telescope to Jack. "Miss Remington's hair is flying in the wind. Have a care, Jack. She may actually smile."

Jack Quincy had known Jonna Remington all of her young life. He had worked for her father, and at John's death had worked beside her until she reached her majority and took control of the company herself. Jack defended her now. "She was a wee thing when her mother passed on," he said. "And only fifteen when her father was lost to her. If she's serious about her responsibilities, then you should take heart. As her employee she considers you one of them."

"I'm not Jonna Remington's responsibility," Decker said. There was no humor in his tone now.

"Perhaps not," Jack agreed. "I'm only saying that she thinks you are. It's not something you can change. It would be easier to change the direction of a prevailing wind than to move Jonna from a course she's set or an opinion she holds."

Decker had nothing to say to that. He walked away.

Huntress officially reached Boston Harbor at ten minutes after eight. The total length of her run from Boston to Charleston to London and back again was calculated at thirty-three days, sixteen hours. It was ninety minutes better than Jonna had quickly worked out in her own head, and a full three hours better than her best estimate upon seeing the clipper off. Her early arrival at the wharf this morning was prompted less by wishful thinking than by her inability to sleep any longer.

When the ship was safely berthed at the pier, the crowd of dockworkers at last breached the distance that had separated them from Jonna. She felt them surge forward just as the gangway was lowered to the dock and Decker Thorne appeared at the taffrail. Her hand that was raised in greeting for Jack Quincy faltered in midair. Her head tilted to one side, and her violet eyes darkened in confusion. She looked past Decker and saw Jack hobbling forward on crutches.

At the angle she was from the ship, it was impossible for her to see the nature of his injury. What she could see, however, as clearly as a lighthouse beacon, was Decker Thorne's careless grin.

Jonna's wide mouth flattened, and the effect seemed only

to broaden his smile. She nodded once, curtly, and realizing her hand was still raised, she lowered it to her side. He seemed to find that amusing as well.

There wasn't much that didn't amuse Decker Thorne, Jonna reflected as she was jostled by the men crowding around. When two hands were placed firmly at the small of her back and she was pushed into the drink, her last thought as she tumbled forward was that Decker Thorne would find this very funny indeed.

Only two men moved. One slipped deeper into the crowd and then out of it. The other tore off his jacket and dove into the icy water.

Jack Quincy clutched the woolen coat Decker had tossed him. He found himself staring helplessly at the spot where Jonna had been standing a moment earlier. Her fall, and now Decker's rescue attempt, had transfixed him. Quincy knew himself to be standing at the taffrail of the *Remington Huntress*, but there was a part of him that had suddenly been transported back in time. Nearly a quarter of a century ago he had been standing in a similar place on another ship of the Remington line. The clipper was *Sea Dancer*, and on the Boston wharf was a woman waiting for the ship and the ship's master.

Jack could see the events unfold as clearly now as he had all those years before. Charlotte Reid Remington stood patiently and proudly at the end of the pier, waiting for her husband John to reach her. In her arms she held her infant daughter Jonna. John hurried toward her. He hadn't seen her for almost three months, and it was his first sighting of his only child.

Jack never did know how Charlotte lost her balance. One moment she was landfast, and in the next she was in free fall.

It was her husband who leaped to her rescue and the crowd who had gathered to welcome the ship cheered the recovery. Jack himself experienced a considerable lightening of his heart when he saw Charlotte brought to the surface.

It was the young cabin boy beside Jack who saw what others did not. While John Remington had been able to bring up his wife, she had not been able to hold onto her child.

Before Jack understood what Charlotte's forlorn cries meant, the lad at his side had leaped into the water for Jonna. Jack had marveled at the boy's tenacity as he dove repeatedly for the bundle of blankets and baby. Jack remembered thinking when he'd paid for the boy at Cunnington's Workhouse for Foundlings and Orphans that he'd be burying him at sea before they reached Boston. The child had claimed to be ten; the headmaster had said he was twelve. If he was nine, Jack would have been astonished.

The lad, though, had a way of surprising Jack. He took to the sea and the ship, and as each day put them farther from London, he seemed to grow stronger. His duties as cabin boy were menial but not backbreaking, and John Remington was not a tyrant or a petty and demanding taskmaster. The fresh air may have had something to do with the boy's recovery, but more likely it was the food.

When Jack first laid eyes on Colin Thorne he knew the boy was starving.

Jack Quincy was brought abruptly to the present as he saw Decker surface with nothing to show for his efforts. Even from the distance that Jack viewed the rescue attempt, he could see that Decker's skin was pale and his lips were already turning blue. They would have to drag him out of there if he wasn't to die from the frigid water himself.

As Jack thought this, Decker pushed under the surface again.

Jonna's cape and gown took to the water like a sponge, pulling her down as she fought for another direction. She managed to claw open the frog fastening at her throat and get rid of the cape, but it was not as helpful as she had hoped, not when she couldn't swim a stroke.

The current tossed her against the pilings. Her shoulder slammed the barnacle-encrusted wood. Pain made her gasp, and icy water replaced air in her lungs. She had no sense of up or down as darkness edged out her vision. With a clarity that astonished her she understood she was losing consciousness and that she was going to die.

Something floated past Decker's face. His hands reached out blindly for it. Jonna's cape. Somehow she had gotten out of it. He surfaced, tossed it to the onlookers, and ignoring the oars and hands they stretched out to him, he dove for what he knew would be his last time.

The current pushed him toward the pilings, and he went with it this time instead of fighting it. Was this what had happened to Jonna? Kicking hard, he pushed himself deeper. It was impossible to see. His lungs burned with the need to breathe and icy fingers of water seemed to have slipped under his skin. His bones ached with cold. He was so numb that he almost missed the first brush of her hand against his leg.

Decker instinctively turned away from the touch, pulling up his knees to his chest. When he realized what he was doing he changed direction and reached out for the thing that had held him so briefly. His hand clamped over Jonna's forearm. He yanked, bringing her close so that he could grasp her shoulders, and began swimming for the surface. It was like dragging an anchor, he thought. She was a dead weight in his arms. The thought chilled him in a way the water couldn't.

A dead weight. He hoped it wasn't true.

There was help aplenty when Decker surfaced with Jonna.

He pushed her limp body toward the small boat that had been lowered into the water and waited until she was hauled in before he dragged himself over the side and then collapsed.

He had a vague memory of being covered with blankets before he was lifted to the pier. He recalled turning his head and seeing Jack Quincy bent awkwardly over Jonna, his splinted leg thrust out to one side as he pressed on her back. Men crowded around him and circled Jonna. She was lost to his vision and then his vision was lost.

Decker was not familiar with his surroundings upon waking, but he had a good idea where he was. He had been in enough well-appointed bedrooms, either as a guest or an intruder, to recognize the quality of the furniture and linens in this one. It could only mean he was somewhere in the Remington mansion. That meant Beacon Hill.

Decker pushed himself upright. The heavy covers fell away to the level of his waist. Looking down at himself, he saw he was wearing a nightshirt. The tautness of the fabric across his shoulders made him sure it wasn't his own. If that hadn't been enough, there was the faint scent of cedar that clung to the material, hinting at a season or more in storage. His own clothes were not clearly visible. Even his boots were missing. He could only imagine that somewhere in the house, servants were working on laundering and drying and polishing.

A fire had been laid. It burned with enough intensity for Decker to feel its warmth across the room. The flames were reflected in the polished surface of the walnut wainscoting and in the spindles of the great four-poster. Above the mantel was an oil painting. Decker leaned forward to study it closer. It was a portrait of a couple, but the pair were not brother and sister. The rather stiff, clean-shaven young man had his hand lightly resting on the shoulder of the woman. The dark-haired beauty was not looking out from the canvas. Rather, she was looking up at the man. There was a profound sense of calm in her gaze, an expression of such tenderness that it defined the notion of a heart at peace and filled with love.

Decker had seen that expression before. When she wasn't exasperated with him, Marie Thibodeaux had looked at Jimmy like that. She'd looked at him like that right at the end, Decker remembered, just before he swung from the gallows and the trap dropped from beneath her own feet. Marie had loved Jimmy Grooms with the same sense of rightness and conviction that the woman in the painting had about her feelings for her husband.

Decker turned away from the mantel, no doubt in his mind that the couple captured in the gilt-framed portrait above it were Charlotte Reid and John Remington.

Jonna's parents.

He could no longer pretend to himself that he wasn't thinking about her. His eyes may have been wandering about the room, taking in the armoire and highboy, the exquisitely scrolled workmanship on the vanity, the expensive rug from the Orient, but his mind was wondering. He strained to hear movement in the hallway outside his door or beyond that, something below stairs that would tell him what had happened after Jonna had been pulled out of the water.

What did so much silence signify? A vigil? Or mourning?

On the bedside table was a silver tray and tea service. Decker would have preferred something stronger than milk in his tea, but he made a cup anyway. Sliding his legs over the side of the bed, he hooked his heels on the frame and drank the tea. It was the first time since jumping into the Atlantic that he had the sensation of being warm on the inside.

He stood. If no one was going to come to him—

"Now where do you think you're going?" The no-nonsense voice belonged to Mrs. Davis, Jonna Remington's housekeeper. She was carrying a warming pan in front of her as if she meant to do battle with it. Though small of stature, she had a militant look about her even when she wasn't harried as she was at this time. Normally her apron was as crisp as her speech and stiff as her upper lip. The wrinkles in it now suggested Mrs. Davis had indulged herself briefly in a little hand-wringing. Her white cap was slightly askew on her graying hair, and there was a hint of puffiness beneath her eyes. The tip of her thin nose was pink. Her handkerchief was a visible bulge under her sleeve. "Back in bed with you," she ordered. Brooking no argument, she advanced with the warming pan.

"Miss Remington?" The weakness in his voice was unexpected. He wasn't sure he was even understood.

Her face looked about to crumple, but she busied herself exchanging the warming pan in her hand for the one under Decker's sheets, this bit of industry helping her recover. "The doctor's been and gone," Mrs. Davis said.

What exactly did that mean? "Then Miss Remington is . . ."

"In her room." Mrs. Davis plumped the pillows, smoothed the covers, and, pressing Decker's shoulder firmly, directed him to lie down again. Her eyes watered as she studied his drawn features. There was a certain tightness in his jaw that she could not recall seeing before, and a muscle worked in his cheek. She thought of his careless smile only because it was absent. "You should rest, Mr. Thorne," she said quietly. "Though I suppose it's Captain now. Mr. Quincy tells us you mastered the clipper when he took to his bed." Mrs. Davis felt absently along her forearm for the handkerchief she'd tucked under her sleeve. Tears threatened to fall. "He told us what you did in the harbor . . . how you risked yourself to pull Miss Remington free. We're grateful." A tear that she could not blink back fell over her delicately lined cheek. "I just thought you should know." Her cheeks pinkened. She gave up trying to find the handkerchief and began to walk hurriedly away.

Decker pushed himself up on his elbows. "Here, Mrs. Davis. I think you're looking for this."

She stopped, turned, and saw Decker holding her handkerchief between his thumb and forefinger. She'd heard stories about him. All the servants had. It seemed an odd time to verify there might be some truth in them. Her tears dried of their own accord. She would have to set the maids to counting the silver as long as he was a guest. Mrs. Davis took the crumpled square of linen back. "How did you do that?"

The incorrigible grin surfaced now. "Habit."

Decker waited several minutes before he left the room. He belted the dressing gown he had found in the armoire and stepped into the empty hallway. He had only been in the Remington home on two occasions, both times with Jack Quincy on business matters, and he had never been above stairs. He knew from the view from the street that the mansion was laid out in two distinct wings. If the portrait above the mantel was any indicator, then the bed-chamber in which he had been placed to recover had belonged to the master and mistress of the house. Would Jonna's room have been in the same wing as her parents' or would it have been elsewhere?

Decker thought about the woman in the painting. Charlotte Reid would have wanted her child close. He started to open the door to the room next to his, then stopped. Jonna would have struck out independently sometime on her way to adulthood. Decker was sure of that. He closed the door carefully and padded on bare feet to the west wing.

He really hadn't expected to make it to her room without discovery, and he had no hope that he would find her alone. Yet no one stopped him in the hall, and when he found her bedchamber she was quite without company.

Decker shut the door behind him and approached the bed. Laid out in the middle, the covers neatly folded back across her breasts, she was wearing a plain, long-sleeved cotton shift that was buttoned to just below her throat. Her arms had been positioned outside the blankets, the pose serene but not entirely natural. Her long fingers were pale, the nailbeds faintly blue in color. Someone had taken time with her hair. It had been dried and braided, and the long plait had been drawn over her right shoulder. The oil lamp at her bedside lent her hair a blue-black sheen. The contrast with the porcelain texture of her skin had never been more profound.

There was a rocker beside the fireplace. The flames had not been attended to recently. Decker added two logs, then ignored the heat he had afforded himself by moving the rocker closer to the bed and sitting there. He stared at her until his vision blurred and his eyelids grew heavy.

He could make his peace with Jonna Remington, but how would he ever tell Colin?

Jonna bolted upright in bed the moment she realized she was not alone.

Startled out of his sleep by Jonna's rise from the dead, Decker gave a surprised shout.

Panicked now, Jonna yelped.

That brought Decker leaping out of the rocker to his feet. He stared at her.

Jonna blinked owlishly and stared back. Decker Thorne

was looking considerably wild-eyed and not at all amused. To Jonna's way of thinking it was rather funny. The beginnings of a smile tugged at the corners of her wide mouth. "You look as if you've seen a ghost," she said. "Or what I expect *I* might look like if I ever saw one."

Decker's hand was reaching out before he thought better of it. He placed the backs of three fingers against Jonna's forehead. When she flinched, his hand dropped to the curve of her neck. His thumb found her racing pulse just to one side of the hollow of her throat. Her skin was not nearly so cool as it looked, and her heartbeat, though racing, was strong.

He stepped back from the bed as she moved to push his hand away. "You're alive," he said.

She touched her throat. Had he been set to throttle her? "Well, yes," she said slowly, confused. "Of course I'm alive. That was the point in jumping in after me, wasn't it?"

There was no sarcasm in her tone that Decker could discern. She was asking the question quite honestly, with her usual directness. Decker shook his head, not believing it himself. He raked one hand through his hair in an absent gesture. The dark, coffee-colored strands fell back in precisely the same position as before his fingers combed them. "Yes," he told her, "that's why I went in. But I . . ." He shook his head again.

"Do you mean you came in here thinking I was dead?" she asked. That was an astonishing thought.

"I wasn't sure. Mrs. Davis wasn't completely clear about the matter when I asked. So I thought I'd find out for myself. When I saw you . . . well, you looked . . ." His brows furrowed. "Do you always sleep on your back with your hands at your sides?"

Jonna blinked again. Her thick lashes slowly lowered and then rose over her violet eyes. It seemed a terribly personal question. "I don't suppose I can say how I sleep, can I?" she said. "*I'm* the one sleeping." She stuffed a pillow behind the small of her back. The pressure there brought back an unwelcome memory.

"What's wrong?" Decker knew he should go. Clearly she was uncomfortable with him in her room and he hadn't meant to compromise her, but something in her expression prompted him to ask the question.

"It's nothing." She was not a skillful liar, and Decker's skeptically raised brow told her she was not good at it now. Jonna tried again. "My shoulder," she said. "I hit the pilings. Dr. Hardy says I'm fortunate not to have dislocated it or broken my collarbone." That was true enough, but not the real answer to Decker's question. Two hands pressing at the small of her back, shoving hard, that's what had been wrong.

Decker could see that she was favoring her left side as she eased back against the headboard. The current had pounded him against the pilings too, so it was a reasonable response. It was only the fact that she couldn't quite meet his eyes that gave him pause. He was used to Jonna's directness, but as her employee he was in no position to challenge her. He stood and turned to go.

"That was my father's dressing gown," she said.

He looked back at her. "I thought as much. Your housekeeper put me in your parents' room."

Jonna nodded. "She must have thought you would be comfortable there."

"I think it was because your father's clothes were easily available." He indicated what he was wearing. "My own things were spirited away."

She smiled faintly. "All will be returned to you, Captain Thorne."

His head came up, and Decker's clear blue eyes narrowed on Jonna's face.

"I know what I just said," she told him. "It was no slip that you heard. Mr. Quincy informed me he placed you at the helm of *Huntress* and that you're responsible for the record run."

"I didn't do it alone," Decker said.

She waved aside his modesty. The simple gesture with her left hand caused her to wince. Pain radiated from her shoulder to her wrist, but she continued speaking as if it were of no account. In truth, she acknowledged that it could have been worse. If not for Decker Thorne she could have been lying in this bed feeling nothing at all. "You know you were not my choice to master *Huntress*," she told him. "In spite of Mr. Quincy's recommendation I thought you were too inexperienced to take the helm for this run. I will always believe it was probably more luck than skill that brought you in ahead of schedule." She saw one corner of Decker's mouth turn up. Most men would have been sputtering a defense when she presented this opinion. Decker Thorne appeared more amused than offended. She quelled her own irritation with his response. "Still, I don't dismiss luck. It's a force like wind and fire and water, and some people know how to make it work for them. I think you're one of those people, Captain Thorne. Perhaps, if I'm completely honest with myself, I can even admit to being a little envious of you for it. So you see, however it was accomplished, I believe you've earned the right to be called captain." And to be certain there was no misunderstanding, she added, "It has nothing to do with your heroics on the wharf. But for that action today, I thank you."

Fascinated, Decker nodded slowly. Was there another woman like her anywhere else on the globe? She was totally without guile and possessed remarkably little tact, yet he found her approach as refreshing as a cool spring rain. In one breath she told him he wasn't skilled enough to handle her ships and in the next, gave him his due for being able to command good fortune. And to be sure he knew it wasn't his rescue that she was rewarding, she made a point of thanking him.

Jonna swiped at the tip of her nose with her index finger. "Why are you looking at me like that?" she asked when he continued to stare.

Decker blinked and came out of his reverie. Did she know she had a dimple at the corner of her mouth when she pressed her lips together? Probably not, and he wasn't going to be the one to tell her. "It's nothing, Miss Remington," he said. "I'm glad you're well."

He turned on his heel and left.

Grant Sheridan took the stairs two at a time. Mrs. Davis's protests were ignored, and she could not summon help quickly enough to keep him from mounting the steps. She heard doors open and close in the west wing as he tried to locate Jonna's room.

Jack Quincy limped out of the library on one crutch, a tumbler of brandy in his free hand. "What is it, Mrs. Davis? What's the racket?"

The housekeeper's hands twisted in her apron. "It's Mr. Sheridan. He heard about the commotion at the harbor this morning, and he's come to make certain Miss Remington's all right."

Jack grunted as he glanced down the hallway at the staircase. "I'd like to know what's kept him. If I was planning on marrying Jonna I damn well would have been here before now." A glance over his shoulder at the library's mantel clock assured him it was every bit as late as he thought it was. "It's been almost twelve hours since she fell in the harbor. Where's the pup been all this time?"

That was not Mrs. Davis's concern now, though she had wondered it privately some hours earlier. "But Dr. Hardy said Miss Remington was to rest. She's not past chills and fever yet, he said. And her shoulder's horribly bruised. She requires quiet, not visitors."

Jack knocked back a third of his drink. "Do you want me to go up there and drag him down?" he asked only half in jest.

Mrs. Davis eyed his splint as if she was seriously considering it. Finally she said, "No, you're supposed to be in a chair with your leg up. That's what the doctor advised."

"I *was* in a chair with my leg up," he told her. "That is, until I heard you caterwauling out here." Before she could object to his description, he held up his arm so he could fit it around her shoulders. "Now, if you'd be so kind as to help me back, we'll give Mr. Sheridan a few minutes with his fiancée before we mount a rescue."

The housekeeper let Jack's arm settle around her before she looked up at him. She was biting the inside of her cheek, her expression still worried. "There's been no official announcement, so I don't think he's properly Miss Remington's fiancé."

Jack nodded sagely. "Then we'll give him a little less time, Mrs. Davis. Just to satisfy your notions of what's proper."

Jonna was sleeping soundly when Grant walked into her room. He went immediately to the bed and sat on the edge. His weight depressed the mattress and moved Jonna closer to him. He touched her cheek with his fingertips, stroking

45

softly. As tired as he knew her to be, he couldn't stop himself from waking her.

"Jonna," he said softly. Bending low, he kissed her cheek. Her skin was warm, flushed with sleep. "Jonna, dear. It's Grant." She moved a fraction, adjusting the hand that lay palm down near her face. Beyond that she didn't stir. He tried one more time, this time placing his hand on her shoulder and shaking her gently.

Jonna came awake, gasping for breath. Stinging darts of pain brought tears to her eyes. She caught enough air to finally cry out. The effect on Grant was the opposite of what she could have wished for. He gathered her in his arms and hugged her. The words were soothing, but the action was not. She screamed this time, and then her screams became sobs. She struggled against him, wrenching her shoulder until the pain threatened to make her pass out.

"For God's sake, man, let her go!"

Grant turned sharply on the bed. He recognized Decker Thorne, but the man's presence in Jonna's home was more confusing than helpful. "Get out!" Grant snapped. "And fetch the doctor. There's something wrong with her."

Disgusted, Decker crossed the room and wrested Grant away from Jonna. That was not accomplished easily. Sheridan was as tall as Decker but thirty pounds heavier, and not one of those pounds was soft. Pulling him up from his sitting position on the bed took the last vestige of Decker's strength.

"Miss Remington?" He turned to Jonna as he pushed Grant away. "Are you all—"

He saw it in her eyes. He knew the blow was coming a full second before it connected. With his strength sapped and his reaction time stretched, Decker couldn't duck the roundhouse punch. Grant Sheridan came from behind, and his fist

46

slammed into Decker's temple. The force of the blow knocked Decker sideways against the rocker. He was out cold before he hit the floor.

He didn't hear Jonna Remington call his name.

Two

"I don't think you're listening to me," Grant said.

Jonna heard the discreetly tempered anger in Grant's tone and finally put her pen down. She looked up from the ledger she was reviewing to regard him with the full attention he thought he deserved. He was standing on the opposite side of her wide desk, his arms braced stiffly on the edge while he leaned forward. It was a posture she knew he used to intimidate shippers and clerks and business associates. He had never done it professionally with her, and she had to remind herself that he still hadn't. This was personal.

Jonna sighed and found a measure of patience she hadn't had a moment before. "I'm not agreeing with you," she said carefully. "That doesn't mean I haven't heard what you've said." She watched Grant react visibly to that. His head jerked back as if she had slapped him lightly on the cheek. "I know you believe you've presented your opinion in language so clear I *must* agree with you, but"—now she shrugged to emphasize her point—"I don't."

Grant's first instinct was to tell Jonna that she couldn't possibly have been listening. He held the words back because he knew he would win no favor by insisting on his point again. He waited until he had reined in his anger before he pushed away from the desk. He walked to the window on the other side of her office, where he had a clear view of the harbor. Rain pounded the wharf and churned the waters. In spite of the downpour Grant could make out his own ships from this vantage point. Bad weather hadn't stopped work and he watched one of his sleek clippers being loaded while he considered his position.

Jonna was quiet. Her eyes followed the rather stiff line of Grant's back to the breadth of his shoulders. His jacket stretched tautly across his solid frame as he crossed his arms in front of him. Jonna's gaze dropped from the fringe of sandy brown hair touching his collar to his narrow waist. He dropped his hands to his sides, but his shoulders didn't relax. There was tension in the hard muscles of his back and at the nape of his neck. It was clear he felt strongly about his view. Jonna only wished he would respect hers. She stared at him, wondering what she might say—or do—to convince him. Her eyes dropped to his lean but powerfully built legs, and her mind wandered. When he turned on her suddenly her cheeks were hot with the direction of her thoughts.

"Are you all right?" he asked.

She nodded and reached for the cup of tea that had been ignored this past hour. It was cold now and faintly bitter—just what she needed. Jonna pretended not to notice that Grant was still studying her. There was concern in his expression, but more than that, there was interest. His eyes were so brown they were very nearly black, yet Jonna could tell they had just darkened as he watched her. She could feel herself going warm again, and she took another sip of tea.

Grant smiled slowly, a beautifully telling smile that said he knew something of what was going through her mind. His features were transformed by that smile from merely handsome to arresting. He shook his head slowly, and the lift of his lips became a trifle self-mocking. He ran a hand through his hair. Anger had dissipated to mild exasperation. "There's nothing I can say that will change your mind?" he asked.

"I think you've said it all," she told him, setting her cup aside. "I'm not throwing Captain Thorne out of my home."

"You make it sound as if you'd be tossing him into the streets. He has a place of his own, doesn't he? He could stay aboard *Huntress* for that matter. It's been two weeks, Jonna." Now he added something he had *not* said before. "There's been talk."

Jonna did not take the bait. "I assumed that's why you brought this up again," she said. "I'd find it very odd indeed if people weren't talking, but I have no control over it, and neither do you." She knew that did not set well with Grant, especially when he still harbored some notion that he had control over her. "Tell me, Grant, do people know how it is that Captain Thorne came to be bedfast?"

"They know about his rescue of you," he said.

"But I was in that water, too. And worse for the experience than the captain. Why do they think he hasn't recovered?"

"I couldn't say."

Jonna noticed he hadn't the grace to look at all contrite. That irritated her. "Then you haven't told anyone that you knocked the man senseless."

"He deserved it."

"He was *trying* to help me."

"He was interfering," Grant said.

"You were hurting me."

Grant's dark eyes softened, as did his tone. "And for that I'm profoundly sorry, but I thought you were having a nightmare. I was trying to comfort you. Must I apologize the rest of my life for mistaking the situation?"

"No, of course not," she said immediately.

"Then . . ." His voice trailed off, but his expression was hopeful.

Jonna frowned. "Then what?" she asked. "Your apology to me changes nothing about Captain Thorne's situation.

Until Dr. Hardy releases him from my care, he will remain a guest in my home."

"You're maddening. Do you know that? Absolutely maddening."

"If you want to be mad at someone, try being mad at yourself. You're fortunate that the blow you gave Captain Thorne only set back his recovery instead of killing him. In his condition he was in no way prepared to fight you."

"That's not how I remember it."

Jonna ignored that. She pressed her fingertips to her temples, closed her eyes, and began massaging away the first hint of a headache. "I can't discuss this any longer, Grant. You're not wearing me down. You're wearing me out. There's a difference, you know."

He crossed the room again and this time rounded her desk. Pushing aside the ledger, he sat on the edge. "Jonna," he said quietly, persuasively. "Jonna. You must listen to me. For appearance's sake, if not for reason's, you should put Thorne up somewhere else. I'll take care of the arrangements and pay for them. That should show you I'm willing to make amends for my behavior that morning. Think what you're doing, Jonna, by having him live in your home. You're my fiancée. Surely you can see it isn't right."

Jonna's hands dropped to her lap. She leaned back. The soft leather upholstery cushioned her head. She opened her eyes and stared at him. "Saying it often doesn't make it so, Grant," she said tiredly. "I've never said I would marry you. Don't press that point on top of the other."

He said nothing for a long minute, then reached for her wrists. Taking them in one of his large hands, he easily pulled Jonna to her feet. She came without resistance to stand between his splayed and outstretched legs. For Grant it was something of a surprise and a disappointment. Overpowering her would have made the moment sweeter. He let go of her wrists and placed his palms on either side of her face. She was watching him intently now, the centers of her violet eyes darkening.

He bent his head and kissed her. Long and thoroughly. There was no consideration for her lack of response. In his own time, he set her from him carefully, with more thoughtfulness than he had shown in taking her. "I'll concede victory to you on the matter of Thorne," he said quietly. "But not on the matter of the other. You *will* be my wife."

It was after eight o'clock when Jonna arrived home. The long day in Remington Shipping's offices had been largely unproductive. Grant Sheridan's departure had in no way meant she could return to business as usual. Not with the imprint of his mouth on hers. Not when he left her feeling uncertain and unsettled.

It was the first time he had kissed her on the mouth. He had taken her hand before and pressed it to his lips. He had unbuttoned her glove and kissed the back of her wrist. He had touched her cheek briefly in greeting when they were in the privacy of her salon or his carriage, but he had never asked for nor taken a more intimate liberty. Until now. She wondered at it, wondered at his timing.

Before this morning all she had wondered about was the kiss. At least the dreaded anticipation of that was behind her.

Jonna slowly removed her damp coat and hat and handed them to Mrs. Davis.

"Is everything all right, Miss Remington?" the housekeeper asked, her brow furrowed.

"What? Oh, yes. Nothing's wrong." Realizing her thoughts were still back at her office, Jonna made an effort to come to the present. "I think I'd like to have dinner in my room," she said. When she saw the housekeeper frown she asked, "Is there some problem with that?"

Mrs. Davis quickly shook her head. "No, not at all . . ." She glanced down the hall toward the dining room. The crease between her brows deepened.

"Mrs. Davis?"

"It's just that Captain Thorne dressed for dinner this evening," the housekeeper said in a rush. "He's waiting for you in the dining room. It was supposed to be a surprise." Her worried expression remained unchanged. "And now I've given it away."

Jonna was not able to school her reaction. It was still a surprise. "Should he be up?" she asked. "What did the doctor say?"

"Dr. Hardy hasn't been here today. As for Captain Thorne, well, there's really no telling him one way or the other what he should do. He has his mind quite made up on the matter."

Just like someone else she knew. Unbidden, her fingers came up to lightly touch her lips. She wished the kiss had gone on longer, wished she knew if time and familiarity would have made her more responsive. Jonna's hand dropped away slowly and she became aware that the housekeeper was waiting for some answer from her. "I'll join the captain, then," she said. "He is a guest, after all."

Decker came to his feet as Jonna opened the pocket doors to the dining room. He made a slight bow and crossed over to close the doors behind her. His light step hardly made a sound on the hardwood floor.

"Captain," Jonna said in acknowledgment.

"Miss Remington."

"You're looking well," she said, surveying him from head to toe. She was vaguely aware that her scrutiny, bold as it was, could have been interpreted as improper. It was justified in her own mind because she had some stake in his good health, or the lack of it.

Amusement brightened Decker's blue eyes. "Are you going to make a bid on me?" he asked. "Shall I show you my teeth?"

"Don't be vulgar."

Rather than being offended by her reprimand, his grin merely deepened. He offered her his elbow. "Allow me, Miss Remington."

Jonna's mouth flattened slightly at his air of gallantry, but she laid a hand lightly on his arm and allowed him to escort her to the table. He held out the chair at the head, seated her, then returned to his place at the other end.

The hearty meal of thinly carved roast beef, baby carrots, and buttered potatoes was served by a young black woman under the watchful eye of Mrs. Davis. Jonna noticed the maid's trembling hands as she held out the platter of meat. "You're doing fine," she said gently.

The young maid said nothing, but in her dark eyes there was instant relief as well as gratitude for the encouragement.

Decker watched this exchange with interest. When the maid came around to him and offered the platter he told her, "Mrs. Davis isn't watching you. She's watching me." His voice, though it was lowered in a confidential tone, was perfectly audible to everyone in the room. "She's afraid I'll steal the silver."

The maid's sloe eyes widened, and she swallowed visibly. It was the very thing she had been warned about. "Yes, sir. I count it myself." She jumped back in alarm as Mrs. Davis called her name sharply. The platter bobbled, but Decker helped her keep her grip on it. As soon as he had served himself, the maid hurried out of the room with the housekeeper only a narrow step behind her.

Decker looked down the length of the table at Jonna, fully expecting her to be scolding him with her sharp glance if not her sharp tongue. Instead, she seemed to be concentrating hard, perhaps too hard, on cutting her meat. Was that a glimmer of a smile he saw her fighting back? He thought he spied the shadow of a dimple at the corner of her mouth.

"I sent Mr. Daniels to the harbor today," Decker said conversationally. "I wanted my clothes from *Huntress*."

Jonna looked up politely and nodded. She had noticed as soon as she walked in the room that Decker had not borrowed the clothes he was wearing from her father's armoire. The shirt and jacket fit him too well, and the trousers were trim around his waist. These clothes were tailored in London. Jonna recognized the precise workmanship because Grant also had his suits made for him there. She was struck by the odd thought that their clothing may have been cut from the same cloth. She wondered about the men.

"It was good of Mr. Daniels to go," he said.

"I'm sure he thought it was what I would have wanted him to do," Jonna said. It was a subtle message that *her* orders were being followed, not his.

"And wasn't it?"

Jonna didn't answer the question directly, but asked one of her own. "Has Dr. Hardy given you leave to be out of bed?"

"He didn't say I couldn't."

Raising one brow, Jonna gave him a knowing look. "Mrs. Davis said the doctor wasn't here today."

"Then you already knew the answer to your question. I think you were trying to trap me in a lie, Miss Remington."

"What I was trying to do was make certain you're well enough to be down here. I wouldn't think you'd want to prolong your recovery."

Decker considered that. He let his eyes wander about the room, making a point to take in the superbly carved mahogany sideboard, the expensive damask drapes, the crystal vase, and the silver candlesticks clustered at the center of the table. When his eyes finally rested on Jonna's face again he said carelessly, "Why not? I find I quite like it here." He regarded her steadily, his expression going from straight-faced to curious. "Are you going to throw something at me?"

Jonna blinked. She realized she was holding her breath and her hands were clenching and unclenching around the napkin in her lap. Her smile was too sweet to be sincere. "Do you think you deserve it, Captain Thorne?"

"I suppose it depends on what you have under the table." He quickly surveyed the silver and china pieces in front of her. Everything seemed to be accounted for. "It must be a napkin. I don't think you'll get much satisfaction from pitching it at me, but yes, it's about what my comment deserves." He watched her visibly restrain herself and kept his own smile in check. There was no point goading her until he got a water goblet thrown at his head. Even if he managed to duck the glass, he'd surely get wet. There was no dignity in that. He was satisfied when she picked up her fork and began eating.

Decker also applied himself to his meal. The roast beef was rare, basted in its own juices, and had been making his mouth water since he'd smelled it being prepared hours earlier. If he was being strictly honest with himself it was more than Jonna's company he had sought this evening. He was tired of the sickroom fare the doctor had ordered for him. In the last few days he had pressed Tess and one of her equally nervous friends into bringing him something more substantial from the cook's larder. But they were rightly afraid to be caught out and lose their positions in the house. It wouldn't be easy for them to find other work, even in Boston where there was considerable tolerance for freeborn blacks and fugitive slaves.

"I noticed you have a number of Negro servants working for you," Decker said.

Jonna wondered at what thoughts had taken him to that observation. Just then young Tess parted the doors and stepped in to offer more food. Had Decker heard her approach? Jonna refused to talk about the servants in front of them, as if they were deaf to what was being said. She waited until Tess quietly left again before she answered. "Five or six, I think. I have as many white servants. You'd have to ask Mrs. Davis. She hires them. I leave the running of the house up to her."

"They're all free men and women, I assume," he said idly.

That comment brought Jonna's sharp-eyed glance. "I should hope so, Captain Thorne. I don't hold with abolitionist talk if that's what you're getting at."

"I wasn't aware I was getting at anything," he said. "It was merely an observation. But since you mentioned it, Boston is quite a stronghold in the abolitionist movement. It wouldn't be surprising if you shared some of those beliefs."

She made a small dismissive motion with her hand. "You're speaking of people like William Lloyd Garrison and his following. Grant thinks he has a level head, but I think Garrison is a fanatic. I take a more tempered view."

"And that is?"

"I don't agree with slavery, but I also don't agree with legislating morality—and that's what Garrison and those like him want. If they can't get it done legally, then they're not above using illegal means. What do they call it? The Underground Road?"

"I think it's the Underground Railroad now," Decker said.

Jonna nodded. "Yes, I believe you're right. Conductors. Stations. Passengers. They can dress it up any way they like, it's all against the law. This country still recognizes slave states and even allows territories to enter the Union under those conditions. Short of taking up arms, I don't see that there is any way to stop it. Remington Shipping does a lot of business in Southern ports, as you well know. I suppose I could make a stand and only take on cotton that's been picked by freeborn men and women, but we'd be out of business in two years, perhaps sooner. It's not prudent to bite the hand that feeds you, Captain. Remember that."

Decker's keen blue eyes narrowed. He was thoughtful. "I wonder if your thinking is perhaps dictated more by your business sense than it is by moral imperative."

Jonna's response was unhesitating. "Business is a moral imperative . . ."

"I see," he drawled.

"I doubt it."

Decker gave her an arch look. "Oh?" he asked softly. "What do you mean by that?"

Jonna opened her mouth to speak, then closed it, thinking better of what she had been about to say. Decker Thorne was her guest. She would not insult him. "Nothing," she said. "It's of no consequence."

But Decker knew it was. He had been treated with nothing but respect since he had been in her home, yet Decker had always known that Jonna Remington didn't respect him. It hadn't been that way at first. When he'd come to the United States and presented himself at Remington Shipping, looking for work, she had not regarded him differently than any of the other men working for her. In fact, he thought, she hadn't noticed him much at all.

That was as he'd wanted it to be. No favors. No additional

expectations. He'd been determined to make his own way. It was the last thing he'd told his brother when he'd left London three years ago.

It had been Colin's idea that he seek out Jonna Remington and apply for a position with her company. Decker had had no experience with ships or sailing, but he had confidence in his ability to learn. What was more, he knew Colin had confidence in his ability as well.

Decker had introduced himself only as Pont Épine, taking the name that Marie Thibodeaux had christened him with when she was teaching him French. It was an awkward translation of his own name and eventually had been Anglicized to Ponty Pine.

It was as Ponty Pine that he had worked for Remington Shipping for the first six months. Then, in an innocent correspondence between his brother and his employer, his identity had been betrayed. Jonna Remington had summoned him to her office and had asked directly if he'd intended to make a fool of her.

Decker had never given any consideration to Jonna's feelings about his deception. Had he considered them at all, he would have concluded that she would have had no feelings. He was aware of the relationship that existed between the Remingtons and his brother. He knew that as a boy Colin had saved Jonna from drowning and so had been given every opportunity to advance his career in the aftermath of that rescue. He knew that Colin had made his fortune working for the Remingtons and that his brother's eventual return to London, his marriage to Mercedes Leyden, even his success in finding Decker, all could be tied to Remington Shipping.

What Decker hadn't anticipated was that Jonna Remington would dislike him so much for not being Colin.

She had never said as much, and Decker suspected she

might never say it. Hell, he acknowledged to himself, she might not even know it.

So he goaded her from time to time. Tweaked her a little here and there, just to see if he could make her say the words aloud. She never did though, or at least she hadn't yet. Watching her now, her features very still and grave, the dark centers of her violet eyes giving away nothing, Decker was again struck by what a private person she was.

More than private, he thought. Alone. Lonely.

"I think it is important," he said, picking up the threads of their conversation. Silence had hovered over the table for too long. "What do you mean I don't understand that business is a moral imperative?"

Jonna set down her water goblet without drinking. "Do you really want to hear this, Captain Thorne? I promise you I will speak plainly."

"I can take it, Miss Remington."

Still, she hesitated. They were not in her office on the waterfront. Decker Thorne was not an employee here. He had saved her life and then come to her assistance only to be laid out cold for it. His recovery had been slow as a fever took him, and two days past the point where she had regained all her strength, he was still fighting for his life. She was not unaware of the debt she owed him, yet, she wondered, had anything really changed?

His act of heroism on the wharf made no essential difference in the way she thought of him. In all likelihood that behavior was an aberration. For all she knew, Jack Quincy had pushed him into the water. What choice did he have then but to attempt a rescue?

Some part of her knew she was being unfair, but she wouldn't consider it now. It was far simpler to interpret his actions to fit her view of him than it was to change her view.

"Very well, Captain," Jonna said. "I have doubts that you know much about the morality of work. Until you came to Remington Shipping, it's my understanding that you never worked in your life. I'm aware that you've been jailed for stealing and that you might well have been hanged for your crimes. I believe it was a lucky encounter with your brother that kept that from happening, and as I told you before, I think you know how to command good fortune."

Jonna paused, wondering if she should go on. Except for the smallest hint of a smile edging the corners of his mouth, Decker's features were passive. That flicker of amusement decided her. She wanted to wipe it off his face. "I like to know the people who work for me, and I suppose I know you no more or less than any of my other employees. What I do know I don't particularly trust. I don't think I need to count the silver or inventory the linens while you're in my home. My sense is that though you tease us with your criminal past from time to time, those days are behind you. By the same token, I don't believe you're a reformed man. You may not take from others any longer, but neither do you give anything. Your attitude, indeed, is quite as careless as your smile.

"Frankly, I find it irritating, but then, you know that. I'm very aware you do it for just that reason. I only regret that I can't seem to ignore it. It would be so much less amusing for you."

Jonna's appetite had fled. More than that, she was drained. Decker was simply studying her now, his expression carefully neutral. She had no idea what he was thinking, and perversely, she wished he would flash that reckless grin. She pushed her plate away, then came to her feet. "If you'll excuse me, Captain Thorne, I—"

"Sit."

Her head snapped back at the tone as much as the command. "I beg your pardon?" It was a stupid thing to say, given that her reaction clearly told him he had been heard. Jonna didn't wait for him to point that out. She sat.

"Good," he said. "Now I have something to tell you." Decker leaned back in his chair, his posture casual as he crossed his long legs at the ankles. "I told you I could take it, Miss Remington. I have no intention of mounting a blistering defense on my behalf. Is that why you were going to run off? Because you thought I meant to argue with you?"

It was, though Jonna didn't like to admit it. "I'm weary of arguments today," she said.

"Jack Quincy told me once that I could sooner turn back a prevailing wind than make you change your opinion. I've always found his counsel to be sound. It certainly seems to hold true for your opinion of me." He pointed to the plate she had pushed away. "Now eat something, then tell me who was brave enough to beard the lioness."

Feeling his eyes on her, Jonna was flooded with an unfamiliar sense of calm. He sat there across from her, unruffled and unrattled by anything she had said. To be that certain of oneself, she thought wistfully, and knew she envied this about him as well. Her eyes dropped away from his untroubled gaze and went to her plate. She picked up her fork and continued eating, surprised to find that she was hungry after all.

"Did Jack really say that about me?" she asked when she had finished most of what was on her plate.

"Would you believe me?"

"Yes," she said without hesitation. "Yes, I would."

"They were Jack's words as near as I can remember them," he confirmed.

She thought about that. "A blistering defense would serve no purpose, would it?"

One corner of his mouth kicked up in a grin. "None."

Tess arrived to clear the table and bring cherry cobbler and coffee. The dishes rattled in her hands as she removed them. She was aware that her presence, where it had been welcomed before as an interruption, was now an intrusion. There was waiting in the silence, and Tess bobbed her curtsy and hurried from the room as quickly as she could.

The moment to laugh had passed, but Jonna wished it could have been otherwise. She poured a small measure of milk in her cup. "Would you prefer liqueur with your coffee?" she asked. "There's some in the sideboard."

"No, nothing. Thank you." He drank his coffee black. "Tell me about all the arguing today," he said.

She found she did want to talk about it. "Most of it was the usual sort of thing that goes on every day. Mr. Edwards wanted another price for his shipment of finished goods, one that was totally unacceptable to me. He thought he could get a better price with the Sheridan Line, then he remembered that Grant wasn't likely to undercut me. That frustrated him, and he started complaining that we controlled all the shipping. I told him to go to Garnet or Canning if he didn't like my prices. In the end he knew he was getting a fair deal from me, but I heartily disliked having to prove it to him."

Decker imagined that some days she was energized by the challenge. Today, he could tell, had been different. "And then?" he prompted.

So Jonna recounted the squabbles and haggling she had been through. Even leaving out her quarrel with Grant, she found herself unburdened at the end.

Decker listened without comment. His posture was at odds with his formal surroundings. Loose and relaxed, his eyes lazily hooded, he was a study in contrasts to the rigid high-backed chair he sat in. He held his coffee cup in front of him, never once replacing it in the saucer, while he heard Jonna out.

He wondered if she would tell him everything. The odds were against it. She spoke soberly about her day, as if each decision she'd made had the same magnitude of consequence for Remington Shipping. She used few gestures as she talked; mostly her slender hands rested quietly in her lap. Her voice was cool and steady, and her spine remained as inflexible as the chair under her.

But then there were her eyes. Even down the length of the table they had the power to arrest Decker's attention. In their darkening violet depths he glimpsed her passion.

"There you have it," she said, coming to a close. She picked up her cup, a bit uncomfortable with the way Decker was staring at her. His lazy regard unnerved her as a more direct approach would not. Jonna found herself brushing back a loose tendril of hair that had fallen across her cheek. She tried to make it a casual gesture, but it felt very much like a vain one. It was out of character for her, and that added to her discomfort. "Would you like something else, Captain?" she asked. "More coffee? A drink?"

Decker smiled slightly as he shook his head. "You've had a day of it, then," he said.

Jonna nodded.

"It must have been a relief to have Mr. Sheridan visit you in the middle of all of it." He saw her fingertips press whitely on her cup. "The eye of the storm, as it were."

Anything but, Jonna thought miserably. If she had recounted her day accurately Decker would have known that Grant Sheridan *was* the storm. "How did you know Mr. Sheridan came to my office?" she asked.

"Mr. Daniels told me," Decker said. "Remember? He went to get my clothes from the ship. I suppose he felt a need to explain his presence at the harbor in case you heard about it from someone else, so he stopped at your office."

"While Mr. Sheridan was there."

"Yes."

The silence was drawn out while Jonna considered what it was that Mr. Daniels might have overheard and, more importantly, what he might have related to the captain. There was no clue from Decker himself. The slight smile and watchful blue eyes, even the single arched brow, only made him more inscrutable. He could be aware of everything or nothing, and he still would maintain that quietly amused expression.

Decker decided to make it easy for her. "I'll be leaving tonight," he said. "Jack's been paying on the room I let, so I still have some place to go. He tells me that *Huntress* is scheduled to make a run to Charleston in two days. I'd like to be at the helm if you're agreeable."

Jonna blinked, trying to take it in. "There's no reason for you to leave tonight," she said.

"There's no reason for me to stay."

"Are you quite recovered? I think I would prefer to hear from Dr. Hardy before you leave." She could hardly believe she was saying these things. His departure would ease the tension between her and Grant. She wondered again what he knew. Was this a gallant gesture on his part or a selfish one? He had mentioned *Huntress*. Was that behind his desire to leave? "You can go in the morning after Dr. Hardy examines you," she said.

Decker's grin deepened. Jonna spoke as if she could actually stop him from leaving.

"I won't let you take out *Huntress* if you go tonight," she told him.

Decker sobered immediately and leaned forward in his chair. So she *could* keep him here. He wouldn't underestimate her again. "Do you always get your own way?" he asked.

"Yes," she said simply. "I do."

Decker considered that. His eyes fell on the dimple at the corner of her mouth. She was looking as pleased with herself as her aloof expression allowed. "Your fiancé must hate that. Sheridan seems like a man of similar mind."

"No matter what you've heard to the contrary, Grant Sheridan and I are not engaged. As for wanting his own way, he's no different than any other man of my acquaintance."

"Really? I thought I just gave in to your blackmail rather easily."

Jonna shrugged. "That's because you have no backbone."

Decker was aware he was slouching in his chair again. "Literally or figuratively?" he asked, idly curious.

Her mouth flattened. "Both."

He had no clear idea how he might have responded to that, but he was saved the effort of thinking about it by voices in the hallway. Even though it was muted by the closed pocket doors, Decker recognized Grant Sheridan's curt, commanding tone as he ordered Mrs. Davis to show him to the dining room.

Jonna was on her feet and moving toward the doors when they opened. "Grant," she said in greeting, holding out her hands. "This is a surprise."

Sheridan all but ignored her, looking over her head to spear Decker with a sharp glance. There was no challenge in Decker's expression. He returned Sheridan's gaze, his own features remaining impassive. It was Grant who finally looked away. He took Jonna's extended hands in his. "I was on my way back from the meeting at Faneuil Hall," he said. "I thought I would stop and offer my apologies for this afternoon."

If Grant had not been holding her hands Jonna would have touched her lips. Was he apologizing for the kiss? Their argument did not seem to warrant an apology. They were simply of two different minds on the matter of Decker Thorne's presence in her home. "Please, Grant, won't you sit down?" She looked over her shoulder at Decker. "Better yet, why don't we retire to the parlor? It's more comfortable there."

Decker declined. "I'm away to bed," he told them. "I expect to be released by Dr. Hardy in the morning."

Grant looked to Jonna for an explanation.

"Captain Thorne is anxious to take back his command," she said. "He leaves tomorrow if the doctor approves."

"That's good news."

Decker rose from his chair and walked almost soundlessly to the doors. He caught Sheridan's eye as he passed. "I thought you would think so," he said. Then he left the couple alone.

It was much later when Decker left his room. The house was quiet. The servants who lived in the mansion were asleep in their own quarters, and Jonna had long ago retired to her room in the west wing. Decker's progress through the hall and down the back stairs was quiet. He slipped soundlessly through the kitchen and opened a door in the pantry to go even farther into the bowels of the house. At last he found the laundry.

His clothes had never been returned to him. Lying abed these past two weeks, he hadn't needed them. On the brief occasions he did get up, he had a nightshirt and dressing gown compliments of the late John Remington. He had asked Mrs. Davis about his things but she had avoided answering him directly. He understood then that Jonna was concerned he would leave if they were returned. That had been behind his decision to send Mr. Daniels to the harbor. While the man wouldn't disobey Jonna's orders to leave Decker's clothes in the laundry, he was willing to retrieve things from *Huntress*.

Decker found his clothing just where Tess had told him he would. He separated the clean and neatly folded stack until he had his vest. Setting his candle down, Decker held up the article. All evidence of saltwater stains had been removed from the buff material. A loose button had been sewn on tighter. Decker noted these things, but they did not interest him.

The purpose of his late-night trek through the silent house was to retrieve something from inside the vest. He laid his hand across the concealed pocket and felt the familiar bulge. His talisman was there. He knew relief then, something he hadn't felt in all the days it had been out of his sight and beyond his touch. It was not superstition that had brought him to this place. It was his heritage.

Decker slipped two fingers into the small pocket and caught the earring. He drew it out. The gold pendant glowed in the candlelight. The pearl was almost luminous. He let it slide into the heart of his palm and studied it. It looked none the worse for its dip into Boston Harbor or the drubbing it took in the laundry. He knew he was lucky to still have it. He could have lost it to harbor water or wash water. Anyone handling the vest could have found it, and probably had, yet no one had taken it.

There was a time in his life when he would not have been so generous.

Decker's hand closed over the earring. He picked up the candle and the rest of his clothes and mounted the stairs to the kitchen. He stopped on the threshold of the pantry. Jonna was sitting alone at the table, a mug of warm milk in her hands. There was no surprise on her features when she looked up and saw him.

"I couldn't sleep," she said.

Decker didn't offer the same excuse. He hadn't even tried to sleep. He had purposely waited for the rest of the household to do so. Obviously he had misjudged her. "I needed to get the rest of my belongings."

Jonna didn't comment on the absurdity of the hour he had chosen to do that. "Are you leaving?" she asked quietly.

"You mean now?" He shook his head. "No, in the morning." He watched her eyes drop back to the mug in her hands. Her lashes were thick and every bit as dark as her hair. The steam from the warm milk had flushed her skin. She looked very young in her plain cotton shift and worn dressing gown. Her hair was loosely plaited but not secured, and the end that had been pulled over her shoulder was already unraveling. He had an urge to glance under the table to see if her feet were bare.

In this unguarded moment she did not look at all like the woman who ran a shipping empire.

Decker felt a drop of hot wax splash his thumb. He pushed away from the door frame and laid his clothes on the table. He set his candle beside Jonna's and peeled back the wax.

"Did you hurt yourself?" She put her mug down and without asking his permission took his hand in hers. His fist was still closed over the earring. "Let me see."

"It's nothing."

"Your thumb will blister. You should put cool water on it."

Decker withdrew his hand. Her fingers had been very gentle as they moved over his skin. "It's nothing," he said again.

She shrugged. "Would you like some milk? I can warm it for you."

"I don't like warm milk."

Jonna's glance went to her mug, and her faint smile was wry. "I don't either."

"Then why . . . ?"

"Habit, I suppose. Comfort, perhaps."

Decker saw her eyes drop immediately as if she were embarrassed by the confession. He was uncertain what he should say. He wondered what she would do if he slipped his fingers in her hair and raised her face and kissed her tremulous mouth. Would she stop him if he laid one hand over her breast?

"I used to make my father a cup of warm milk when he couldn't sleep," she said after a moment. "We'd sit here in the kitchen and talk, sometimes just a few minutes, sometimes until the sun came up."

"You miss him."

"Most every day," Jonna said.

She seemed not to mind his company. Decker pulled out a chair and sat down at a right angle to her. "Do you miss your mother like that?" he asked.

"No," she said. "But he did. I know that now. I didn't have many years with my mother so the time with my father was especially precious." She glanced at Decker again as if to gauge his reaction to her next words. "He wanted a son, you know."

Neither Jack nor his brother had ever mentioned it. That may have been another reason Colin had become so important to the Remingtons. "No, I didn't know."

"It's true. Mother died giving him a boy. The boy died, too. I'm not sure Papa ever forgave himself." Jonna straightened in her chair, laughing a bit uneasily. "I can't imagine why I told you that," she said.

Decker pushed the mug of milk completely out of her reach. "Perhaps you should stick to the hard stuff," he said lightly. She smiled then, and it had the power to pin Decker back in his chair. It occurred to him that she was right to keep her expression guarded and her thoughts to herself. In Boston Harbor women who looked like Jonna Remington did now weren't in command anywhere but the backstreet bedrooms.

Jonna's smile wavered, then finally faded as Decker continued to stare at her. She made a swipe at her upper lip to remove any vestige of a milk mustache. "What do you have there?" she asked, pointing to his closed hand. "Is it the earring?"

Both of Decker's brows shot up. "You know about it?"

"Of course," she said simply. "One of the maids found it in your vest when it was being laundered. She showed it to Mrs. Davis who brought it to me. I assured her it wasn't stolen and told her to put it back." Jonna extended one hand, palm up. "May I?"

With some reluctance, though he couldn't say what was at the root of it, Decker unfolded his fist and dropped the earring into Jonna's hand.

She admired it, turning it over in her palm so she could see the *ER* inscribed clearly on the raindrop of gold. "It's beautiful," she said. Her tone was hushed, a shade reverent. "Elizabeth Regina. Colin described this to me. It was made for her coronation, wasn't it? That makes it—"

"Almost three hundred years old."

"It's very valuable."

"It's priceless," Decker said tersely.

Jonna heard the unfamiliar edge in his voice. She returned the earring and this time he tucked it back into the pocket of his vest. "I'm sorry," she said. "I didn't mean to offend you by assigning some dollar amount to it. I have some idea what it means to you."

"You can only know what Colin's told you about it," he said coldly. "You haven't the vaguest notion what it means to me."

Jonna's brows rose slightly. "I'm sorry," she said again. "You're right, of course."

Decker didn't indicate what he thought of her apology or even if he'd heard. He came to his feet as she was making it, and the chair scraped noisily on the hardwood floor. "I think I'll have that drink after all," he said.

"The milk's in the cooler on the back—" She stopped because Decker was heading back to the pantry. He returned with a half-used bottle of whiskey that he had spied on his way to the cellar.

"Glasses?"

Jonna pointed to a cupboard to the left of the sink. "Two, please."

Decker didn't comment, but took a second one from the cabinet. He carried them both to the table along with the whiskey and poured a good measure in each. Raising them, he eyed both carefully, and finally gave Jonna the one that he judged to hold a fraction less. "So why can't you sleep?" he asked. "Did you and Sheridan argue again?"

"Again?" She started to make a denial, then thought better of it. What did it matter if Decker knew about her earlier discussion with Grant? What did it matter if he knew about this one? "You heard him say he went to Faneuil Hall this evening. Garrison was speaking."

"An abolitionist meeting."

Jonna nodded.

"You don't approve."

"It's not that I disapprove exactly," she said. "I think it's dangerous. He was very excited when he came back here. He has some idea that he might be able to meet Falconer."

"Falconer?" He looked at Jonna blankly. Clearly she expected him to react. "I don't know the name."

"Then you're the only one in Boston who doesn't. Don't you read the papers, Captain Thorne?"

"I haven't recently."

"Falconer has been news long before you took to a sickbed."

"Then I overlooked that column," he said carelessly.

Jonna's snort clearly indicated it was much as she'd expected. She went on to explain. "Falconer is the name some freed slaves gave to their liberator. Garrison heard about it and published it in his paper."

"Then it's not the man's name."

Jonna's look was frank. "What makes you think their liberator is a man?" she asked. "She could be a woman."

"Point taken." He sipped his whiskey.

"It's probably a man," she conceded. "And I doubt Falconer is remotely close to his real name. That would be rather foolish, wouldn't it? It certainly wouldn't be the slaves intention to betray him."

Jonna had sat back in her chair and pulled her knees up to her chest. Her toes peeped out from under her dressing gown. They were indeed bare, Decker noticed. "Why does Grant want to meet him?" he asked.

"He has some idea that he can help Falconer. Money. A ship. Another connection to the Underground. Any of those reasons or all of them. Grant wants to act on a cause he believes in."

"Mr. Sheridan is a man of backbone, then. How lucky for you."

Jonna's violet eyes searched Decker's face for a trace of sarcasm. It was as absent from his cleanly carved features as from his tone. "Yes," she said at last. "Yes, to both."

Decker wondered that she didn't sound convinced. He recalled she had made a point earlier this evening of saying that Sheridan was not her fiancé. "You're worried about him," Decker said.

"I think I have reason to be."

Decker rubbed the side of his face where Sheridan had clipped him. "I think he's able to take care of himself."

"In a fight, perhaps. I'm talking about something that could get him hanged."

"Not here in Boston."

"But Grant goes aboard his ships from time to time. And he goes south. If he were to take on fugitive slaves . . ."

"I see." He hesitated, finished his drink, then plunged in. "Tell me something, Miss Remington. With so much to admire about the man, why haven't you agreed to marry Sheridan?"

Jonna didn't answer immediately. Until the words came out of her mouth, she didn't know what she would say. "Would you mind very much kissing me?"

Three

Studying her face, Decker said nothing. It was an earnest request, quite sincere, but he wondered how much she was already regretting it. "I wouldn't mind at all," he said finally, quietly. *But is it a good idea?* That question was not given a voice. He leaned forward in his chair.

Jonna blinked. "No," she said.

Decker's expression indicated neither disappointment nor relief, both of which he felt in some measure. He stopped, paused, then pushed himself back again. "All right."

"No," she said, shaking her head. "You don't understand."

Decker didn't doubt it for a second. "You're probably right."

"Could you stand first?"

He considered that. Apparently she wanted to direct this kiss. He fought the urge to laugh out loud and pull her into his arms right then. How typically, refreshingly Jonna Remington. "Very well," he said, coming to his feet. He added in what he hoped was a helpful tone, "But from this distance the best I can do is blow you a kiss."

A small vertical crease appeared between her feathered brows as she frowned up at him. "If you're not going to be serious . . ."

"Yes," he said. "Of course."

She continued to stare at him, searching his features for some hint that he was laughing at her. He merely looked expectant now. Jonna spoke before her courage faltered. "You need to come around here," she said, pointing to the edge of the table on her side.

Decker moved around the corner. Without any prompting from her this time he sat on the edge, his legs stretched out in front of him, his hands resting casually on either side of his hips.

She nodded, satisfied. "Yes, that's it."

"I thought it might be," he said dryly.

Jonna ignored that. "Would you take my wrist?" she asked.

He reached for her.

"Both of them," she said.

"You have to be specific."

"Both of them," she repeated.

He took a wrist in each hand. He knew what should happen now, but he waited for her instructions.

"Could you bring me to my feet?"

Decker didn't act immediately. "Is it just a gentle urging?" he asked. "Or should it be more commanding?"

"The latter," said Jonna. "Almost impulsive."

He nodded sagely. "Masterful, then." He pulled her to her feet in a single motion, and she came to rest quite naturally between his splayed legs. He continued to hold her wrists. Beneath his thumbs he felt her pulse racing, then acknowledged that it could be his own. Decker's head tilted slightly to one side as he continued to regard her with more detachment than he felt. "And now?" he asked.

"Now you should kiss me."

He began to lower his head.

Jonna's eyes closed in anticipation of the touch of his mouth. She waited, wondering how it might be different than with Grant, wondering if he would pull a response from her or find that she had very little to give.

Nothing happened.

She opened her eyes slowly and found herself staring directly into Decker's startlingly blue ones. "What is it?" she asked. She did not care at all for the breathlessness in her voice or for his brief, wry expression that said he noticed it. "Well," he said, drawing out the single word. "I was wondering what sort of kiss it should be."

Jonna frowned. "What do you mean?"

"There *are* different kinds, you know."

"I'm sure I don't," she said primly.

"You don't?" Decker straightened now, putting some distance between them. Her face remained raised toward his, her violet eyes wide and unwavering, her mouth slightly parted. Her glossy black braid still lay over her shoulder. For a moment his attention was caught by it, caught by the curling end, the way it curved around her breast. "I thought this was an experiment of sorts. Was I mistaken?"

Jonna shook her head slowly.

"Then you must know the sort of kiss you want."

"Yes, but—"

Decker's voice was compelling. "Tell me."

Heat flushed Jonna's face. She started to pull away only to discover he was holding fast. The distance he had put between them disappeared again. It was when she opened her mouth to speak that his lips covered hers.

Decker had anticipated Jonna's startled, rigid reaction. His thighs tightened to keep her intimately in place, and he did not release her wrists. Her mouth was warm, the sweet taste of milk lingering on her lips. It was a taste he thought he might come to like, and he pressed the kiss more deeply.

He felt the first tentative stirrings of her response when she relaxed against him. His tongue traced the shape of her upper lip, then the ridge of her teeth. Her mouth opened wider, and he felt her breath catch. She leaned into him. He felt the outline of her breasts through their clothes. If she moved any closer she would feel the outline of his arousal. He didn't think she was prepared for that.

It was with more than a little reluctance that Decker broke off the kiss. "That would be one kind of kiss," he said. The steadiness of his voice was a wonder to him. "There are others."

Jonna opened her eyes slowly and found herself being studied with irritatingly frank regard. "That one will be quite sufficient," she said.

"I thought it might be. That's why I started there." He bent his head, but Jonna turned hers aside.

"I meant that one *was* quite sufficient," she told him. "There's no need for you to do it again."

He shrugged. "I don't mind."

"I do." She looked down at her side, where his hand still covered her wrist. "You can let me go now."

"I could."

Jonna's head snapped around. "It wasn't a suggestion."

Decker kept her right where she was. "You know, Miss Remington, you could get into a lot of trouble inviting men to kiss you. It's something you should think about before you offer yourself up the next time." He felt her stiffen at the rebuke, but she didn't offer a response. "Very well. Just so you understand there won't be any more experiments at my expense." Letting go of her wrists, Decker allowed her to step back. He crossed his legs at the ankle and folded his arms across his chest. His look was considering now. "Did you discover what you wanted to know?"

"Yes," she said quietly. "Yes, I did."

"And?"

"And the experiment wasn't about you at all, Captain Thorne. It was about me." She began to turn away. Softly, more to herself than to him, she added, "I don't suppose marriage will suit at all."

Then she was gone.

Dr. Hardy visited his patient the following morning and pronounced Decker fit for duty. Although the doctor offered to inform Jonna himself, Decker wanted that pleasure. He had heard her leave for the harbor before it was light out, and he couldn't help but wonder if she had been to sleep at all. He hadn't. "But perhaps you might write something down," he told the physician. "She won't be entirely sure I'm telling the truth."

Hardy laughed. "Just so," he said. "You know her well."

Decker thought about her parting words last night. He didn't know her at all. "Well enough," he said to close the subject. He waited for the doctor to scribble down the order, and as soon as he was gone Decker began packing.

Jonna was seated behind her desk when Decker was announced by her secretary. She didn't get up to greet him. "The doctor's been to see you?" she asked.

"I'm sure you were an influence there. I was his first house call." Decker's eyes suddenly narrowed on Jonna's face. Her skin was pale, and there was a tightness about her mouth that spoke more of pain than disapproval. "Are you feeling well?" he asked. "Perhaps I should—"

She waved his concern aside. The gesture ended with her hand coming to rest on her lap, outside of the line of his vision. Her fingers knotted with the fingers of her other hand and she pressed hard enough to make her knuckles white. It kept her from thinking about the throbbing pain in her ankle. "I take it he thinks you're able to work."

"That's why I'm—" He stopped this time without any prompting from Jonna. Tossing his valise on a chair, he rounded her desk. At first he couldn't see what was wrong, but he didn't miss the white-knuckled fist. His eyes lifted to her face, then dropped again, this time following the raised line of her dress under the desk. The skirt of her gown and a full complement of starched petticoats hid her legs from his view, but he could tell she had one limb propped on something. He hunkered down for a closer look. Without asking permission, he lifted the hem of her gown.

Jonna pushed at her dress and tried to move out of his reach. Shifting her weight only caused her pain, and he was already allowing her hem and petticoats to fall back into place. Mustering what dignity she could, she asked stiffly, "Are you quite through?"

Decker's brows rose at her tone. "No," he said. "But you are."

"What is that supposed to mean?"

"I'm taking you home."

Jonna pushed herself upright in the chair. Her ankle fell off the stool and her heel bumped the floor. She thought she would faint from the pain. "No, you're not." As a protest it was rather pathetic, and she wasn't surprised when he ignored her.

Decker came to his feet and went to the door, calling for her secretary in a tone that had the older man stepping lively. "Get Miss Remington's carriage," he said. "She's going home now."

"Thank God," the secretary said. He looked past Decker's shoulder to see that Jonna was glaring at him, branding him a traitor with only her eyes. At the moment he didn't care. "I wanted to send her home when she hobbled in here, but she wouldn't go." He glanced down at his own slight frame and then with a touch of envy at Decker's. "Twenty years ago I'd have carried her out of here myself," he said.

Jonna called out tartly to him. "Twenty years ago I was

four, Mr. Caplin. Everyone carried me."

Samuel Caplin pulled himself up to his full height and straightened his narrow shoulders. "And you weren't half so sharp with that tongue," he said smartly. He looked back at Decker. "I'll be happy to get her carriage."

Decker let the door stand open and turned to Jonna. "Twenty years ago someone should have turned you over their knee." Before she could come back at him, he was crossing the room and pulling back her chair. "Put your right arm around my neck," he said.

"I need my coat." She pointed to where it was hanging beside the door. She was in too much pain to smile at Decker's frustrated sigh. In other circumstances she would have enjoyed seeing him lose his air of implacable calm. This was a moment worth committing to memory and savoring later. Jonna let him help her slip into her dark green velvet coat while she hobbled unsteadily on one foot. "My hat," she said. He crossed the room again and handed her the matching velvet bonnet. She put it on, but it was Decker who tied the satin ribbon under her chin.

"Now will you put your arm around my shoulders?"

"My boot," she said. "It's under the desk. I had to take it off."

"A mistake," he said. "But I think you already know that." Decker scooped up the black kid boot. The side lacings hung open. "There's no chance of putting this on your foot again. You can hold it." He handed it to her, then turned to offer his shoulder. "If there's nothing else . . ."

"You will not find me a lightweight, you know. And you've only just recovered yourself."

Decker eyed Jonna's slender build critically. "Miss Remington, soaking wet you're hardly more than a handful. Now, come aboard."

Jonna could not think of another thing to delay the inevitable. He did not seem to find her height at all intimidating. "Very well," she said, sighing herself now. "But you can't say I—"

He picked her up smoothly, one arm at her back, the other under her knees. He noticed she naturally slipped her other arm around his shoulders. Her weight, such as it was, was distributed evenly and Decker had no difficulty in carrying her from the second floor offices of Remington Shipping to the carriage waiting at the door. The driver helped him assist her into the carriage and then they were off.

"You forgot your valise," she said. Why was it, she wondered, that she was more breathless than he?

"What?" Decker was sitting opposite her. He had her injured foot in his lap and was lifting her dress to get a better look at it.

She could not take her eyes off his hands. "I said, you forgot your valise."

"I'll get it later," he said absently. Decker ran his fingers lightly over the swollen area. Even through her stockings he could make out the livid discoloration of her skin. He felt her stiffen and glanced up. "Am I hurting you?"

She shook her head. In truth, she could hardly feel his fingers on her skin, but watching his hand move over her flesh was powerful in another way. "No, there's nothing you can do to make it hurt worse."

"Can you move it?"

Jonna rotated her foot, a motion she already knew she could do. "There. You can see for yourself that it's not broken. Merely sprained."

She started to remove her foot from his hands, but Decker cupped it gently and cradled it in his lap. "You will keep it right here," he said. "And when we reach your house I will carry you inside and up the stairs and directly to your room. We will not stop in the foyer for you to remove your hat and coat or bark orders at Mrs. Davis or Mr. Daniels. We will not stop in the library so you can get work to do, and we won't wait for Dr. Hardy to get some laudanum down your throat."

"I don't bark."

He smiled. "No, you don't. You don't have to."

She wondered what that meant.

"How did this happen?" he asked.

Jonna had known he would get around to asking the question. She was only uncertain as to how she should answer. What part of the truth did she want anyone to know? "I fell," she said.

Decker's eyes darkened, and he pinned her back with the glance. "Does your lack of respect for me extend to my intelligence?"

Not accustomed to be taken to task, Jonna felt herself flushing. "No," she said softly. "I have never thought you unintelligent."

"Then give my question the full response it deserves."

Jonna winced, as much at the rebuke as she did at her attempt to find a more comfortable position. "It happened moments after I stepped down from my carriage," she said, as she settled back against the leather seat. "Cargo was being unloaded from wagons onto one of the ships. It was all the usual activity. I paid it hardly any attention until one of the wagon drivers couldn't control his horse. It got away from him, wagon and all, and came right in my direction. He ran alongside but couldn't catch it. It was stupid of me, I know, but I couldn't move out of the way. Not, that is, until the last possible moment. People were shouting at me, of course, but I couldn't seem to make sense of what they were saying. I just kept staring at the horse. Then, I did move, or at least I think I did. I heard someone say the horse actually knocked me aside, but I'm not sure that's what happened. I only know that I went head over bucket. I collided with a pyramid of crates, knocked two of them over and wrenched my ankle."

"Then you put on a calm face and went to work anyway."

"Well, yes," she said simply. In Jonna's mind there had been no other choice. "I couldn't let anyone know I was hurt." She remembered looking up into a sea of concerned faces. How many of them, she wondered, had seen her fall into the harbor only two weeks earlier? She had let herself be helped up, but had declined any further assistance. "I hadn't been able to move out of the way," she told Decker. "I felt very foolish."

And that emotion would have dictated her actions, Decker realized. "Standing still probably saved your life," he said. "You let the animal make the decision. If you had leaped you might well have charged right into him."

Jonna's eyes widened. "I hadn't thought of that."

"What happened to the driver?"

"I don't know."

"He didn't come around to apologize? You mean there was no offer to make amends?"

Jonna looked out the carriage window. They were turning the corner to Beacon Hill, and she was grateful their ride was nearly at an end. Decker's questions didn't bother her half as much as the way he was watching her answering them. It was as if he knew what she said was not nearly so important as how she said it, almost as if he were anticipating a lie or perhaps that she would not tell the whole truth. Carefully schooling her features, she returned his steady stare. "I suppose he had his hands full with his animal. I was probably gone by the time he had the poor thing calmed."

Decker didn't dispute her theory. He eased her foot off his

lap as the carriage slowed in front of her home. The door opened and he helped Jonna up, then delivered her into the hands of the driver. She leaned against the driver until Decker stepped out and lifted her. Her arms slipped around his shoulders without prompting. Decker carried her up the walk while the driver ran ahead to get the door and announce their approach. Although Decker was only ten paces behind the man, Mrs. Davis was already hovering by the time he and Jonna crossed the threshold.

Jonna dropped the boot she was carrying into the housekeeper's outstretched hands as they passed. True to his word, Decker didn't pause to let her remove her bonnet or slip out of her coat. Without once pausing in his stride, he took her directly up the stairs to her room. Mrs. Davis's presence behind him was no more annoying than a puppy nipping at his heels.

In spite of Decker's careful handling, Jonna's eyes were glazed with pain by the time they reached her room. He set her on the bed before he helped her with the bonnet and coat. "Cold compresses, Mrs. Davis," he said. "And laudanum. It's a severe sprain."

"I'm going to send for the doctor."

"That's fine," Decker said. "In the meantime, cold compresses and laudanum."

The housekeeper turned to find two of the maids hovering in the doorway. Their large brown eyes were anxiously taking in the scene, and there was a grayish pallor to their dark complexions. "Tess, you fetch the doctor. Emily, get the other things Captain Thorne wants." The girls disappeared immediately, but not before Decker had glimpsed them.

"What's wrong with them?" he asked.

The housekeeper sat on the bed beside Jonna. "I don't know what you mean."

"It's a sprain, not a fatal disease," he told her. "Those girls looked frightened."

"I'm sure I don't know what gets into their minds," she said dismissively. "They're like children."

Decker was surprised by the housekeeper's tone. It was not a statement merely about Tess and Emily. She was speaking of every person of color. He was about to ask why she hired them when Jonna's wince drew his attention. "I think we should elevate her foot," he said. He leaned across Jonna, drew a pillow from the other side of the bed, and slipped it under her ankle.

When there was nothing else for him to do but wait, Decker elected to wait elsewhere. He excused himself and went downstairs. Neither Jonna nor the housekeeper heard him leave by the back door.

Mrs. Davis's voice was hushed. "God forgive me, I dislike the things I have to say sometimes. Captain Thorne must think me the worst sort of person."

"He probably has no opinion on the matter," Jonna said, wondering that the housekeeper cared. She closed her eyes and tried to block out the pain. "He rarely has an opinion on anything."

Mrs. Davis laid her hand across Jonna's brow. Her employer's skin was clammy. "Let me help you change," she said. "And cover you up. The captain's right about the cold compress and laudanum. You need both." She helped Jonna sit up, then began to unfasten the back of her gown. "How did this happen, Miss Remington?"

Jonna told her, offering no more or less of the story than she had offered Decker. The housekeeper said nothing until she had finished helping Jonna change into a shift and had tucked the quilts around her. When she spoke she didn't offer Jonna sympathy. She went directly to the problem that was uppermost on her mind—and Jonna's.

"What will we do?" she asked. "Did you see Tess and Emily? Captain Thorne didn't mistake their feelings. They are most definitely frightened."

"Then you will have to calm them. As the captain said, it's a sprain, not a fatal disease. You'll have to make them understand that nothing's changed except the timing. A week is all I'll need. Two at the most."

"Isn't there someone else?" she asked. "Perhaps I could—"

"No." Jonna was firm, and pain made her voice harsh. She caught her breath and tried for a softer tone. "I'm sorry . . . but, no. I won't let you."

"Then Mr. Sheridan. He's the most logical choice."

"I won't have him involved either."

"But surely . . . if I went to him and explained—"

"No!"

Mrs. Davis sat back. She frowned disapprovingly but said nothing. Emily had entered the room with the laudanum and compress. The housekeeper took both, laid the compress carefully across Jonna's ankle, then ladled two spoonfuls of laudanum down her throat. "You can go, Em," she told the maid. "I'll speak with you and Tess later."

Emily looked uncertainly from the housekeeper to her employer. Her eyes remained troubled, but she didn't question the order. "Me and Tess," she said shyly, "we both hope you feel better soon." Then she seemed to realize how that might sound and added quickly, "Not because of us. I mean, we wish—"

The housekeeper came to her feet. "Miss Remington knows what you mean, Emily. Please wait outside. I'll be with you in a moment."

Emily bobbed a curtsy and fled.

"I think she's frightened of me," Jonna said.

Mrs. Davis straightened her apron and smoothed the front. "Emily's in awe of you," she said. "She's *frightened* of me."

That made Jonna smile because she knew how untrue it was. "Would you ask Captain Thorne to come up here? I'd like to talk to him before the laudanum dulls my senses."

It was Emily who returned a few minutes later to inform her employer that Decker Thorne was nowhere to be found.

Jonna was able to walk with a cane after two days of bed rest. She suffered the confinement, rather than embraced it. Conducting the business of Remington Shipping from her bedroom, in spite of Dr. Hardy's orders to the contrary, Jonna managed to see that contracts were honored and cargoes were held.

Decker never explained his disappearance from the house that morning, and Jonna, less sharp with the effects of the laudanum, forgot about it until after he had sailed. As the days passed it didn't seem so important.

It was not that she didn't think about Decker Thorne. On the contrary, and somewhat to her annoyance, Jonna found his likeness appearing in her mind's eye at the oddest moments. She told herself it was because she had entrusted him with *Huntress* and a valuable cargo of rugs and rum. He was returning with cotton, for which the New England mills were paying the best money in two years for a shipment. She concentrated on that when she thought of him. It was less troubling than remembering the kiss in her kitchen.

Grant visited her daily while she was confined to her room and came for dinner when she was able to move easily up and down the stairs. After meals they would retire to the music room, where he would play the spinet. Jonna shared the bench and turned the sheet music, and while she watched his beautiful hands move over the keys with fluid grace, she thought of Decker's lean fingers sliding over her ankle, his hands disappearing under the hem of her gown, his thumbs caressing the undersides of her wrists.

"I'm leaving for Charleston tomorrow," Grant told her ten days into her recovery. "I hope you understand I wouldn't go unless it were absolutely necessary."

Jonna looked past Grant to the doors of the music room. A maid was framed in the entrance, holding a tea service in front of her. Her dark eyes betrayed her uncertainty. Jonna motioned her to enter. "Bring the tray here, Mattie. I'll pour."

Mattie nodded once and proceeded into the room slowly, carefully balancing the tray with its delicate china cups and heavy silver service. She set it down on the table beside Jonna.

"Thank you," Jonna said when the girl simply stood there. "You may go."

The young woman didn't respond immediately. She smoothed the front of her neat apron in a perfect imitation of the housekeeper. Her wide mouth was tremulous, and there was heat rising in a face that was the color of cocoa. It was difficult for her to keep her hands from pressing her cheeks.

"Yes?" Jonna asked. "What is it?"

"Miz Davis tol' me to ask if there's anythin' else."

"And now you have," Jonna said. "Please tell Mrs. Davis that nothing further is required."

"Yes, ma'am." Mattie did not so much take her leave of the room as flee it.

Jonna began to pour tea while Grant, who had watched the exchange with interest, got up to attend the doors that Mattie failed to close. "Where do you find these girls?" he asked as he returned to the settee. He took the cup and saucer Jonna held out to him. "That one can't have any experience in service."

89

Jonna set the silver pot down and stirred sugar into her tea. "I couldn't say. Mrs. Davis hires all the help. But you're right about Mattie. She doesn't have experience. Mrs. Davis has been training her these past few days, and I think she's coming around. She's just nervous about pleasing me."

"That, at least, I can understand."

Jonna's head tilted to one side as she regarded Grant consideringly. "Now what do you mean by that?"

"Well, my dear, you cannot be the easiest employer to work for. You seem to change your staff as regularly as you change bonnets, and with no more consideration."

"What *are* you talking about, Grant?"

"I haven't seen that one colored girl who served us dinner a few evenings ago."

"You must mean Tess," she said.

"Yes, I think that was her name."

"And I'm certain that's still her name," Jonna said tartly. "If you're really interested in what's become of her, you'll have to get the details from Mrs. Davis. I believe the girl was let go because of some missing silver. And before you ask, her friend Emily elected to go with her. Apparently she thought her friend was wrongly accused."

"Well," Grant said somewhat stiffly, "you *did* have Decker Thorne staying in this house."

"Are we going to argue about that again?" she asked. "I'd really rather not."

"It doesn't have to be an argument."

"Not if I agree with you, it doesn't."

Grant leaned back on the settee and raised his cup. His distant and dark eyes regarded Jonna over the rim before he drank. "When does *Huntress* return?" he asked.

"A few days from now," she said. "No more than a week."

"You're confident he'll return with your ship."

Jonna poured more tea for herself and spoke when she could do so lightly, without sarcasm. "I don't think he'll steal the clipper, Grant. It's not as if he could slip it into a pocket and not be noticed."

Grant set his cup and saucer aside. "You're too trusting, Jonna. He's not his brother."

"I've always been aware of that," she said. "But it's an interesting observation coming from you. You never bore Colin any particular fondness that I can recall."

"My concern was the amount of influence he had on Remington Shipping. He and Jack Quincy were allowed to manage your holdings much too freely."

"Which is precisely as my father intended," Jonna reminded him. "Your family, on the other hand, particularly your father, would have liked nothing better than to take over Remington. I haven't forgotten that, Grant. I haven't forgotten that it was your father who thought a marriage between us would solve his financial problems and negate the concerns about my youth and inexperience."

Grant's head snapped back as if he'd been struck. "My God, Jonna. Have you been thinking this way since I proposed? Is that why you won't give me an answer?"

"I've given you an answer," she said. "The answer is no. You simply ignore it."

Grant took the cup and saucer from her, then he took her hands in his. He leaned toward her, his handsome features compelling her to listen. "My father's been dead four years now. You can't think I'm influenced by his wishes in regard to marriage. I was just a young man when he came up with that idea, and you were little more than a child. The financial problems that he thought a merger could solve have long since been righted by me. They've never been a factor in my proposal to you. We're not those young people anymore,

Jonna. Sheridan Shipping is a solvent enterprise and will continue in just that vein, with or without a firm connection to your business."

Jonna searched his face. She found she very much wanted to believe him.

"Who put this idea in your head?" Grant asked, giving her wrists a small shake. "Did Jack or Colin make you think you aren't desired for yourself? That I could only be interested in what you have and not who you are? Don't you know how often I think of you or how much I want you?"

Jonna raised her face, her eyes unwavering in their regard. "Do you want me, Grant?" she asked softly. "Would you love me?"

Grant stared back at her, wondering what she was about.

The boldness of Jonna's words was at odds with the flush in her cheeks. "I mean would you make love to me?"

"Now?" He came to his feet. "Here?"

"Now," she said. "Here, if you like. My bedroom, if you prefer." She stood and took a step toward him, holding out her hand.

Grant's astonishment faded as his beautiful smile lighted his face. He took her hand and pulled her into his arms. Hugging her close, he kissed the crown of her dark hair. "Your sense of humor always confounds me," he whispered. "You never let on." His mouth moved to her ear. "I should take you up on your outrageous suggestion, you know. Ravish you right here on the settee and not give a damn which one of your maids walks in on us." His hands moved up and down along her back then he held her from him long enough to study her face. "If you could have managed the thing without blushing," he said, "I might have been taken in." His smile was more teasing than wicked. "I might have taken you."

Jonna found herself held loosely in his embrace again. Her

cheek rested against his shoulder, and his hands lay lightly on the small of her back. She could feel his breath stir her hair.

"It's a good thing I know you so well," he said deeply.

"Yes," she said. "Isn't it?" She pushed gently at his chest to free herself. Her features were perfectly composed, and the color that had crept into her face was gone now. Taking his hand in hers, she urged him back to the settee and picked up the threads of conversation as if there had never been a moment's interruption. "Tell me about Charleston," she said evenly. "How long will you be gone?"

Michele Moreau had never cared for the term "fancy house." If there must be a euphemism for her brothel, then she preferred it simply be called an establishment. That was less painful on the ears of the well-bred Charleston ladies who sometimes had to hear of it. Though the business was discreetly run, any married man who sought refuge or comfort there ran the risk of discovery. He could learn that his wife had always known about Michele's establishment and that she had grown up knowing about it. The knowledge had been passed from mother to daughter just once, usually on the eve of the daughter's marriage, then never spoken of again.

Michele Moreau was sensitive to the wife's dilemma, so she did not mind when they used the euphemism.

The two men sitting at a table by themselves did not have a care for such things, she knew. They did not represent her usual clientele as neither of them was married.

Michele idly ran an index finger along the edge of her bodice and straightened the pearls at her throat. She did not have to glance in the mirror above the bar to have confidence in her appearance. She knew that at fifty she was still a handsome woman and that many of her regulars would be surprised to discover she was not ten years younger. It was not often that she experienced any regret about aging. These two men made her think of that now. If she had not liked them half so well she would have thrown them out for the inconvenience they caused her emotionally.

She walked over to their table and placed her hand on the back of an empty chair. Her slim, jeweled fingers tapped lightly on the uppermost wooden slat. Their conversation ceased, and they raised their heads simultaneously. "Gentlemen," she said, basking momentarily in their welcoming smiles. "You might at least invite a girl to sit with you. My other customers may think you find the women lacking; worse, that you only have eyes for each other." Her glance darted between them, her own eyes dancing with humor. "And if that were true I swear I would have my best girls jumping out windows in despair." She touched them both on the shoulder. "Do not flatter yourselves over much. They are only silly girls, after all."

"Aaah, Michele," Decker said, laying his hand over hers. *"Vous êtes très amiable."*

"You know I don't understand a word of French," she said. But her handsome face was alight with pleasure anyway. "Come. I will let you use my private rooms. I would have taken you there immediately if I had seen you come in. You should have asked for me."

Both men rose and followed the madam to her private apartment at the rear of the house. She gave them brandy to drink from her bar and saw to it that they were comfortable before she left them alone.

Decker leaned back in the large leather chair he'd been shown to. It held the faint rich fragrance of cigar smoke, and he wondered if it was Michele's vice he smelled or that of one of her customers.

Graham Denison watched Decker's attention wander about the room. "It's quite something back here, isn't it?" he asked. "Less is never less with Michele. And more is never quite enough."

It was true, Decker thought. Michele's apartment was opulent to excess. Tapestries hung on the walls, and the floor was overlaid with Oriental carpets. Porcelain and jade figurines crowded the marble mantelpiece and every other available surface. Heavy gold tassels held back blood red drapes at each window. The furniture was large and thickly upholstered in brushed velvet. There was more of it than the room could strictly handle.

"I take it you've been here before," Decker said.

Graham nodded. He had a reserved smile that did not always reach his eyes, and a flinty, blue-gray stare that rarely let others see past his guard. His Southern drawl was tempered by a New England education, and he could use either accent to great affect. With Michele Moreau he had a voice like honey over velvet. With others it was clipped Yankee tones that offered no quarter. Occasionally, with someone he respected and trusted like Decker Thorne, it was a smooth mixture of the two. "It's good to be seen here from time to time," he said. "Not just when I need to be."

That brought them to the reason for their meeting. "I know someone who wants to meet Falconer."

"Oh?" Graham rolled his snifter of brandy between his palms. "Who would that be?"

"His name is Grant Sheridan."

Graham was thoughtful. He had dark brows and even darker lashes. He stared at the brandy in his hands, his eyes shaded by his lowered lids. "I know him, don't I?"

"Perhaps. The Sheridan Line. They make runs to Charleston from time to time, though I understand his trade isn't well received here. He's also Jonna Remington's fiancé."

"Your employer."

"Yes."

"I see." His flinty stare lifted to meet Decker's gaze. "And what would his interest in Falconer be?"

Decker shrugged. "Jonna says—"

"Jonna?"

"Miss Remington."

"Oh, I knew who you meant," Graham said. "I just wondered at the familiarity. But then you did tell me earlier that you fished her out of the harbor. I suppose that gives you some leave."

"Have a care, Graham. I may decide I won't tolerate being upbraided by a young pup, plantation aristocrat or not."

"Well," he drawled. "You be sure to tell me when your patience is at an end, and I'll be sure to duck." He lifted his brandy. "Right now I want to hear what Jonna says."

Decker raised his own snifter in a return salute. "She says that Sheridan might be willing to offer ships or money or some other kind of assistance to Falconer."

"Why did she confide this to you?"

"She was worried about Sheridan, actually. He's very active in the Boston abolitionist movement. One of Garrison's soldiers."

"Really?" Graham sipped his brandy. It went down smoothly, warming the pit of his empty stomach. "That's interesting. There are rumors here . . ." His voice trailed off as he reconsidered his words. Finally he shrugged. "It bears some thinking. I take it Miss Remington doesn't approve of Sheridan's involvement with Garrison."

"She thinks he's a fanatic. Lunatic was the word she had for some of his followers."

"And she would be right. They have a vision but no plan

save violence. At least that's all I'm familiar with." Graham studied his brandy as he gently swirled the snifter. "What about Jonna? Does she hold any part of Sheridan's views?"

Decker almost laughed, thinking about his conversation with her. "She is ever the voice of temperance and reason," he said. "She's against the practice of slavery, of course, but for economic reasons. And never doubt that she's thinking of her own economy."

"Then her position is not so different from every other Boston merchant's."

"Perhaps a little different," Decker said. "She employs freeborn blacks, or at least she doesn't object when it's done. Her housekeeper hires the staff in her home, and Jack Quincy does most of the hiring at the shipyards. He takes men of color for construction jobs, but says Jonna won't let him use them on the clippers."

"Why not?"

"She's afraid of losing them. Thinks they'll be pulled off ships that do business here in the South and worries that they'll jump ship in European ports."

"She's probably not far off the mark."

"I told you: the voice of temperance and reason." He finished his drink. "You have some special cargo for me this trip?"

Graham nodded. "Upstairs. Do you want to see? It will be hours yet before we can load."

"I'd better have a look. I have to be sure I have accommodations."

"Very well." Graham stood. "Come with me."

Decker followed him through Michele's rooms to take the back stairs to the attic. Their passage was nearly soundless, though there was no reason for stealth. Beyond the stairwell was enough music and laughter and chattering to swallow a stampede of noise.

It was Graham Denison who opened the attic door, but it was Decker who raised the candle to illuminate the small closed space.

Six shiny black faces turned in their direction. Twelve dark eyes looked to the light. Save for a single word there was silence.

"Falconer."

It sounded like an answered prayer.

These people were not related. One was a mother without her children. Another a husband without his wife. A brother and sister were among the group, but they had different parents they barely remembered. The oldest was a grandfather who had seen his family sold off until no one remained; the youngest was a girl of seventeen, so new to these American shores that she spoke only the language of her native village.

The importation of men and women as slaves had been forbidden by the federal government since 1808, but the ban had yet to be enforced. Slavers saw the enormous profit and little in the way of risk, so ships still plied the waters on the African coast, bearing away human cargoes purchased for goods from victorious tribal chiefs, whose enslaved captives they were, or from the slave markets.

The people huddled in Michele Moreau's attic were no family, yet they had nurtured and supported one another as if their bond were blood. When Decker hunkered down beside the youngest in the group, she shied away fearfully into the arms of the mother.

Decker set the candle down. He had moved toward the girl because of the heavy bandage on her hand. Now he glanced over his shoulder at Graham. "What happened to her?"

"She got out of her irons by biting off most of the ball of her hand."

"Jesus," Decker said softly. The beads of perspiration that edged his upper lip had little to do with the close quarters. "She's from a slave ship?"

Graham nodded. "She doesn't speak any English, and no one here knows her dialect." He knelt beside Decker and held out his hand to the girl. She was gently urged to go to him and finally, shyly, laid her uninjured hand in his. Her skin was as smooth and creamy as dark chocolate. Graham's fingers closed over her slender ones. "The best we can determine, she escaped from *Salamander*. The ship was in the harbor a week ago. It carries legitimate cargo, but it's known to be a slaver. We think she freed herself then hid somewhere on board until the search moved to the wharf. Somehow she ended up here."

"Here? At Michele's?" Decker was incredulous.

"Amazing, isn't it?" He squeezed the girl's hand. She was watching them warily, seeming to know intuitively that they were talking about her. "Not directly, of course. She was passed from hand to hand and was lucky enough not to be passed back to the slaver. But this is where she finally landed."

"Did she swim ashore?"

"That's what we think."

"And you want to send her north with me?" Decker ran a hand through his hair as he considered what this meant. "I'm not going to London this trip," he said. "It would be easy to deliver her there. But not Boston. No one's going to mistake her for freeborn, not when she can't speak any English."

"She *is* freeborn," Graham reminded him. "Just not on these shores."

Decker sighed and looked sideways at his friend. "You

knew I'd do this, didn't you?"

Graham was smiling at the girl, but his words were for Decker. "Let's just say I hoped and leave it at that."

Jonna let Jack Quincy help her up from the table. He had abandoned two crutches in favor of one and was managing to do better than she was with her cane. "We're a fine pair of bookends, Jack," she said, leaning on her ebony-handled walking stick. "I had expected to be getting around without any assistance from this."

"Sprains take their own time."

"Whatever that means."

"It means it will be better when it's better," he said. "And not before."

Jonna glanced at his splinted leg. "And don't you think you're taking too much on yourself?"

Jack slanted her a grin. The weather-beaten lines of his craggy face deepened with amusement. "I find that sage advice works best when I give it, not take it."

Looping her free arm in his, Jonna leaned toward him and kissed him on the cheek. "What would I do without you, Jack? What would I ever have done?"

He shrugged, embarrassed.

Jonna opened the dining-room doors and led him into the hallway. Drinks were waiting for them in the salon. Jonna had tea. Jack sipped port. "I mean it," she said to him when they were seated. "You're the only person I truly trust."

Jack frowned. "I don't think I want that burden. Don't know that any man would. What if I failed you, Jonna?"

"You never have."

"Even when I turned *Huntress* over to Thorne?"

"Even when you pretended to break your leg in order to do it," she said.

Jack Quincy almost lost a mouthful of good port. He managed to choke it back, but it was a narrow thing. "You know about that?" he asked.

"Let's say I had my suspicions and you just confirmed them."

Rather than being disappointed by his failure, Jack was admiring of her success. "There's no getting anything past you, is there?"

Jonna's humor faded, and her violet eyes were grave now. "I'm not certain about that any longer," she said. "I wondered if I—"

She was interrupted by Mrs. Davis who had entered the room without knocking. "I'm sorry," the housekeeper said. "But there's someone here from *Huntress*. The ship's just arrived, and there's a problem at the harbor." Mrs. Davis moved aside to make room for the young man who came up behind her. He was holding his hat in hand and shifting his weight from one foot to the other. He looked nervously at Jonna who was coming to her feet.

"It's about the captain, Miss Remington. He wanted you to know they're putting him in jail."

Four

Jonna had never been to the jail before. Until now there had never been any reason. She did not thank Decker Thorne for providing one.

Jack Quincy offered to handle the matter himself. Over the course of his employment with Remington Shipping, Jack had had occasion to visit both the jail and the magistrate's office. Decker Thorne was not the first employee he had had to provide bail for, only the first employee of rank and considerable responsibility.

Jonna had politely refused his assistance but agreed to his company. Jack wondered that she had even accepted that. The few times he broached conversation during the carriage ride to the jail he was met with silence. It wasn't simply that she was ignoring him, he realized, but that she had not even heard him.

Now that Jonna knew his injury was a sham, Jack abandoned any pretense of a limp along with the props. He hopped lightly down from the carriage and helped her out. Her hand was cold, and her eyes were only marginally less so.

"Jonna," he said. "You don't have to—" He broke off because she was already moving up the steps of the jailhouse. Sighing, Jack motioned to the driver to wait down the street and then hurried after her to open the doors.

As cells went, it was not the worst one Decker had ever been in. It was cleaner than Newgate and for the time being, at least, it was private. He imagined that would change as the night wore on and the constable gathered up vagrants and drunks and whores from the waterfront. He rather hoped it was a slow night. If he had to spend it in jail, he preferred to spend it alone.

Decker sat on the edge of his cot, his forearms resting lightly on his knees, his hands folded together, and took stock of his situation. There was no escape from the basement cell, not without hurting someone, and Decker had no wish to compound his problems by laying out the turnkey. He had been in Boston four years now, yet this was his first acquaintance with the legal system. He supposed that might be seen favorably, at least by some people.

Decker's slightly crooked smile was rueful. He had no expectation that Jonna Remington would be one of them.

If there had been a way of not involving her, Decker would have taken such a measure. His smile vanished as he thought about the six people who were hidden in the hold of *Huntress*. Their freedom depended on him, and now he was depending on Jonna.

He drew in a slow breath, then let it out with even more care. In spite of this precaution there was still a sharp pain in his left side. Easing himself back on the cot, Decker leaned against the cool stone wall. He drew up his knees, and the position supported his rib cage better. The next breath was slightly less painful.

Decker's hand went to the back of his neck, and he kneaded out the tension there. Informing Jonna of his incarceration had been a gamble. He couldn't be sure if she would get the message this evening, and if she did, he was even less certain of her response. The one thing he knew without any doubt was that if she decided to act on his behalf he would be out tonight. That was the kind of power she could wield. Much to Decker's regret, it was the kind of power Jack Quincy did not have.

Decker's head swiveled in the direction of the heavy wooden door as the observation panel slid open. He would have raised an eyebrow at the turnkey's cursory glance, but he recalled even that small movement made his face ache.

The door opened, and the turnkey poked his head in. "You're free to go," he said. "They're waiting for you upstairs."

"They?"

"Miss Remington and Mr. Quincy. They came together."

Decker didn't dwell on how Jack had heard about what happened; he was simply grateful that he had. Jack's influence would have had something to do with Jonna's quick response. Indeed, Jack's presence now was going to make it a little easier for Decker to do what he must. "Is there a back way out?" he asked.

The turnkey blinked. "You're not serious?"

Decker slid off the cot and came to his feet. He straightened slowly, wincing again as pain knifed his side. "In my place, would *you* want to face her?" Decker saw immediately that he was understood. The guard's expression was sympathetic. In other circumstances Decker would have laughed. Right now it would have hurt too much.

"She did manage to get the magistrate out of his house," the turnkey said thoughtfully. He opened the door wider so that his substantial bulk was framed by the entrance. "Not everyone can do that this time of night."

"My point exactly."

There was a hesitation. "I don't know. . . ."

Decker went to the door and placed a hand on the other man's shoulder. "I don't expect you to let me out the back for nothing," he said. Decker's knees buckled a little under the effort of standing, and the turnkey had to support him momentarily. "I'd be willing to give you something for your trouble."

The guard was interested. He made sure Decker could stand on his own before he let go of him. "How much?" he asked, his eyes narrowing.

Decker reached into his coat pocket and extracted two silver dollars. "Is this enough?"

The turnkey thought about the two coins he had in his own pocket. Four dollars would pay his bill at Wayfarer's Tavern and set up credit for a few rounds. "Is that all you have?"

Decker wavered on his feet as he held up his hands. "Search for yourself. This is the best I can do."

"All right," the turnkey said. He turned out his palm for the coins.

"When you show me out," Decker said.

There was another hesitation, but greed and a taste for liquor won out. Decker was halfway to the ship before the turnkey realized the coins his prisoner had given him were his own.

"Decker Thorne no longer works for me," Jonna told Jack as soon as they were back in the carriage.

Jack didn't argue. While he believed there was some good explanation for Decker's behavior, he wasn't wasting breath to convince Jonna. If her eyes had been like ice chips when they'd entered the jail, now they were glacial. Jack figured silence was his best recourse.

"And you won't be the one telling him," she said. "I will."

Jack nodded but said nothing. He looked out the window, took note of the landmarks they passed, and estimated their arrival at the harbor to have taken about four minutes. God help Decker if he is there, Jack thought. Then he reconsidered. God help him if he isn't.

Decker was supervising the unloading of the last six crates from the hold when he saw Jonna's carriage approaching. She had wasted no time in searching him out, and he had no illusions about what it meant to his future with Remington Shipping. He waved off the wagon driver when the crates were secure, then held his ground as the carriage stopped directly in front of him.

Jack jumped out of the carriage first. The hand he put out for Jonna was ignored. Armed with her cane and her anger, she managed quite well.

The night sky was overcast. The harbor was illuminated by lanterns on the ships and wagons and by the ones the dockworkers held. Light shifted and shadows lurched as the lanterns swung in concert with the movements of tide, wagons, and workers. Decker raised the one he carried. It lighted a circle around them. It also revealed his face.

Jonna had opened her mouth to speak, but now there were no words. The thought that rolled through her mind could not be said aloud, not in front of Jack Quincy, perhaps not even in front of Decker Thorne.

Jack found his voice when Jonna lost hers. "What the hell happened to you?"

Decker's smile was a pathetic parody of his careless grin. The right side of his face was swollen, and there was a cut on his bottom lip. There was a certain amount of humor in his eyes, but even that was tempered by the discoloration and bruising around his brow. Decker indicated Jack's leg with a small nod. "I was going to ask you the same thing. Where's your splint?"

Jack shrugged and pointed to Jonna. "She told me tonight that she knew I was faking. I thought the splint and crutch were a bit much after that."

"Faking?" Decker's puffy eye narrowed to a thin slit. "Do you mean you didn't break it?"

Jonna stepped forward and took the lantern from Decker's hand. "You needn't pretend you didn't know for my benefit," she said. "Get in the carriage."

Jack started to come to Decker's defense, but Decker gave him a look that said he shouldn't bother. "It can't matter one way or the other," he said quietly. "She'll think what she wants to."

Jonna's mouth flattened at the reproof. It was never a pleasure to be considered small-minded. It was even worse to be small-minded *and* wrong. In this case she didn't believe she was either. "The carriage, Captain Thorne."

"I have duties here," he said. He indicated the men milling around behind him on the wharf as well as the ones still on the ship and the gangway. He could imagine they were all trying to look busy, but in a way that would give them the best view of this confrontation.

"It appears you've unloaded the last of the cargo," she said. "I don't see the men bringing anything else up from the hold."

"It's unloaded," Decker said. "But you know that's not the end of it."

"It certainly isn't." Her voice was pleasant enough, but the words were not meant strictly as a reply. "You can get in my carriage on your own, Captain, or I swear I will have you thrown in."

Jack gave Decker a frank assessment. "She'll do it, and you can't fight it. Go on with you. I'll do what's needing to be done here." He tapped Decker lightly on the shoulder, not missing the younger man's wince. "And I'll come round to your room to check on you."

"That won't be necessary, Jack," Jonna interrupted.

"He'll get good care in my home." Ignoring Jack's unflattering astonishment and Decker's raised brows, she tapped her cane once and pointed to the carriage. "Now, Captain Thorne."

Decker climbed in. He braced himself in one corner, fully expecting Jonna to sit on the bench seat opposite him. Instead she sat at his side, and when the carriage rolled forward she held him still.

"I was told you were in a fight," she said. "From the look of you I'd say I was misinformed."

"No, you heard correctly."

"I didn't say I misheard. I said I was misinformed. I'm not naive, Captain. A fight is between two people. No one person did this to you. You were in a brawl."

Decker let his head be cushioned by the padded leather. He closed his eyes. "Perhaps I just couldn't defend myself."

"I don't believe that." She thought about it a moment. "Not unless you were held down."

He opened his eyes long enough to give her an arch look.

Jonna's own eyes widened. "That's what happened, isn't it? You were held down."

"Close enough."

"Then why were *you* arrested?"

"I suppose because I was the only one left when the authorities arrived."

"The magistrate told me it was because you started it."

"That would be the other reason," he said dryly.

His quiet amusement bewildered Jonna. "Do you shrug off everything with an ironic comment?" she asked.

"Not everything." His tone was serious again. He let her think about that. "Why didn't you tell me about the wagon driver?"

The change of subject set Jonna off balance. "What driver? What are you—"

Decker raised one finger. It was as much energy as he could muster, and it was the least painful movement he could make. It was enough. It got her attention and stopped her from talking. "The day your ankle was injured on the dock," he explained. "Why didn't you tell me it wasn't an accident?"

Jonna stiffened and knew her reaction did not go unnoticed. Decker's arm tightened slightly over hers as if he expected her to pull away. It was his injuries, not his strength, that stopped her from doing just that. "It *was* an accident," she said. "Why should I say otherwise?"

"Before I left for Charleston I spoke to three people who remember the incident a little differently than you."

"Who gave you leave to do that?"

One corner of his mouth turned up at her rather priggish tone. "I don't need your permission to talk to people," he reminded her.

"When I'm the subject you do." The effect of this statement was the opposite of the one Jonna wished for. Instead of being put in his place, Decker actually laughed out loud. Her only satisfaction, and it was a small one, came from the fact that it hurt him to do so.

He had opened his eyes and was watching her out of the corners of them. He didn't miss that smug smile hovering about her mouth. The hell of it was, he thought, he liked that expression. He liked the faintly haughty lift of her chin, the shadowed dimple at the corner of her lips. He liked the controlled steadiness of her breathing and the way she sat so still against him. Jonna Remington was a singularly beautiful woman and didn't know it. Decker thought he liked that best of all.

"Your permission aside," Decker said, "the fact remains

that I asked some questions."

"Why would you do that?"

"Because the driver of that wagon should have come back to make amends, and he didn't."

"I told you I was gone by the time he had his horse under control."

"He could have found you," Decker said. "He *should* have found you. Everyone at the harbor knows who you are. The only reason he didn't come back to apologize or to inquire about your condition was because what was done was done deliberately."

Jonna said nothing, and she noticed that Decker did not seem to require a response. She looked past him to the carriage window, beyond that to the lamp-lighted street. She realized that they were within minutes of reaching her home, yet she still knew almost nothing about the fight that had caused his injuries and his arrest.

Then, suddenly, intuitively, she *did* know. She had been asking about the brawl, and he had begun talking about the accident. What she thought had been a change in the subject had merely been one part of the whole. He hadn't shifted the subject as much as brought it around to what was important to him.

As the carriage slowed she felt it sway when the driver leaped down from his perch to help them out. "The fight was about me," she said softly, just before the door opened. "You fought about me."

Her tone was neutral as if she couldn't decide whether she were astonished or appalled. That uncharacteristic indecisiveness made Decker smile. "It was a brawl," he reminded her. "And I lost."

Decker woke in the middle of the night. At first he

couldn't identify his surroundings. The fact that his cabin wasn't rocking was in itself disconcerting. Then there was the softness of the bed, the scent of freshly laundered sheets, and the cocoonlike warmth of several thick blankets. It was the portrait above the mantelpiece that finally oriented him.

John and Charlotte Remington were looking at each other, but Decker felt as if they were watching over him.

He sat up. Instantly there was a movement on the other side of the room as someone rose from the rocker. Backlighted by the flames, the figure at first seemed to be one of the servants. Only as it approached the bed did he recognize Jonna.

"Can I get you something?" she asked. "Water? More laudanum?"

He frowned. There was a muzzy memory of something being spooned down his throat as he was put to bed. Laudanum would explain the cotton head he had now. And unfortunately, although his mind was dull, the pain was still sharp.

Jonna reached for the dark bottle of opiate on the nightstand, but Decker put out his hand to stop her.

"I don't want any," he said. His hand closed over her wrist, and even though she made no further move to get the bottle he did not let her go. "What time is it?"

She looked over her shoulder at the mantel clock. "Just past four."

"Have you been here all night?"

"Only this last half hour. I woke a while ago and couldn't fall asleep again. I thought I would check on you and discovered the maid in attendance wasn't having the same difficulty with sleep that I was. I sent her to her room." Jonna felt the lightest pressure on her wrist. It was all that was needed to draw her down beside him. Her eyes slipped over his bruised

111

and battered face and came to rest on his mouth. "I suppose if you don't need anything I should go back to my room," she said.

"I suppose you should."

He didn't let her go, and she made no move to leave.

Jonna's gaze dropped away from his mouth and fell on the hand that lay over her wrist. "I had planned to tell you I don't want you working for me any longer."

Decker nodded. It was what he had expected to hear when Jonna arrived at the harbor.

"It wasn't because of the fight," she said. "Or even the arrest. Those things happen from time to time, and though Jack thinks I don't understand how or why, I do." She could feel him watching her. Even without looking at him she sensed his quiet amusement. "I know the men work hard on board ship. The sea may be open, but the quarters are confined. Disagreements that aren't settled on board sometimes get settled in port, usually after a few drinks and some intemperate words."

"And you thought that's what happened tonight."

Still looking at his hand, Jonna nodded. "I didn't like it," she said. "It sets a bad example for the men under you and I expect . . . no, I *demand* better."

Decker knew that she did, and no one who worked for her minded, least of all him. It was the gravity of her expression that made him want to needle her. "But you were prepared to forgive me."

She gave him a sharp glance. "I was prepared to flay you."

His eyes dropped to her mouth this time. "With your tongue?" he asked. "Or were you thinking of using the cat on my back?" He watched in fascination as her face flamed and her lips parted on a breathless little sound of surprise. It was only then that he took pity on her. His gaze lifted to her eyes again. "You were about to take me to task for disappearing at the jail," he said. "That was why you were going to relieve me of my employment, wasn't it? Because I embarrassed you?"

Jonna's wrist came away easily from his grasp, and she knew it was because he had let her go. The distance she was able to put between them now was there as much by his permission as by her desire. "You did embarrass me," she said quietly. "To leave the way you did, instead of coming forward to talk to the magistrate, or thank me, it showed neither regard nor respect. That was cause enough to end your employment."

Decker didn't disagree. "Yes," he said. "It was."

Jonna sighed. She stared at the flames in the fireplace. Her voice was hardly more than a whisper. "And it would have been impulsive and petty for me to have done so."

This admission was not what Decker had expected. Jonna Remington's pained honesty had taken an inward turn. He supposed it was that kind of thinking that had kept her up and eventually had brought her to his room. When she showed no inclination to go, but continued to stare steadily at the fire, he asked, "What makes you happy, Jonna?"

She didn't answer. He studied her profile, the pure, clear lines that were almost without expression. He knew she had heard him and knew now that she wouldn't answer him, that possibly she couldn't answer him. Nothing about her profile changed as tears welled in her eyes. They clung to the edge of her lower lashes for the longest moment before one, only one, escaped. The lone tear, sparkling like a liquid diamond, slipped down her cheek. She made no move to brush it away or blink back the others. They hovered, then fell in quick succession, and finally disappeared.

Jonna stood. "I think it would be better if you wouldn't ask any more questions," she said.

"Of you?"

"Of anyone." Then she closed the discussion by crossing the room and closing the door.

The rocker made an alarming creaky protest under Jack Quincy's weight. He paused, waited to see if it would support him, then finished tipping it back while he placed his boots flat on the bed frame. He picked up his end of the conversation with Decker as if there had been no interruption. "What the hell is that supposed to mean?" he demanded. "Damn, if you're making any sense."

"I'm making sense," Decker said. "You just don't want to believe it." He sat up, pushed the pillows more firmly behind his back, and leveled Jack with a hard look. It was difficult to be taken seriously when his right eye was almost swollen shut and he grimaced with pain every time he moved. "Listen to me, Jack, because Jonna won't. If she believes that business on the wharf wasn't an accident, then she's not admitting it, at least not to me. But she might talk to you. You've had her ear almost all of her life, and she trusts you. I think she has suspicions about what happened but doesn't know what to do about it." Decker paused, judging Jack's interest.

"Go on," Jack said. "You've got my attention."

"Three men, all separately, were willing to tell me that the driver who lost control of his horse and wagon ran the animal directly at Jonna."

"Either he had control or he didn't," Jack said.

"They say he grabbed the bridle but didn't pull the mare in."

"Maybe he couldn't."

"Maybe he didn't want to."

Jack's feet dropped back to the floor. "There were more

114

than three witnesses. You must have talked to others."

"I did."

"Well? What did they say?"

"The ones I talked to before I left for Charleston told mostly the same story."

"The same one Jonna's telling," Jack said.

Decker nodded. "But even some of them wondered why the driver didn't come back to ask after Jonna's well-being. When I probed a little more, no one could identify the driver." Decker saw this information finally yielded a reaction from Jack. "I know," he said. "That struck me as odd, too. You know someone always knows somebody else on the wharf. I don't think I worked more than a half day before people I'd never seen before were calling me by my name."

"Ponty." Jack couldn't resist reminding him. "They were calling you Ponty. And it wasn't your name." He held up his hands, surrendering when Decker gave a hard, very nearly angry look. "All right. So no one knew this man. I'll grant that's unusual, but it makes him a stranger, not a killer."

"I don't know that he meant to kill her," Decker said. "But I believe he meant to frighten her."

"Frighten Jonna? Why?"

"I don't know."

The rocker began to creak with the precision of a metronome as Jack moved fore and aft. He considered what he'd been told. "Tell me about the fight," he said after a few moments.

Decker's jaw was stiff. He worked it back and forth until it gave a satisfying pop. "Jonna's right about one thing," he said. "It wasn't much of a fight. There was a message waiting for me when *Huntress* docked. It said if I had more questions I should inquire at Brown and Birney's."

"You read this note yourself?" Jack asked. "Are you sure you got it right?"

A faint flush crept under Decker's skin. "I read it good enough, Jack. I've been practicing. It wasn't as complicated as logging my journey."

"All right," Jack said. "I didn't mean anything by it. It's just that—"

Decker brushed the explanation aside. "I went to B and B's."

"You left the ship?" asked Jack. "Before you had the cargo unloaded?"

"I know. It's against regulations, but I had to go." Decker's frank look was unapologetic. He would do it again. "I waited in the tavern only a few minutes before someone approached me. I didn't recognize him. I suppose that should have raised an alarm; if it did, I was deaf to it. He wanted to talk to me behind the tavern, and I followed him out."

Jack winced, knowing what was coming now. "He had friends, I take it."

Decker held up three fingers. "They blindsided me immediately. I went down, and I don't think I ever came up."

"Did you tell Jonna you started the fight?" asked Jack.

Decker tried to remember the carriage ride back to Beacon Hill. "I probably did," he said. "Is that what she told you?"

"She said the magistrate told her that and you confirmed it. You have a talent for making her think the worst of you."

"That doesn't matter." Decker knew it was more than a mere talent. He practiced it like a craft. "What do you think, Jack? Is there substance to what I've told you?"

There was a pause in the creaking again, while Jack regarded Decker with a keen and knowing eye. "I don't think you gave yourself that shiner and two broken ribs," he said finally. "It's a mercy you weren't killed."

Last night, when he had been taking the blows to his chest and head and groin, Decker would have considered a quick end very merciful. "Mr. Brown walked out back . . . or maybe it was Mr. Birney . . . whoever it was frightened them off. Mr. B. sent for the authorities, and somehow I ended up being the one carted off to jail."

"I think their purpose was to ask you some questions. Apparently you weren't very cooperative. You struck some of them."

"I did?"

Jack nodded. "Best I can put it together, Jeremy Dodd came looking for you from the ship and arrived in time to see you being taken away. You must have sent him after Jonna."

"I remember doing that."

"You could have asked for me."

Decker had wondered how he would explain that. The answer presented itself simply enough. "Bloody hell, Jack, I don't recall hitting anyone. Who knows why I sent Jeremy after Miss Remington instead of you."

"What about at the jail?" Jack asked. "Why did you leave like that?"

"I wanted to get back to the ship. I knew that if the two of you saw me, you wouldn't let me go to the harbor—which is what happened when you did catch up with me. I had duties to finish. With everything else that had already occurred, I didn't want to neglect them." Decker watched Jack take it in, consider it, and finally accept it. "Will you talk to her?" asked Decker.

Jack sighed. "Aye," he said heavily. He had no liking for the task that Decker had set for him. "I'll talk to her."

Decker slept off and on throughout the day. Maids came and went, changing the bindings on his ribs when he soaked

117

them through in his sleep, bringing trays of tea and toast, tending the fire, and placing fresh compresses on his eye. By nightfall Decker had had as many intrusions on his privacy as he could tolerate. He was considering locking the door when a trio of servants trooped in again, this time with a hip bath and buckets of hot water.

They helped him out of bed, even when he insisted he could manage the thing himself, and didn't leave him to his own devices until he was stripped to his drawers. When they were gone Decker finished undressing and eased himself into the hot water. Ribbons of steam rose from the surface as it rippled around him. Decker's contented sigh was audible in the quiet room.

At first he didn't want to move. The water was like a liquid bandage, supporting and caressing every part of his sore body. Gradually he unfolded himself as much as the copper tub allowed; then he reached for a towel one of the maids had left at hand. Folding it in quarters, he placed it behind his head. Decker's eyes closed almost immediately, and he was asleep soon after that.

Jonna had no intention of staying long when she went to check on her house guest. She had been up early that morning, at the harbor office before eight, and after a near sleepless night it had been a difficult day. There were the usual annoyances: untimely delays, spoiled cargoes, complaints about the costs. A bit more rare, but not without precedent, was the problem with *Huntress*'s manifest and her bills of lading. Too much time was spent, first by her secretary, then by her, on a matter she thought shouldn't have been a problem at all. What was so difficult about matching the cargo list with the cargo? She had seen the crates in question being hauled away from the harbor herself, so she knew they existed. She had a bill of lading to state that they had been paid for by the shipper, yet she had no record of them on the manifest the cargo master kept. If Jeremy Dodd had been doing his job in Charleston, the crates could hardly have come aboard without his noticing.

Jonna pushed the problem to the back of her mind. It wasn't important enough to have consumed so much of her time, and that in itself made it more frustrating.

The door to Decker's room was not completely closed. Jonna entered soundlessly, then came up short as she registered the sight of Decker in the hip bath. Expecting to be ordered out, and quite willing to comply this time, she let her hand rest on the doorknob. It was only when he said nothing that she concluded he was taunting her, and Jonna's nature was to accept a challenge rather than shy away from one. Good sense told her to back out of the room. Defiance moved her to close the door.

He was facing her, watching her . . . or so she thought. Jonna didn't realize he was sleeping until she was standing beside the tub. Defiance disappeared and left a wave of foolishness in its wake. What did it say about her, she wondered, that she could allow herself to be goaded by Decker Thorne even when he was sleeping?

Shaking her head, her slight smile more wry than regretful, Jonna bent and picked up the bandages that had been around his ribs. She laid them over the back of the rocker with his nightshirt and dressing gown. She should go, she told herself, but her feet only moved in the direction of the large wing chair by the fireplace. She sat down, curled her feet beneath her, and waited.

The water cooled to the point that the chill of it woke Decker. He groped for a towel and raised himself up, drying off his shoulders and damp hair as he stood. He was on the point of stepping out of the bath when he saw Jonna.

"Bloody hell," he swore.

She didn't stir.

Decker peered in her direction more closely. Firelight bathed her face in warm hues of gold and crimson, and Jonna's long black lashes left a shadow just beneath her closed eyes. Sleeping. He swore again, more softly this time, and went back to the business of drying himself. It was her small gasp that alerted him to changing circumstances.

Decker considered his options. He had the towel, but it was around his shoulders. The water was too cold to use it for cover. And his ribs ached too fiercely for him to dive for the refuge of the bed. "Since my modesty is already compromised," he said, "I suppose you can look as much as you want."

Jonna blinked rapidly several times.

Annoyance faded as Decker began to appreciate the farce unfolding in his bedchamber. "I hadn't thought of that," he said dryly. "Do you only get half an eyeful that way?"

Groaning, Jonna placed both hands over her eyes. "Please put something on," she said.

Decker did not see any reason for hurrying now. He stepped out of the tub carefully. "You could always leave, Miss Remington."

"I can't see," she said. "Not with my hands over my eyes. I'll fall on my way to the door."

"Your logic leaves something to be desired, but I won't dispute it." Decker picked up his drawers and put them on, then slipped into the dressing gown. He left it unbelted. His ribs had to be wrapped anyway, he thought. He was not in favor of expending any unnecessary energy. Sitting on the edge of the bed, he finished toweling his hair dry. When he was done he combed it with his fingers.

"You can come out from behind your hands now," he told her. He watched her do so slowly, splaying her fingers first, risking only a peek from between them. "Your lack of trust is hardly flattering, Miss Remington. Your maids were more circumspect in carrying out their duties than you've been."

"My duties?" she asked, letting her hands fall away and into her lap. "What duties?"

"To make me comfortable," he said. "Isn't that the first obligation of a hostess?"

"Are you saying you haven't been treated well?"

"I'm saying that you could acknowledge my right to privacy by not appearing in this room every time I open my eyes."

Jonna wondered if Decker could see the rush of heat to her cheeks. It was an effort not to raise her hands and touch them. She came to her feet instead. Her striped silk gown was a deep shade of plum, and the movement lifted the hem around her ankles, giving it an almost iridescent quality before it fell back. Jonna's hands were folded quietly in front of her. "You're right, of course. It won't happen again."

Decker's dark brows creased. He held one hand over his swollen eye to get a better look at her with his good one. "You may as well stay now," he said. "I need help with my bandages."

"I'll ring for Mattie."

"Not Mattie," Decker said. "She's all thumbs."

"Janie, then."

"She pulls them too tight."

"Dorcas."

"Too loose."

Exasperated, Jonna placed her hands on her hips. "Who is it you want, Captain Thorne?"

The answer came without hesitation or reservation. "I believe I already said that, Miss Remington. I want you."

Jonna's heart hammered in her chest. It didn't make sense to her that she was reacting so strongly to his words. He had not said them suggestively, but rather matter-of-factly. It did not seem that he required her services in any personal way, yet she felt herself responding as if he had. Annoyance flattened the lush curve of her mouth.

Decker watched her cross the room. There was the whispered rustle of silk as Jonna approached the bed. He liked that sound, liked the contrast of its softness to Jonna's staccato step. Her limp was barely noticeable now and she was no longer using the cane. She had a serious stride, one that could never be taken as lacking in purpose, yet there was a certain reckless elegance in her walk that invariably turned heads. Decker had never seen her give any indication that she noticed.

Jonna picked up the linen wraps. "I've not done this before," she said. "I might be no better at it than any of my maids."

Decker opened the front of his dressing gown wider. "You can't be any worse," he said.

"Perhaps you'd better stand." She followed his pained progress as he complied. "What did the doctor say when he was here?"

He gave her the report. "I shouldn't wear out my welcome this time," he said. "I can leave tomorrow or the day after."

One of Jonna's brows arched. Her glance was skeptical. "You can't even see out of your right eye."

"The swelling's actually gone down from what it was this morning. Anyway, it won't heal faster here than aboard *Huntress*." Decker expected her to argue. He knew a moment's disappointment when she didn't. It wasn't until much later that he realized the lack of a response on her part wasn't the same as agreement. "Can you raise that bandage higher?" he asked.

Jonna slipped her index finger between the linen wrapping and Decker's chest, loosened the bandage, and slid it upward. She kept her eyes focused on what she was doing, but when she heard his sharp intake of air, she risked a glance upward. "Have I hurt you?"

The catch in his breath had nothing to do with physical pain. "No, keep going."

"Very well," she said. She was standing very close to him now. Her arms were around him, under the dressing gown, as she unrolled more of the wrapping across his back. If he lowered his arms he could have enclosed her in the dressing gown, cocooned her in silk.

Decker could feel her breath on his skin. It was very light. Warm. He remembered that she had tasted sweet. He needed to think about something else. "What happened to Tess?" he asked.

There was a brief pause then Jonna continued wrapping. "She left."

"I gathered that. I wondered why. She seemed happy enough here. Or at least she did until that day you were hurt at the wharf. Then she and that other girl . . . what was her name?"

"Emily."

"Yes, Emily. Well, that night they both looked scared witless, but I suppose it was their concern for you. I didn't expect they'd be gone by the time I returned from Charleston."

Jonna pulled the wrapping more tightly than she meant to, eliciting a small groan from Decker. She eased back before she tied off the ends. "Tess was dismissed for stealing. Emily left as some sort of protest."

"Tess? Stealing? That doesn't sound right."

Jonna stepped away, surveyed her work, and indicated Decker could close his dressing gown. He let it fall but still didn't belt it. Without pausing to consider what she was about, she did it for him. "I didn't concern myself with the particulars. Grant asked me about her, too. Apparently she made quite an impression on you both."

"She was kind and eager to help."

"She was pretty."

Decker had no illusions that Jonna was jealous of his attentions to Tess. The edge of jealousy he heard in her voice was there because of Grant Sheridan's interest in the servant. "Yes," he said. "She was pretty. She also wasn't any thief. What was she accused of taking?"

Jonna shrugged. "Silver, I think." She turned her back on Decker and went to the fireplace. Adding a log, she poked at the flames. When Decker was quiet for so long she glanced over her shoulder. He was staring at her in a way he had never done before. His features were set hard, his eyes cold. "I have Remington Shipping to run," she said, straightening. "I told you before that Mrs. Davis is in charge of my home."

"Perhaps you should take the same interest in your employees here as you do at the harbor."

"What is that supposed to mean?"

"Tess wouldn't have taken your silver. She had opportunity to take my earring. That piece is worth much more than a few spoons and forks or a tea service." Decker thrust his hands into the pockets of the dressing gown. It was a better place for them than around Jonna's neck. "Did your housekeeper find the silver on Tess?"

"In her room, I believe."

"Did you put it there?"

At the accusation Jonna's slender frame snapped to attention. She fairly vibrated with anger. "I think you had better explain that remark."

"Did you put it there to set her up . . . to get rid of her? I don't think I can be more clear than that."

"I'm clear on the question," she said. Jonna put the poker down, very much afraid he might give her cause to use it. "What I don't understand is what motive you think I have for doing it."

"Sheridan."

Jonna simply stared at him.

"You said yourself that Sheridan had shown an interest in Tess."

Now Jonna's mouth parted and her violet eyes widened considerably. "Jealousy?" she asked. "You think I was motivated by Grant's attention to Tess?"

"Why not?"

"Why not?" Jonna repeated. "Because the notion's absurd."

"Because Tess is black?"

"Because I don't love Grant Sheridan!"

Except for the crackle and hiss of the fire there was no other sound in the room. It was as if the larger silence held substance and grounded them separately, holding them still. Their eyes locked, but the exchange was without meaning, their expressions quickly and skillfully guarded. She did not take back the words she had spoken. He did not ask if they were true.

Jonna could never say how long she stood there. She only knew that she was the first to move. Her silk gown swayed as she spun on her heel and headed for the door.

Decker called to her. When she didn't stop he moved quickly to block her path. He held out his hands to keep her from bumping into him, but the effort was only marginally successful. Thrown off balance by his sudden appearance in front of her, she ended up toppling into his chest sideways.

The edges of his vision darkened as Decker rocked back on his heels. Excruciating pain forced a guttural cry from his throat. He staggered, thought he would fall, then felt something catch his weight. He leaned heavily, and the support for his shoulder began to sag.

Jonna's breath came raggedly as she struggled with Decker's weight. She pushed against him, forcing him upright and steadying him at the same time. "I can't do this alone," she said under her breath. "And neither can you."

The first wave of pain had receded. Decker now felt just ripples. He let himself be helped back to the bed because Jonna was right—he couldn't do it alone. She turned down the covers with one hand while she kept her shoulder under his arm, then she lowered him onto the bed. When she would have moved away she found he was holding a fistful of her dress. She looked at him pointedly.

"Let me go."

Decker shook his head. "I didn't go through all that just to have you leave anyway. In case you didn't realize it, I was trying to stop when you plowed into me."

"It was a very clever ruse," she said dryly. "And it worked temporarily."

Decker looked down at the fist of material he still held and then back at Jonna. "It's still working. Sit down." He saw her hesitate. "You could fight me, and given my present condition, you might even win. Or, and I like this idea better, you could take off that dress and leave me holding it while you walk away."

Jonna sat down.

"That's better."

"I don't want to talk about Grant," she said.

"Neither do I."

"Then why—"

Decker gave a little tug on her gown, cutting her off. "I want to know if Jack spoke to you today."

"He was at the warehouse and in and out of my office several times. Was there something in particular he was supposed to say?"

Decker's good eye narrowed fractionally. "Do you imagine I have endless patience, Jonna?" He had never addressed her familiarly before, and she wasn't able to hide her surprise. "You've seen me naked," he said. "Circumstances that would seem to require less formality. You can call me Decker."

Jonna's smile was sweetly beautiful and completely insincere. "Hateful arrogant bastard comes to mind, but it's a mouthful." Her smile changed to complacent and confident as Decker's bark of laughter ended in a very real groan of pain.

He caught his breath, wincing as he sipped the air. "You did that on purpose," he said when he could speak again.

Her features were without a trace of guile. "Did what?"

"Made me laugh. You knew it would hurt."

"That would be cruel."

Decker's mouth twisted to one side in a wry smile. His accusation hadn't cracked her composure. She was still regarding him coolly, patiently. "All right," he said, conceding the round to her. "Now tell me what you thought of Jack's concerns."

Jonna no longer pretended she didn't know what Decker was talking about. "They're really your concerns, aren't they?" she said. "You simply filled Jack's head full of them and sent him on to talk to me."

"Did it work?"

"If you're asking if I listened to him, I did. I simply don't draw the same conclusions as either of you. I don't have any enemies. Quite frankly, I don't inspire that sort of passion."

And because she said it so naturally, as if she had long ago come to terms with it as fact, Decker was moved to show her something different. He released her dress so he could push himself upright. "Close your eyes, Jonna," he said softly, insistently.

"What—"

His face was near enough to hers that he could feel her breath. She was searching it, not afraid, merely uncertain. "Close your eyes."

She did.

That was when he kissed her.

Five

Jonna felt the heat of his mouth a moment before he kissed her. She could have pulled away or turned her head or pushed at Decker's shoulders. It even registered in some remote area of her brain that any of those responses would be acceptable. She did none of those things.

Her lips parted instead. His mouth was warm, his touch gently exploring. He changed position, tilting his head, and pressed the kiss from another direction. His tongue swept her upper lip, then the lower one. He teased her by running it along the ridge of her teeth, but never pushing its entry.

It was Jonna who leaned into the kiss. A small sound at the back of her throat signaled her frustration, and she could sense the shape of his smile against her lips. When his tongue slid along the sensitive underside of her lip, she engaged him with a like response. She had the satisfaction of knowing the smile vanished.

She caught a hint of tea and lemon on her tongue and realized it was the taste of him. The kiss somehow seemed more intimate, her awareness of his touch more complete. Her senses were opened now to the warmth and fragrance of his skin, the sound of his breathing. Only her sense of sight went unsatisfied, and she knew it would have to remain that way. If she opened her eyes this would end.

God help her, she thought. She didn't want this to end.

Decker felt the swell of passion in her. Her responses echoed his own as she returned his kiss full measure. The press of his mouth became hungrier and more demanding, and Jonna didn't shy away. His hands had settled on her waist when she leaned into him. Now they grazed her sides slowly, his fingers sliding up her back. Decker felt her stiffen, but he didn't release her and she didn't ask him to. He swallowed her small gasp as his thumbs passed once over her breasts.

Layers of clothing were of little consequence. Decker felt her nipples rise and harden before he cupped the undersides of her breasts; then his hands slid higher, this time across her upper arms and shoulders. He held her face for a moment, deepening the kiss just once before he raised his head.

Her lush mouth still invited him. He touched her closed eyes instead, briefly, lightly, then he let his hands fall back to her shoulders and finally freed her.

It was ending anyway, Jonna thought. Even with her eyes closed it was ending.

She blinked once. His hands were at his sides, but she could still feel them on her arms, at her waist, and then ever so gently on her throat. Her mouth bore the imprint of his, and she resisted the urge to raise her fingers to seal it there. The warmth and fragrance of him clung to her. She knew she would breathe it tonight when she went to bed. And finally there was a faint roar in her ears that made her deaf to the thrumming of her own heart.

Jonna didn't look away from him. His eyes grazed her face, watching, searching. He wasn't smiling. He just seemed to be waiting.

Her voice was hardly more than a whisper. "Grant didn't want me. I offered myself and he didn't want me."

Decker said nothing. A muscle worked in his cheek.

"I'm not certain I even like you," she said.

"I know." He said it softly, without a trace of humor.

Then why, she wanted to say, *why did I explore your mouth with my tongue? Why did I let you touch me? Why would I let you do it again right now?* Jonna's hands rested quietly on her lap. She looked down at them, willing her heart to be as steady and still. "I don't think you should kiss me anymore," she said.

"You're probably right."

Jonna wasn't certain she welcomed his agreement this time. She stole a glance at him. "It was an experiment for you, wasn't it? You wanted to see what I would do."

The slightest smile edged Decker's mouth, but his eyes remained grave. "Not the way you think," he said.

She frowned, wondering what he meant.

Decker cupped the underside of Jonna's chin and raised her face. He spoke to clear her troubled expression. "You should never doubt that you inspire passion."

Jonna's violet eyes cleared, and the crease between her brows vanished. She felt a tide of color and heat wash her cheeks. The words were out of her mouth before she had a clear thought of them in her head. "Did you want me?" she asked. "I mean, did you—"

Decker's grin finally came to the forefront, and it silenced Jonna. He lowered his hand and levered himself back against the headboard. "Never say you didn't know."

But she hadn't. "I just thought . . ." Her voice trailed away uncertainly. She didn't know what she thought.

Decker plumped the pillows behind his back. There was a newspaper on the nightstand. He picked it up and pretended interest in it. "Go to bed, Jonna," he said. The grin was gone again, and he did not look at her. "You may not like how I answer the rest of your questions."

It was at breakfast the next morning that Jonna learned Decker was gone. She surprised Mrs. Davis by not insisting that someone be sent to bring him back. "Jack will look after him," she said and the subject was closed.

When she saw Jack Quincy at her offices she only inquired briefly after Decker's health. Assured he was resting comfortably in his rented room, she didn't mention him again. Jonna found it easier not to think about Decker Thorne if she didn't have to talk about him. Her cool, rather remote expression whenever his name was brought up encouraged the silence of others.

Grant Sheridan returned from Charleston one week before Christmas. Jonna was hardly aware that he had overstayed the expected length of his voyage south. He was the one who reminded her he had hoped to return days earlier.

"What's wrong?" he asked as they retired to the salon. Grant caught her inside the room when she closed the doors and held her in his arms. "You've been very quiet this evening. I confess I had expected a warmer welcome."

Jonna raised her face. She saw his eyes drop to her lips. He looked at her mouth a long time before he lowered his head. Even though she knew that she didn't love him, Jonna wondered if she could learn to like Grant's kiss. She surprised them both by turning her head at the last moment and giving him her cheek.

"Jonna?" Grant said.

She eased out of his arms and put some distance between them. His eyes were very dark now, almost black, but they watched her without expression. She had no sense of whether he was hurt by her response or annoyed.

Jonna turned to the small pie table where the tea service had been placed. She picked up the silver pot and realized her hands were shaking.

"I think I'd prefer a more substantial drink," Grant said.

His voice came from immediately behind her. Jonna put the pot down slowly and smoothed the front of her gray silk dress. She found herself taking a deep, calming breath. "Of course," she said. "In the sideboard." She waited, expecting him to go get it or to move out of her way. Caught between the table and Grant's powerful frame, Jonna couldn't take a step without bumping into one of them.

Grant placed his hands on the curve of Jonna's shoulders. Her silk gown was smooth and cool beneath his palms. Her skin would feel that way, he thought. He leaned forward, bent his head, and touched his lips to the side of her neck. He had been right. Smooth and cool.

Jonna closed her eyes. His hands lay heavily on her shoulders. He didn't force her to turn, but the weight of them kept her in place. His breath was hot, his mouth faintly damp. She felt a tug on her flesh as he sipped her skin. The knowledge that he was going to leave a mark there, like a brand, made her stomach turn over. She did not want him to touch her. "Grant," she said. "I don't want—"

That was when he twisted her in his arms. She thought later that it was almost as if her protest had excited him. At the moment it was happening she couldn't think at all. His mouth closed over hers hard. It was an act of ownership, of possession, and Jonna recoiled at the stamp of his lips on hers. She pushed at his shoulders, but her strength had no impact on his solid frame. At her back she felt the edge of the table.

Jonna bit his lip.

Grant's head snapped back. He tasted blood on the inside of his mouth. Letting go of Jonna, he took out a handkerchief and raised it to his lips. "What was that for?" he demanded, his black eyes cold and flat.

Jonna slipped sideways, out of his reach. Even though his voice was muffled by the handkerchief, it lost none of its angry edge. "I'll get your brandy," she said quietly.

"Forget the brandy. Tell me why I deserved that."

Jonna's chin lifted a fraction, and she regarded him steadily. "I didn't want you to kiss me," she said. "I don't think I want you to touch me at all." Before he could respond she continued quickly. "Please, won't you sit down? You asked me what was wrong. I think perhaps I can tell you."

Except to lower his handkerchief and tuck it away, Grant didn't move. "I think perhaps you had better," he said.

Jonna realized that he was not going to make it easy for her. She couldn't fault him for that. He deserved better than what she could offer him. "I don't love you," she said. "I'm sorry, Grant, but I never have and I don't believe I've misled you on that account. You know that I admire you, respect you, and value your counsel. I will always appreciate your friendship." She glanced at the floor a moment, gathering the threads of her composure. When she faced him again her voice was surprisingly steady. "It's not enough for a marriage. It never will be. Not for me."

"Jonna." There was a hint of condescension in his tone, as if he thought she didn't know her own mind. "What's happened while I've been gone? This isn't where we left things."

"Nothing's happened." It wasn't entirely the truth, but there was no explaining Decker Thorne to Grant. Not when she didn't fully understand that encounter herself. "And it's precisely where we left things. I don't believe I can say it more clearly. We're not engaged. You're not my fiancé. We will never be married." Jonna watched color leave Grant's face. It was his only visible reaction. "Please, Grant, I'm sorry. You must know I wish it could be different. I wish *I* could be different."

He took a step toward her and stopped when she immediately backed away. "Are you afraid of me, Jonna?" he asked. "Have I given you some reason to fear me?"

"No," she said. "No to both your questions."

He raised one eyebrow, his look patently skeptical. To prove his point he took another step forward. While Jonna didn't move he saw the effort it took on her part to stand her ground.

"It's not what you think," she said. "I don't want you kissing me again. You seem to believe you can change my reasoning that way."

"Can't I?"

"No."

Grant studied her for a moment longer. Every line of her slender frame was set stubbornly, and her mouth was mutinously flat. "I wonder who you're trying to convince," he said. He didn't let her answer. "I think I'll have that brandy now."

Jonna turned to the sideboard only as Grant sat down. She poured the brandy, served him, then took tea for herself. She took the wing chair at an angle from the settee, guaranteeing he could not choose to sit beside her. "I'd like us to remain friends," she said finally.

"And business associates."

"Of course."

"But not partners."

Jonna didn't know if he was speaking of marriage or business. She supposed it didn't matter. Her answer was the same to both. "No," she said. "Not partners."

Grant regarded her thoughtfully over the rim of his snifter. "I see," he said.

But Jonna did not think he sounded convinced. She was wondering what more she could say when the doors to the salon opened. Mrs. Davis stood on the threshold with a young black girl at her side. The girl wasn't touching the housekeeper in any way but her posture suggested she was trying to cling to the older woman.

"She's come to take the tray," Mrs. Davis said. "We've practiced what she should do."

Grant glanced over his shoulder at the door and then back at Jonna. He was calm now, his smile was almost teasing. "Another new one, Jonna? You must really find some good help and stay with them. Or is it Mrs. Davis who's the ogre?"

The housekeeper blushed. "Go on with you, Mr. Sheridan." She gave the maid a little push to enter the room. "I knew you wouldn't mind if we tried her out on you," she said. "She's frightened, poor thing. And she doesn't speak a word."

Grant watched the girl's passage with more interest than Jonna. "Is she deaf?" he asked.

"No," Mrs. Davis said. "She hears everything, but it's as if she doesn't understand. And no one can get a word out of her. I think she's mute."

"What's her name?" he asked Jonna.

Jonna looked to Mrs. Davis for the answer.

"Rachael," the housekeeper said.

Rachael recognized her name and swiveled around to face the housekeeper. She looked at Mrs. Davis expectantly, her dark eyes large and apprehensive. The housekeeper made a number of motions with her hands, indicating Rachael should go on about her business and remove the tray. The girl picked up the service quickly, aware of the scrutiny of the housekeeper, her employer, and the guest. Her hands shook, and the silver and china rattled noisily. The more she tried to steady herself, the more awkward her positioning became.

Grant set down his brandy and came to her rescue. "Here," he said quietly. "Allow me to help."

The small dark face stared up at him. There was worry

first, then gratitude, but both expressions were shaded by fear.

Grant took the tray to Mrs. Davis. "I think more practice is in order, but you can't fault her effort."

The housekeeper smiled gratefully at Grant's understanding. "You're right about that." She stepped aside, let the girl pass, then left herself. Grant shut the doors and turned on Jonna. "You're a fraud, Jonna Remington."

She noticed he sounded quite pleased about it. "I am? How so?"

"You have nothing good to say about the abolitionists, yet you have set up this house to help one poor young Negress after another."

"One has nothing to do with the other," she told him. "That child's freeborn. Mrs. Davis plucked her out of the colored orphanage and has made a cause of her. She thinks the girl is perfectly trainable, but I have my doubts."

"How old is she?"

"Seventeen . . . eighteen."

Both of Grant's sandy brows rose. "Really. I would have thought younger."

"Apparently the records indicate otherwise."

"What happened to her hand?" he asked.

Jonna had suspected he'd noticed the girl's maimed hand when he'd reached for the tray. "You're not thinking of taking her on as a cause yourself?" she asked. "I thought you and your abolitionist friends only wanted to free slaves."

"That's a narrow view," Grant said. "But I'm not surprised you entertain it." He couldn't resist adding, "You and every other Boston merchant with Southern interests."

"Be careful, Grant. You'll tar yourself with that same brush. What are you if not a Boston merchant?"

He chuckled, raising his glass in a small salute. "As a

matter of fact, I *was* thinking of taking up that girl's cause. Even abolitionists need to be reminded that slavery is not merely a problem in the South."

Jonna sat up straighter. "That girl is not a slave in my home. She earns a wage and her room and board."

"Of course she does. But I wonder how much freer she is here in Boston than she would be below the Mason-Dixon line."

"Well, you're not going to put her on display at one of your meetings to ask that question."

He smiled at her protectiveness. "See, Jonna, you are a fraud." He saw her mouth flatten as she dismissed this observation. "Tell me about the girl's hand."

"A dog bite, I believe. Fairly recent. Mrs. Davis asked Dr. Hardy to treat it. Apparently there's nothing to be done. He can't repair what's left of the ball of her hand, but at least there is no infection. He thinks she will always have some numbness in her fingers."

He nodded slowly. "That explains that business with the tray. I thought she was going to upend it on you."

"I suspect she was nervous as well. This evening is the first time she has worked in front of company."

Grant considered that. "Is it because you haven't had any guests in my absence or because she's only been here a short time?"

"Both," Jonna said.

Setting aside the snifter, Grant leaned forward. His elbows rested on his knees, and his hands were folded together. "Not even Decker Thorne?"

Deception did not come easily to Jonna. On the occasions it was necessary it was something well thought out, and she practiced it with considerable effort. She could not deceive Grant now. His question had come too unexpectedly. Besides, she knew she had already, in one manner or another, given herself away. What bothered her more than this knowledge was the fact that she had wanted to lie. "Captain Thorne was here one evening," she said. "But I suspect you knew that."

He nodded. "I heard about the fight within a few hours of arriving in Boston," he said. "And naturally the same people wanted me to learn that you were responsible for his release from jail. Knowing you as I do, I was surprised that he only spent a single night here."

"That was his choice."

"I thought it might have been." Grant stood, but he didn't approach Jonna's chair. "I wonder at your interest in him. It was not so long ago that you dismissed Decker out of hand." His smile did not light his flat black eyes. "It always seemed to me that it was Colin Thorne you favored. Or is it just that you find Decker a more acceptable substitute for his brother than I?"

Jonna recoiled as if struck. Grant's accusation took her breath away. She came to her feet, her hands curled at her sides, and forced herself to speak calmly. "Perhaps we cannot even be friends any longer."

Grant Sheridan had never found it easy to be contrite, but he knew how to make an apology. Clearly he had overstepped himself with Jonna. "I'm sorry," he said stiffly. "I suppose I was getting some of my own back. Did you think I wouldn't be hurt by what you've said tonight? I love you, Jonna."

It was the first time he had ever said the words. She was struck by the fact that they made no difference. "I'm sorry, too," she said quietly. "But I don't return your feelings."

Grant hesitated, wondering what he could say that would change her mind. It was with deep regret that he understood there were no words. He walked to the doors, opened them soundlessly, and made his exit. He was standing on the sidewalk in front of her house, well outside of her hearing if not her sight, when he finally swore softly to himself. "Nothing's changed." He recalled the kiss. His mouth against hers. The way she pushed at his shoulders and twisted in his arms. He remembered the texture of her skin under his lips. Cool and smooth. "You *will* be my wife."

Jonna stepped away from the salon's large window as Grant continued down the sidewalk. She let the velvet drapes fall back into place. Hugging herself, feeling chilled by this last glimpse of Grant, Jonna approached the fireplace. She knelt in front of it, raising her face and hands to the heat. What had he said, she wondered, just before he turned away from the house? It was too dark for her to make out the words, yet she had the distinct impression he meant for her to know them.

It wasn't fair, she thought, that she had never fallen in love with him. She had willed it to happen on any number of occasions. Once or twice she had even permitted herself to believe it was true.

Flames lighted Jonna's rueful smile and colored her complexion. She had never thought of herself as a particularly foolish person. Now she was revising that opinion. She mocked herself with soft laughter. She knew one or two people who would require no convincing.

Jonna spent Christmas Day alone. She gave presents to the staff, then dismissed those who wanted to spend time with their own families. The others she knew would gather in the kitchen and share a specially prepared feast in front of the hearth. She took her own meal in the afternoon, spending the rest of the day working in the library. There was the occasional interruption as Rachael brought tea and replaced wood in the fireplace, but save for these moments, Jonna was alone.

In other years she had accepted invitations. Most recently she had shared Christmas Day with Grant. She had no regrets about choosing solitude this Christmas, and she had none about Grant's absence. She told herself there was really no one she wanted to spend the day with, and for the better part of the afternoon and evening, she believed it.

It was only when she heard a pair of familiar voices singing cheerfully off-key that she knew herself to be a liar as well as a fool.

Jonna pushed her chair back from the desk and went to the window. Falling snow was illuminated by the lantern Decker held. Jack's lantern dangled from his fingertips, and the light it gave off swept the crusty, glistening ground cover. Their faces were raised above the lines of their scarves. The wind had flushed their cheeks with color, and Jack's nose looked dangerously close to frostbite. Jonna pressed her forehead to the cold pane of glass, peering down at them. She revised her opinion of Jack's nose as he shot her a broad, slightly loopy smile. More likely he had been drinking.

Jonna pointed to the front of the house and waved them inside. She knew her opinion of Jack's condition was correct when he leaned heavily on Decker. His lantern sprayed snow as it hit the ground every time his knees sagged.

She met them at the door. Jack stomped in noisily, shaking off flakes of snow from his coat and boots with the abandon of a wet mongrel. Jonna and Decker couldn't do a thing until he was finished.

"You take his coat and muffler," Decker said, sweeping off Jack's hat. "I'll keep him upright. Steady as you go there, Jack."

It was not a simple thing to accomplish. Jack bobbed and weaved as if he were fighting to keep his honor instead of his coat. Jonna found herself laughing helplessly.

"Now there's some sweet music," Jack said to Decker. "Can't say I've heard much of it lately."

Jonna saw Decker narrowly avoid being poked in the ribs. She sobered immediately. "I'll hold him," she said. "You get the muffler. Just put it all on the stairs."

"Where's Dorothea?" Jack asked. He craned his neck to look around the entrance hall.

It took Jonna a moment to realize he was talking about her housekeeper. "Mrs. Davis is visiting her children today."

Decker brushed snow off his shoulders before he tossed his coat on the newel post. More flakes clung to his dark hair. He raked it with his fingers, and the ends curled damply at his collar. "There's no one here at all?" he asked.

"A few servants with no family of their own," she said. "I don't want to bother them. Here, take Jack into the library. I'll put away your coats." Jonna joined them a few minutes later. She carried in a tray of cookies from the kitchen and a pot of hot tea. "There's liquor if you prefer," she told Jack when he eyed the pot suspiciously.

"You only have the good stuff here," he groused. "Never sets well after a few tankards of stale ale."

Jonna shook her head, affectionately exasperated, and set the tray down. Her gaze swept over Decker when he reached for a cookie. It was the first time she had seen him since he had been a guest in her home. He moved easily, without any stiffness from his injuries. She didn't think he could possibly be healed, yet he didn't seem troubled by his ribs. Then she remembered how quickly he had moved to avoid Jack's wayward elbow in the entrance hall. It was not outside all possibility that he was making an effort to appear more fit than he was.

Decker picked up a sand tart, held it to his lips, and

glanced up at Jonna. "Assured yourself yet that I'm all of a piece?" he asked. He dropped casually back in the large wing chair and plopped most of the cookie in his mouth. His bright blue eyes were watching her, and they were laughing.

"You're not so far in your cups as Jack," Jonna said.

"True enough," he admitted. "But that's not why you were looking at me like that."

"Like what?"

Sharing a few pints of ale with Jack had transformed Decker's careless smile into a reckless one. "Like this," he said. Then his eyes narrowed a mere fraction and grazed Jonna slowly from head to toe.

She forgot about Jack's presence. For this moment there was only Decker, and that easy, reckless smile of his made her heart trip over its own beat. She had never looked at him the way he was looking at her now. She didn't know how to. She wouldn't have dared. This look was as substantial as a touch. Jonna could feel his fingers in her hair, at her nape; feel his thumb pass over the pulse in her throat.

She was wearing an emerald gown cut from glacé silk. It shimmered when she stood perfectly still; when she drew a breath it glittered like green ice.

Jonna drew a breath now. Decker's gaze slid over her shoulders, her breasts, then down the length of her long legs. Jonna was so thoroughly undressed by his eyes that she had an urge to raise her hands to preserve her modesty. His expression never changed, never indicated approval or dislike until he raised his eyes to hers again. Then she saw his frank appreciation.

"You're looking well," he said casually. He reached for another cookie. "Are you going to sit?"

Jonna dropped like a stone into the chair behind her. She glanced at Jack. His head had lolled sideways onto his shoulder, and his eyes were closed. She hoped he had been sleeping throughout Decker's scrutiny. "I've never looked at you like that," she whispered heatedly.

"You should."

Jonna's mouth flattened in disapproval. "I think you've had rather more to drink than is immediately evident."

He didn't deny it. "I didn't match our friend Jack here, but I lifted my share." He pointed to the pot of tea. "May I?"

"Of course." She moved to pour, but he stopped her. Jonna sat back in her chair while Decker served both of them. "Jack's going to have a stiff neck in the morning."

Decker looked at his sleeping friend. "His sore head will keep him from noticing it."

"Should we move him to one of the bedrooms?" she asked. "He'd be more comfortable."

One of Jack's eyes opened. "Fine just where I am," he said. He shifted slightly in his seat, adjusted the angle of his head, and closed his eye again. "Chaperoning, don't you know." Almost immediately he was asleep, this time snoring softly.

Jonna blinked. She looked at Decker. "How does he do that?"

Decker was already on his feet, picking up the tray. "I have no idea. I think it's a trick he mastered at sea. He hardly ever used his cabin to sleep. During storms he'd be strapped in his chair at the helm and catch a moment's rest when he could." He raised the tray a little higher. "He can stay here. We can go somewhere else." He paused when she didn't move. "Unless you think you need a chaperone."

Jonna stood. "That's silly."

Decker turned, smiling to himself. He let Jonna precede him into the hallway, then followed her into the salon. He put the tray down and gave her back her cup of tea. Taking another cookie for himself, he went to the fireplace and added a few logs. Jonna was already positioning two chairs to get the most heat from the fire.

"It's chillier in here than I thought it would be." She took a rug from the back of the settee and laid it over her legs as she sat. She sipped her tea. "Except for dinner I've been in the library."

Decker was still hunkered in front of the rising flames. He looked over his shoulder at her. "Working."

"Well, yes," she said a bit defensively.

"It wasn't an accusation, Jonna." He watched her react to his use of her given name, but she didn't comment. Decker stood and brushed off his hands. She held out his cup to him as he sat. "Thank you."

As she watched, Decker stretched out comfortably in the chair beside her. She envied him his complete ease, his perfectly settled posture. "Was it Jack's idea to come caroling here this evening?"

"It was Jack's idea to sing at the top of his lungs when we left the tavern. It was my idea to do something productive with all that vocalizing. There was no sense landing both of us in jail." Decker put aside his saucer and simply held the china cup between his palms. "Have you been alone all day?"

The shift in subjects startled her. Somehow this question seemed more personal than the appraising look he had given her earlier. "There are a few servants here," she said.

He gave a brief, sideways glance that told her he wasn't satisfied with that answer.

"All right," she said. "You and Jack are the first company I've had."

"Then I'm glad we came. You shouldn't spend Christmas Day by yourself."

"Is that a rule?"

"Yes," he said. "My rule." He reached in his pocket and drew out a small package. "I have this for you."

"Oh, but—"

Decker held it out to her. "Please, I want you to have it."

Jonna put aside her cup and took the neatly wrapped gift. She undid the string, then folded back the plain brown paper to reveal a wooden box. Having no idea what to expect, Jonna lifted the lid.

A polished piece of ivory not much bigger than her thumbnail lay inside. Jonna had no difficulty recognizing the scrimshaw on the piece. It was *Huntress*. The exquisitely carved clipper was outrunning the wind, her graceful sails fully extended, water rushing along the sides of her hull. Jonna picked up the ivory and laid it in her palm. She ran her finger lightly over the carving. It was almost possible to feel the speed of the ship.

"It's beautiful," she said softly. She had no glance to spare for Decker until she was certain he wouldn't see her tears. "Thank you. Really, it's beautiful." With some reluctance she put it back in the box and replaced the lid. She removed the string and paper from her lap, but kept the box there. "Did you do the scrimshaw?" she asked, finally looking at him.

He nodded. "I've had the ivory for a few years. I just never knew what I wanted to put on it."

"I'm flattered you chose *Huntress*." And she meant it. She believed he had captured some part of her in the exquisitely detailed carving. She wondered if he knew that. "It must have taken you a long time."

Decker shrugged. "It passed the hours while I was waiting for my ribs to mend."

Jonna realized she was absurdly disappointed by that answer. She did not want her gift to have been a diversion for him; she wanted it to be its own purpose. "And your ribs," she asked. "Are they quite healed?"

"I'm seaworthy," he said. Which was not precisely an answer to her question. He spoke again before she could pursue the subject. "I wasn't sure we'd find you at home this evening. I thought you might be with Sheridan."

Jonna's fingers tightened imperceptibly on the box. "It's really none of your business, Captain Thorne, but—"

"Decker."

She ignored that. "But Grant and I are agreed that we do not suit."

Both of Decker's brows lifted. "Oh? When did this happen?"

"Just after he returned from Charleston."

Better than a week ago, Decker thought. "Are you certain Sheridan shares your feelings?"

"I couldn't have been any clearer about my own."

"That isn't what I asked," Decker said. "The rumor on the waterfront is that you'll be his wife by spring."

Jonna hoped her sigh masked her irritation. "Rumor has always had it that we were engaged," she said. "I can't be responsible for what other people think."

"Then it's not true?"

"That I'm going to marry Grant? No, it's not true. I'm self-sufficient, Captain. Even if I chose not to run Remington Shipping, my inheritance would be more than adequate to meet my needs. I don't require a husband to support me, and I won't marry a man who can't."

"Then you have the luxury of marrying for love."

She had never considered it quite that way. "Yes," she said thoughtfully. "I suppose that's true."

"As long as he's rich," Decker added.

Jonna was no longer looking at Decker but staring at the

147

fire. "As long as he's rich," she repeated quietly. "Otherwise I'd wonder about the money, you see."

"What would you wonder?"

"If that's why he married me." Her smile was rueful. "The silver lining in having Grant as a constant companion has been to keep the fortune hunters away. My father worried about them. I don't have my mother's looks, you know." She said this last piece simply, as if it explained everything.

Decker said nothing. He studied Jonna's profile as she watched the fire. His scrimshaw work was clumsy compared to the delicately carved lines of her face. There was a master's stroke in the arch of her brow and cheek, in the slant of her nose and chin. He wondered if she knew these same proud angles were in her clipper's sails and canted deck as it was lifted by the surf and wind. He had set the shape of her ship in ivory, but he hadn't scribed one line without thinking of her.

"I suppose I should be going," he said at last. "Getting Jack on his feet will take some doing."

Jonna was jerked out of her reverie. She held Decker's present in her hands as she came to her feet. "You can leave him here," she said. "I have enough help to get him situated in a room. He'll be fine."

"Are you certain?"

She nodded.

"I imagine I'd have to be pretty well battered and bruised to get the same invitation."

Jonna smiled. "I'm afraid so."

His look of disappointment was only slightly exaggerated. It had the desired effect of deepening her smile. "Thank you for bringing us in out of the cold."

"I couldn't think of any other way to stop the singing."

Decker's eyes dropped to her mouth. Firelight caressed the dimple at the corner of it. He forgot what he was going to say.

148

"Thank you for the gift," she said.

His eyes lifted to hers. They were more blue than violet now, and their centers were very large and very dark. "I don't suppose there is any mistletoe over us right now."

She shook her head. "I shouldn't mind if you kissed me anyway."

So he did. His mouth was gentle and gently seeking. He held her face lightly in his hands. He captured her sigh. The taste of her was sweet and warm. He wanted more of what he couldn't ask for and shouldn't take. Decker raised his head and felt Jonna lift on tiptoe. His hands fell to her shoulders, pressing her back lightly. "I'm going now," he said.

She opened her eyes and looked at him. "All right."

"My coat?" he asked. "My scarf?"

It took Jonna a moment to collect herself. She was glad he didn't seem amused by her just then. She had never felt more like crying. "This way," she said.

Snow was still falling when Decker stepped outside. He hunched his shoulders forward, burrowing deeper into his coat. He heard the door close behind him and resisted the urge to glance back. His boots made fresh prints in the snow as he tripped lightly down the steps. He smiled when he saw the half-covered, haphazardly placed impressions he and Jack had made earlier as they'd staggered up the walk.

Then Decker's smile faded. He bent, lowering his lantern, and examined this path more closely. It went off in a direction other than the one he and Jack had taken and these footprints were only covered with a dusting of snow. That meant they were almost as fresh as his own trail from the house.

Curious, Decker followed them. Though he had done his share of poaching in lean times, he was no expert tracker. Even so, he could see that the person who made the prints had stopped for a while about four yards from Jonna's salon window. The snow where he had stood was trampled smooth, and there were multiple prints, as if he had shifted his weight repeatedly or stamped his feet to stay warm.

Decker stood in the same space and turned around slowly, looking for the view that had kept this visitor's attention. He stopped when he faced the window squarely. When he had been in the salon he had never noticed that the drapes were tied back. Now he regretted this oversight. At this angle he could not see the lower portion of the room, but he had a clear view of Jonna crossing it, bending slightly, then lifting the tray of tea and cookies in front of her. He stood there until she left the room, then just a bit longer. It took those extra minutes to become accustomed to the tight, sinking feeling in his gut.

Someone had seen him embrace Jonna Remington. Someone had seen them kiss.

Decker's eyes traced the remainder of the trail until it turned the corner of the mansion. He let the lantern fall again and set his mind to considering the possibilities.

On the second day of the new year Decker Thorne was in command of *Huntress* again. From her office window, Jonna watched the ship taking on its London cargo. Her payload was a rich one. She was carrying barrels of cured tobacco from Virginia, silk and carpets from the Orient, and machinery for some newly developed railway system. There would be no passengers this voyage. The cabins normally set aside for their use held cotton from a recent Carolina run. It would fit nowhere else.

Jonna took a small bite of the apple she had brought as part of her lunch. Thus far it was the only thing she had eaten. Nothing else in the basket held much appeal to her. Idly she pressed one hand to her chest. Beneath the material of her gray gown she could make out the shape of the ivory piece Decker had given her. The day after Christmas she had taken it to a jeweler. It had been fitted with a slender gold chain and returned to her two days ago. She had been wearing it ever since.

She let her hand drop to her side. An odd odor had her turning away from the window and wrinkling her nose. Jonna sniffed. It wasn't that the odor was odd at all, she thought, dropping her apple and running for the door. It was that it was out of place.

There was never any good reason for smoke to be coming from her warehouse.

The outer office was empty, and Jonna remembered Mr. Caplin had said he had business at the ship. She hurried down the narrow stairs and through the doors at the bottom which took her right into the warehouse. She caught her breath and lifted her face, trying to catch the odor of smoke that was so clear to her upstairs.

The warehouse was like a cavern and Jonna's steps echoed eerily as she began her inspection. Because of the loading there was no one around and the storage area itself was largely empty. *Huntress* was the fourth clipper to be loaded in three days, and no ship was due in any sooner than tomorrow. Jonna hoped that would turn out to be a blessing as she searched amid the crates and barrels that remained.

Several minutes passed. She was calm now but not convinced that the smell of smoke had been in her imagination. She was just not that good at imagining things.

There were a half-dozen small rooms on the left of the warehouse. They were sometimes used for space for clerks whose services were required. Since these rooms could be locked, they were mainly used to store more valuable items scheduled for shipping. Paintings that were insured for amounts larger than the typical manifest were kept there. At the specific request of a passenger, personal possessions could be stored.

Even though two of the rooms were situated very nearly under her office, Jonna hadn't started her search there. She had no reason to believe they were anything but empty.

This turned out to be the case with the first one she looked into. She was not right about the second.

Smoke billowed out as soon as she opened the door. The draft from the warehouse swept the small enclosure and fanned the flames, which shot out, licking at her hand and the hem of her gown. She opened her mouth to call for help. Searing heat crawled down her throat and words turned to ashes on her tongue. Acrid smoke burned her eyes. She beat down a spark that singed her hair.

Jonna tried to pull the door shut, but the knob was already too hot to touch. She ran for the warehouse entrance and waved frantically for the attention of a passerby. It was not her wildly flailing arms they noticed but the fact that her silk skirt was burning like a candlewick.

Jonna felt a blow to her midsection that took the last of her breath away. She was thrown to the ground and rolled roughly across it. Frightened and disoriented, she struggled at first, pounding at the person who was beating at her legs. She heard someone yell for a bucket brigade. Then everything around her erupted into jarring footsteps and discordantly raised voices.

The weight on Jonna's legs was lifted as Decker picked up Jeremy Dodd and practically flung him aside. Jack helped the hapless young man to his feet while Decker knelt beside Jonna.

"Quick thinking, lad," Jack told Jeremy. "You probably saved her life. Now get a bucket and get in line. No time to rest on your laurels." He watched Jeremy take off at a run. At his back, he could feel the heat from the fire. "Get her out of here, Decker. We can manage without you."

Jonna was sitting up now, supported by Decker's arm. "No," she said. It was difficult not to choke on the single word. "I want to stay here . . . I want to—"

Decker stood and pulled Jonna to her feet. The skirt of her gown was mostly gone. What remained were pieces of four singed petticoats. Still, there was enough material to cover her modestly. She wobbled on her feet when he let her go, but she didn't faint. "It's your warehouse," Decker said. "Pick up a bucket."

He strode away and Jack followed. Jonna stared at the flames rising to the ceiling of her building; then she ran after them.

Like worker ants driven by instinct to protect their queen, every man at Remington Shipping rushed to the scene to help Jonna. They were joined in short order by dockhands from all over the harbor. Taverns and warehouses emptied as word of the fire spread. A pumper wagon arrived, but the horses shied away from the intense heat. In short order they were unhitched so men could pull the wagon close enough to the warehouse to hose down the adjoining buildings.

The firefighters did not have the wind in their favor. The breeze off the ocean fanned every flame their buckets missed. Jonna joined the line in the middle and passed the full pails forward. Her cramped and blistered fingers gripped the rope handles, and her shoulders ached with the effort of hefting the heavy buckets. A thin sheet of ice glazed her blackened clothing and frosted her hair. Stubbornly she refused to give way, and there wasn't a man around her who didn't work harder because of it.

Twice the men thought they had it beaten, and twice they

were proved wrong. They didn't let themselves hope too much when the flames were finally confined to the small side offices and storerooms again.

Jonna didn't know they had won until she heard the cheer from those closest to the source. Even then she was too tired to fully understand what it meant. Dazed, she looked around her.

With more care than they'd showed for the buckets, Jonna was passed forward along the line until she was handed into Decker's arms at the head of it. "It's done," he said. His arm at her waist was all that was holding her up.

Jonna stared at the charred remains of half of her warehouse. She knew she was fortunate to have any part of it standing, yet she didn't feel particularly lucky right now. "I'd like to go home," she said hoarsely.

Decker shook his head. "Later. Right now I'm taking you to the ship."

Jonna stiffened. "No. I don't want to go aboard."

The brigade had lost its form. Men from the end of the line were moving closer to the warehouse to inspect the success of their efforts. They crowded around and speculated on the cause of the fire. Jonna and Decker were quickly hemmed in by them. Decker saw Jack pushing through and waved him over. "I'm taking her to the ship, Jack," he said. "Can you handle things here?"

Jack raised his hat and wiped his forehead with the sleeve of his coat. Soot creased his wrinkled brow. He tried to read Decker's expression. "Aye," he said. "I can. For as long as it takes, I expect."

Decker nodded. "Jonna?" She didn't answer him. Her attention was elsewhere. Decker followed the line of her vision and saw Grant Sheridan moving toward them. Nothing about Grant's sudden appearance was welcome, especially the fact that he was still neatly turned out in a clean coat and creased trousers. His handsome face, though expressing concern and a sense of urgency, showed no trace of sweat or soot.

Grant held out his arms to Jonna. "I'll take her now," he said to Decker. "My carriage is waiting."

"Only if she wants to go. Do you, Miss Remington?"

It was increasingly difficult to think clearly. Jonna shifted unsteadily on her feet and was grateful for Decker's support. Pressing three fingers to her temple, she closed her eyes. The arm around her waist tightened uncomfortably and drawing a full breath became an effort.

She was thinking she should ask Grant where he had been when she felt herself slump into unconsciousness.

Six

Jonna came awake slowly. She stretched under the thick quilt and raised her eyelids to half-mast. This narrow view of the world was enough to make her bury her face in her pillow.

The roll of the ship cradled but did not comfort. The forward surge was unfamiliar to Jonna, yet completely recognizable. *Huntress* was out to sea.

Groaning softly, Jonna threw off the covers and sat up. Her fingers curled around the edge of the bunk. She steadied herself as the cabin rocked under her feet and her stomach lurched. Closing her eyes helped marginally, but the humiliating truth was that she was going to be sick. Jonna propelled herself out of the bed in the direction of the commode. She opened the cupboard and removed the basin. Hugging it all the while she was sinking to her knees, Jonna emptied the contents of her stomach.

She was still on the deck in this almost penitent posture when Decker found her. It was no accident that he came upon her then. Anticipating that she might be unsettled and disoriented upon waking, he had positioned a man outside the cabin with orders to get him the moment Jonna stirred.

Decker waited until the last wave of sickness had passed before he took the basin. He poured a glass of water and handed it to her. "Rinse," he said when she simply held it between her palms.

Jonna rinsed.

Decker extended the basin. "Spit."

Closing her eyes, Jonna did as she was told. She leaned

weakly against the foot of the bunk while Decker put the basin away. "I want to go home." Even to her own ears, her words were largely unintelligible. She wasn't surprised when Decker ignored her.

"Back to the bunk," he said, kneeling beside her. "You haven't found your sea legs yet."

"Don't have any." Jonna didn't see Decker smile at this small protest. She let him help her to her feet, then ease her onto the bed. She lay down without any prompting from him. "We'll have to turn around," she whispered tiredly.

Decker didn't reply. He sat with her until she fell asleep, knowing all the while there would be no turning back.

It was dark by the time Jonna woke again. The oil lamp secured to the captain's desk had been lighted, and the stove had been fired. It was evidence that someone had come and gone while she slept, and Jonna wasn't grateful for this invasion of her privacy even if thoughtfulness had been the motive.

Her stomach growled when she sat up, but it didn't turn over. She supposed it was progress of sorts that she entertained even a moment's awareness of being hungry.

Jonna teetered when she first stood, but the unsteadiness passed quickly. The layout of the cabin was familiar to her, first as a two-dimensional plan, then later as a model. She had toured it once when the ship was being built, but had never seen it furnished.

The cabin was not much larger than her own dressing room. The built-in bunk took most of the space on one wall. The commode closet and a trunk were at the foot, bookshelves were at the head. Storage space beneath the bunk was closed off by small louvered doors. The cabin's only chair was pushed far under the desk, and there were more shelves behind that. A wooden bench ran the length of the bow wall directly under two tiers of leaded glass panes.

Jonna moved to the stove and held out her hands in front of it, warming them. She found the cabin oddly sterile. It seemed that Decker had done little in the way of making it his own. There were no mementos of voyages, no figurines or lacquered boxes. The linens and quilts were from Boston, not London, and the books were dry maritime tomes that she suspected belonged to Jack.

The item that was out of place in the cabin was the trunk in the middle of the floor. She knew it hadn't been there when she awoke earlier. Even ill, she would have recognized it for what it was and understood its significance. She doubted she would have been able to sleep so easily or for so long if she had known it was aboard her ship.

The trunk belonged to her.

Jonna looked down at herself. She was still wearing the clothes she had fought the fire in. The bodice and sleeves were all that remained of her gown and her charred and tattered petticoats hung limply around her legs. Smoke clung to the material and to her hair. Every breath she took brought back some memory of the fire.

She didn't open the trunk. Instead, she sat down on it. Burying her face in her hands, Jonna wept.

Decker dismissed the man outside his cabin. "You won't be needed," he said. "Get some sleep. You have early watch." Decker watched the sailor hurriedly and gratefully leave his post. His footsteps cleared the gangway before Decker knocked softly on the door.

"Come in."

It was with a certain cautious air that Decker opened the door. Jonna's tone did not invite, it granted an audience. He was prepared to duck in the event something was thrown at his head. She had nothing in her hands, and was sitting on the hard window bench, her eyes turned toward the sea. The night sky was revealed only by a crescent moon's light, and Jonna's face was reflected in the glass. Her features were almost devoid of expression; none of the ravages of her earlier bout with tears were evident now.

In spite of the lateness of the hour, she had not dressed for bed when she changed her clothes. Jonna had not wanted to be at a disadvantage when she saw Decker again. She wore a wine-colored gown, high-necked, severely cut, with tight sleeves and a fitted bodice. Her black hair was loosely braided in a thick plait that fell down the center of her back. It hid the three tiny hooks she had not been able to fasten on her own.

Jonna looked past her own reflection and watched Decker enter the cabin. When he had shut the door behind him and was leaning against it, she swiveled around on the bench and came to her feet. Her arms remained still at her sides; her fingers didn't sift the material of her gown. Her manner was composed and poised and cool, and she spoke with the serene confidence of one who expects to be obeyed.

"You will turn this ship back to Boston," she said. "You will do so immediately and without argument. The matter of whether you had any right to take it out with me aboard will be addressed later. I think you know you acted precipitously and contrary to my wishes. The cost of the delay in reaching London will be levied against your future earnings with Remington Shipping. Once the fine is paid in full you will be relieved of your employment with the company. You may assure *Huntress*'s crew that I do not hold them responsible and will not seek similar reparations." Jonna's head tilted slightly to one side in an attitude of gracious condescension.

"Have I been quite clear, Captain Thorne?"

"Quite," he said.

She nodded once, almost regally, and waited for him to go.

Decker pushed away from the door, but didn't open it. He skirted the trunk which still remained in the middle of the room and stepped over the pile of Jonna's discarded clothing. When he reached the desk he kicked out the chair with the toe of his boot and sat down. Lifting the cover, he removed the ship's log along with ink and a quill from the drawer beneath. Decker opened the log and painstakingly recorded his heading and the weather conditions. He took several more minutes to record Jonna's demands.

He turned the book toward her. "Have I set it down accurately?" he asked.

Jonna approached the desk and read what he had written. His script was careful, each letter formed with exactness. There was no flourish in the handwriting, no carelessness, and it was not only what he had just recorded that had such discipline, but all the entries on the page before it. Somehow it was like the cabin, Jonna thought, sterile and without the stamp of his character.

It struck her then how new he was to both things. She raised her head a fraction and stared at him, a question in her own eyes now.

"Have I set it down accurately?" he asked tersely.

Jonna's reply was hushed. "Yes," she said.

"And the spelling?" he pressed almost defensively. "Have I got it right?"

"Yes."

Decker spun the log around and penned another line. "My reply," he said, pushing the book back in her direction.

Jonna glanced at the entry: Huntress *will stay her course.*

"What? You don't mean that."

Decker blotted the log before he closed the book. "I mean exactly that," he said. He put everything inside the desk. "If there's going to be an argument, it will be from your end. My mind is made up on the matter." He watched Jonna react as if she'd been struck. Her head came up, her jaw clenched, and color flushed her face.

"It wasn't a request," she said.

Some part of Decker admired her restraint, but he wasn't swayed. "It can be nothing else," he said. "Your position here doesn't give you the right to make demands."

There was a cold fire behind Jonna's violet eyes. "I own this ship," she said.

"And I command it." He held up one hand, stopping her. "You don't own me, Jonna. Don't ever think you do."

"The men will—"

"The men respect us both. Don't make them choose sides or divide their loyalty unless you're prepared to take command of this ship yourself." He paused a beat and studied her face. "Are you?"

Jonna's features were pale now, her lips bloodless. The chill she felt went all the way to her marrow. "No," she said. "You know I can't take command."

Decker nodded once, satisfied she understood. He rubbed the back of his neck wearily. "How are you feeling?" he asked. "Are you hungry?"

She didn't answer him. The certain knowledge that they were not returning to Boston had closed Jonna's throat. Her stomach roiled, not from lack of food or the motion of the ship. It was a deeper panic that twisted her insides.

"Perhaps you should sit down," Decker said. "I'll bring you something from the galley. I haven't had anything myself." He was gone twenty minutes, but he didn't think she

161

had moved in his absence. He placed the tray on the bench beside her. Without asking if she wanted any, Decker poured a mug of tea and passed it to her. "Warm your hands or your insides," he said, as if it were a matter of indifference to him.

Jonna held the mug between her palms and raised it to her lips, but didn't drink. She was grateful Decker didn't urge her to do anything else. Steam rose from the mug and bathed her face in warmth. "Why did you bring me here?" she asked finally.

Decker had uncovered a plate of chicken and biscuits for himself. He carried it over to the desk, away from where the fragrance of something more substantial than tea might offend Jonna, and sat down. Hooking one leg over the arm of the chair, he began to eat. "I couldn't very well look after you otherwise," he said simply.

Jonna frowned. "I don't understand. I would have had Dr. Hardy to look after me."

"True, but I wasn't thinking of your physical health. Or at least not in that regard."

Jonna cautiously sipped her tea. Her confidence increased slightly when it settled in her stomach. "You're not my keeper," she said.

"I am now."

"But—"

"Do you really want to argue, Jonna? You're here. You may as well accept it." Decker wasn't fooled into believing her silence signaled agreement. He suspected she was merely marshaling her forces. "Jack is taking care of the business," he said. "He taught you what your father didn't so you know the enterprise will not suffer."

"That's not the point."

He went on as if she hadn't spoken. "Your offices and the warehouse will be rebuilt by the time we return from London.

You don't have to be there to oversee every detail. Mrs. Davis has the running of your home in hand and will send around regrets for your social commitments." He didn't add that he knew there were few of those. "She packed your trunk herself. I trust you'll find everything you need."

Jonna's shoulders sagged a little at hearing of this betrayal. She hadn't expected her housekeeper to willingly support her abduction. "And Grant?" She had a vague recollection of him appearing after the fire was put out. Hadn't he offered to take her home? "Didn't he have anything to say about you taking me on board?"

"He had a lot to say. No one listened." Not after Grant had been leveled by Decker's fist. "Should his opinion have carried any special weight? I thought you weren't engaged any longer."

"We were *never* engaged," she said crisply. When she saw one corner of Decker's mouth lift Jonna knew she was being needled. She wondered if she would ever learn to ignore him. "I suppose I'm your prisoner then."

Decker glanced up from his plate. "Hardly."

"I can't think what else to call it," she said. "I'm not here willingly, and there's nowhere for me to go. You even posted a guard at my door."

"An attendant," Decker corrected. "And he's gone now. That was only for as long as it took you to come around. There's no need for anyone now. You're free to come and go as you please. I trust your common sense to keep you clear of the crew's quarters, but other than that, you may have freedom of the ship."

The thought of going on deck made her stomach clench again. "I'll stay here," she said.

He shrugged. "If that's what pleases you."

"It does." Jonna finished her tea and set the mug on the

tray. "I'd like to retire now," she said.

Decker wondered how weary she was and how much she simply wanted to be rid of him. "Very well." He got to his feet in a single, effortless motion and crossed the small space that separated him from Jonna. He laid his empty plate on the tray and bent. It wasn't the tray he reached for though. When he straightened he had Jonna in his arms.

She was surprised, but she didn't try to move away. She looked up at him, her eyes wide and searching.

"Good night, Jonna." He touched his lips to her forehead, then kissed her lightly on the mouth. "I'm sorry."

Decker was gone before Jonna knew why he had apologized or if she had forgiven him. She sank slowly back on the window bench. Sleep was a long time claiming her that night.

With a brisk North Atlantic wind at her back, *Huntress* cut the water effortlessly. Most days she traveled at twelve knots an hour, sometimes thirteen. Her passage was unmarred by storms though the wind was steady and strong. White-capped waves curled around her hull and kept her decks awash in saltwater.

The business of mastering a clipper was topside. In any twenty-four-hour period Decker rarely left the helm for more than two or three hours. On those occasions he napped in a sling in the crew's quarters. His visits to Jonna's cabin were only long enough for him to write in the ship's log. During these brief encounters he made it a point to inquire as to her health and her comfort. He always asked her to take a turn with him on deck or accept the escort of another member of the crew. Her answers were perfunctory, civil but cool, and did not invite further conversation. She refused every offer to leave the cabin.

Jonna passed the time reading and writing. Decker's

books were of some interest, but the ship's log captivated her. She was only disappointed that *Huntress*'s brief history meant she concluded reading it in a day. She began a journal of her own, keeping an account of her conversations with the crew and her thoughts about the voyage. She gathered recipes and remedies, and faithfully recorded the lyrics to four sea chanteys she had never heard before. Two of them contained *words* she had never known.

She kept a list of things she didn't miss: Grant Sheridan and haggling with merchants. She kept another list of things she did: tub baths, Jack Quincy, fresh air, and having her hair brushed out before bed.

Huntress was still two days out of London when Jeremy Dodd shyly presented Jonna with a great wooden cask. "Captain says we've enough fresh water for you to have a proper bath," he said. His freckles disappeared beneath a rosy flush.

"This is Captain Thorne's idea?" she asked.

Jeremy's weight shifted uncomfortably. "No, Miss Remington. The captain says you'll want to know that it was my idea and that he only approved it." He said it exactly the way Decker had told him to. No lie there, he thought. Jeremy could see it *was* what Jonna wanted to know, even if there wasn't a speck of truth in it. "Hot water's coming up for you from the galley," he went on before she could see through him. "Buckets and buckets of it."

The brigade arrived a few minutes later and left when the tub was near to brimming over. In their eagerness to please they had forgotten to account for Jonna. When she eased herself down into the water a cascade of it slipped over the side and made rivers and puddles on the floor. She found she didn't care at all.

It was twenty minutes later that Decker walked in. He stopped just inside the door. Jonna's complexion was beautifully flushed from the heat, and the sheen of water on her skin made it glow.

She sank lower in the water so nothing below the line of her collarbone showed. "You didn't knock."

"No," he said. "I didn't."

His matter-of-fact honesty startled Jonna. She realized that his presence here was planned, not accidental. "Please go," she said.

He closed the door, produced a key from his jacket pocket, and locked it. "I think you know I'm not going to do that." He returned the key to his jacket. "At least not yet."

Jonna ducked another fraction as Decker walked by the tub. She realized she needn't have bothered. He didn't glance in her direction when he passed. Behind her, she heard him open her trunk and begin to root through it. "Perhaps if you tell me what you're looking for—" She was cut off when he dangled her robe in front of her.

"You can put this on. I'll turn my back."

"I want my clothes," she said.

"This." Now he glanced significantly at the water. "Or nothing."

Jonna held out her hand for the robe and Decker dropped it. True to his word, he turned his back while she stood and shrugged into it. It clung to her damp skin. Jonna moved to the small stove to warm herself. From under the robe, water dripped on the floor. Where it splashed the stove it sizzled. She looked over her shoulder at Decker and found he was watching her.

"Come here," he said. It was more of a command than an invitation.

Jonna felt a rush of warmth that had little to do with her proximity to the stove. She turned but didn't move in his direction.

"Jonna." He said her name quietly this time and held out his hand. Though his direction was softer it still carried the weight of a demand. "Come here."

Jonna found herself walking toward him. Without knowing she was going to do it, she placed her hand in his. He drew her closer. She had no idea what he was going to do until he touched her throat. She started to twist away, but he caught her and held her fast.

"Don't struggle," he said, his fingers closing around the gold chain at her neck. "You'll break it."

Except for her racing heart, Jonna was still. She looked away from him as his fingertips traced the length of the chain. They slipped under the edge of her robe and came to rest on the ivory pendant. He lifted it away from her skin and the loss of warmth was replaced by the heat of the back of his hand.

"Look at me, Jonna." She raised her face. "I had to be certain."

A small vertical crease appeared between Jonna's brows as she frowned. "I don't understand."

"I think you do."

Jonna's frown deepened before it cleared. Yesterday she had worn the necklace outside her dress. It was an oversight and one she corrected after the sailor who brought her breakfast commented on the ivory. "Mr. Eddies told you about it."

Decker's hands moved lightly to Jonna's upper arms. "He does scrimshaw himself. He admired the piece."

"He hardly saw it," she said.

"He saw enough to make an idle comment about it to me," Decker said. "Enough to make me think it could be the ivory I gave you."

"You're acting as if there's some significance in that."

"Isn't there?"

It was difficult to swallow, even more difficult to work

words past her throat. The pads of Decker's thumbs gently massaged her arms. The friction of her robe was pleasantly abrasive against her skin. "I told you I admired the gift when you gave it to me. Wearing it doesn't mean I admire the giver." He was smiling at her now. Not widely, not openly. His amusement was quieter than that. It was in the depths of his eyes and the faint lift of one corner of his mouth. "You didn't have to arrange my bath this evening," she said, striving for cool accents. "That's why you did it, didn't you? It was all in aid of seeing the necklace yourself. You could have asked me. I would have told you."

"Really?"

Jonna's eyes dropped away. She knew he was right to question her. She wouldn't have told him at all. "Of course," she said.

"Liar." There was nothing unforgiving in his tone. His voice was more of a caress. "Is it possible you like me just a little?" he asked.

She shook her head. "I can't . . . I won't."

Decker's quiet amusement deepened. "Because I'm aimless," he said. "And have a serious lack of principles."

"Because you don't care about anything," she said.

"Yes," he said, as if suddenly remembering. "There's that."

Jonna leaned into him suddenly. Her forehead rested on his shoulder. "And you're not rich," she whispered.

Decker's arms slipped around her waist. His mouth was near her ear when he spoke. "Possessions make it hard to move quickly," he told her. "I can carry everything I value."

She hardly heard him. He was lifting her, and she felt weightless in his arms. Jonna clutched the collar of his jacket until he set her on the window bench. He left her side only a moment, but when he returned he produced a brush from behind his back.

Decker sat in the corner of the bench and drew Jonna between his legs. She went without protest, her eyes closing as his fingers began to unwind her hair. Her sigh was nearly soundless.

Decker separated the thick strands as delicately as ropes of silk. Her dark hair crested in smooth waves like a calm sea at night, and the texture was almost liquid. He spread her tresses across her back; then he raised the brush and ran it through them.

Jonna hummed her pleasure. Her head felt too heavy to keep upright. She let it sag forward. The brush bristles lightly scraped the back of her neck and a frisson of heat spiraled down her spine. The brush followed the same path a moment later.

"I should tell you to leave," she said on a thread of sound. The words ran together as if she had been drinking.

"Yes," he said. He didn't pause a beat in brushing out her hair. "You should."

She didn't though. Jonna continued to sit nestled between Decker's thighs, her head bent and knees drawn toward her chest, and let him pull the brush through her hair. Energy the hot bath hadn't sapped was taken away by Decker's hypnotically smooth motions. "There's my reputation to consider," she whispered. "Those men on deck are my employees."

"Those men are my crew," Decker said. "I have a reputation, too."

She didn't think they were talking of quite the same thing. "Really?" she asked, interested. "Have you seduced a great many women?"

"You would have to define 'a great many.' "

Jonna was aware of the slowing of the movement of the

brush. She kept her eyes closed, not wanting it to end just yet. "More than a hundred," she said.

He pulled part of her hair to one side and exposed the curve of her neck. His lips touched her there just once. "Then, no," he whispered against her skin. "I haven't seduced a great many women."

"Oh."

Decker smiled. Jonna sounded almost disappointed. "Will you have to revise your opinion of me?" he asked.

"A little."

"I'm sorry for that. I usually try to live down to your expectations."

That caught Jonna's attention, the words and the edge of cool irony in his tone. She twisted her head, trying to look at him. "Is that true?"

Decker gently turned her face forward again and continued brushing. "No," he lied without regret. "It's not true. Why would I care one way or the other about your expectations and have none of my own?"

Jonna didn't want to think it through. It made sense when he posed it like that. She sighed, closing her eyes again. "How many women *have* you seduced?"

"Is it so important?"

"Yes," she said flatly.

"Do you require an exact figure?" he asked, amused.

"An estimate will do."

Decker considered what number would ultimately satisfy her. He had no idea if it was close to the mark. "Fifty-eight."

"Oh my."

"It's just an estimate." He stopped brushing for a moment and reached around her so she could see his hand. Decker unfolded his palm. Jonna's ivory pendant lay in the heart of it. "Here," he said. "You haven't missed this yet."

She gasped softly. "When did you—" She stopped, remembering his mouth on her neck, his fingers lightly moving in her hair. She hadn't felt him open the clasp at all. "How did you—"

"Practice," he said simply. He helped Jonna refasten the necklace. Decker was tempted to tell her that profit rather than pleasure had guided his seductions, but he suspected she was arriving at that conclusion herself.

Jonna placed her hand over the ivory pendant. He wouldn't get it so easily from her again. "Did you always give back what you took?"

"I wasn't performing parlor tricks then, Jonna. I was a thief. I never returned anything willingly." Decker resumed brushing and let her think about that.

"You were a good thief," she said quietly.

"Yes, I was."

She was silent for a long time. Her thoughts gradually ceased to take on form or substance. "I could fall asleep here," she said at last. "Just . . . like . . . this."

Decker said nothing but each subsequent stroke of the brush was lighter than the one before it. Finally he felt her body give up the last line of tension. He put the brush down and adjusted them both so she was more completely cradled in his arms.

They both slept for a time, but when Jonna awakened, Decker was gone.

Huntress reached London within hours of her scheduled arrival. Jonna had to shield her eyes as she was lifted topside. The early morning sun had burned off banks of river fog and now shone brightly over the city. Jonna took the bonnet Jeremy Dodd held out to her and put it on. She allowed him to escort her to the taffrail; then she dismissed him. "I'll be

fine," she said. "There's no need to watch my every move."
The young man hesitated. "The captain says—"

"I'm not going anywhere," she said. Then she turned away. Although Jonna's attention was on the teeming harbor, she was aware that Jeremy hovered uncertainly. "Leave me, Mr. Dodd." Her voice caught the perfect, imperious inflection to send him scurrying.

Jonna smiled to herself, pleased with this small victory. Decker Thorne had had his way far too long. It was rare when she could get one of the crew to do as she wanted.

Jonna huddled in her cape and leaned against the taffrail. In spite of the sunshine there was little warmth in the air. She could see her breath mist with each exhalation. Similar clouds rose from the men as they exerted themselves moving cargo down the gangboard and hauling in sail overhead. On the wharf horses snorted their displeasure at having to stand idly while their wagons were being loaded. The drivers clapped themselves on the arms or stamped their feet to keep warm.

Huntress rocked gently in her berth, but Jonna had no difficulty keeping her balance. She had found her sea legs long ago.

London was not so different from Boston, she thought. Certainly the scale was far grander. There was more of everything here: ships, men, wagons, and warehouses. The accents were changed, but the activity was not. All in all, she was glad they wouldn't be in the city long. Everything she saw made her want to be again in Boston Harbor.

Turning away, Jonna searched out Decker. She had no difficulty finding him. His voice caught her attention first. It wasn't raised in the least, but it carried the quiet certainty of authority and registered at a different pitch than the other strained voices. Jonna had never really seen him with the crew before, and now she recognized the respect they had for his command. He was in charge of the rhythm of this ship, the sequence of furling sails and hoisting cargo. He was not the one shouting orders, but there was nothing accomplished that wasn't under his control.

She had wondered about the hours he spent away from her on the voyage. She read what he logged, but the accounts had not satisfied her curiosity, and pride had kept her from asking him. Even without prompting Jonna heard things from the crew. She learned he slept very little, that he lent a hand when needed, and that there was no task on the ship that he hadn't done himself at one time or another. She accepted these things as true because they were offered offhandedly and she had heard them first from Jack Quincy.

If that weren't enough, there was always the fact that Decker had no reason to ingratiate himself with her. He'd made it clear he didn't care at all for her good opinion.

Watching him, Jonna tilted her head to one side. The brim of her bonnet threw a shadow across her eyes. He seemed oblivious to her presence at the taffrail, and Jonna found she liked it that way. Decker had never treated her with the solicitousness that Grant Sheridan had shown her, but neither had he patronized or coddled her, two things that Grant had been apt to do. Decker respected her as someone who knew her own mind, even when she didn't. Grant most often expected to change her mind.

Still observing him, Jonna walked along the taffrail. He stood a head taller than all but a few men, yet he didn't use his height to achieve a commanding presence. His manner was confident, not arrogant. He held himself loosely and walked lightly on his feet, his trim, athletic frame completely synchronous with the ship under him.

The collar of his woolen navy jacket was turned up against

the cold, but he was hatless. The wind whipped strands of coffee-colored hair past his forehead. He raked it back carelessly.

Jonna's shiver was not because of the icy Thames air. She was remembering those fingers in *her* hair, separating the strands, testing the weight of it. She wished she had not fallen asleep in his arms, and she wished he had been there when she woke.

Jonna turned away and closed her eyes briefly. Even if he were a man she could admire, there would always be the matter of his fortune. Or the lack of it. Hadn't that been what he was trying to tell her the other night? He seduced women for what they could give him. It was of little consequence that he had returned her necklace when she had a shipping empire he could raid.

Decker joined Jonna at the taffrail. "I'll be done here in half an hour," he said. "Mr. Jeffries has my instructions and will carry them out. The cargo we contracted for from the Manchester mills won't be here until Thursday."

Jonna's head jerked up. "Thursday. But that's six days from now."

"That's right," he said calmly. "And if we leave without it there will be no profit in the run."

"There must be something else we can carry. I thought we were taking on Indian tea."

"Another delay. Again, not our fault. But if we sail without the tea *or* the material . . . well, you know the problems better than I."

She certainly did. Whether Decker was any less familiar was open to debate. Jonna did some calculating in her head. "Send Mr. Jeffries to Manchester and tell him to push for the product to be in London by Tuesday. Unless there's been an accident at sea the tea shipment should arrive by then. The loss in time and money will not be as damaging if that can be accomplished. And we'll accept passengers for the return."

Decker shook his head. "No passengers."

"Why ever not?"

"Because there's your reputation to think of. You may be the owner of Remington Shipping, but you're still a young woman traveling alone. The crew will always be discreet. I can't say the same for anyone we bring aboard."

"You should have thought of this before you abducted me," she said, annoyed. "And why would there be anything to tell? Unless you mean to interrupt my bath again and announce it to one and all." Her words would have carried more weight if she had been able to look him squarely in the eye. As it was, her flushed cheeks warded off the cold.

Decker leaned back against the taffrail and crossed his arms in front of him. "I'll take on passengers under one condition," he said.

"You're in no position to make conditions, but I'll listen to this one."

"Marry me."

Jonna's mouth flattened. "You really have the most abysmal sense of humor," she said. "I'm going below."

Decker caught her elbow. He was grinning. "And you have none."

She looked pointedly at the hand that was on her arm.

He didn't release her, but he tempered his smile. "Don't leave. The carriage I hired will be here soon, and your trunk has already been brought up."

Jonna stared at him. "Carriage?" she asked. "My trunk? What are you doing now?"

"Abducting you again, I'm afraid." He said this without a shade of regret. "To Rosefield, Miss Remington. Colin's home."

Jonna's suspicions did not silence the sudden slamming of her heart. "Colin lives at Weybourne Park," she said.

"That's right. And Rosefield is one of his residences. The ancestral home, as it were. He inherited it when Lord Fielding, the old earl, died last year."

Jonna nodded. "Colin wrote me about it," she said. "But Lord Fielding was your grandfather, too."

"I never knew him though, not like Colin came to know him. And then there was the matter of my thieving. It seems he found something objectionable about my occupation."

"Imagine that," Jonna said dryly. Her violet eyes regarded Decker curiously. "Tell me something. Are you still a wanted man here in England?"

There was a glimmer of a smile on Decker's mouth. "I'd say no one's much interested in Decker Thorne," he said. "But Ponty Pine? *He* could still face a hangman's rope."

Jonna wondered if that was really true, and if it were, why he had entrusted her with the knowledge. "Why Rosefield? Won't Colin be expecting you to stay at Weybourne Park?"

"Rosefield borders the Park and Colin knows I prefer not to be underfoot."

Jonna didn't pursue the matter, though she suspected there was something left unsaid. "If you're certain it will be all right," she said. She strived for evenness in her tone and achieved it. "I confess it will be a pleasure to see Colin again. We will see him, won't we?"

Watching her closely, Decker nodded. "And Mercedes, of course."

"Oh, yes. I'm looking forward to meeting her. Their children, too."

Decker could almost believe she meant all of it. "Then we're agreed? You'll come to Rosefield."

She liked him for giving her the illusion of choice. "Yes,

we're agreed." Jonna watched Decker go to finish his business with the ship. Was it her imagination, she wondered. Or did his step seem even lighter than usual?

It was dark by the time they reached Rosefield. Jonna thought the lateness of the hour was good enough reason for not announcing themselves at Weybourne Park first. They were met in the drive by a full complement of servants and Decker immediately dispatched one to Weybourne Park with the message of their arrival. Some of Jonna's weariness faded as she mounted the wide stone stairs to the entrance.

The housekeeper let them in. At the first sign of the carriage in the drive she had ordered the staff to be sharp. Rosefield was kept in a state of readiness, but there were always small details that required an extra touch. It was not often that the staff performed their duties with guests in residence. Now Mrs. Shepard would see if their preparation met the exacting standards of the earl's brother.

"Good evening, sir," she said, inclining her head. "May I extend the best wishes of myself and the staff?"

"Indeed you may, Mrs. Shepard." Decker helped Jonna with her coat and bonnet and then handed both to the housekeeper. "Your spies must be everywhere," he said. "I think you knew I was coming before I knew myself."

Mrs. Shepard's round face flushed with pleasure. She beamed at him. "Right you are, m'lord."

He gave the housekeeper his own coat. "This is Miss Remington. She'll be staying here as well, or did your spies already tell you that?"

"You know all is as it should be. Shall I show you to your rooms?"

Decker looked at Jonna. "I don't think I could sleep just yet," she said.

"Refreshment in the library, then," Decker told the house-keeper. "Something light. We ate dinner at an inn on the post road." He offered Jonna his elbow. "This way."

Jonna's own home on Beacon Hill was impressive by any standard, but in size and grandeur it was a mere carriage house compared to Rosefield. The hallway dwarfed them as they made their way to the library, and their footfalls echoed upon crossing the polished floor. Mrs. Shepard ushered them in, then went to oversee the preparation of their repast.

The library was a veritable cavern of books. Jonna barely noticed. She spun on her heel to face Decker as soon as they were alone. "Mrs. Shepard called you m'lord," she said accusingly.

Decker shrugged. "Habit, I expect," he said. "Colin's an earl now, and I'm his brother. It signifies nothing. I think she means it as a courtesy." One of his brows kicked up. "You're not impressed by titles, are you?"

"No."

"That's what I thought. A thorough Yankee."

It seemed to Jonna that since arriving in England Decker's accent had sharpened. As hard as it had been to imagine Decker Thorne here, it reminded her now that she was the one who didn't belong. "This is all Colin's?" she asked.

"Impressive, isn't it?" He walked past her to the large fireplace and held out his hands. "Tomorrow you can have a tour of the estate. Colin will probably come in the morning. He'll show you around."

Jonna was careful to keep her hands still. "Why don't you?"

"I don't know where everything is myself. I don't think I've been here three times since Colin inherited it. When I'm in London on the business of Remington Shipping—*your* business—there's little time to come out this way. If I know when I'll be in London, Colin and Mercedes will sometimes meet me at their townhouse. There hasn't been much opportunity. Colin and I mostly exchange letters."

She spoke without thinking. "How can that be when you've only just—" Jonna stopped herself as her thoughts caught up with her tongue.

"When I've only just learned to read and write myself?" he asked. "That's what you were going to say, wasn't it?"

She nodded. "I'm sorry. I didn't—"

"Do you think I'm ashamed of it?"

"No, I hope not. There's no reason to be." She remembered the first time he had shown her his ship's log. There had been an undercurrent of challenge in the gesture that had nothing to do with what they were talking about at the time. He had been waiting to see if she would comment on his careful script and attention to spelling. He was sensitive to it no matter what he said to the contrary. "I thought perhaps it caused you some embarrassment."

Decker rarely showed his hand. He realized that somehow he had this time. Embarrassment was the exact thing he felt, but that emotion didn't register in either his startling blue eyes or his careless smile. "It's all right," he said. "You can say whatever occurs to you to keep me under your feet."

Jonna flushed. "I didn't deserve that."

"Yes, you did." Decker turned and picked up a poker. He nudged at the fire. "But you're correct about my reading and writing. I wasn't entirely illiterate when I joined Remington Shipping but near enough. Jack helped me with the letters to Colin, and I studied on my own. He wouldn't have recommended me to take command of *Huntress* if he didn't think I could log the journey."

Jonna was relieved when Mrs. Shepard appeared with a tray. It was set on the cherry wood table between two leather arm chairs. She thanked the housekeeper and offered to pour herself. When she and Decker were alone again she didn't touch the tea or cakes. Her appetite for even this light fare had fled.

She walked over to the fireplace and stood beside Decker. "I've read your logs," she said quietly. "I've no complaints."

Decker shrugged and replaced the poker. "Jack's a good teacher."

"That's something we have in common. Jack's been a teacher to both of us."

"And Colin," Decker said. He was staring at the fire, but he was watching her out of the corner of his eye.

"Colin, too. I suppose Jack's responsible in some way for bringing us all together."

"He'd like to think so," Decker said dryly.

"It makes me wonder what he could do about your other brother."

Decker reached in his vest pocket and withdrew the heirloom earring. He held it out in his open palm so it caught the firelight. "Jack knows what to look for. There's only one other like it."

"Do you think Greydon still has it? He was only an infant when Colin slipped it into his blankets."

"Who can say? The couple who took him from Cunnington's Workhouse may have recognized the worth of the piece and kept it for him."

She watched Decker repocket the earring. "That's everything you own, isn't it?"

"You sound amazed. I told you I could carry everything I valued."

"If you've never cared for possessions, then why did you make a career of stealing the possessions of others?"

"Because I could, I suppose."

Jonna's mouth flattened at the flippant remark. "I think

I'll retire now," she said. "I find I have no appetite."

"And no particular fondness for the company."

She did not attempt to soften his observation. "Not just now," she said.

Jonna woke early the following morning. She took special pains with her appearance, pinching color into her cheeks and asking one of the maids to dress her hair. She forced a certain gaiety into her expression that was at odds with the tight knot of dread in her stomach.

Decker only glanced at her when she entered the breakfast room. She was seated at the far end of the table and served dishes from the sideboard. "You slept well?" he asked.

She had slept hardly at all. "Very well, thank you. My room is quite lovely. I have a view of the grounds to the south. I imagine the gardens are magnificent in the spring and summer. Have you seen them then?" Jonna was chattering, and she knew it. The thing of it was, she couldn't seem to help herself. "Even covered with snow they have a certain charm. I could make out the paths and the maze."

Decker had the same view from his suite of rooms. Although Jonna didn't know it, they shared the east wing of the manor. "I've seen them," he said. "I haven't Colin's eye for that sort of thing, so I can't judge their charm."

The forced brightness in Jonna's violet eyes faded at the mention of Colin's name. She smoothed her napkin in her lap to hide her nervous fingers. "My mother taught Colin about gardening," she said. "She loved flowers. I think she passed more of that love on to him than she did me. I've never thought it took a special eye to judge beauty or charm. You know what you like, don't you?"

Decker held Jonna's glance. "Yes," he said. "I know what I like."

"There you have it," she said simply. When he didn't look away Jonna's own gaze dropped to her plate. She picked up her fork. "Now, if you're talking about creating a garden, or anything beautiful for that matter, it helps to have an artist's eye."

"Like Colin."

Jonna felt her pulse quicken again. She placed her free hand just above her heart. Beneath her gown and camisole the ivory pendant lay solidly against her skin. "Actually, I was thinking of you," she said. "Your scrimshaw is the work of an artist." Her hand fell away, and she began eating. "I would judge your eye to be every bit as good as your brother's."

Decker wondered if she realized it was the first time she had ever compared him favorably to Colin. He found his next bite of food to have more taste than the one before. It occurred to him that bringing Jonna to Rosefield was an inspired idea after all.

His sister-in-law would certainly think so. Mercedes had suggested it almost a year ago.

Seven

Colin Thorne stepped down from the carriage. Snow crunched beneath his feet. His blond hair glinted in the sunshine like a helmet of light. In startling contrast to his pale hair were dark brown eyes that had more in common with polished onyx than chocolate. As he turned to hold out a hand to the carriage's other occupant a smile softened the line of his square-cut jaw.

Mercedes Leyden Thorne took her husband's hand gratefully. It was not so simple a thing to alight from a carriage these days. The shape of her small, slender body had been noticeably redefined by pregnancy. In her seventh month her high, narrow waistline had disappeared along with her view of her feet. Consequently she almost missed the step.

Colin caught Mercedes easily and set her down in front of him. The hood of her cape fell back, exposing thick hair the color of bittersweet chocolate. Her gray eyes were shining as she raised her face and laughter was hinted at in her open smile.

"There's no need to look so fierce," she said. "I'm quite all right."

Colin's dark eyes still examined his wife from head to toe. He didn't feel fierce at all, just frightened. "You nearly stopped my heart, madam. From now on, I'm going to carry you everywhere." From somewhere behind him he heard a familiar chuckle. "Better yet, I'm going to spare my back and let *him* carry you." He stepped aside so Mercedes could see Decker.

"Ponty!" She was immediately caught up in his arms. Her

183

own arms went around his neck as he swung her off her feet, her protest lost in laughter. "Oh, put me down! You'll hurt yourself!"

Decker rolled his eyes as he looked at his brother. "She practically fits in my pocket, and she thinks I'm straining my back. I've stolen purses that weigh more than she does."

Colin grinned at his wife as he clapped his brother on the back. "He has you there. Now, just enjoy the ride."

Mercedes looked over Decker's shoulder at her husband and smiled sweetly. "I believe I will."

Colin's brows lifted at her smug and flirty smile. "Tease me, madam, and just see if you don't pay the piper."

"I'll look forward to it," she said softly.

Laughing, Decker jogged up the front steps. "I see why you wanted to save your strength, brother. She's a handful." A servant held the door open for him, and he set Mercedes down inside the entrance hall.

Colin stamped his feet and brushed a few flakes of snow from his hair. "More than a handful these days," he said. "And always needing to have the last word." His coat was taken away. "I can tell you, Decker, she's not to be—" He stopped, his attention caught by the figure on the wide staircase. He stepped around his brother and his wife, unaware their eyes followed him.

As though uncertain of her steadiness, Jonna let her hand hover above the banister rail. She remained poised on the stairs, caught in midstep as Colin approached.

Mercedes laid a light, restraining hand on Decker's arm when he would have stepped forward. She, too, was regarding the young woman on the stairs with interest, but felt none of Decker's urge to interfere.

The guarded, watchful expression faded from Jonna's violet eyes as Colin began to climb the stairs. The shape of her mouth changed, her smile tentative at first, then losing all hint of reserve by becoming broad and open and genuine. The years they had been apart were no longer of any account, and Jonna went into Colin's arms eagerly and without inhibition.

"My God," Colin whispered. He held her tightly, his mouth near her ear. "You really *are* here. I didn't dare believe it when the message came last night. I thought there must be some confusion."

Laughing a little breathlessly, Jonna pulled back. Her eyes remained on his face, searching for changes and finding few that weren't for the better. His smile came more easily, and there was less distance in his dark eyes. His expression welcomed her and unabashedly displayed his happiness. That emotion was one she had rarely associated with Colin, and she understood it existed because of something deeper and more abiding than her sudden appearance in his life.

"No confusion," she said simply.

Colin shook his head as if he still couldn't believe it. He glanced back over his shoulder at Decker. "How did you get her out of Boston?" he asked. "She refused to leave each time I made the offer."

"Abducted her, I'm afraid."

Colin grinned. "I could almost believe you." He looked back at Jonna. "Did he have to knock you out to get you on board?"

Her smile became noticeably more restrained. "Something like that," she managed to say lightly.

Slipping his arm under hers, Colin escorted Jonna down the stairs. "She's afraid of the water," he explained to Mercedes. "Always has been. Or at least she always was. She wouldn't step foot on a Remington ship once it left dry dock."

Jonna felt Decker's eyes on her, but she wouldn't look in

his direction. Trying to conceal her discomfort, she fixed her smile on Mercedes. "It's a pleasure to finally meet you," she said. "Colin has written so much about you, I feel as if I've known you almost as long as he."

Mercedes inclined her head. Her smile was soft and engaging. "I had a very similar greeting prepared," she said without guile. "But I'm certain we must have a few secrets held back. He can't know *everything* about us." She took Jonna's arm and led her away from Colin. "For instance," she said conspiratorially. "Did you know that . . ."

Colin strained to hear what bit of information his wife was giving up, but her voice faded beneath her footfalls. He watched Mercedes and Jonna disappear into the library before he turned to Decker. "How the hell *did* you get her here?" he asked.

"I told you. I abducted her."

The answer didn't raise a smile this time. Colin studied his brother's face critically. There was no easy grin evident, and the light blue eyes were remarkably cool and remorseless. "You're serious," he said.

Decker nodded. "Half the Remington warehouse burned to the ground," he said. "She was almost killed in the fire. I had no choice but to get her out of Boston."

Colin's look sharpened. "No choice? That's a slim explanation. What's the rest?"

There had never been any intent on Decker's part not to tell his brother everything. "Later," he said. "When I know we won't be interrupted. We should join Mercedes and Jonna now." He didn't wait for Colin's reply, but began walking in the direction of the library. Just outside the doors he paused and quietly asked the question he had been turning over in his mind. "Is it true about Jonna being afraid of the water?"

"Yes. She won't put her toe in anything larger than a tub,

and she can't swim a stroke. Her father drowned at sea. As near as I can tell she's been afraid of it all her life, at least since I pulled her out of Boston Harbor."

"But she was just a baby then," Decker said. "How could she—"

Colin shrugged. He placed his hands on the doors to the library but didn't part them. "Who's to say how she remembers? She just does. Ask her about it." His look was frank. "You didn't know, did you?"

Decker shook his head. "She never let on."

"Did she come topside even once while the ship was out to sea?" Colin asked.

"No."

"Then she was telling you," he said, shaking his head slowly. "You just weren't listening." There was something close to disappointment in his eyes as Colin opened the doors and stepped inside.

Decker followed but not immediately. Jonna had called herself a prisoner once, and he had dismissed that assertion out of hand. Now Colin had confirmed it was exactly what he had made her. Decker felt a certain hollowness where his heart had been. He took a deep breath and exhaled slowly, then steeled himself to face her.

It was Mercedes, not Colin, who took Jonna on a tour of Rosefield. In construction it was similar to the manor at Weybourne Park, and Mercedes was quite comfortable answering Jonna's questions about the architectural layout and the use of the rooms. Although much of the house was rarely visited by guests, no part of it had been allowed to go uncared for. The conservatory's flowers and greenery thrived, and the spinet in the music room was tuned. The ornate, gilded frames that held family portraits and scenes of the English countryside were free of dust. The furniture was uncovered in all but a few of the bedchambers, and the woodwork gleamed warmly from frequent polishings.

Many of the rooms had fires laid in them, inviting company to linger near the marble mantels. "I can't abide a drafty home," Mercedes told Jonna as they entered the long gallery. "Colin thinks I'm foolish for wanting to keep Rosefield ever at the ready, but I know what it's like when a house falls into disrepair. I don't want to see that happen here as it did at Weybourne Park."

"It's hard to believe that you choose not to live here," Jonna said.

Mercedes's smile was serene. "That's only because you haven't visited the Park, though I admit to a particular bias, of course. I was born and raised at Weybourne, and it will always be dear to me. Colin has no particular attachment to Rosefield so it was an easy decision for us."

Jonna stood back from the portraits on the wall and studied them individually, then as a group. "Family has always been important to Colin. I can understand why he wouldn't want to sell it." She laughed lightly at herself and glanced at Mercedes. "I suppose I've shocked you with the talk of selling. Decker says I'm a thorough Yankee."

"So is Colin," Mercedes said. "For all that his roots are here in this room, he spent too much time with—"

"Me and my family?" Jonna interjected, one of her dark brows rising archly.

"I was going to say with Jack Quincy," Mercedes said.

Jonna felt her prickles fade. "Forgive me," she said softly. "I fear I'm too sensitive."

"Just Yankee proud." Mercedes's smile was gentle now. "I love Colin for it." She paused, sighing. "And for any number of other reasons."

Jonna was silent. Mercedes's words confirmed what Jonna had already observed in the exchanges between Colin and his wife. In Mercedes's burgeoning figure she saw further tangible evidence of their love. Jonna turned her attention back to the portraits. They were a dour group of ancestors, with austere countenances and rather grim smiles. "It's hard to imagine Decker sprouting from this family tree," she said dryly.

Mercedes laughed, as much at Jonna's tone as her observation. "You are so very right." Stepping back, she gave the portraits the same critical attention as Jonna. "Not a rogue among them, though perhaps that's not fair to Ponty."

"Do you always call him that?" Jonna asked. "It's a ridiculous sort of name."

"I doubt he hears it that way. Mère gave it to him."

"Pardon?"

"Mère," Mercedes repeated. "Marie Thibodeaux. His mother." Out of the corner of her eye Mercedes watched Jonna begin to scan the portraits again. "You won't find her there. Even the mother who bore him isn't among these paintings, and Marie wasn't that mother. She and Jimmy Grooms are the ones who took Decker from the workhouse. You know about Cunnington's Workhouse, don't you?"

Jonna nodded. "Colin told me some things. That's where Jack Quincy found him."

"That's right. All three boys were taken there after their parents were murdered. Lord Fielding, the earl here, had been estranged from his son for years. Colin's father, his wife, and the boys were on their way to Rosefield, when their carriage was stopped by highwaymen. The children survived but none of them, not even Colin, knew enough about their journey to say where they were going. There was some attempt to find relatives, as you probably know, but nothing came of it. Greydon left the workhouse first, still a babe in arms. Ponty was next, then Colin. Lord Fielding searched for the boys for years, much as Colin searched for his brothers, but in the end it was mostly serendipitous events that brought Colin and his grandfather together."

Jonna's eyes studied the portrait of the former Earl of Rosefield. He was in his middle years in the painting and there were fine lines around his eyes and at the corners of his mouth. None of them seemed to have been earned through laughter. He had a narrow jaw and fine, aristocratic features. His hair was covered in a powdered wig, but his brows were dark. He was not a startlingly handsome man, but he was not unattractive. There was a certain authority in his features, or perhaps in his carriage, that she had long associated with Colin but only recently with Decker.

"Tell me about Marie," said Jonna. She felt Mercedes's hesitation, and she added softly, "Please. Decker says so little about himself."

Mercedes's nod was slight but knowing. "Colin can be that way. And he uses his eyes to keep distance and privacy. Ponty manages it with a smile. It seems welcoming at first, then you realize he's as remote as the moon."

Jonna's gaze dropped to the floor. Her hands were folded in front of her, fixed and still. "Sometimes," she said softly, in the manner of someone making a confession, "sometimes I want to slap him when he smiles at me like that."

Mercedes wasn't startled by the sentiment, only that Jonna admitted it. She managed to keep her own smile in check. "Marie and Jimmy were accomplished actors," she said. "But they were even better thieves. Decker has never really been clear on which calling they enjoyed more. They traveled off and on as part of a troupe; sometimes they struck out on their own. They posed as missionaries to take Decker from the workhouse, but what they taught him to do was pick pockets. He worked the crowd while they performed, and by all accounts—mostly his—he was quite good at it."

Jonna remembered the way Decker had deftly removed her necklace. "Yes, I believe that."

"I think the odds finally conspired against them," Mercedes went on. "The three of them worked together for eight years, and Ponty became every bit their son. He has nothing but affection for them. For all intents and purposes, Mère and Jimmy were his parents, and when they were gone he never worked with another partner or attached himself to another family."

"What happened to them?"

"They were hanged."

Jonna's eyes widened. "Hanged?"

"You were expecting to hear they were transported, I suppose. I know that's what I'd first thought had happened to them when they were caught. Decker never told me, nor did Colin, the whole of it. We only know that Marie and Jimmy were arrested in London for stealing. Decker somehow escaped, but he was in the crowd that saw them hanged three weeks later."

Pale as salt now, Jonna concentrated on the portrait of Lord Fielding. His expression did not soften. She imagined he could have watched the hanging without flinching. She, on the other hand, had only to think about it and her knees threatened to buckle.

Mercedes was watching Jonna closely, gauging her reaction. "When Ponty left Weybourne Park for Boston he told us he wanted to make his own way, but he'd been doing that for years. From the time he was twelve he'd lived by his wits on the London streets and had managed to avoid the fate of Marie and Jimmy. I don't think he was ever arrested until he was a young man."

"I never knew how much to believe in that regard. There were rumors that he had been in prison."

"Several times, I think. Colin never shared any of this with you, even after Ponty began working at Remington Shipping?"

"No. For months I didn't know there *was* any relation between the two of them."

"That would have been at Ponty's request," Mercedes said. "Colin's not ashamed of his brother or anything Decker's done. After all, it was Decker's stealing that brought us together." She caught Jonna's questioning glance. "Oh my! Colin has been much less informative than I thought. Whatever does he write you in those long letters?"

Jonna found she had it in her to smile. "In one way or another they're mostly about you. He writes about his life at Weybourne Park, managing the property, the politics, the taxes. He speaks fondly of your cousins and lovingly of your two little girls. I know about the thoroughbreds he is raising and crop rotation, but he failed to mention that you were expecting another child."

Amusement made Mercedes's gray eyes bright. "That's because he's hoping for a boy and the less said about it, the better."

Jonna watched Mercedes's hand linger lightly on her swollen abdomen. "You're the lens through which he views his life now, and there's little he writes that doesn't reflect your influence. Oddly, it doesn't take anything away from who he is. He seems a richer person for it. I never thought I would say this about Colin, but I find I can state it with complete certainty: He is truly, deeply happy."

It meant a great deal to Mercedes to hear this from Jonna. "He's not alone," she said.

Jonna nodded. "Yes, I can see that." Her next thought was left unspoken as that very happy man entered the gallery.

Colin eyed the two women suspiciously. "Dare I hope you're comparing me favorably to the ancestral line?"

"We weren't talking about you at all," Mercedes said, taking immediate exception. She looked at Jonna for support. "Really, why do men think that if women are engaged in conversation, it must be about them?"

Jonna's expression was carefully neutral. She found she very much liked Mercedes. "I suppose it's because they think they're so terribly interesting."

Colin held up his hands, palms out. The gesture was less to ward off his wife's advance and more in the nature of complete surrender. He kissed the cheek that Mercedes offered him and placed one arm around her back. "Would you mind keeping Decker company while I show Jonna the grounds?"

"The grounds?" Mercedes asked. "Colin, everything is knee deep in snow."

"She's a Boston girl," Colin said.

Mercedes protested. "That doesn't mean she has ice water in her veins."

Not any longer, Jonna thought. And not for some time.

Jonna sat at her vanity and idly pulled a brush through her hair. The maid who had drawn her bath and offered to assist with the bedtime rituals had been dismissed. The reflection in the mirror and in the black-leaded panes of glass was Jonna's lone figure.

Outside it was snowing again. Had Jonna moved to the window and peered closely through the white curtain of flakes, she would have seen that the trail she and Colin had made crossing the gardens was disappearing. Their path to the stables and their ride along the southern wall of the property was similarly being obliterated. The evidence that they had passed by a hunting lodge or paused in the clearing in front of it was also gone. The white woods would not give up the route they took. All traces of the time spent with Colin that afternoon were being erased everywhere but in Jonna's heart.

There, those hours in his company were deeply engraved, not for what she'd learned about him or his brother, but for what she'd learned about herself.

She put the brush down. Her face was lightly flushed, but her skin was cool. She stared at her reflection. It was no beauty she saw looking back at her. The oddly colored eyes were too frank, the jaw too defined, the mouth too wide. Drawing her hair over one shoulder, she began to loosely plait it.

Colin and Mercedes were gone now, though not before they had extracted a promise from Decker and Jonna to visit Weybourne Park. Jonna wished they would have stayed the night. It would have made it harder to set out on the course she had planned, perhaps impossible. In Colin's eyes she had been like a younger sister. Jonna had to accept that he might never see her as a woman grown.

She stood. Behind her on the bed was her robe, but she didn't put it on. Her feet were bare, and when she stepped off the carpet the wooden floor was cold. She picked up the lamp from the bedside table, adjusted the wick to give her a sliver of light. Her nightshift was plain white linen, and the hem brushed her ankles as she walked to the door. The material caught the draft in the hallway, flickered with the same motion as the lamplight.

Had it not been for Mercedes's tour that morning, Jonna would have had no idea where Decker might be found. They had come across his bedchamber as they were going from room to room. Jonna had been startled by the proximity to her own chamber, but Mercedes, if she'd noted it, was kind enough not to comment. Jonna had reasons to appreciate Decker's arrangements now, though she didn't believe he had made them for her convenience. She doubted he was expecting her.

In that, she was wrong.

Decker's hair was still damp from his bath. A few strands of it curled darkly at the nape of his neck as he knelt in front of the fireplace. Orange and red flames seemed to dance across his glistening shoulders. He was wearing only a pair of drawers, and they rested low on his hips. There were two small dimples at the base of his spine. Jonna was narrowly caught staring at them.

Decker rose slowly. "I thought I might see you tonight," he said.

That gave her pause. It was not only that he had anticipated her, but that he did not sound particularly pleased that she had proved him right. "Should I go?"

"No." He motioned to her to shut the door. "Not now. Not before you've said what's brought you here."

"You don't know?" she asked. He seemed to know everything else.

He didn't answer her. Instead he picked up his dressing gown and shrugged into it. He belted it, then pointed to the wing chair in front of him. "Are you going to hover there where it's cold or come closer to the fire?"

Jonna did not mistake his words for a real welcome. There was nothing inviting in his tone. The lamp trembled in her hands as she crossed the room. Decker relieved her of it before she sat down, then placed it on the mantel. "Aren't you going to sit?"

"I'm comfortable standing, thank you." His words were

clipped, and there was no characteristic amusement in his eyes. They were ice blue now, and they pinned Jonna back in her chair.

She cleared her throat. She had not given any thought to what she actually might say, nor to how it might sound. "It has always served me in business to speak directly," she said. "May I do so now?"

"Is this business?"

"Yes," she said. "Yes, it is."

He made a small flourish with his hand. "Then by all means . . ."

Jonna started to come out of her chair, but Decker motioned her back. She felt the disadvantage keenly. "It's occurred to me that a man may have a mistress," she said. "Society hardly blinks an eye at the convention as long as the thing's managed discreetly. I thought there might be instances where the reverse is true. I mean, that a woman might take a lover. If the woman is wealthy then she could provide for him, set him up in a residence or even a business, and the two might reasonably agree on what favors would be exchanged. He would be faithful to her, of course, as long as they were each satisfied with the arrangement. In the event that was no longer the case, then either of them would be free to leave. He would have some settlement placed upon him, and she would have his assurance that he would not speak of this particular association with her to anyone."

There was small lift to Decker's mouth, but his smile had an icy edge to it. "And I thought you just came here because you've finally realized you can't have my brother."

Jonna's head snapped back. "What?"

"I expected that seeing him with Mercedes would make your heart bleed," Decker said coldly. "I didn't anticipate it would open that tight little Yankee purse." He couldn't resist adding, "The one you carry on your wrist *or* the one between your legs."

Jonna shot to her feet. Except for her glittering violet eyes, there was no color in her face. She stared at him for a long moment, then she turned to go.

Decker caught her elbow. "Never say you're leaving."

She tried to shake him off, but he held her fast. "I intend to do exactly that," she said. "Let me go."

"Don't you want to hear my answer?" he asked. "Although you didn't strictly ask a question, did you? It was more of a proposal, nevertheless one deserving of a response. Do you know what mine is?"

"Go to hell," she said tightly.

There was no humor in his curt laugh. "No, that isn't it, though it probably should be." This time when Jonna tried to loose herself she was twisted in Decker's arms and brought flush to his taut frame. Only a hairbreadth separated his mouth from hers. "Yes," he said. "My answer's yes."

Decker closed the distance between them, crushing her mouth with his. It was not so much a kiss as a first volley on the field of battle. Jonna's entire body jerked in reaction. The movement didn't free her, but made her intimately aware of the shape and power of the man who held her. Her arched back flattened her thighs against his, and Decker thrust his hips forward so she cradled him.

Jonna's breath came shallowly as Decker lifted his mouth. She couldn't turn in his embrace. The arm at the small of her back was like an iron bar, and the fist he made in her hair tilted her face toward his. He watched her, his blue eyes burning cold as he took in her pale complexion and the flushed, swollen line of her mouth.

Decker bent his head slowly, tugging on her braid and exposing her throat. His lips settled on the curve of her neck, and he tasted her skin with the edge of his tongue. Her pulse beat frantically against his mouth. He touched the hollow of her throat, the underside of her jaw. His lips sipped her flesh. His teeth caught the delicate gold chain at her neck, and when he pulled the ivory pendant was lifted from between her breasts.

Jonna felt as if her heart were being torn from her chest. She caught the necklace in her palm and closed her fingers around it. Her lips parted around the word "no," but it was a soundless protest. Decker let the chain drop, and when he looked at her again triumph edged his cool smile.

He caught the corner of her mouth as she tried to turn her head. His tongue traced the closed line of her lips, not pressing, merely learning their shape. He moved on, grazing her cheek, her temple, then lower to the sensitive hollow behind her ear.

Decker released Jonna's braid, and she didn't move. His fingers slipped around her throat. He kept her head tilted upward with the lightest pressure of his thumb. Then even that was taken away. His hand drifted to the small buttons at the neckline of her nightshift, and he began to unfasten them.

Jonna released the pendant when Decker's hand brushed hers. She didn't push against his shoulders or try to slip from his grasp. Her arms dropped to her sides and she closed her eyes.

Parting the material, Decker's mouth found her exposed shoulder. His hand slipped over her gown and cupped her breast. His thumb made a pass across her nipple, and he felt its rise through the fine cotton nightshift. Jonna was arched over Decker's arm as he began to lower her to the floor, his tongue making a damp trail from her shoulder to her breast. His teeth caught the material first, then her nipple. He felt her shudder.

Firelight glanced off her hair. The carpet was under her knees now, and the fireplace was at her back. Decker opened a fourth button, then a fifth. Jonna's nightgown slipped completely off both shoulders, trapping her arms at her sides. When Decker's mouth closed over her breast this time, there was no damp and abrading material between them. His lips were on her skin, his tongue laved the swollen tip of her breast, his teeth worried the hard bud.

Where firelight licked her skin Jonna was warm. Where Decker did the same she was warmer. His hand slipped under her gown and stroked her flat belly. Each pass brought his fingertips closer to where her thighs were pressed tightly together; each pass forced a fractional parting.

Decker lifted his head from her breast. This time when he touched her cheek with his lips he tasted the salty wetness of Jonna's tears. They pooled at the underside of her dark lashes like beads of dew, then slipped soundlessly over her cheeks. He found one at the corner of her mouth and kissed another away before it fell.

There was no anger in the way he touched her now, no edge of steel or hint of conquest. Neither did he give any quarter.

Decker's lips moved over hers, insistent rather than forcing. His tongue slipped along the ridge of her teeth, and her mouth parted under his. He pressed the entry and engaged her in the kiss, drawing a response that he sensed she resisted even as she gave it.

He guided her the rest of the way to the floor and removed his arm from behind her back. He deepened the kiss, winding his tongue around hers, then teasing her with just the taste of him at the tip of her mouth. When she raised her face slightly in response to his withdrawal, he drove his tongue against hers. The intent of the kiss was clear.

Decker raised himself on one elbow and looked down at her. Firelight bathed her face. Her mouth was damp. The lower lip was faintly swollen and it was thrust forward in a sulky, sensuous line. She was watching him, the centers of her violet eyes were very dark and very wide. Long, spiked lashes presented the only evidence that there had been tears.

His fingertips grazed her cheek, then her jaw, and finally slid along her throat. He watched his hand move slowly over her skin, following the flicker of light and shadow. Her breasts were pale and tipped in virginal pink. Her flesh swelled in his palm as he made an almost weightless pass across one.

His fingers drifted down and were dragged lightly along the center of her abdomen. The edge of her parted nightshift was pushed lower until her arms and hips were free, then her thighs. Finally he removed it altogether and held it away when she tried to reach for it.

Decker tossed it in the fireplace, silencing her cry with his mouth. His body restrained her but not heavily. One hand rested on her shoulder, and his leg lay across both of hers. Jonna was weighed down more by her own need than anything that was done to her. She moaned softly as he lifted his mouth.

The ivory pendant lay between her breasts. Decker's eyes fell on it again. Save for where it covered her skin she was naked. He didn't try to remove it from her. There was something erotic about her wearing nothing but what he had given her.

He fingered the ivory. "You should never wear anything else," he said lowly.

Jonna's eyes closed against the intensity in his. She turned her head.

"And in bed," he added, "I won't let you."

She bit her lower lip as he let the pendant fall against her skin. Her chin was cupped in his hand, and her face was lifted in his direction.

"Look at me," he said.

He would not even allow her this one small rebellion, she thought. Her eyes opened and she stared at him. His face was close to hers, the lines tautly drawn. His mouth hovered about hers, and when he spoke his breath was warm on her lips. He told her she was beautiful.

The flush that filled Jonna's breasts and cheeks with heat vanished. She was suddenly cold all over. For a moment she didn't breathe. Her body was still as stone beneath his and almost as lifeless. "I'm not paying you to lie *to* me," she said tonelessly. "Only *with* me."

Decker stared at her.

"Don't say it again," she said. "Ever."

For a long moment he said nothing at all. "As you wish," he whispered. Then his mouth punished hers.

Decker's knee wedged between her thighs. His hand slipped along her rib cage, past the inner curve of her waist, then across her hips to finally press lower and more intimately between her legs. He cupped her mons and his fingers parted her moist, silky passage.

Jonna pushed against the floor, trying to escape at first, then only trying to feel more. Her back arched and her hips lifted. As the heel of his hand pressed against her, sensation rocked her forward. She was damp where his fingers touched her at first and wet where he explored later.

"Do you know what you want?" he asked against her mouth.

She shook her head.

"Shall I show you?" Before she could answer he slipped one finger inside her and on the next stroke, he slipped two.

Jonna raised her knees; her heels pushed against the floor. Her eyes were closed again, and if he had asked her to look at him just then, she would have only been able to look away.

He swallowed her low keening cry with his kiss. He could almost feel the shimmer of heat under her skin. It rushed up from the center of her and spread out across her taut belly and breasts. A flush followed in its wake, and tension extended the tips of her fingers outward, strained the smoothly muscled line of her legs.

A log jumped in the fireplace, and the flames crackled. The sound accompanied the sudden jerk of Jonna's slender frame, the spiraling of heat along her limbs.

Decker held her there, teetering on the brink of pleasure, letting her experience the first faint stirrings. The rhythm of his stroking changed and slowed and finally stopped. She was breathing hard. He was hardly breathing.

Jonna grasped his wrist as he started to lean away from her. He merely stared down at her hand until she lifted it. She let it fall to her side where it curled into a loose fist. He looked at it and smiled. That made her want to hit him.

He kissed her briefly, tugging on her lower lip and running his tongue sweetly across it. He'd let her hit him later, he thought, if that's what she wanted or needed. But not now, not just yet.

Decker sat up. He removed his dressing gown and then his drawers. Unashamed of his nakedness or his arousal, he knelt between Jonna's thighs. Drawing her legs up and around him, he lifted her bottom and leaned forward slowly.

He had not asked her to watch him now, yet Jonna's vision was filled with him. His shoulders and arms were trim and athletic, the muscles cut cleanly so their shape and movement was defined under his skin. His chest was smooth, yet still held a hint of summer color from working shirtless on board the clippers. A lock of dark hair fell over his forehead. It lent an oddly youthful look to a face that had seemed older and harder than mere years could explain.

His blue eyes held hers until they closed briefly, and only once, as he guided himself into her.

All of Jonna's senses were filled with him, just as she was filled with him. Her hands lifted and she touched his shoulders, lightly at first, then tightly as he pressed himself forward and her body stretched to accommodate him.

There was a moment's pain, no more, before it was replaced by an aching sort of fullness that had pleasure at its center.

He rested on his elbows and looked down at her. She was searching his features, her violet eyes darting across the planes and angles of his face. He liked the fact that she was looking at him, that he didn't have to command her attention, that she couldn't mistake his possession of her for anyone else's. He thought it might be enough. It wasn't.

"My name," he said, brushing his mouth across hers. "Say it."

She resisted at first because she knew why he was asking and why he needed to hear it. She felt him begin to withdraw. "Decker," she said. The ease with which she capitulated frightened her. It made her want to strike out, to hurt him, and she was too vulnerable not to let him see it.

"Do you want to hate me, Jonna?" he whispered. "Would that make it better for you?"

If only it were so simple, she thought, then even that thought died away as he thrust into her again. He buried his face in the curve of her neck as he began to move in her. The cadence was slow and deep and hard. Her body lifted. His plunged. Her breasts were crushed against his chest, the nipples hard and aching. His mouth moved over her throat, her shoulder. She held him close, and firelight caressed her hands as she moved them along his back.

Sparks of heat returned to her skin, spreading outward from the place where they were joined. As her body tightened around him she heard him groan softly. He rocked her back, harder now, faster. His open mouth captured hers, and he kissed her over and over, making her seek his face, his lips, each time he paused.

There were no sounds outside herself. She heard only her own body: the roar in her ears, the thrumming of her heart, the caught breath at the back of her throat. The pitch changed as sensation accelerated and the power of pleasure shifted.

Decker watched her neck arch and felt the surge of her body under his. She cried out, shuddering, and his own body quickened as the vibration seemed to slip under his skin and ripple through him with equal intensity. He raised himself up and drove into her one last time.

Jonna wasn't prepared for the second skimming pleasure that pulled her taut and then left her limp. Unaccountably embarrassed by her body's aftershock, she avoided Decker's probing eyes and turned her face in the direction of the fireplace.

Careful not to let her see his smile, Decker eased away from Jonna. One hand lingered near her breast for a moment, then he withdrew that as well. "Don't move," he said. Scooping up his drawers, he got to his feet and padded soundlessly into the adjoining room. He returned a few minutes later, this time wearing the drawers and carrying a basin of water.

Jonna was sitting up, her legs curled to one side. Most of her braid had been unwound and she was combing it out slowly with her fingers. She didn't look at him as he knelt beside her.

Decker set the basin on the carpet. He touched her throat and fingered the lapel of his satin dressing gown which she was now wearing. "I thought I told you not to move."

She kept her face averted, but her fingers stopped their idle combing. "You weren't serious," she said.

"I thought I was."

"I don't take orders from you." There was no anger; it was only a statement of fact.

Decker nodded slowly. "That's right," he said softly, as though the truth of it had just occurred to him. "I take them from you."

Jonna's head lowered once in agreement. "Yes," she said. "You do."

He said nothing for a moment. If she had turned just then and seen the look in his eyes or the set of his steely smile, she would have had good reason to question who held the upper hand. By the time Decker's silence captured her attention and she glanced at him, he had drawn a shutter over his features.

"I shouldn't let you wear this robe," he said. "I burned your nightshift for good reason."

"What good reason?"

"I want you naked."

Jonna averted her head and gave him her shoulder. "We should discuss the terms of our agreement," she said without inflection.

"I suppose you'll want to insist on clothes."

His amusement cut her. Tears welled in her eyes, and she dashed them away.

"Jonna?"

"Don't make light of me," she said quietly. "I can accept anything else, but not that."

Decker's fingers slipped along the length of her hair. He

stroked her back. He knew she was feeling the enormity of what had passed between them and she hadn't yet looked ahead to the consequences. He didn't apologize for his humor, but he didn't goad her with it again. Decker dipped the washcloth hanging over the edge of the basin into the water. He wrung it out. "Look here, Jonna."

When she turned he bathed her face, erasing all traces of tears. He let the cloth glide down her throat and lower, between her breasts, where her skin glowed with a sheen of perspiration. He unbelted the dressing gown, parted it, and moved his hand to her abdomen. Dipping the cloth again he drew her up on her knees. Her thighs were parted. The dark centers of her eyes reflected his own gaze. She gasped a little as he placed the damp cloth between her legs but she didn't move. Jonna laid her hands on his shoulders while he washed away the evidence of her virginity and his seed.

Decker dropped the cloth into the water and pushed the basin under a wing chair. He took Jonna's hands from his shoulders, encircling her wrists, and brought her to her feet with him. He led her to the bed where the covers had long ago been turned back by a thoughtful servant. Decker drew the dressing gown off Jonna and let it fall on the floor. He kissed her lightly once, then more thoroughly a second time. The backs of her thighs were pressed to the mattress, and then she was lying across it, covered more by Decker than the sheets.

There was no place he could touch her that didn't bring a response. Every inch of her was sensitive to the passage of his fingertips. Her nipples rose in anticipation of his touch; her skin retracted when he drew his hand across her belly. She moved restlessly under him, wanting more, wanting less. Her soft cry was the inarticulate expression of her need to make him stop and of her desire that he never should.

Decker responded to her uncertainty this time. His mouth gentled on hers. There was a soft sigh of satisfaction that could have belonged to either of them. He felt her relax, felt her yield without surrendering. He couldn't have taken her just then, in spite of his desire. What he could have done, *would* have done, he didn't think she was ready for. His hand between her thighs had shocked her. She couldn't suspect he wanted to place his mouth there.

Decker rolled away and off the bed. He held up the covers for Jonna to slide under them, then he shucked his drawers and crawled in with her. When he turned back to her after extinguishing the bedside lamp, he found she had already moved to the far side of the bed.

"Are you going to sleep over there?" he asked.

"I was going to sleep in my own room," she said.

"I thought you wanted to discuss terms."

She stared at the ceiling. Her voice was almost inaudible. "Tomorrow morning."

Decker shook his head. "We're speaking of my payment," he said. "I've learned that's the sort of thing that shouldn't wait. Tell me what you had in mind."

It had been too easy to imagine that he had really wanted her. In those moments when he was touching her gently, seeking a response from her body to match his own, Jonna could believe that his desire was prompted by something other than her proposal. She died a little inside knowing it wasn't that way at all. Her suggestion had knocked him back, her terms had insulted him, yet his pride was insufficient to tell her no. It wasn't because he wanted her, but because he wanted what she had.

Jonna mocked herself with a small, wry smile. She was a fine one to speak of pride when she had so little herself. He could have had her again on this bed and she would have let him. She would have given him license to do anything—*everything*—except amuse himself at her expense. She was not so wretched a creature that she could tolerate that.

"I thought I would buy you a house," she said quietly. "Somewhere in Boston where I'm not known."

"So you can visit."

"Yes," she said. "You'll be away for weeks when you're at sea, but I'll give you money for a good staff."

"Better than those girls Mrs. Davis trains."

She shrugged. "You may hire them yourself. Train them yourself. I don't care if you have a hundred or five. I just don't want any of them there when I am present."

Decker plumped a pillow under his head and stared at her, fascinated. "I should have some sort of allowance."

It had occurred to her as well. "In addition to your wages I can pay you something quarterly out of my trust account. I have no idea how much that should be."

"I suppose it depends on how well I perform my duties," he said dryly.

Jonna shook her head. Her brow knit, and her mouth flattened seriously. "No, I don't think that should enter into it. I mean, there should be a standard amount you can count on to pay your employees and run the house, separate of what . . . separate of our . . . that is, not dependent upon . . ."

"My ability to pleasure you," he finished helpfully. Decker regretted putting out the lamp. The firelight was insufficient to see Jonna's flaming face. He had to be satisfied with imagining it.

She nodded in agreement and named a sum she thought he would require for his household and personal needs.

Decker just managed not to choke. "Aren't you afraid of making me a rich man?" he asked. "Then you'd have to marry me."

"I'd have to love you first, and I'd have to like you before that."

The verbal blow had the impact of a physical one, driving the breath from Decker's lungs. It was a moment before he could speak. "Then there's no danger of you accepting my proposal."

She turned her head toward him. His face was mostly in shadow, but she could make out his ice blue eyes regarding her steadily. "No danger," she said. "Were you going to make one?"

"I may have," he said, "in the event you found yourself pregnant."

Jonna managed to still her panic. "I wouldn't expect it," she said evenly.

"Good. Because I won't offer." He raised himself on one elbow. "This business of liking and loving has to be mutual, Jonna. I don't have many finer feelings where you're concerned, only baser ones." His hand snaked under the covers and found Jonna's wrist. He pulled her toward him, pinning her back when she struggled. His hands held her face so she couldn't look away. "Shall I tell you what *I* want?" he asked.

Caught between his hands, Jonna could only make a small nod.

Decker smiled. His eyes dropped to the ivory pendant between her breasts then came back to her. "*Huntress*," he said. "I want your flag ship."

Eight

Jonna simply stared at Decker. When there was no change in his expression, no relaxing of his hold on her gaze, she realized he was serious. She wedged her hands between their bodies, found leverage against his chest, and pushed hard. Even then she knew she was free because Decker allowed it.

He rolled over and lay back on the bed as Jonna sat up. He let her yank one of the blankets free and tuck it around her breasts. He sighed. "I suppose I should have made my terms clear at the outset."

"I suppose you should have," she said. "I'm not giving you *Huntress*. You can't really believe that is a reasonable request."

He shrugged. "I don't think that matters. It's what I want." He turned on his side, giving her his back. The discussion was over as far as he was concerned.

"I'm not going to change my mind," she said.

He plumped the pillow under his head and closed his eyes. "Go to sleep, Jonna."

The thing that surprised her was, she did.

Slim beams of light from a cold, white winter sun slipped through an opening in the drapes. Neither Decker nor Jonna stirred. She was comfortably cradled by his body, her bottom snug against his groin, his arm tucked under her breasts. Their breathing was soft, almost in unison. They shared the same pillow. In time they shared the same dream.

The need was mutual. It began with the heat that lingered where they touched. It was there at her breasts and at the

210

backs of her thighs. He felt it run the length of him. The fragrance of her hair made him draw a deeper breath. The warmth of his breath made her turn her head.

They moved together, his mouth on her neck, her body stretching sleepily. He kissed her shoulder. Her hand moved along his thigh. Above his arm her breasts swelled slightly. At her back he was hard.

She turned, murmured something under her breath, and pressed against him. Her thighs parted and then he was inside her. Her mouth found his, and she kissed him deeply. Her hands caressed his shoulders. She rubbed against his chest to satisfy the ache in her breasts. Her thighs tightened as she felt him move.

There was no urgency yet. Positions changed slowly and the kisses were languorous. She rocked against him. Her slender frame stretched sinuously. She kissed the underside of his jaw, his throat. The edge of her tongue traced his collarbone. Her mouth was warm, and the hum of her pleasure caused a vibration just under his skin. He whispered her name, and there was heat now even where she didn't touch him.

She was under him, holding him with her thighs. She unfolded against him and ran her feet down the length of his legs. He arched, deepening his thrust. She sighed.

He moved in her slowly. His selfish pleasure satisfied them both. He kissed her breasts and took a nipple into his mouth. He tugged lightly with his teeth until she cried out softly.

It was his own name he heard. He opened his eyes and stared at her. She was watching him, alert now, as if she too had been awakened by the sound of her own voice. They said nothing. His head bent slowly, giving her time to avert hers. She didn't. Their mouths touched, just in a whisper at first, then deeply, hotly, and with purpose.

Awareness changed the rhythm of their joining. There was no sleepy arch to her body as he thrust into her this time, no light caress across his back. Jonna's heels dug into the mattress as she raised herself against him and her fingertips pressed whitely into his shoulders. He moved in her hard and she accepted him, accepted his urgency and need because it mirrored her own. She accepted the faint edge of anger which drove him now. She understood it, even embraced it. There was no denying that she wanted him. She only wanted to deny it. He was no different. Their bodies had betrayed them; the anger was there because their minds had not.

Tension pulled her body taut. Her throat arched. She closed her eyes as the first wave of pleasure shuddered through her and opened them again as she felt his.

Afterward she thought he would let her go. He didn't. He remained inside her a little longer, until their breathing slowed and their heartbeats settled. Even when he eased out of her he kept her close, laying an arm across her waist. She didn't try to move away. She didn't want to.

"This doesn't change anything," he said quietly. There was enough light in the room that he could see her face clearly now. He wondered how much longer they had before servants would intrude. "I want you, but I need *Huntress*."

"You already command her," she said.

"I want to own her."

Jonna's eyes narrowed fractionally as she searched his features. There was an edge to his tone that hinted of something else. "We're still talking about the clipper, aren't we?"

Nothing in Decker's face changed. "What else?"

She tried to make out what he was thinking. His blue eyes were cool as his smile and just as impenetrable. "For a moment . . ." Her voice trailed off.

"Yes?"

She was mistaken, of course. He hadn't been speaking of her. "Nothing," she said. Uncomfortable, Jonna looked away. Over Decker's shoulder she could see the shifting pattern of white light on the walls. "I want to go to my own room."

"A few more minutes," he said. "This is the last time you'll be in my bed after all."

Jonna nodded and kept her eyes averted. She felt very much like crying. "Why is she so important to you?" she whispered.

"I could ask you the same thing."

"I built her," Jonna said.

"You've built other ships." He shrugged. "You'll build more."

Perhaps she would, Jonna thought. But never would she put so much of herself into the design of a ship. She had started with a vision and a cause, and *Huntress* was built to serve both. "Not like *Huntress*," she said. "Never again."

Decker's fingers trailed lightly between Jonna's breasts. He picked up the ivory pendant and examined it as if for the first time. "She's like you, you know," he said. "Graceful. Proud. A bit aggressive." He felt her stiffen at that appraisal, but he didn't apologize or elaborate. "Her lines are your lines. Elegant. Fluid. She has character, and I think you meant her to. I think she has your spirit and your bravery and more than a little of your arrogance."

Jonna could hardly draw a breath. "You can't know that."

"I can feel it," he said. "Walking her deck is like having you under me. She rises up to meet me the way you do."

A rush of heat swept up from Jonna's breasts to her face. She closed her eyes. There was a small shake of her head but her denial had no voice.

Decker let the pendant drop. His fingertips brushed her

cheek. "She's as responsive as you are," he said quietly. "She's quick and agile, and she knows her master."

That opened Jonna's eyes.

He was perfectly unmoved by her glare, but he rather liked the dimple at the corner of her mouth. "Responsive," he repeated, kissing her. "Just like *Huntress*."

Jonna ducked her head. He kissed the sensitive hollow at the back of her ear. "I can't give her to you," she said. She stared at the cold fireplace while his mouth settled on the curve of her neck. "If you believed what you were saying, you wouldn't ask for *Huntress*."

Decker's teeth nipped her skin lightly. "She's a ship, Jonna. She's *like* you. She's *not* you. I can't own you." He paused. "Can I?"

"No." She slid out from under him and dragged a sheet with her. "I'm not property," she said sharply, coming to her feet. She wrapped the sheet around her. "Of course you can't own me."

Decker sat up. "Give me *Huntress*," he said. "Prove that you know you can't own me either."

Jonna was quiet for a long time. She thought of why she had built *Huntress*, of the purpose it had yet to realize. She couldn't give it to Decker when it was intended for someone else. "I know I can't own you," she said. "I'm a Yankee trader, not a slaver. I told you my offer, and you refused it. And I can't pay what you ask. *Huntress* wasn't built for you." Jonna turned away to pick up Decker's dressing gown. She didn't see the grim smile that changed the shape of his mouth or brought an edge of frost to his eyes. She didn't hear him leave the bed or come up behind her. The first Jonna knew that Decker was at her back was when his hands came down on her shoulders and she was being turned around.

"Tell me," he said. There was nothing else he needed to

say. He saw understanding flicker in her eyes.

She couldn't tell him the truth, so she told him what he expected to hear. The lie would assure that they would never be intimate again. "I think you already know," she said. "I built it for Colin."

Decker's hands dropped away. A moment ago they had been too close to her throat.

Jonna's gaze remained squarely on Decker's face. "I thought he would come back," she said. "I thought a ship like *Huntress* could put him on the sea again."

"In your bed, you mean."

"If you wish," she said almost graciously. It was an effort to shrug off the accusation, but Jonna managed it with careless elegance. She wondered if Decker knew how well he had taught her that attitude.

"He'll never leave Mercedes," Decker said.

"I think that's true." Jonna realized she was clutching his dressing gown in her fists. She loosened her grip and slipped it on. "We'll find out, won't we?"

Decker watched Jonna flinch as he raised his hand. He only used it to rake back his hair but the truth was, he had never been so close to striking a woman as he was at that moment. "Don't try it, Jonna. You won't like the consequences."

"You have no say in it."

"He's my brother."

"I've known him longer," she said. "And I've known him better."

Decker caught the lapel of the dressing gown in his fist and slowly pulled Jonna toward him. "Then think of him as a brother, Jonna. Not a lover."

He bent his head and kissed her hard. As a punishment it was more thoroughly humiliating than a slap. When he set her from him the sheet she had been wearing under the dressing gown was lying on the floor at her feet. Jonna rocked back on her heels. She stared at him mutely for a moment, then fled the room.

It wasn't until she was in her own cold bed, waiting for her heartbeat to calm, that she realized he had stolen more than her confidence with that last kiss. He had stolen the ivory pendant.

Some part of *Huntress* was his after all.

It was Decker who decided they would visit Weybourne Park immediately after breakfast. He didn't invite Jonna's opinion on the matter. He simply announced his own, then left her to finish her meal in silence.

Jonna did not mind that the carriage ride was accomplished without conversation. As long as she was not forced to talk there was no chance she would take back anything she'd said the night before. Decker wouldn't have to know how his response to her lie had unsettled her. Jonna thought she might welcome never having to talk to him again.

Weybourne Manor was a formidable presence on the landscape. It had the monolithic power of a gray stone vault, and it seemed to rise higher out of the ground as their carriage approached. Snow frosted the north and south turrets and outlined the recessed windowsills. Glistening icicles hung from the slate roof, emphasizing the mansion's stark beauty.

Jonna turned away from the window as the carriage slowed. Decker was watching her. "This place is more like Colin than Mercedes," she said. "That's why you wanted me to see it, isn't it?"

"Yes," he said. "You should know all the reasons you can't tempt him to leave."

"He hasn't seen *Huntress*." Goaded by his arrogant smile,

Jonna found the words were out before she had considered them. It was as if she had issued a challenge.

Decker raised a single brow and nodded faintly, his expression implacable. He reached inside his outer coat to his vest and withdrew the ivory pendant. Holding it up, he said, "And he never will."

Jonna didn't try to take it back. The door to the carriage opened as Decker pocketed the piece. He jumped to the ground, then turned for her. His smile was in place, but it didn't touch his eyes. It was with a great sense of foreboding that Jonna put her hand in his.

Mercedes and Colin greeted them in the manor's great drawing room. Mercedes didn't rise as they entered. She had one child in her arms and another scrambling to be held in what remained of her lap. Laughing helplessly, she made her apologies.

It was Decker who rescued her, stealing both of his nieces as easily as he stole handkerchiefs. At just a year, Elizabeth fit neatly in the crook of his arm. She laughed and struck out with her small fists. Emma was more of a handful, but Decker expertly raised her to the height of his shoulder and perched her there.

Watching this, Jonna felt a surge of fear, but she saw that neither Mercedes nor Colin was particularly disturbed and the children were delighted. It didn't seem to matter that he was almost a stranger to them. They were easily engaged by his smile and his laughter and his nonsense chatter. So simply did they surrender to his roguish charm that Jonna counted them as Decker Thorne's latest conquests.

Decker introduced his nieces to Jonna with great ceremony. She had never held a child before and it was with some trepidation that she accepted Elizabeth. The baby's face screwed up immediately, reddened, and she let out a squall that made Jonna wince.

Mercedes whisked the baby away and scolded Decker. "That was very bad of him," she told Jonna as she soothed her daughter. "He thinks it's so very easy to placate them. He gives no thought to how hard it is for the rest of us."

Seeing Mercedes with her daughter, Jonna knew she was being kind. She made it appear as effortless as Decker had. Elizabeth's face was no longer mottled with color, and she seemed quite content with her thumb in her mouth.

Decker hoisted Emma high in the air. The young girl's fine blond curls fluttered around her cherubic face. She giggled happily at her uncle's attention. "Mercedes," he said casually, swinging Emma up again, "I wonder if you would show Jonna the nursery, the whole house for that matter. I would like a moment with my brother."

Jonna felt blood rushing from her face. There was no subtlety here. Decker clearly wanted to be rid of her for a while. She looked from Mercedes to Colin and realized neither of them had reason to regard Decker's request suspiciously. Jonna considered that perhaps she was making too much of it. She and Decker had only just arrived at Weybourne Park. She had had no opportunity to seek out Colin alone, and more importantly, she had no intention of doing so.

Jonna felt a little weak in the knees. Decker didn't know she wouldn't be speaking to Colin about *Huntress*. She had taken great pains to make him think differently.

Mercedes held out her hand for Emma, but she was watching Jonna. "Perhaps Miss Remington has no interest in Weybourne Park," she told Decker. "I can just as easily ring for the children's nanny. You and Colin may speak in the library while we take tea here."

Jonna interrupted Decker's reply. She would never be able to mask her anxiety sipping tea with Mercedes. It would be better to have a distraction. "If Decker has not pressed too insistently on your hospitality, I would very much like to see all of your home. At first viewing from the road, I was struck that the manor seemed more like Colin than you. I doubt the same can be true of the inside."

Mercedes smiled at this observation. "Oh, my husband has made his mark here as well, but mostly it has been in his attention to the deep structure of the house." She took her older daughter's hand and hefted the younger one more comfortably in her arms. "Come. It will be a pleasure to show you what Colin has accomplished with the rooms in the north wing. I think you'll find the turret especially interesting."

Decker watched Jonna fall into step with Mercedes and the girls. He gave her full marks for pretending she was unconcerned by his desire to speak privately with Colin. He had noted her pale features and the fingers that nervously smoothed the silk skirt of her gown, but he had been looking for these things. It was clear that she had not expected him to remove her as a threat so early in their visit. What was less clear was whether she had any idea of the tack he intended to take.

Jonna looked at Decker only briefly as she closed the doors to the drawing room behind her. She was not comforted by the slight smile that lifted one corner of his mouth. It was the faintly feral grin of a predator.

Decker's expression stayed with Jonna throughout the tour. Even knowing that was precisely what he'd intended did not help her remove it from her mind's eye. She knew she made all the proper comments as they passed from room to room and that she asked the right questions to demonstrate her interest, but she registered little of what Mercedes gave as responses. It was not that her attention wandered as much as that it was never fully engaged.

Only as they were approaching the grand staircase to descend to the main floor was Jonna able to return her mind to a single focus. This was accomplished because Mercedes brought the conversation around to what was most important to her.

"Do you think we've given them enough time?" she asked.

Jonna drew a calming breath and tried to look unconcerned. "I have no idea," she said. "Decker's business with Colin is a mystery to me."

"Really?"

Jonna hesitated. Her palm was damp on the banister. "Well, yes," she said. "How would I know?"

A small vertical crease appeared between Mercedes's brows. "I've probably mistaken the matter," she said quickly.

Now Jonna stopped on the staircase. "Do you mean you think *you* know what they're talking about?"

"I'm quite sure I don't."

Jonna was not accepting this answer. She was certain Mercedes was trying to extricate herself from misspeaking. "Please," she said. "You must tell me."

"I may be wrong. I couldn't forgive myself for raising your hope."

It was a peculiar phrasing to Jonna. She had no hope concerning Decker's private audience with his brother, only dread. "In what way should I be hopeful?" she asked.

Mercedes's frown deepened. "I'm convinced I'm mistaken. You could not be so bewildered if I were right. I would judge you to be a perceptive woman, and you would know this." She paused and studied Jonna's features. "You see? I've only confused you with this explanation. It must be that I've made an unwarranted assumption."

Jonna almost stamped her foot in frustration. "What assumption?" she asked. "What is it you think you know?"

Mercedes took a deep breath. The words came out of her in a rush. "Why that Decker loves you, of course. I thought he was applying to Colin for your hand."

It was as if Jonna had been winded. There was no breath in her lungs, and it was painful to draw one down. She used the railing to steady herself. She waited until she was certain her voice would not betray her anxiety. "You were right," she said coolly. "You have mistaken the matter." In response to Mercedes's stricken look, she added, "But you mustn't think you've dashed my hopes. The prospect of marrying your brother-in-law is in no way a welcome one, and you would receive much the same answer if you posed the arrangement to him." Having said her piece, Jonna descended the remainder of the stairs. Her hand glided along the banister, and only she knew it was trembling.

Colin and Decker both came to their feet as Jonna entered the drawing room. Mercedes followed a moment later. She immediately sensed the tension and knew she had no place here. A fleeting look passed between her and her husband, and Mercedes responded to the unspoken request.

"If you'll excuse me," she said. "I'd like to speak to Cook about our dinner." She was gone before anyone made a polite protest.

Colin waited for the doors to be closed before he pointed out the empty space beside Decker on the love seat and asked Jonna to sit. She obeyed only part of his command, taking a wing chair instead. Colin thought this small rebellion did not bode well for what he was about to say.

"I can arrange a special license," he said without preamble. "You and Decker will be married in three days' time. The chapel here at Weybourne Park will serve, and Mercedes and I will witness the event. Mr. Fredrick will perform the ceremony. He is the vicar in Glen Eden. It is a distance for him to travel here, but he is a cousin of my wife's by marriage and will be more discreet than our local vicar. Discretion may not be of paramount concern to either of you, but this is my home. I will not have another scandal attach itself to Weybourne Park or Rosefield."

Jonna stared at Colin, astonished as much by his delivery as by the content. "You pompous ass," she said when she had composed herself. "I believe your title has caused you to take yourself too seriously. Certainly you've concluded it gives you the right to dictate terms to me." She stood and looked squarely at Decker. "I only regret that you have not found your youngest brother. If he's the least like you and Decker, it would be a rare pleasure to tell all three of you to go to hell at once."

Decker was on his feet immediately, blocking Jonna's exit.

She didn't attempt to skirt him or push him aside. "Let me pass," she said coldly.

"Where is it you think you're going?"

"London," she said. Jonna had the satisfaction of seeing his slight smile fade. "And Boston after that. I'll book my own passage home. I have no need to wait for *Huntress*."

Colin stepped away from the fireplace. "Decker, let me speak to Jonna alone."

Jonna's head swiveled in Colin's direction. "I have nothing to say to you. It's clear that you've taken your brother's side."

"Side?" Colin asked. "There are no sides here. There is a need for amends to be made, and Decker is agreeing to marry you." Colin looked significantly at his brother again, but Decker was not as easily removed as Mercedes. Perhaps Jonna is right, Colin thought. He might be acting less like a friend to these two and more like the pompous ass she had called him. "Sit down, both of you." He sighed. "Please."

Decker was the first to yield ground. He returned to his seat and gave Jonna the opportunity to come to her own decision. She knew he wouldn't bar her way again. Turning slowly, obviously reluctant, Jonna found the wing chair again and sat.

It was Colin who broke the tense silence. "Decker told me you would not accept his offer. I find myself confused by that. Most women, once compromised, would be grateful."

Jonna could do nothing about the heat that flushed her cheeks. The warmth was at odds with the ice around her heart and the frost in her violet eyes. "Do you intend to be so insulting, Colin, or is it simply a happy accident? I am not 'most women.' There was a time when you would have taken some pride in that, a time, certainly, when you didn't see me so differently from yourself. Why, then, must I be grateful for your brother's proposal? In what way have I been compromised? I hold the same beliefs and values I did the previous day. I am still the head of Remington Shipping. Papa . . . Jack . . . even you, Colin, warned me to be wary of offers of marriage. I know it's my money that draws a man's attention." She ducked her head and missed the look that Colin and Decker exchanged over it. "I've turned down Grant Sheridan for years. Why should I treat Decker's offer any differently?"

"Sheridan never bedded you," Colin said bluntly. As if he'd had an afterthought, one brow kicked up. "Did he?"

It was Decker, not Jonna, who answered. "No," he said. "There's never been anyone else."

Jonna's heart was slamming in her breast. "Did Decker tell you he seduced me? Is that what he said?" She felt bubbles of hysterical laughter touch her lips. "It wasn't like that. Not at all. I'm the one who—"

Decker leaned forward and drew Jonna's attention to him. "It's no good, Jonna. I already told Colin that you would lie to protect your fortune at the expense of your reputation."

"You may be carrying Decker's child," Colin said. "Have you considered that?"

Jonna felt cornered. It was as if they were physically pushing her deeper into the large brocade chair. Her large eyes darted between the two of them, and she saw no compromise in their expressions. It was of little comfort that she saw no triumph either.

"Decker wants no part of your fortune," Colin said. "He is quite—"

Decker caught his brother's eye and made a small negative shake of his head. "I am quite willing to sign an agreement allowing you to keep your trust your own."

Jonna's eyes widened. She looked at Colin. "Can that be done?"

Colin nodded. "Something can be prepared. You will not have to turn over control of Remington Shipping. Does that ease your mind?"

"I don't know," she said softly, thoughtfully. "I never considered such a thing." Her eyes darted to Decker again. "It would all remain mine? You'd own none of it?"

"None of it," Decker repeated.

He wanted nothing from her, nothing except the knowledge that he had kept her away from Colin. Jonna understood that all of Decker's maneuvering had been prompted by her lie. Even now, faced with these consequences, Jonna was honor bound not to reveal the truth about her great clipper. That truth was meant for only one man, and he wasn't in this room with her. She pressed her lips together to keep from saying his name aloud.

"I may not be carrying your child," Jonna said. She knew it had no relevance one way or the other. It wasn't why he wanted to marry her. She parroted Colin's question to her.

"Have you considered that?"

Decker tempered his smile. Jonna would have understood that he felt a certain victory over her in this moment, but Colin would not. "I would make the same offer," he said. He glanced at his brother. "I suspect Colin would insist."

Jonna nodded. It did not surprise her that Decker had somehow engaged Colin in believing that he was acting in her best interests. Colin may have even been the one to suggest it. "Is this true, Colin? Would you insist?"

"I would."

"I suppose it has something to do with the fact that you fished me out of Boston Harbor." Her attempt to say it lightly failed. There was a trace of sadness in her tone. "You have always felt unaccountably responsible for me because of that."

Colin's dark eyes grazed her face. "And never once has it been a burden," he said gravely. "Your mother and father were kind to me, Jonna. So much of what I have is because of their guidance. Seeing to your welfare is the very least I can do. It's not a matter of repayment to them but out of sincere affection for you. Can you doubt that I care very much what turn your future takes?"

Jonna lowered her head. Tears hovered very close to the surface, and her throat was constricted. She wasn't prepared for Colin to cross the room and pull her out of the chair and into his arms. She pressed her face against his jacket and wept. Neither of them was aware that Decker left the room.

Three days later in the chapel at Weybourne Park, Jonna and Decker were married. The vows were witnessed by Colin and Mercedes and their children. It was not lost on the newly-weds that those in attendance found more joy in the occasion than they did themselves. There was a wedding breakfast served afterward, and Jonna did her best to fix a bright smile. It faltered only when Decker looked in her direction. She found herself longing to see his careless grin.

The bride and groom did not return to Rosefield. Upon leaving Weybourne Park they went to London and boarded *Huntress*. Decker put the word out that they were married, and he and Jonna received the congratulations of the crew. She retired to their cabin hours before he did, and was asleep before he joined her.

The moonlight was sufficiently bright to guide Decker about the cabin. He had no need to light a lamp and disturb Jonna's rest. He wondered that she didn't wake when he entered the cabin. He had not been particularly quiet until he saw she was sleeping.

She lay on her side, facing him, one arm curved in front of her protectively, the other supporting her head. Her heavy black hair was confined in a thick braid that fell across her shoulder and curled around her neck. Her lashes fanned out darkly, and they emphasized the shadows under her eyes. Her lips were slightly parted; each breath came deeply.

Where he had only noticed a wan smile and a brittle temper, he now recognized the exhaustion that had forced those things on her. Jonna's nights of late, it seemed, had been as restless as his own.

Decker finished undressing. Jonna occupied the near edge of the bed, and he had to climb over her to get in. He managed to do so without disturbing her, then slipped under the covers naked. She smelled of lavender. The fragrance wafted from her hair and skin as she turned with childlike confidence toward him. Never waking, she settled into a position that was agreeable to her, her arm wedged warmly between them and one of her knees solidly against his thighs. He didn't move her away. It occurred to him that one of them should be comfortable.

Decker moved her braid, pulling it away from her throat. The unsecured end of it unraveled in his hand and he rubbed the silky strands between his fingertips. The light scent of lavender stirred his senses again.

Today, when they had exchanged vows, he and Jonna had spoken more to each other than they had in any day since Colin had brokered their marriage agreement. This morning they had plighted their troth. This evening, after accepting the best wishes of the crew, they stood alone on the bridge of the clipper and Jonna quietly told him how much he was despised. It was the very calm of her words, the lack of animation in her cool expression, that lent credibility to her statement.

Decker closed his eyes. It was easy to imagine Jonna in Colin's arms again, weeping at the prospect of a forced marriage to the wrong brother. At least she had not wept today when Colin had held her. She had proffered her cheek for his affectionate kiss and had managed a tolerably warm smile, then, stepping away, had gone into the arms Mercedes extended toward her, and nothing about her expression had changed. The only real emotion Decker had seen was when Jonna was with the children. Emma and Elizabeth, one towhead, one with hair like midnight, crowded around Jonna and tugged her skirt, begging for their share of attention. Jonna had bent, kissing each one in turn, then hugging them both to her at once. She was easy with them now, unafraid that young Elizabeth was too fragile to hold or that she wouldn't see Emma underfoot. Decker had entertained a fleeting vision of Jonna with her own children—*his* children.

He bent his head slightly, his forehead almost touching hers. Moonshine cast a pale silver light over them. She looks angelic, he thought, wearing moonlight like a halo. He wished she hadn't worn a shift to bed. He wanted to pull back the covers and see all of her bathed in the translucent glow.

She unfolded her legs. Her knee brushed his groin. He was already hard, and the movement of her leg against him was exquisite torture. Decker wanted to be inside her. He wanted to be between her open thighs, moving in her, taking pleasure, giving it.

Decker's hand found the hem of her shift. He gathered it slowly, letting it slide upward over her calves, her knees, and finally her thighs. He laid his palm on her hip. Her skin was warm. The caress of his fingertips was like a whisper across her skin. She sighed in her sleep. The sheer contentedness of that small sound made Decker smile.

Edging closer, he kissed her lightly on the mouth. Her lips moved under his. Encouraged, Decker pressed again. The tip of his tongue traced her upper lip. This time she made a small humming sound.

"Jonna?" He said her name softly, tentatively. She moved, lifting her thigh across his legs so that her own were parted. A single thrust of his hips would have put him inside her. Except to kiss the corner of her mouth, Decker didn't move.

She raised her arms. Her hands slid across his chest and came to rest on his shoulders. She ducked her head a fraction and nuzzled the curve of his neck. Her cheek lay warmly on his skin. Through the fabric of her shift he could feel the tips of her breasts. He palmed her bottom, then let his hand slide upward to the small of her back. She shivered lightly.

"Jonna." Although his voice was still quiet, this time there was nothing hesitant in the way he said her name.

Her mouth stirred against his skin, and she pressed a kiss to his throat. She did not really want to be awake. It would have been easier to accept that her body was responding in spite of her conscious wish that it might be otherwise. He could have had her if he was as willing to pretend as she was. Under her shift his hand moved again, trailing up her spine and then across her rib cage. He cupped the underside of her breast, his thumb making a pass across her nipple. She could not hide her response any more than he could hide his. It was then she realized he could have her anyway.

"I want you, Jonna."

There were any number of ways she could have answered him. What she did was to place her hand over the hard, hot length of him and guide him into her. "This only means you can make me want you," she whispered. Her hips thrust forward, and he was joined to her deeply. "Nothing's changed."

It seemed important to her to believe that, and Decker let it go unchallenged. As she turned on her back, he followed her with his body. Her thighs pressed his hips on either side, and her arms slid around his back. He kissed the corner of her mouth, her jaw. She arched under him. Where their bodies were joined her muscles contracted and she held him tightly. Her breasts were flattened against his chest. His skin rubbed hers deliciously and the friction raised heat along her arms and legs. Her fingers curled around his shoulders. His flesh was marked by small crescents where her nails scored him.

They shared both hunger and a sense of urgency. Their mouths touched fleetingly, then clung. He moved in her. She moved around him. He watched her face, watched her mouth part, saw her tongue touch her upper lip. She sipped the air, and when he lowered his head, she sipped his skin. He felt her teeth tug. Tension stretched his legs taut, and he pushed inside her deeply. Their rhythm changed. Her head tilted back as heat rippled through her. She closed her eyes.

He didn't ask to hear his name. She said it without prompting and without embarrassment, naked in her need.

He held her closely as she cried out her pleasure. Her body shuddered under his, and he absorbed the vibration until her release was part of him. His thrusts quickened. His face lay in the curve of her neck. She said his name again, this time against his ear. Her breath ruffled his hair. Raising himself up just once, he spilled into her.

Jonna waited for the feeling of regret to wash over her. It never did. She expected some sense of remorse for having found this guilty pleasure. There was none. She reasoned it was the same with him.

It wasn't, but she couldn't know that. There was no apology from Decker as he rolled away from her, only silence. It mattered to him that she still lied to herself, that she was convinced he could somehow make her want him. That wasn't in his power and he knew it, even if she refused to accept it. If she had told him to stop he would have. There was nothing he wanted from her any longer that wasn't given freely, and the next time they lay so intimately coupled it would be because she initiated it.

Under the covers Jonna drew her knees up and pulled her shift over them. Doubly cocooned, she felt less vulnerable now. Decker was turned on his side away from her; the blankets lying loosely at the level of his waist. She stared at his naked shoulders and back. She had an urge to see her hand flat against his skin in the moonlight. Her splayed hand drew closer to his back. It hovered just above his spine before she pulled it back and curled it into a fist. She wondered if he had felt the heat of her palm before she had taken it away.

Why didn't he say anything? While she felt no regret, neither was she settled or sleepy. He appeared to be both. "Decker?" she whispered, nudging him with her voice. "I think we should talk."

It was an opinion he didn't share. He continued to give

her his back and his silence.

"Are you in love with Mercedes?"

Of all the things he thought she might say, he hadn't considered this one. She must have known he wouldn't ignore this overture. He turned over. "No," he said calmly. "I'm not in love with my brother's wife."

Jonna's brows puckered slightly as she frowned.

"You don't believe me?" he asked.

It wasn't that at all, she thought. What bothered her was that she *wanted* to believe him. His answer was more important than she'd known it would be when she'd posed the question. Jonna smoothed her shift over her knees and suppressed her unease until her features cleared. "Colin told me that you saved her life."

"I think that's putting it too strongly."

"He showed me the hunting lodge at Rosefield."

So that was where Colin had taken her when they'd toured the grounds, he realized. Decker wished he hadn't.

"He said you gambled your own life to save hers."

"Have a care, Jonna." His tone was wry. "You may have to revise your opinion of me."

As he had intended, she remembered what she had told him only hours ago on the bridge. "There's no danger of that," she said coldly. "I didn't imagine that you helped Mercedes without considering how it might benefit you. I've only mistaken your motive."

He smiled, but narrowly and without amusement. "You thought I did it for love?"

"It occurred to me."

"And now?"

"I suppose you hoped to ingratiate yourself in some way. Did you know that Colin was your brother then?"

"I suspected."

"Did he share your suspicions?"

"Not at all."

That satisfied Jonna. "There you have it," she said. "He only knew you as a thief. You needed him to think better of you. What if you had shown him the heirloom earring and he'd only thought you had stolen it? You wouldn't have been welcomed into the family then."

"I wasn't precisely welcomed," Decker said. "I left England."

"Because you were awaiting sentencing. Mercedes told me how you met her in jail."

"It seems as though my family did a great deal of talking. Did they offer this information or did you ask for it?"

"They offered," she said. Then, because the lie did not go down easily, she added, "Mostly."

"Mostly?"

Jonna defended herself quickly. "I admit to some curiosity. I'm aware not everyone shares my opinion of you. Mercedes, for instance, finds much to admire."

"You shouldn't place too much emphasis on that. As you already noted, she has reasons for being biased in my favor."

"She cares more that you saved Colin's life than her own," Jonna said.

"She said that?"

"Not in just those words, but it was just as clear from the things she *didn't* say." Jonna searched Decker's impassive features. "Mercedes and Colin are very much in love."

Except to watch Jonna more closely, nothing about his expression changed. "Can't you be happy for them?" he asked.

It took Jonna a moment to understand what he was saying. Decker still believed her affection for Colin ran more deeply than a sister might feel for a brother. "I am happy for them," she said quietly. She counted on sincerity to speak for her.

She would not defend herself in this regard. "Do you regret leaving England?" she asked.

"We haven't left yet."

"I meant before. Mercedes seems to think you were determined to make your own way."

His response was casual. "I believe I said something like that."

"Did your plans include a rich wife?"

"My plans always included a rich wife," he said dryly. "I only supposed that she'd be married to someone else." He caught her wrist as she would have turned away angrily. "You deliberately tried to needle me, Jonna. Don't be surprised when it's turned back on you." He released her and watched her draw her hand back quickly. He knew he hadn't hurt her, only stung her pride. "I don't regret leaving England," he told her after a moment. "I don't regret anything about it. You're right that I had a motive for helping Colin and Mercedes. It gained me my freedom."

Jonna was struck by the husky resonance of his voice. Here was a passion she had not expected, and Jonna wondered what to make of it. "I know you risked it for them," she said. This time when he said nothing the silence was powerful. Jonna had the oddest sensation that he didn't speak because he couldn't speak. "Decker?" Without thinking she reached out and touched his face. Moonlight gave a gunmetal cast to his blue eyes, and she found she couldn't look away. "You won your freedom and risked it again. Did it mean so little to you?"

"It meant so much," he said quietly.

Jonna stared at him wonderingly. She felt as if her heart were being squeezed. Suddenly it was difficult to breathe.

His fingers curled lightly around her wrist, and he removed her hand from his cheek. Her confusion was so palpable that her emotional struggle raised Decker's gentle amusement. "Perhaps you should sleep on it, Jonna. You may find I'm easy to despise again in the morning."

It would have been so simple to say she found him easy to despise at that moment. The words were on the edge of her thoughts, at the tip of her tongue. She would never know what held her back, but her discretion was rewarded by the flicker of surprise in his eyes. Her smile was vaguely smug as she withdrew her hand from his. Decker Thorne was not the only one who could respond in unpredictable ways.

Jonna turned on her side, away from him, and curled one arm under her head to support it. Reaching behind her, she found Decker's arm and brought it across her waist. Her fingers threaded through his. Several moments passed before she felt the tension wash out of him. He moved closer, and she found herself curving naturally into the cradle of his body.

Jonna had no idea what to make of this man or this marriage. What seemed clear to her now was that she liked being held by him, liked the heat and strength of his lean frame next to hers. This morning when she'd thought of sharing a bed with him she could find no comfort in the prospect. Just now it was difficult to imagine feeling anything else.

She closed her eyes. "When do we leave London?"

"At first light."

It would come too soon. In the morning she would be less certain of what she wanted. Jonna knew that now. It would be hard to justify that she found pleasure with him in this bed and that she had let him find pleasure with her. "Then you should sleep," she said.

He didn't think he would, at least not quickly, but the steady rocking of *Huntress* in her berth, and the even cadence of Jonna's breathing, brought him to that gentle state long before her.

★ ★ ★ ★ ★

Captain Thorne was on the bridge when Jonna saw him again. Framed in the doorway that led from the lower decks, she watched him for several minutes without being seen. His head was tilted upward as the first mate directed attention to something in the rigging. Jonna's eyes fell on his strong throat and his dark, wind-ruffled hair. He raised a hand to shield the sunlight. He might have been saluting the sky.

She liked the way he stood there, light and lithe, his body slightly arched to balance him on the rolling deck. He spoke to his first mate, pointed out something overhead, and waited for his order to be carried out. The last thing Jonna expected was for him to move toward the taffrail, make the graceful leap to its ledge, and climb into the rigging himself.

In spite of her fear she was compelled to move out of the doorway and follow Decker's progress onto the ropes. All of her life she had been watching men do just what he was doing now and had never given it a second thought. Now she felt as though her heart was in her mouth. It didn't matter that his ascent was sure and swift, every step he took pushed her pulse a little faster.

Jonna didn't think she moved. She didn't think she could have. Yet something caught Decker's attention, and then he was peering down at her. It was the first time his foot faltered. He missed one of the cross pieces and hung there in midair upside down, his ankle caught but his grip having saved him.

Wind beat hard against the sails and flattened Decker's shirt against his chest. He thought he heard Jonna call his name, then realized it had to be a trick of the wind and water. He couldn't have heard her above the hand that was covering her mouth. She was pale as salt, and her eyes were huge.

Decker pulled himself back into the rigging easily, but he knew it was too late.

Jonna fainted before he was out of the ropes.

Nine

Jonna recovered from her faint as she was being carried to the cabin. Her lashes fluttered once, and she caught a glimpse of Decker's taut and impassive features. "You may put me down," she said.

"I may," he replied easily. "And I may throw you overboard. I'm not yet set on the matter." Seeing Jonna's lips flatten and the appearance of that elusive dimple, Decker smiled for the first time since she had collapsed.

Inside the cabin, he set her on the bed. She tried to sit up immediately but the pressure of his hand on her shoulder kept her in place. "I assure you, I'm quite all right," she said. Indeed, she was more embarrassed by what had happened than physically discomforted.

Decker was not entirely convinced. He studied her face for a moment, then touched her brow and cheek with the back of his hand. "You're warm." His fingers grazed Jonna's throat. Her pulse was racing. "I think you should rest. There's some good reason why you fainted. You may be sickening."

There was a good reason, she thought. Decker had been dangling upside-down by his ankle twenty feet above her. That sight had been enough to stop the blood flow to her head and buckle her knees. "I don't feel sick," she said. Nothing could induce her to tell him what had gone through her mind before she fainted. He could put any construction he wanted upon her warm cheeks and racing heart as long as he didn't suspect the real cause.

Decker's thumb passed lightly across the hollow of her

237

throat. "What possessed you to go topside?"

The truth served her well enough here. "Boredom mostly," Jonna said. "I can't bear it in this cabin any longer."

Her tolerance for those four walls had exceeded all of Decker's expectations, but something more had prompted her visit. "And what else?" he asked.

"I'm tired of being afraid." She stared him straight in the eye as she said it, daring him to laugh at this confession.

"Aaah," he said softly, one brow arched. This was perfectly believable. "So you decided to confront your fear by stepping out on a rolling and pitching deck with no warning to anyone that you were about. You might have pitched yourself right into the Atlantic."

That had occurred to her only belatedly. "I didn't make it even half the distance to the rail. I'm not so brave as you might think."

Decker almost smiled. Failure did not sit well on Jonna's shoulders. "You're fearless to the point of being senseless." This observation was softened by the kiss he placed on her mouth. Her lips parted under his. Her breath was warm and sweet, and he had the sense the kiss was welcomed rather than merely suffered. He was of a mind to linger, to draw out the kiss in the hopes that it would become another and yet another, and eventually something more altogether. He liked the thought of making love to her in the daylight, of being able to see her pale skin pinkened by sunshine, of watching her unshadowed features respond to pleasure.

His own body stirred. Hiding the effort it cost him to do so, Decker pushed himself up. It was just last night that he'd told himself it would be Jonna who initiated their lovemaking the next time. He wondered how long he was obligated to keep a rash promise known only to him. Decker sighed. Probably longer than twelve hours. His brief grin mocked himself.

He was quite capable of being as senseless as Jonna.

"Here," he said, helping her up. "If you think you can manage it, I'll take you on deck myself. Just a few feet out at first and you have to hold my arm."

Jonna thought she would be grateful for the opportunity, but now that it was presented, she wasn't as certain. "What if I faint again?"

"Then I'll bring you back here and you can try tomorrow if you like, or the day after that."

"But the crew . . . I don't know if I want them to realize I'm afraid of the water. That won't look very good, will it? I mean, what must they be thinking?"

"They think you fainted because I was caught upside down in the rigging. I've already been scowled at and cursed for scaring you." He saw Jonna's eyes widen. Panic flashed briefly. "Don't worry. I didn't tell them that my imminent demise would have had quite the opposite effect."

"That's not true," she said softly, looking away. "I don't wish you ill."

"But you wish me gone."

"Something like that."

Decker nodded. He had expected nothing better than the answer she gave him. "Will you come topside? The men will want to know you're feeling better. I think they'll believe me if you're on my arm."

"Did someone really curse you?" she asked suspiciously.

"Under his breath."

"And scowl?"

"Every one of them."

"Oh."

Her surprise amused him. "They admire you, Jonna. They'd string me up sooner than see me hurt you." He stood and held out his hand. "Ready?"

She wasn't, but neither did she hesitate. She placed her hand in his and let him pull her to her feet. "Just a yard or so from the entrance," she told him. "That's as far as I want to go. And if my sea legs turn to water you'll have to prop me up. Don't carry me. I don't want anyone to know I've fainted, so you mustn't make a fuss."

Decker let Jonna continue to chatter her orders and conditions while he led her along the companionway. When they reached the narrow steps that would bring them topside he placed one finger lightly over her lips. She quieted immediately. Satisfied, Decker pulled the hood of her cape over her hair. For a moment his hands remained on either side of her cheeks, framing her face. "Follow or lead?" he asked.

"Hmmm?" She was staring up at his face, at the blue eyes that were watching her with unwavering intensity. Jonna couldn't make sense of what he was asking.

"Do you want to follow me or lead the way?"

She decided it depended on whether she wanted to be pulled or pushed. "I'll lead." Jonna glimpsed the smile he couldn't quite conceal. She supposed he had expected that answer as being part of her character. What he couldn't know was that when fear made her faint, she wanted to be in a position to fall into his arms, not out of them.

Decker gave Jonna a nudge at the small of her back. It was like lighting a fuse. Jonna was up the steps before she could think better of it, and Decker had to scramble to stay with her. When she fairly exploded out of the hold it was only Decker's hand on her cape that kept her from going too far. Brought up short by the fistful of material he held, Jonna vibrated like a plucked string.

She was aware of several things at once: winter sunlight on her face, the surprised expressions of the crew, and how difficult it was to breathe. Decker stood at her back, his arms closing around her waist. She could feel his chin nudge her head and heard his soft command.

"Breathe."

Jonna sucked in air. Cold North Atlantic wind filled her lungs, almost robbing her of a second breath. She tasted frozen nettles of sea spray on her tongue.

"Smile."

She fixed the corners of her lips upward.

"Open your eyes."

Her smile actually became a genuine one. "They're open."

"You *are* fearless. Can you look around?"

Jonna's eyes darted from crew member to crew member, but her head remained perfectly still. Her lips barely moved as she spoke. "No, I can't mo—" The clipper rolled beneath her, and Jonna felt herself begin to lose balance.

"Spread your legs."

That intimately spoken order brought Jonna's head around. Her violet eyes were wide. "What?"

Decker grinned. His hands moved to either side of her waist to steady her. "You have to meet the ship's pitch," he said. "Widen your stance."

Jonna's lips pursed prudishly. "You might have said that in the first place."

"I might have," he agreed easily. "But then you'd still be as immobile as *Huntress*'s figurehead. Stiff-armed . . . stiff-legged . . ." There was a decidedly teasing light in his blue eyes. "Stiff-necked."

Jonna marveled at his ability to make her laugh at herself. "How do you do that?" she wondered aloud.

"What?"

She shook her head, bemused. "It's nothing." More relaxed now, Jonna turned in his arms and quite naturally leaned back against him. This time she was able to tilt her head in greeting to Mr. Leeds and to nod hello to an astonished Jeremy Dodd. When the ship rolled again she shifted her weight naturally. "I want to go to the rail," she said.

"Are you certain?"

"No," she said honestly. "But it's what I'm going to do."

Frigid air buffeted Jonna's cape and skirt about her legs. It wasn't the icy wind that caused her to shiver as she approached the taffrail. It was terror. Whitecapped swells of water were all she could make out for as far as she could see. When *Huntress* rolled, the rail seemed to dip so low she could imagine herself simply stepping over it and disappearing in a froth of churning water.

"Head up," Decker said. "Eyes on the horizon."

That meant she would have to open them again. For a moment it seemed the safest recourse had been to close them tight. Jonna looked out. She felt Decker's hands curl in the material of her cape. She was secure in the knowledge that he wasn't going to let her go.

"Put your hands on the rail."

Jonna steadied herself.

"Breathe."

A whisper of a smile crossed Jonna's features. It was good of him to remember what she had forgotten. She took a shaky breath and confronted the vastness of the ocean.

"You're right to respect it," Decker said.

Jonna laughed uneasily. "That's putting it kindly."

"Not at all. There's not a man on board who doesn't share some of the same fear."

She wondered if he included himself. Jonna started to glance over her shoulder, but Decker caught her head and turned it back to the horizon.

"Including me," he said. "I'd be a fool to think I could tame this force. The best any of us can hope to do is outwit it."

Jonna's stomach sank as *Huntress*'s deck seemed to fall out from under her feet. She grasped the taffrail with fingers that turned white at the tips. The hood of her cape fell back. The wind flattened tendrils of glossy black hair against her temples.

"Steady," Decker whispered near her ear. "I'm not going anywhere."

Jonna held on to the rail, but it was not really her support. "I think I should go below," she said.

"All right."

She wished he would try to persuade her otherwise. A few more minutes like this were what she wanted. Her smile was a trifle sad, a trifle self-mocking.

"What is it?" Decker asked.

She shook her head at first, not certain she wanted to answer him. Then she said it anyway. "I'm reminded again that my life is a cliché," she said. "Here I am standing between the devil and the deep blue sea." Jonna didn't have to see his face to know that he was amused by her observation.

"And if you were forced to choose?"

Jonna felt his hands resting lightly on her waist and the warmth of him at her back. His chin nudged her hair. In front of her was the relentless north wind and an ocean of icy water. It should have been an easy choice. Jonna's hesitation spoke when she could not.

"Never mind," Decker said. "It was wrong to ask."

If it was possible the sun seemed to grow colder. Jonna missed Decker's support immediately as he stepped back to allow her room to move away from the rail. She hurried to the entrance to the hold and braced herself on the stairway by putting a hand on each wall. She was in the gangway below before she realized he was no longer following her. Glancing back, she saw him silhouetted in the entrance, his expression shadowed. Jonna did not think he was smiling. He had never looked more alone.

"Tell me about your parents," she said. They were lying side by side in the bunk, eyes on the ceiling, arms at attention beside them. The covers were virtually undisturbed. Jonna had hoped he would reach for her this night, at least to put an arm around her waist. He hadn't, and she was angry at herself for being disappointed. By her reckoning it had been ten days since he had been with her. The last kiss they had shared was the one he'd given her before taking her topside. She had been on the bridge every morning since then and on three evenings besides, but short of taking her arm in his, Decker had not touched her. He had never given the slightest indication that he wanted to do so.

The devil was now as cold and remote as the deep blue sea.

"I don't remember them very well," he said. "Most of what I know I've learned from Colin."

"I was thinking of Marie Thibodeaux and Jimmy Grooms. Mercedes told me you consider them your parents."

"In a way I do, it's true. What do you want to know?"

His tone was not particularly inviting, but Jonna was not going to let that deter her. "Were they really actors?"

"Always," he said. "Though not only on the stage. Every pinch we made was a little drama to Jimmy. He had a certain flair for it, and Mère liked that about him."

"Mère," Jonna said softly. "That means mother, doesn't it?"

"Yes. That's what I've always called her."

Jonna turned carefully on her side. She slid one arm under her pillow to raise her head a notch and studied Decker's shaded profile. "Were there other children?"

"No. Just me. Mère couldn't have babies. Before Jimmy found her she had been used pretty roughly."

"She was a prostitute?"

Decker smiled faintly, remembering how Marie would have answered. "She'd tell you that was putting too kind a light on what she was. 'Until Jimmy came into my life,' she'd say, 'I was a whore. But it took you, *Pont Épine,* to make me a saint.' "

"And was she a saint?"

"I thought so. She was smart and funny and cheerful. She had an almost endless well of patience, and she loved me and Jimmy to distraction."

"Did she always call you by that name?"

"Mostly. It was my professional name, she said. Part of the drama."

"How were Jimmy and Marie caught?"

Decker didn't answer immediately. Finally he told her what he had told no one else. "They weren't. Not really."

"But—"

"I was."

That silenced Jonna for several minutes as she considered what it meant. "Mercedes didn't tell me," she said quietly. "I wouldn't have—"

Decker interrupted her. "Mercedes doesn't know."

"Oh."

"Mercedes and I shared a cell, Jonna. Not every detail of our lives."

"She was too refined to ask some direct questions, you mean."

"Something like that," he said dryly.

"I can be very forthright, you know, even tactless. I'm not good at diplomacy. I don't have the patience for it, and I'm almost insatiably curious."

He had observed all that about her. Her guileless approach to most things still had the power to charm him. He wondered if tonight would be the night she would reach for him. Better the devil you know, he wanted to say. If she thought her life was a cliché, then she should grasp one that could change these intolerable circumstances. "Well?" he asked finally. "Have you really finished the inquisition?"

Knowing that she was being challenged didn't make Jonna think better of responding to it. "How were you caught?"

"I got careless," he said. "I let my mind wander while I was lifting a watch fob. I had done the very same maneuver twice already that day. I had done it hundreds of times since Jimmy first let me try it on my own on my tenth birthday. This time I forgot the cardinal rule."

"The cardinal rule?"

"Jimmy's rule, anyway. 'Every mark is different,' he'd tell me. 'Them that seem to have their mind engaged elsewhere, might be they're just thinkin' about the time.' He only meant that the mark's preoccupation might not be quite what it seemed. I reached for the fob, my little blade ready to cut it free from a certain dandy's breeches, at the same time the dandy decided to check the hour. He caught me by the wrist, and I sunk the blade into his palm. I thought it would make him let me go, but he held on tighter and started shouting for the constable."

Jonna's eyes were wide now. She edged closer to Decker. "What happened then?"

"Jimmy and Mère were watching. They had been working the crowd with me, and now they joined in the middle of it. Jimmy pulled me loose and tossed me to Mère. She spun me out and away, but somehow my blade caught her pocket. It ripped open and spilled her morning's work onto the street. There was a cameo, a pair of earrings, some silk ribbons. I tried to get back to her when she was grabbed, but the crowd closed in around her. I think Jimmy must have dove for her because I heard someone yell to hold him back. People were shouting and pushing, and I couldn't see over them anymore."

"You were forgotten."

"I'd like to think the dandy that I stuck remembered me."

Jonna thought she saw a glimmer of a smile, but this one was bittersweet. "You got away," she said.

Decker nodded. It was a moment before he spoke again, and this time his voice was husky. "Mère and Jimmy were taken to Newgate. I couldn't visit them for fear of being taken myself. In light of the fact that they had risked everything to save me, I would have been ungrateful to present myself at the gate." He paused. "At least that's what I told myself."

"I'm sure you were right."

"I don't know. If I had given myself up all three of us might have been transported."

"Or you might have hanged with them."

Decker shook his head. "They hanged because they wouldn't give me up. That dandy I stuck turned out to be the Duke of Westport, and that small cut I gave him almost took his life. The authorities were so certain he was going to die that they made Mère and Jimmy hang for it. The charges against them were theft, but no one will ever convince me it wasn't the duke's condition and the fact that they wouldn't lead anyone to me that sent them to Tyburn Tree." Decker drew in a breath and let it out slowly. "Westport began recovering three days later. I had a mind to run him to ground and stick him again, but there was really no sense in it. Mère and Jimmy were gone to me."

"What did you do?"

"What makes you think I did anything?"

Jonna merely raised one eyebrow.

"I waited three years and found a position in the duke's country home as a cook's helper. I made off with two place settings of silver, a chalice from the chapel, and a ruby necklace that had been in the family for three generations." For the first time Decker turned to look at Jonna. Her expression was difficult to read. "Isn't that more or less what you expected?"

"It depends," she said. "Did you keep any of it?"

"No."

"Did you sell it?"

"No."

"You threw it away."

"Tossed it in the river."

Jonna's smile was slow to surface, but she didn't hide it. "Then it's exactly what I expected. Not more. Not less." Pleased that she was not always so predictable, her smile deepened. "Now I've surprised you. Did you think I would make a rush to judgment? I really can't say what I would have done in your shoes but I like to think I would have done *something*." Under the covers Jonna's hand closed the distance between them and covered his wrist. "Have you ever wondered how your life would have been different if your own parents hadn't been murdered?"

Decker didn't answer the question directly. "It sounds as though you've given it some thought."

"I don't think you would have been raised to be a thief."

He wouldn't be here now, he thought, with her, in the dark, her palm lying possessively across his wrist. What about his past could he regret when all the events conspired to bring him to Jonna? "I would be the dissolute middle son of a titled family, with a small estate of my own and a hunting lodge. I would dabble in politics and horse racing, and have a rake's career of breaking hearts."

"You would not." Then Jonna considered his reckless smile. "Well, perhaps the last would be true." She found she didn't want to think about that. "Do you remember the circumstances of your parents' deaths?" she asked.

"I take it you mean my real parents."

"Yes. I know you were young."

"I was four," he said. "Old enough."

"You don't have to—"

"It's all right," he told her. "I don't mind talking about it." He wondered if that were strictly true. The only person he had ever spoken to about it was Colin, and that was only to compare memories of what had happened. "For a long time I chose not to remember it at all. I was hardly aware that it was a choice, but when Mère and Jimmy were gone it seemed pointless to pretend any longer. I had another family somewhere, the earring was proof of it. It was my only real link with my brothers. It was odd, still I had more of a sense of being part of them than of my parents. The night they were killed I remember Colin thrusting Greydon in my arms and telling me to keep him quiet. I thought that somehow everything that was happening was my fault, that I hadn't done my part right and my parents had died because of it."

Jonna's hand tightened over his wrist. "Oh, Decker."

"I didn't see anything outside the carriage, not the highwaymen, not their horses. I heard my father offering what money he had. I heard my mother pleading with them not to hurt her children." He paused. "I heard the shots."

Jonna edged closer. She laid her head on his shoulder. Her arm slid across his chest.

"Colin ran after them, but there was nothing he could do. It was later that night we were taken to the workhouse. No one understood that the Earl of Rosefield was our grandfather, and he didn't know we were on our way to visit him. It was at Cunnington's that we were separated."

"But the earring brought you back to Colin."

"Eventually it did exactly that."

"Do you ever think it will lead you and Colin to Greydon?"

"I think it will lead Greydon to us."

"How?"

He shrugged. "I don't know."

Jonna was quiet. She yawned once, covering her mouth with the back of her hand. "Do you really think you would have dabbled in politics?"

Decker realized she had picked up threads of their earlier conversation. "And horse racing."

She smiled sleepily. "I think you would have been good at both those things," she said more to herself than Decker. "I think you can do most anything." Her cheek nudged his shoulder as she fit herself more comfortably against him. "May I sleep here?" she asked.

"You only had to ask."

Jonna stood at the rail as *Huntress* approached Boston Harbor. If there was even the slightest possibility that Jack Quincy was watching, Jonna wanted him to see her on the deck of the clipper. For years Jack had tried—and failed—to get Jonna on board one of the Remington ships. She knew he would appreciate her success now. Raising the spyglass, she eagerly scanned the wharf for a glimpse of Jack.

"Have you seen the warehouse?"

Jonna turned so suddenly that she almost knocked Decker in the head with the spyglass. He managed to duck under it as she pivoted in place.

"Careful with that thing." He took it from her. "You should remove it from your eye before you start dancing around." Holding it up to his own eye, he adjusted the glass for a clear look at Jonna's rebuilt warehouse. "Jack and the men must have been very busy. It seems completed to me." He collapsed the spyglass and tucked it in his trousers. "As promised."

"Did I even once entertain the notion that Jack wouldn't have it done?" she asked.

"Not aloud," said Decker.

Jonna glanced sideways at him, frowning. "What do you mean by that?"

"I mean that you've obviously been preoccupied these last ten days." He recalled most of their conversation the last time they had talked at any length. He had been over it in his own mind half a dozen times, wondering what he had said that kept her at arm's length for the remainder of the voyage. When she had curled herself against him and asked if she could sleep in his arms, he had been hopeful. Each evening since then, when she made no other overtures, he had felt a little more of that hope slip away. Perhaps she did despise him every bit as much as she had first said.

Jonna scanned the harbor again. "Preoccupied," she said quietly. It was true, but she hadn't thought he'd noticed. He always seemed busy himself with some aspect of running the ship. "You never said anything."

"I asked you on several different occasions what you were thinking."

She remembered that he had. And each time she had fixed a smile on her face and made up something to placate him. Now she realized he hadn't once believed her. She wondered how much it mattered since she could never have shared the truth. "I suppose I've had too much practice at keeping my thoughts to myself," she said. "Did you think marriage would change that?"

"No."

"Do you think it should?"

"I'd like to think you could tell me when something's troubling you. More importantly, tell me *what's* troubling you."

Jonna turned her back on the harbor. All around her the crew was making ready for docking. Decker's second in command was issuing the orders, and no one was paying them the least attention. It was as good a time as any to tell him at least one of the things she had been thinking since they'd left London. "I'm not certain I want to announce our marriage, at least not right away."

"Have you forgotten?" Decker asked. "We already announced it to the crew. How long do you suppose they'll keep it a secret?"

"We can ask them not to say anything."

Both of Decker's brows rose. His expression was patently skeptical. "That will guarantee the news will be out to every matron and scandalmonger in half the usual time." Decker studied her face. There was a small vertical frown between her dark brows, and she was worrying her lower lip. "You're serious about this, aren't you?"

Not sparing him a glance, afraid of what she would see, Jonna nodded.

Although Decker was fairly certain of the answer, he asked the question anyway. "Is there someone specific you don't want to hear about our marriage?"

Jonna didn't flinch from his tone, though it felt like ground glass against her skin. "Grant," she said. "I'd like to tell him myself."

"So you *do* intend to tell him."

"Of course. I just think he should hear it from me."

"I have no problem with that, as long as I'm with you."

"There's no need," she said.

"There's every need." Decker saw she was about to make another protest. He cupped her chin and brought her face toward his. "If I even suspect you're going to visit Sheridan without me, I'll make certain every town crier has the news of our wedding." He let that sink in. "Now, if you don't want to hear the announcement from the street corners, you'll let me accompany you when you tell your fiancé about your husband."

"He was never my fiancé."

"Exactly."

Jonna watched him walk away. Her response had been feeble, while his parting shot had been quietly triumphant. What did it matter? she wanted to ask. It wasn't as if they had a real marriage.

Jack Quincy caught Jonna in his expansive arms as soon as she set foot on the wharf. "A good thing it was," he said heartily, "to see you standing at the rail. Couldn't believe my eyes at first. Thought you'd be holed up in the cabin until *Huntress* was berthed."

"That was the voyage over," she said breathlessly as she was set down. "I found a bit of courage on the way back."

Holding Jonna by the shoulders at arm's length, Jack looked her over carefully. Her violet eyes were bright but watchful. The smile was fulsome but strangely unanimated. There was an air of barely contained energy about her that seemed more nervous in origin than excited. There was no doubt in Jack's mind that Jonna was happy to see him, but there was also no doubt that she was not entirely happy.

253

"The warehouse is finished," he told her. "Do you want to see it?"

"I'd like that."

Jack looked up the gangway. He could see Decker was discussing something with Mr. Jeffries. "Perhaps we should wait for Captain Thorne."

"He'll be along when he's able," she said. "He won't have any trouble finding me."

Jack thought her tone was decidedly cool. He shook his head. "I suppose there are some things time alone can't change."

Puzzled, Jonna stared back at him. "Now, what does that mean?"

"It's just that I thought—" He glanced up at Decker again. The captain was thoroughly occupied with his crew. "Wishful thinking, I suppose." His hands dropped from Jonna's shoulders, and he looped his arm in hers. "This way, Miss Remington. I'm thinking you're going to be very pleased by what you see."

Jonna was. There was no evidence of fire damage left at the warehouse. The collapsed walls had been rebuilt with new brick; the offices on the first floor had larger dimensions, and deep shelves had been added along one wall for cargo storage. Jonna's own office had been refinished and refurnished. The floors were as polished as her desk, and the walls had been papered instead of painted. Jonna sniffed the air, expecting some residue of smoke to fill her lungs. Instead she caught the sweet scent of the hothouse flowers that had been set out in vases in her office and that of her secretary.

"One might think you were expecting me today," she said.

Jack laughed. "The work's been eight days done. By my reckoning, Mr. Caplin's changed the flowers three times so they'd be fresh."

Jonna smiled, pleased by her secretary's thoughtfulness. "You've outdone yourself, Jack. You have the cost figures, of course."

"Of course." Jack couldn't help himself. He was grinning broadly. Before Jonna could ask him what foolish notion he had taken into his head, he said simply, "Damn, if it's not good to have you back at the helm. Cost figures, indeed."

Decker was waiting for them outside the warehouse with a rented hack. He opened the door for Jonna and held out one hand to assist her inside. "I take it you liked what you saw."

She nodded. "Am I so obvious?"

"Not often." Decker thought she seemed unaccountably pleased by his answer. He leaned in the carriage, made certain she was seated comfortably, then turned to greet Jack. His hand was grasped warmly. "Good to see you, Jack. It seems you've pleased her highness."

"I heard that," Jonna called from the carriage.

"I intended you to," Decker replied.

Jack laughed. "Still sparring, I see. Don't know why I thought that might change." He pointed behind him to the warehouse. "Do you want to see the renovations?"

"Later," Decker said. "Right now I want to go home."

"Sure. Shall I get another hack for you?"

"Not necessary."

Jonna leaned forward and caught Jack's attention. "Captain Thorne is coming with me."

Jack's thick brows drew together first; then one lifted archly, squeezed to that higher plane by the strength of his confusion. "Decker's place is not exactly on the way."

Decker glanced back at Jonna. "You didn't tell him."

She merely shook her head. How could she explain that there had never seemed an appropriate moment?

"Tell me what?" Jack wanted to know.

255

Decker climbed into the carriage and signaled the driver to go. He leaned out the window as the hack began to move. "I'll be sharing Mrs. Thorne's Beacon Hill address from now on."

Jack stood rooted to the wharf, clearly dumbfounded. "Sharing an address?" he said to himself. The carriage was turning the corner when he found his larger voice. "Mrs. Thorne?" he shouted after them. "What the hell does *that* mean?"

Jonna's mouth flattened disapprovingly as she looked at Decker. He was leaning casually back against the leather cushions, for all appearances completely at his ease and pleased with himself. "You might have found some discreet way of breaking the news." Jack's voice was still ringing in her ears.

"I said I would hire a town crier," he reminded her. "Consider Jack the first if you don't change your ways."

"I had every intention of telling him."

"Then you shouldn't be sorry he knows now."

"You made it sound as if we're going to be living together."

"We are."

"But you made it sound . . ." Words failed her. "You might at least have the decency to look less pleased with yourself. This news is going to cover the ground more quickly than our hack. I shouldn't be at all surprised if Mrs. Davis knows before we arrive."

Decker doubted she was very concerned about that possibility. "Afraid Sheridan will learn of it first from someone else?"

"Not afraid," she said. "Apprehensive. I already told you I didn't want that to happen. I believe I owe Grant something more than a rumor."

Unapologetic and unsympathetic, Decker said, "Then you'll have to tell him sooner rather than later." He settled his head back and closed his eyes, blocking out Jonna's violet-hued glare.

The news of Jonna's marriage did not precede her home, but she did not wait long to inform her housekeeper. Mrs. Davis was no less visibly shocked than Jack Quincy, only better at keeping her voice down. When she recovered from the initial surprise, the creases in her gently lined face deepened as her smile widened.

"It's a pleasure to hear, Miss Remington," she said. "You and the captain. If my opinion counts for anything, it couldn't be more right."

"Mrs. Thorne," Jonna said.

The housekeeper was genuinely puzzled. "What?"

"You called me Miss Remington."

"I did?" She thought about it. "So I did. That will take a bit of getting used to. And just when I resigned myself to the idea that you'd be Miss Remington forever." Jonna's deep blush warned Mrs. Davis that she had spoken her errant thoughts aloud. "I'm sorry . . . I didn't mean . . ." She looked to Decker for help in extricating her from her poorly thought-out words.

"If the truth be known, Mrs. Davis," he said, "until very recently, my wife entertained the same notion."

"Then you must be a powerful persuader. Miss Rem—I mean Mrs. Thorne doesn't move easily from a course she's set."

Decker glanced sideways at Jonna. If anything her flush had become a shade deeper. "So I've heard," he said gravely.

Mrs. Davis helped Jonna off with her cape, then held out her arm for Decker's coat. "I think you've brought winter back with you." She brushed a dusting of snow off the sleeve of Decker's jacket. "Will you take some tea in the parlor?"

"Nothing for me," Jonna said. She was assailed suddenly by the oddest sensation that the floor was rolling under her feet. "I'd like to go to my room and lie down. I don't think I feel very well."

Mrs. Davis was instantly concerned, but it was Decker who suspected what was happening and acted. "Hot broth and a few crackers will do, Mrs. Davis. Have one of the maids bring them to her room. Don't trouble yourself." He placed his hand under Jonna's elbow to steady her. "I'll see that she gets to her room."

"Broth," the housekeeper repeated under her breath. Her eyes followed Jonna as Decker escorted her to the wide staircase. "Crackers." The corners of her eyes crinkled, and for a second they glistened with unshed tears. "Oh, my. Broth and crackers. Why, that's wonderful!" She turned and hurried down the hallway, carrying the coats with her.

Upstairs Decker dismissed the maid that was sent to assist, helping Jonna out of her gown and petticoats himself. That Jonna didn't protest spoke eloquently of her distress. Wearing only her shift, she crawled under the covers that Decker held up for her. She groaned softly as her head touched the pillow.

Decker's weight made a depression on the mattress as he sat down at the level of her waist. Leaning forward, he brushed back a tendril of dark hair from her cheek. Her skin was warm, not fevered.

"What's wrong with me?" she asked plaintively.

His slight smile was sympathetic. He began plucking pins from her hair. "Landsickness, I suspect. It happens sometimes when you've been at sea. The floor, the walls seem to move even though you know they don't."

"It didn't happen in London."

"I can't explain it," he said. "Only diagnose it. Is your stomach turning over?"

She nodded.

"And you have a headache?"

Jonna nodded again. This small effort caused her to wince. "Downstairs, I thought the entrance hall was going to fall away from under my feet."

"Then you're landsick."

"Does it last long?"

He was quiet a moment, considering how to answer the question. "Not as long as what Mrs. Davis thinks is wrong with you."

Jonna's brows puckered. She rubbed her temples while Decker placed her hair pins on the bedside table. "What does Mrs. Davis know about being landsick?"

"As far as I know, not a thing. That's why she thinks you're pregnant."

"Pregnant?" Jonna almost sat upright. Immediately the room seemed to tilt on its side. She closed her eyes and fell back. For a moment she thought she was going to be sick.

Watching her, Decker wondered if it was disorientation that was turning her complexion ashen or the thought of carrying his child. "Come here," he said. "Let me help you."

At first she didn't know what he meant, but as he changed position and moved to the head of the bed Jonna saw that he intended she should lay her head on his lap. He had said he wanted to help. When his long fingers began a gentle scalp massage, Jonna was thankful she had let him. "Why would Mrs. Davis think I'm pregnant?"

Even though Jonna's eyes were closed, Decker was careful to temper his smile. For all her business acumen, she could be rather frighteningly naive about other things. "Our hasty marriage," he said. "That wave of sickness downstairs. The fact that I asked for broth and crackers to be brought to your room."

"Oooh." It was a groaning realization. "I'll have to tell her differently."

"Why? It could be true."

"It's not."

"Would it be so awful?"

Jonna's eyes opened. She stared up at Decker. His careless smile was not in evidence. He was studying her face, looking past her set features for the truth she didn't want to reveal. "No," she said softly. "Not awful."

"But not welcome."

"That's right. Not welcome." She would make the worst sort of mother. Spending time with Colin's children had merely confirmed what she suspected about herself: they frightened her. The thought of having even one of her own filled her with a mixture of terror and dread. She knew volumes about ship-building. What she knew about raising children could be written on the head of a pin.

Decker didn't say anything. His disappointment was not visible in his cool glance or his still features. His fingers had only paused briefly on her scalp. Her hair was very soft, and his motions had released the faint scent of lavender. He leaned his head back and closed his own eyes.

A scratching at the door preceded the maid's entrance into the room. The Negress carried a large mug of steamy chicken broth and a plate of unsalted crackers.

"Thank you, Amanda," Jonna said. "Set the tray on the table."

Conscious of Jonna's headache, Amanda set it down carefully. "Mrs. Davis tol' me the news, ma'am. I'm very happy for you."

"Thank you. That's kind of you."

"And the cap'n, he must be poppin' his buttons."

Decker opened one eye and scanned Amanda's cheerful face. "I am. And it's a pleasure to see you again. I suppose now that Jonna's back you'll be running off. It doesn't seem anyone stays here long when she's in residence."

Jonna was too tired to take issue with him. "Don't mind the captain, Amanda. He's convinced I'm an ogre to my servants."

The maid's smile had wavered uncertainly. Now it was back like a bright beacon against her dusky complexion. "Go on with you, Cap'n Thorne." She waggled a finger at Jonna. "Take the soup, ma'am, before it gets cold. It will settle your insides. My mama swears by soup and crackers. There were eight of us, and she had the sickness with each one." Humming happily to herself, Amanda waltzed out of the room, unaware that Jonna tried to call her back.

"I don't think she was congratulating us on our marriage," Decker said when they were alone. "You confirmed Mrs. Davis's suspicions."

"I know that now. You might have said something."

"It will straighten itself out. You don't have to do anything. In a few months time they'll all notice you're not increasing." His fingers continued to sift strands of her silky hair. "If you're not pregnant now, I suppose there's no chance that you will be any time soon."

Since he had no more interest in her, Jonna had to agree with him. "We should discuss sleeping arrangements," she said. "There's really no reason for us to share a bed any longer."

"Other than for appearances, you mean."

"Until we decide how we intend to go on with this marriage, we can manage appearances by arranging adjoining rooms. There are two across the hall in this wing. Mrs. Davis can have the staff prepare them tomorrow."

Decker's fingers stilled. He tapped her forehead lightly with his index finger. "How we intend to go on with this marriage?" he repeated. "Are you entertaining some doubts?"

Jonna pushed herself upright. She reached across Decker for the tray and pulled it onto her lap. She noticed her hand barely trembled as she raised a cracker to her mouth. Decker couldn't possibly suspect how unsettled she was by what she had to say. "I've always had doubts," she said. "I never made a secret of them. It was you—and Colin—who dismissed them. We were in Colin's home then, and you're Colin's brother. I was never really given any choice but to fall in with your plans."

Decker had a good idea where she was heading. "And now that we're on your ground again, you think you can set some new rules? Is that the gist of it?"

"Something like that." She bit into the cracker. Her mouth was so dry she could barely swallow it. Her stomach was roiling more now than it had been at any time since she'd walked in the door of her home. "I do care something for appearances," she said. "In spite of what you might think. I hope that you will maintain at least the pretense of faithfulness. I don't want to end the marriage too quickly. I shouldn't like people to think I acted both precipitously *and* unwisely."

"That would not be good for business," he said dryly.

"Exactly. You understand." Jonna wrapped her cool and clammy palms around the mug of broth. She let the steam rise to her nostrils, then took a sip. Whiskey would have been better, she thought. She should be drunk right now.

"What about you?" Decker asked.

"Me?"

"Do you intend to maintain the pretense of faithfulness?"

"I intend to be faithful," she said.

Decker touched the bottom of her mug and encouraged her to drink some more broth. "But you'll look the other way when I have affairs?"

"It shouldn't matter where I look," she explained. "The idea is for you to be so discreet about it that I will never know one way or the other."

"So even if I were faithful to our vows, you'd merely assume I was very good at planning and carrying out my trysts."

Jonna's brow furrowed. She glanced at him sideways, uncertain.

"Clearly you hadn't considered that possibility. You can see it puts me in something of a double bind. I'm damned in your eyes no matter what I do."

"I was only trying to consider what you might want," she said. Jonna took another swallow of the hot broth. Decker was watching her oddly, looking more through her than at her. There was a glimmer of a smile lifting one corner of his mouth. It was making her stomach turn over in a way that wasn't entirely unpleasant.

"What do you know about what I want, Jonna?"

Ten

She could only stare at him.

Her silence satisfied Decker. "That's what I thought," he said finally, softly. "You don't know anything about what I want."

Caught by his direct, encompassing gaze, Jonna felt a ribbon of heat uncurl in her middle. It slowly flushed her complexion, starting at her breasts and rising up her throat to her cheeks. Dazed, she blinked owlishly. "The room is spinning," she whispered, not taking her eyes from his.

Decker touched her cheek with his fingertips. There was amusement in his voice. "Is that right?"

Jonna nodded.

"Perhaps you should lie back." He took the tray from her lap and put it aside. When he turned toward her again she was still sitting in the same position. Her lips were damp, slightly parted, and there appeared to be a breath caught in her throat. He covered her mouth with his and stole it away.

Decker told himself he wasn't entirely breaking his own promise. This kiss was merely a prompting, a gesture to remind her of what it was she had once wanted from him and what they had once shared. He had no intention of it becoming anything other than a kiss.

Then she responded. He swallowed her breathy little sigh. Her damp lips moved under his. She drew in his lower lip and ran her tongue along the sensitive underside. He felt her lean into him as she shifted position. Her hands came up to hover just above his shoulders, stayed there a moment, then finally gripped him. She seemed to need him for purchase and balance.

It was not so different from her need for him on *Huntress*. That's what Decker told himself when he felt her breasts pressed to his chest. He had steadied her there when the ship had pitched and tilted. It was no more than she wanted from him in her bed.

Jonna's breasts ached deeply. It wasn't enough for her body to be flush with his, not when her shift and his shirt separated them. Her hands slipped under Decker's jacket and pushed it away from his shoulders. With no more encouragement than that, she felt Decker shrug out of it. Jonna murmured her pleasure against his mouth. Without breaking the kiss, her fingers went to the first button of his shirt and slipped it free. She did another, then another, until the opening was wide enough for her to lay one hand flat against his chest. His skin was warm, and his heartbeat thrummed steadily under her hand. She said Decker's name against his lips and felt his response in the heart of her palm.

Jonna lay back and brought Decker with her. The weight of him against her secured and comforted. Until that moment Jonna had no idea that she desired either of those things or that they would heighten her pleasure. Her hands slipped around his back and she held him there, running her fingertips along the length of his spine.

Decker's knee pushed at the blankets that cocooned the lower half of Jonna's body. Beneath them, he felt her respond to the pressure of his knee by opening for him. A fleeting thought, only half-formed in his mind, warned him it was just as well the blankets were there. Inwardly he cursed the obstacle, outwardly he groaned.

Pushing against the bed, Decker raised himself on his elbows and looked down at Jonna. Her lips remained parted, the line of them slightly swollen and berry red. Her complexion was beautifully flushed and her eyes, when she opened them, were dark with the strength of her desire.

She blinked. A fringe of dark hair had fallen forward over Decker's brow. Without thinking Jonna pushed it back, the gesture at once intimate and tender. Her fingertips grazed his temple, then his ear, and finally came to rest lightly on the curve of his neck. An odd thought occurred to her: It was the middle of the afternoon.

"Yes," Decker said, amused. "It is."

Until he spoke Jonna hadn't realized she'd given her thought a voice. It had been easy, with her eyes closed, to believe she was making love to him under the cover of darkness. More disconcerting to Jonna was the discovery that with her eyes open nothing changed. The way he was looking at her now, with that calm and searching and frank regard, made her glad she could see him, too.

She glanced away, unable to hold his eyes. "If you want . . ."

Decker waited. When she didn't go on he bent his head and touched her mouth lightly with his own. "If I want what, Jonna?"

It would not be an easy thing to say the words aloud, Jonna realized. The directness with which she handled most matters of business failed her now. She laced her fingers behind his neck and urged him forward. "This," she said huskily. "If you want this."

The muscles in Decker's neck stiffened as he resisted Jonna's pressure. He saw her surprise in the moment before he extended his elbows and pushed himself away. Sitting up, he put his legs over the side of the bed and stood. He picked up his jacket from where it lay on the edge of the mattress and slipped it on. Out of the corner of his eye he saw Jonna's gaze stray to his groin. He did not button the jacket or make any move to hide his body's response.

"From now on," he said quietly, "it has to be what you want."

Then he left her alone.

Mrs. Davis opened the door to Jonna's room quietly and poked her head through. Her brow creased in consternation when she didn't see her employer in bed.

"It's all right," Jonna called from the window seat. "You may come in." She set aside her book with no care to finding her place again. It was an acknowledgment to herself that she had only been pretending to read it anyway. "I'm glad you're here. I imagine we have a lot to discuss."

Nodding, the housekeeper stepped into the room. "But that's not why I've come," she said. "Captain Thorne urged me to assure myself of your welfare."

"Aaah," Jonna said quietly. She could not credit Decker with good intentions, not when he had left her so abruptly just above an hour ago. The taste of him lingered on her mouth and there was still a heavy fullness in her breasts. He had kissed her with no intention of finishing what he'd started. What had occurred between them had only been for his amusement, not his satisfaction. She would not easily forget his parting words: *From now on it has to be what you want.* Jonna did not think he was being gracious or considerate. In her mind there could not have been a clearer demonstration that his deeper feelings were not engaged. He could take or leave her. He might say that the decision was hers, but the terms were really his.

It had been that way since she had gone to his room at Rosefield. On that occasion she had been foolish enough to imagine she could arrange intimacy between them like she arranged any other matter of business. Somehow Decker had been able to alter the nature of their liaison, turning her proposition into a proposal. Nothing had been as she wanted it since.

"Where is my husband?" Jonna asked. Heat rose in her cheeks as she heard the question. There was a certain proprietary air in her tone that she was suddenly aware of and certain she didn't like. In the far recesses of her mind she heard the faint echo of Decker's voice. *I can't own you, Jonna. Can I?* More strongly she heard his second demand. *Give me* Huntress. *Prove you know you can't own me.*

Jonna lightly touched her throat and cleared it. "I mean, where is Captain Thorne?"

Mrs. Davis looked at her oddly. "The captain went back to the harbor. I don't believe he said what business took him there, not that he should explain himself to me."

"He probably told me," Jonna said. She rubbed her temples. "I'm afraid I was rather groggy for a while."

"Of course you were," Mrs. Davis said solicitously. "Is there anything I can get you?"

Jonna shook her head. "No, but I'd like it if you'd sit with me. We need to talk about how we shall go on from here. Decker's presence will make things more difficult, though I shouldn't think impossible. It will not be so easy as when he was staying in the house before. I can't very well ask him to take his room in another wing."

Mrs. Davis chuckled at that notion, but her laughter faded suddenly as another thought occurred to her. "You haven't told him?"

Although Jonna had been expecting the question, she hadn't considered how she wanted to answer it or how much of an explanation she wanted to make. "No," she said finally, simply. "I haven't told him."

Mrs. Davis turned a wing chair away from the fireplace and toward Jonna. She sat down slowly. Her eyes were grave as she pondered the problems this presented. "Do you have any intention of telling him?" she asked after a moment.

"No." Jonna glanced out the window briefly. The sun ducked behind a cloud and a shadow crossed her face. Fingers of icy air lifted an eddy of snowflakes off the stone balustrade below her. "Not at this time," she said. "Not at any time soon."

"I see," the housekeeper said slowly. It was clear from her tone that she didn't see at all. More than that, she didn't approve.

"The girls must be told they can't say anything to him."

"I'll speak to them before he returns from the harbor. I'm sure nothing has been said to give us away. There hasn't been time."

"I agree." She turned back to Mrs. Davis. "I've already seen Amanda. She brought in my tray. And Delores came in to assist me with my clothes before Decker dismissed her. That's two. How many others are there?"

"Five," she replied. "Three that you know. Two that arrived since you've been gone. No one's left. I've been hard pressed to find enough work for all of them, what with you being gone and the regular staff needing to be kept busy as well."

"Then Rachael's still here?"

"Yes. I'm afraid the girl's somewhat attached herself to me. I don't know that she'll want to move on."

"Her hand?" asked Jonna. "How has it fared?"

"It's healed better than you or I could have hoped for. Mr. Sheridan made certain that Dr. Hardy checked it from time to time."

"Grant? He's been here?"

Mrs. Davis flinched slightly at Jonna's tone. "Why, yes," she said somewhat defensively. "I hadn't thought you would mind. Have I done something wrong?"

Jonna rushed to assure her. "No, not at all." But the truth was, she wasn't sure. "What was Grant's purpose in coming here?"

"I believe he simply wanted to know if I had heard anything from you. Mr. Sheridan was really very kind. Knowing that you left so quickly, he always inquired if there was anything he could do to assist me. I assume it was his way of asking if I had enough money to maintain the house. I assured him Mr. Quincy was seeing to everything. And he was especially thoughtful to Rachael. I think he was much struck by her crippled hand."

"He didn't suggest taking her to one of his abolitionist meetings, did he?"

"No," Mrs. Davis said. "I can't imagine that such a thing would have occurred to him."

Jonna remembered very well that it had crossed his mind. She was only thankful that he hadn't acted on the idea behind her back. "Did he notice the addition of the new girls in my absence?"

"I don't believe so. At least not that he mentioned. There was really no opportunity for him to see them. He was never here very long."

Jonna tried not to let her relief be too easily observed. "I suppose I'm making too much of his coming here," she said. "It was good of him to inquire after your needs. After the way we parted company, I confess I'm somewhat surprised by his interest."

"You mean what happened at the harbor. He doesn't hold that against you," Mrs. Davis said with some authority. "The score he wishes to settle is with Captain Thorne."

"Did he say that to you?"

"Oh, no. He told Mr. Quincy. I understand it was quite a blow Captain Thorne delivered. Mr. Quincy described it as a haymaker. I gather that means Mr. Sheridan was knocked senseless for a time." She blushed slightly at admitting she was privy to Jack's gossip. "Perhaps since you've married the captain, Mr. Sheridan will realize there's really no point in doing anything."

Jonna didn't think Mrs. Davis sounded particularly convinced. Though she didn't say anything, neither was she. "I'd like you to arrange for a new bedchamber for me," she said, closing the subject of Grant Sheridan. "I was thinking that Captain Thorne and I will take the adjoining ones across the hall."

"Adjoining rooms?" the housekeeper asked. Her mouth flattened briefly. "Your parents never—" She stopped, realizing she had overstepped herself. Her hands twisted in her apron.

Jonna did not chastise her. "My parents didn't have the same problems I have to contend with," she said gently. "I'm not so sure they had secrets to keep. I know you wonder at my reluctance to share our mission with Captain Thorne, but I hope I have given you reason to trust my judgment."

"Of course," Mrs. Davis said quickly. "I can tell you I was sorely tempted to speak to Mr. Sheridan while you were gone. When he asked if there was anything he could do to help and I thought of how our house was filling up with girls, all of them needing an escort to the next station, I considered telling him what we were about." The housekeeper paused. "But I didn't."

There was an unfamiliar pressure in Jonna's chest. Belatedly she realized she had been holding her breath. Now she let it out slowly. "I'm glad, Mrs. Davis."

"I remember you said you didn't want Mr. Sheridan to know, and I honored your wishes. I'll do the same now."

"I appreciate that." Jonna felt the beginnings of a headache building behind her eyes. "I believe the fewer people who know, the longer we can keep our station running. And that means we can help more young women. That's still important to me, Mrs. Davis. I don't want anything to interfere with that, including my marriage to Captain Thorne."

The housekeeper was struck again by Jonna's earnestness. It had been like this from the very beginning. Just over three years ago Jonna had approached her with the glimmer of an idea, and since then had done everything in her power to make it a reality. The passion had been in her voice as much then as now.

Mrs. Davis knew her employer cared deeply what happened to the black servants she took into her home. It had been Jonna's plan to make her Beacon Hill mansion a way station on the Underground Railroad and to assign herself the job of conductor.

Besides Mrs. Davis and the young women Jonna helped, there was only one other person who knew of Jonna's role on the Railroad: the conductor of the station immediately before, the one who brought the girls to Jonna. Only Jonna knew that person's identity, just as she was the only one who knew the names of people willing to take the girls on the next leg of their journey. In Jonna's absence the two girls who had arrived came without any escort that the housekeeper could see, yet she knew somewhere nearby the conductor was watching to make sure his passengers had arrived safely and were taken in as usual.

"It will be as you wish," Mrs. Davis said. "The rooms can be made ready this evening."

Jonna smiled at that. "Tomorrow will be fine, Mrs. Davis."

"It's no trouble. We have the additional help, remember."

"Very well. Please speak to Captain Thorne to find out what his needs are. Someone may have to go to the harbor, or perhaps to the rooms he rented, to get all his belongings."

"I understand."

"And I would like the carriage made ready. I'll be going to see Mr. Sheridan."

"Today?" Mrs. Davis asked. "But you only—"

"Now," Jonna said. While Decker was at the harbor she was presented with her best chance to see Grant alone. "I'm feeling well enough," she went on, anticipating her house-keeper's next protest.

Mrs. Davis stood. She smoothed the front of her apron. "Very well. Shall I send Delores to help you dress?"

"Yes. I think I'd like to talk to her."

The housekeeper's smile was wistful. She knew what that meant. It would only be a matter of a day or so before Delores disappeared. "I shall miss that girl. Smart as a whip, she is. Quick to pick up everything. It's hard to believe she only knew field work before she came here."

"That speaks to your guidance," Jonna said. "You do very well with all the girls." It had always been part of Jonna's plan to provide some training for the young women who passed through her station. Mrs. Davis assisted them with needlework and cooking, teaching the skills from scratch if need be or refining talents they already had. More impor-tantly, there were lessons in reading and writing in the eve-ning. Education was the most consequential aspect of what Jonna wanted to provide. She saw it as vital to their survival. The responsibility that came with their newfound freedom meant they had to be able to care for themselves. They had to be able to work.

Jonna considered Delores. She had been under Mrs.

Davis's care for six months. "Does Delores know what she wants to do?"

"A hat shop," Mrs. Davis said. "The dear girl wants to own a hat shop. When I suggested that perhaps she could work in one she told me that working for someone else wasn't part of her dream. I think it's your example she wants to emulate."

"Oh, she can do better than follow my example," Jonna said, smiling. "And I shall be happy to tell her that myself. Please, see to the carriage and send Delores to me."

By the time Jonna arrived at Grant Sheridan's home, her headache had reached pounding proportions. When her driver helped her down from the carriage, she asked him to wait but did not accept his offer to escort her up the walk. She knew she was pale and still unsteady on her feet at odd moments, yet she didn't believe that she couldn't make it to Grant's front door without assistance.

It made her fall on the entrance steps all the more humiliating.

In the end it was Jonna's driver *and* Grant's butler who lent their shoulders to support her into the house. She was shown to the receiving parlor and made comfortable on the divan. In spite of her protests, a pillow was placed under her twisted ankle and the butler ordered a cold compress. There was so much in the way of fussing at first that several minutes went by before Jonna realized Grant wasn't in residence.

"He's expected back shortly," the butler told her. "And he won't forgive me if I let you leave. I anticipate he'll want me to summon the doctor."

Jonna looked to her driver. He was hovering in the parlor entrance, concerned, but clearly chafing from her earlier refusal to allow him to help. Now that she wanted his assistance, he had decided not to offer any. "I will wait half an hour," she said. "Under no circumstances are you to send for a doctor. This sprain is of no consequence, and I won't be mollycoddled."

The butler inclined his narrow head slightly in acknowledgment of her wishes but with no indication that he intended to honor them. He backed out of the room, shutting the doors behind him, and directed Jonna's driver to the kitchen where he could take some refreshment.

Sighing, Jonna leaned her head back against the brocade upholstery. Was nothing ever simple? She rotated her ankle slowly, grimacing as she did so and wondering how this would change the plans she had just made with Delores. On the heels of that thought came another about how she would explain this mishap to Decker.

Her sigh this time was more of a groan. Jonna closed her eyes in response to the throbbing behind them. If she could only rest she was certain a solution would reveal itself.

Grant Sheridan was standing over her when she awoke. He placed one hand on her shoulder as Jonna instinctively made to rise from her vulnerable position. "Don't trouble yourself," he said. "I didn't mean to wake you."

"Did you just arrive?" She glanced past him to the large recessed windows that faced the street. The heavy velvet drapes had been drawn, but through the gold fringe that edged the material she could see that it was already dark outside. "How late is it?"

"It's just after six," he told her. "I arrived thirty or so minutes ago."

Alarmed now, Jonna shrugged off the hand on her shoulder and sat up. "You shouldn't have let me sleep," she said. "I told your man I could only wait half an hour."

"I suppose he was confused. You certainly looked as if you needed to sleep."

Jonna removed the compress from her ankle and put her legs over the side of the divan. She had not even heard anyone come in to attend her. On the table at her side was the tea the butler had promised, stone cold now. Jonna rubbed her temples wearily. "Will you have someone inform my driver I need to leave?"

"I sent him back to your house. I told him I would see you delivered there myself."

Somehow Jonna wasn't surprised by the answer, only disappointed. "I wish you hadn't done that, Grant."

"I'm sorry," he said, no apology in his voice. "But it's done now, isn't it?" Grant twisted the brass knob on the table lamp and raised the wick. The circle of warm light grew wider, casting its glow over Jonna's raised face. "Perhaps you should tell me why you've come. I understand *Huntress* only docked early this afternoon. Had I been at the harbor I would have met you. Dare I hope to be flattered by your presence so soon in my home?" he observed the stillness of her features. "I thought not," he said quietly.

Jonna watched Grant cross the room to where a small gateleg table was set against the wall. It held several decanters of liquor. He lifted the crystal stopper of one and poured himself a tumbler of the palest amber liquid. When he held it up in mocking salute, Jonna had the grace to turn away. The regret in her voice was real. "I never set out to hurt you," she said. "Any number of times I tried to make it clear I saw no future together for us. I thought we would remain friendly competitors."

"But not friends, eh?" Grant asked without inflection. "You've fallen in love with Decker Thorne."

"I've married him."

In spite of the tightness in Grant's chest, he was still thinking clearly. "Are you making a distinction?"

Jonna didn't answer his question. "I've married him," she said again. "It's what I've come to tell you."

Grant nodded and knocked back a third of his drink, never taking his eyes from her. "You didn't want me to learn it from anyone else, is that it?"

"That's right."

"Following your own code of honor."

Jonna felt herself flush at his withering, almost spiteful tone. She didn't deserve that from him. Her chin came up a notch. "I'm trying to do what's right, Grant. I don't require your forgiveness. I've done nothing wrong. If you don't want to associate yourself with me any longer then know that it's your choice."

Grant laughed. He absently rubbed his jaw. The memory of Decker clipping him to take Jonna away was still very fresh even if the bruise had long since faded. "As if your husband would permit that," he said scornfully.

"Decker doesn't have any say in it." She stood. Little of her weight was able to rest on her injured foot. Her militant stance was undermined by a slight bob and weave as she struggled for balance. "I'm still very much my own person."

Grant regarded her thoughtfully over the rim of his tumbler. The rigid line of his powerfully built shoulders relaxed slightly even as his nearly black eyes narrowed. "Yes," he said softly. "I can see that it's true. He hasn't the least idea how to handle you."

Gripping the curved arm of the divan, Jonna steadied herself. "I don't requiring handling, Grant, and I find it particularly loathsome that you think I do. This belief of yours that somehow I should be managed has always been an unattractive quality. Now I discover I'm quite weary of overlooking it. I appreciate that I've upset you. If you think about it, you'll realize that's only because you've held on to hope where I've always told you none existed. I've always been honest with you in saying that there would be no marriage. You have never been honest with yourself."

Grant set down his drink and crossed to where Jonna stood. He stopped within half an arm's length of her. Only her violet eyes flinched at his approach. The rest of her held ground. Grant raised one hand and touched her cheek. "Does Thorne know you're here?" he asked quietly.

"Yes."

One side of Grant's generous mouth curled in a sardonic smile. "You do better when you tell the truth, Jonna. I don't think Thorne is so very different from me in regard to you, and I wouldn't have let you come here."

Jonna wondered at her rising panic. "I'd like to leave, Grant. There's no need for you to drive me yourself. I'll be—"

The fingers that had grazed her cheek fell to curve around her throat. "It's no trouble for me," he said. "I *do* keep my word." He closed the distance between them. "Have I told you before that it's not over between us, Jonna? It's not, you know. Your marriage doesn't really mean very much to me, not when we were promised to each other years ago."

Though there was no pressure from Grant's hand, Jonna felt as if her throat were closing. "Please let me go," she whispered.

He didn't respond to her request. "May I kiss the bride?"

The question wasn't asked out of courtesy. Jonna heard it more as a warning that required no answer from her. She tried to avert her head, but Grant's fingers tightened immediately. His grip wasn't painful, only insistent. Her mouth flattened.

Grant's lips were faintly damp from his drink. She could

smell scotch on his breath as his mouth touched the corner of hers. Jonna's hands came up between them, and she pushed at his shoulders. The effort unbalanced her. Grant's free arm came around her waist. In other circumstances she would have been grateful for the help, but Jonna was not so naive that she couldn't divine his purpose was to secure her, not to offer support.

Grant's mouth moved across hers. The edge of his tongue sought entry between her lips. Jonna's fingers tightened on his jacket, but this was her only response. She was rigid in his arms.

From the doorway a throat was cleared. Jonna was certain Grant heard the sound as well, but he didn't lift his head. His shoulder kept her from seeing who stood there, and Grant's mouth on hers kept her from appealing for help.

Decker Thorne laid his hand over the butler's forearm. "I don't believe clearing your throat again will get their attention." His tone was quiet, his manner calm. There was nothing about his appearance to suggest he was unsettled by what he was witnessing. "Some other action seems to be necessary." Even as he was speaking he saw Grant start to straighten and pull away from Jonna. "There," Decker said lightly. "It only required a few words."

The butler's narrow face became severely pinched with disapproval. His apology was to his employer, not their guest. "I'm sorry, Mr. Sheridan, but he insisted on coming in here without announcement."

"It's all right, Emmerth. You can go. Don't bother having my carriage ready. I'm sure Captain Thorne is here to collect his wife."

The butler inclined his head once, then backed out of the room, closing the doors behind him.

Grant's hand had fallen away from Jonna's throat, but his

other arm still curved around her waist. "I understand congratulations are in order," he said casually. "May I offer mine?"

"As long as you don't kiss me."

For a moment Grant Sheridan was speechless, then his dark eyes saluted Decker and he smiled appreciatively. "I see you understand that's all it was."

"Of course," Decker said. "If I suspected otherwise I'd have to demand satisfaction. I'm not adept at pistols. You?"

"Expert."

Decker nodded. "That's what I thought. Swords?"

"Never lifted one."

"Neither have I. What about bare knuckles?"

Grant knew Decker was thinking of the roundhouse punch that had laid him out cold. "I can hold my own if I'm not blindsided." His smile deepened, but did not reach his eyes. "It's all moot, isn't it? There's no reason to demand satisfaction where no offense has been given."

Decker's cool blue gaze shifted to Jonna. "Is he right?" he asked. "Has there been offense?"

Jonna found she had no voice. Nothing that had happened these last few minutes seemed quite real to her. Not able to meet Decker's gaze directly, she shook her head.

It was Grant who admonished her for this poor response. "Oh, Jonna. You'll have to do better than that. I would be forced to champion you myself were I confronted with that wounded look in your eyes. A more encouraging defense, please."

Jonna raised her eyes. Tears threatened, but she held them back and spoke past the dry, stinging ache in her throat. "Grant was only wishing me well."

Decker studied her pale features a moment longer. His

own expression was closed. "You're ready to leave?" he asked.

"Yes."

"Very well." Decker held out his hand, palm up. When Jonna didn't take even a single step toward him one of Decker's brows arched in question. He glanced at Grant. "Perhaps if you removed your arm from my wife's waist?"

"If I remove my arm," Grant said, "Jonna will most likely fall on her face. You were unaware that she twisted her ankle?"

Decker showed his first real emotion since entering the room. A measure of coolness left his eyes. "Jonna?"

"I'm afraid it's true. I did not have my land legs after all." She rested one hand on the divan again, then looked to Grant. "I'll be fine now."

Grant let his hand fall away. "Of course." He held both hands up in a gesture of innocence. "Steady as she goes."

Mustering the remnants of her dignity, Jonna hobbled forward. She placed her hand in Decker's and felt his warm grip close over hers. It was as if she were being extended a lifeline, and she could not hide the relief she experienced when his arm came around to support her.

"Do you have a coat?" Decker asked.

Grant intervened. "I'll get it."

Jonna was only quiet until Grant's footfalls had receded in the hallway. "Let's not wait here," she said. "I want to go to the front door."

Decker didn't question her request. He escorted her into the entrance hall. Grant was there momentarily with Jonna's coat. He held out the garnet velvet cloak for her to slip into, but Decker politely took it from him. Grant smiled blandly and opened the door for them. No pleasantries were exchanged now. By mutual, though silent, agreement, the farce that had been played out in the parlor had ended.

From the doorstep Grant watched Decker help Jonna into their carriage. No matter how much Grant willed it to happen, she did not at any time glance back at the house. "It doesn't matter," he said under his breath. "It's not over until I say it is."

Decker's silence was unnerving. The anticipation of what he *would* say was more terrible than anything he might have said in that moment. Would he be angry? she wondered. Cutting? Sarcastic? She had disobeyed him. Did he want revenge? Perhaps that was too strong a word, she thought. He might only demand satisfaction.

Jonna blushed. She felt Decker's eyes on her, but he didn't ask any questions and she couldn't explain the wayward thought that had raised a flush in her cheeks. She stared out the window instead and prayed he would say something sooner rather than later.

Mrs. Davis had the staff more than halfway to making the adjoining bedrooms in the east wing ready. It was to this new room that Jonna was shown. Decker deposited her on the unmade bed with the same regard he would have given his carpetbag.

"Can we hope that you'll remain here this time?" he asked. They were the first words he had spoken since leaving Grant's.

"I would be more comfortable downstairs until this room is ready."

"I'm sure you would." As he spoke two maids marched in carrying an armload of gowns. They stopped abruptly, uncertainty in their dark eyes. Decker motioned to them to go about their work. "But here you'll have supervision," he said. "Someone will bring you dinner. I'm having mine downstairs."

Jonna watched him go to the door. That was all? she wondered. He wasn't going to say anything else? "Decker?"

He paused on the threshold. "Yes?"

What was it she could say? What did she *want* to say? Apologizing occurred to her. So did thanking him. Both sentiments clogged her throat along with the tears she refused to shed. "Nothing," she said finally. "It's nothing."

He waited a moment longer, his eyes deliberately holding hers. Then he left.

It was only then that Jonna allowed herself the luxury of sobbing.

The next time Decker entered her chamber it was from the door that connected their dressing rooms. Mrs. Davis's small army of helpers had transformed the unused bedchambers into airy and appealing living quarters. Fresh linens and bedcovers had been brought in, the draperies had been aired and replaced. All of Jonna's familiar things surrounded her again. The dressing table held her brushes and combs and ribbons. Delicate crystal bottles of perfume shared space with her small jars of creams. The chairs that flanked the fireplace were cream brocade now and the rocker was absent, but at the foot of her bed was a spacious trunk covered with a fringed ivory shawl.

It was Decker's thoughtfulness that added the vase of flowers on one bedside table and a small selection of books on the other.

Absent of the flowers and a few lacy flourishes, his own quarters were similarly appointed. The dressing room which joined the bedchambers held two large armoires. His contained less than a quarter of the clothing that filled Jonna's to capacity.

He closed the door behind him and leaned against it. On

board *Huntress* it had been easier to ignore the things that separated them. In Jonna's home they were not so simple to dismiss—and it *was* her home. Marriage had not changed her thinking about his place in her life or in her bed. They might share a suite, but not a room. Clearly, she meant for him to remain a guest. His presence would be tolerated but not welcomed.

Jonna turned on her side. Her complexion was flushed with the warmth of sleep. Lamplight bathed her face. She stirred once, slipping her hand under her cheek, and her breath was drawn in by an abrupt little yawn.

Decker went to the fireplace and stoked the logs. He glanced at his hazy reflection in the windows. The drapes were open and frost had painted ice flowers on each pane of glass. When he set down the poker and turned around it was to find Jonna watching him.

"Mrs. Davis said you didn't eat dinner," he said. "I only came to ask if you needed anything before I retire. It was not my intention to wake you."

Jonna's eyes lifted to the mantel clock beyond Decker's shoulder. It was only a few minutes after ten. She could not remember falling asleep after she refused the dinner tray, but that had been hours earlier. "It's all right. And thank you, but no, I don't want anything."

Decker's quietly amused smile revealed itself as Jonna's stomach operated independently of her mind and rumbled with some force. "Would you like to reconsider?" he asked. "Mrs. Davis gave me a pot of hot cocoa."

Jonna pushed herself upright and somewhat self-consciously brushed a strand of dark hair away from her face. She was aware that her eyelids were still puffy from her self-pitying bout of crying and that her hair was disheveled. "I think I'd like cocoa," she said.

He nodded and disappeared into his room.

Jonna threw off the covers and scrambled out of bed. She ground her teeth as her injured foot struck the floor hard, but managed to swallow her groan. Plucking her brush off the dressing table, she made several hard passes through her hair, then glanced in the mirror, knuckled sleep from her eyes, and all but dove back into bed as she heard Decker passing through the dressing room.

He paused on entering her bedchamber. Observing her flushed features, the tight grimace of pain around her mouth, and her slightly labored breathing, he asked, "Are you well?"

She nodded with less than convincing assurance.

Decker's eyes narrowed on her face, then strayed to her hair. He glanced at the dressing table. His smile was wry. "I would have handed you your brush."

Jonna suddenly had a vision of *Huntress* with her sails taken up. Deflated in much the same way, her shoulders slumped. "It would have been kinder of you not to mention it."

"Possibly." He pushed the vase of flowers and table lamp to one side and set down the tray. Pouring her a cup of cocoa, he said, "I don't know that I'm feeling kindly toward you."

Jonna's fingers wrapped around the cup he handed her. He would say something now, she thought. He would take her to task for her badly thought-out visit to Grant's. She waited . . . and he said nothing. "You're leaving?" she asked as he headed toward the dressing room.

"Yes." He idly raked his dark hair with his hand. "Is there something you need?"

Your company. The words tumbled through her mind, but tangled on her tongue. "I . . . I thought you might want to . . ."

"Yes?"

"Aren't you going to say anything about Grant?" she blurted.

Decker's brows lifted in a parody of thoughtfulness and surprise. "I can't think of even one thing I want to say about Grant Sheridan."

His calm was maddening. "You're deliberately misunderstanding me," she said.

"I'm not sure how. You've said several times that I have no right to interfere where you and Sheridan are concerned. You went to his home expressly against my wishes. What is it that you expect me to say now?"

She said it quickly before she couldn't say it all. "That I was wrong and you were right."

Decker's expression was implacable, but in his silence he seemed to be considering. "And is that true?" he asked after a moment.

"Yes." She nodded once to add weight to her statement. "Yes, it's true."

"Well, if you know that now, there doesn't seem much point in my repeating it. Let's just leave it there, shall we?"

Had their positions been reversed Jonna knew she would not have been so magnanimous. "All right," she said.

Decker only hesitated briefly, then started to go.

"There is one thing," Jonna said.

He only glanced over his shoulder this time.

"I shouldn't at all mind some company."

"I'll send for Mrs. Davis. She said she's—"

"I meant your company." Jonna set aside her cocoa.

Decker didn't say anything immediately. "I don't think so, Jonna. I meant it when I said I'm not feeling kindly toward you just now."

Stunned, she could only watch him leave.

★ ★ ★ ★ ★

Always an early riser, Jonna thought she would see Decker at breakfast, but when she went to the dining room she was informed that he had left an hour before. She did not see him at the warehouse either, though there was no reason she should. Jack Quincy occupied most of her time, reviewing the finances and the warehouse rebuilding figures. Jonna went over the line's schedules and recent manifests. Against Jack's advice she removed Decker's name from the rotation.

"Did you talk to him about this?" Jack asked. "I believe he's planning on making the next run to Charleston."

"I don't have to consult him," she said a little brittlely. "I'm still in charge, am I not? My abduction to London didn't change that."

Jack whistled softly under his breath and pulled on one of his thick, slate gray brows. "You're still in charge," he said.

Jonna suddenly sat back in her chair. "I'm sorry, Jack." She glanced up at him as he leaned over her desk. "Would you mind terribly if we finished this tomorrow? I think I'd like to go down to the ships."

"Decker's not there."

"I didn't say I wanted to see him, did I?" She managed to hold Jack's suspicious gaze without giving anything away. "I've been considering some new designs. I'd like to hear what Captains Thomas and Norton think. Decker's already given me his opinion."

Jack pushed away from the desk. "Very well. I'll take you down myself."

Reaching for her cane, Jonna used it to steady herself as she stood. As casually as she could she asked, "Where is Captain Thorne?"

Jack held out Jonna's cloak to her. "Last I heard he was going to pay Sheridan a visit, at the man's office."

287

All pretense of disinterest vanished from Jonna's face. "Did he tell you that?"

"Jeremy Dodd passed it on. I supposed that was a reliable source."

Jonna was sure it was. Her stomach turned over. "What would you give for Decker's chances in a fight against Grant?"

Jack didn't hesitate. "Not much. Decker would have to get lucky."

"I'd like to go home, Jack. Everything else can wait."

Delores Turner looked down at the envelope Jonna thrust in her hands. Her slim fingers curled around it. Tears hovered on the edge of her lower lashes. "It's too much," she said quietly. "I can't accept it."

"You don't have any choice," Jonna said. "I won't take it back. It will lie here in the snow for some other person to find, someone who might be infinitely less deserving than you."

Delores shook her head. "I heard rumors that you give us girls money for a good start, but I never heard anyone say it could be this much."

"No one's ever wanted to own her own hat shop before."

This generosity took Delores's breath away. "I'll find some way to repay you, Miss Remington." A blush crept under her dusky skin. "Mrs. Thorne," she corrected herself. "I will."

"And I will be happy to accept it, but there's no time limit, and I'd be just as happy with a hat." Jonna pressed the younger woman's hands together over the envelope; then she pointed to the only house on the cobblestone street with a lamp in the window that cast a blue light. "This is as far as I can take you, Delores. Mr. and Mrs. Wright will see that you get from Salem to Montreal. And for your own safety, don't talk about the money to anyone."

Delores nodded quickly. "I understand." She stuffed the envelope inside her bodice and drew her cloak closed again. "If there's anything I can ever do for you, Mrs. Thorne . . ." Her voice trailed away, for she was unable to imagine how Jonna might find her help valuable.

"Actually, there is something," Jonna said. She steadied the horse beside her and leaned closer to shelter herself from the cold wind. The wheels of the small two-seat carriage she had rented for this trip creaked loudly on the deserted street. "I was wondering what you might know of Falconer."

Delores's face betrayed her disappointment. She had very much wanted to be of service. "I know the name. There's few like me who don't. But he's not the one who brought me north." Her dark eyes remained troubled as she added, "There's Rachael, though. You might ask her."

Jonna thought she must have misunderstood. "She doesn't speak."

"I wouldn't put too much stock in that, Mrs. Thorne. It's odd about Rachael. I can't pry a word out of her during the day—no one can—but I've heard her say things in her sleep." Delores's voice lowered to a mere whisper. "And one of the things I've heard her say was that man's name."

"Thank you," Jonna said graciously, but she wasn't hopeful. Delores, in her eagerness to be helpful, was most likely fanciful.

"There's one other thing," Delores said. "I'm only speaking for myself here, and I may not have the right, but I'm glad you married the captain instead of the other one. You couldn't have been happy with the likes of Mr. Sheridan."

Jonna was taken aback by this comment, but she simply inclined her head, accepting it. "You'd better go, Delores. God's speed."

Impulsively, the younger woman hugged Jonna. Then she hurried off in the direction of the next safe house. Jonna waited until Delores disappeared behind the clapboard home and the lamp was removed from the window. Certain that her passenger was in good hands, Jonna climbed onto the carriage and took up the reins with her gloved hands. It would be eight o'clock before she reached the outskirts of Boston, another twenty minutes before she returned the rented hack and walked home.

She wondered if Decker had remarked on her absence at dinner. Had he thought she would be waiting for him, prepared to fuss over his injuries or to thank him for throwing another punch at Grant Sheridan?

Jonna snapped the reins smartly, and the carriage rolled forward. She ducked her head against an eddy of frigid air. Having Delores's welfare to think of provided her with sufficient reason not to dwell on Decker's. It had also provided an excuse to be gone from the house. The foreboding she had experienced at the office, then later at home, had only been marginally relieved by applying herself to helping Delores. Jonna felt the full impact of it return as she considered the inevitable confrontation with Decker.

"I'm not feeling kindly toward you just now," she whispered.

It was just as well, she thought, that the words were carried away by the wind. She couldn't hold them in her heart.

Eleven

Jonna's feet made new tracks in the snow as she hurried up the walk to her home. The skirt of her gown brushed the fresh powder creating a small cloud of flakes behind her that resembled a comet's tail.

She stamped her feet as she entered the foyer and removed her hat and scarf. The house was quiet, almost eerily so. Jonna supposed it was no different than usual at this time of the evening, but she was used to being part of the quiet, not the source of disruption. She was slipping out of her cloak when a servant coming out of the dining room, saw her, and came quickly to her assistance.

"Thank you, Virginia," Jonna relinquished her belongings and placed her hands on her cheeks to warm them. "Mrs. Davis is with the girls?"

Virginia nodded. A dark red curl slipped from under her cap, and she hastily pushed it back. "They're having their lessons. I'm the lookout in the event the captain wants Mrs. Davis for something."

"I see." Jonna thought Virginia seemed pleased with this responsibility. It showed in full measure the trust Mrs. Davis had in her. Virginia was an employee of long standing, but this assignment drew her into the housekeeper's inner circle of confidantes. "He's home, then."

"Hours ago. He's waiting for you in the—"

"Library," Jonna finished for her. "I know. I see the light under the door." She smoothed her skirt and took a calming breath. "Very well. Bring a pot of tea, please." It was not so much that Jonna required a warming drink, but rather that she anticipated needing the diversion the servant's entry would provide. She actually considered ignoring Decker altogether and going straight to her room. It was the very cowardice of that act that prompted her to move in the direction of the library.

Decker looked up as the doors opened. Jonna was framed between them for a moment before she stepped into the room.

"Jonna." He said her name quietly, but not in greeting. His tone was too resigned to be welcoming. Decker folded the newspaper he had been reading and placed it on the table beside him. He started to rise, but she waved him back.

Crossing the room to the fireplace, Jonna warmed her hands in front of the flames. She glanced at the mantel clock. It was almost nine, later even than she had thought. Nearly twenty-four hours had passed since she had seen her husband, and now she was finding it difficult to face him.

"Would you like to go first, or shall I?" he asked.

She felt the unfamiliar weariness of his tone as a weight at the back of her neck. Her head bent forward. She closed her eyes. "I don't suppose it matters."

"No, I don't suppose it does." He stared at her back. "Will you have a seat?"

Trying not to show her reluctance, Jonna took the large armchair opposite him. She sat with her hands folded primly in her lap. Her eyes met his. "Jack told me you went to see Grant this morning."

"That's right."

There were no bruises that she could see. When he had started to rise as she came into the room there had been no hesitation, just his usual casual grace. He didn't appear to be favoring one side over the other. His hands rested lightly on the arms of the leather chair. There were no scraped knuckles. "Was there a fight?"

"Did you think there would be?" He saw her violet eyes flicker. "Never mind. I can see for myself that's precisely what you thought. Perhaps I don't always live down to your expectation after all. Tell me, Jonna, did you decide I wouldn't command *Huntress* again before or after you found out I went to Sheridan's offices?"

"One had nothing to do with the other. I didn't do it to punish you."

"No?"

"Of course not. I resent that you think I'm so small-minded."

Decker sat forward. His forearms rested on his knees. "So why am I not assigned to the Charleston run?"

"No one is taking *Huntress* out," Jonna said. "I have some modifications I want to make. It will be two weeks or more before she's outfitted in the manner I desire."

"You never mentioned this before."

"You're not privy to my every thought."

Decker let that pass. "Jack didn't say anything about changes."

"I don't tell him everything either."

Decker looked down at his hands, half expecting to see open wounds where she'd drawn blood with her stinging tone and the sharp edge of her tongue. Rather than flinching, Decker raised his eyes and regarded her frankly. "And after the modifications are made?" he asked. "Can I expect to command *Huntress* then?"

"I haven't decided."

He nodded once, accepting that answer. "You should know that I'm considering taking a position with another line."

Jonna recoiled as if struck. "What?"

Decker did not repeat himself. "I spoke with Sheridan about a command on one of his ships."

"That's why you went there this morning?" She was clearly incredulous. "But you didn't know that I had taken you off the roster."

"One had nothing to do with the other," he said, turning Jonna's words back on her. "It's occurred to me that perhaps I shouldn't work for Remington Shipping any longer."

"That's ridiculous. You can't work for the competition."

Decker shrugged. "Nothing's been decided," he said. "Sheridan was suspicious of my motives. My proposal took him by surprise. I believe he thought I was there to cause trouble. As it happened, I was very well behaved."

Jonna tried to imagine how the conversation might have gone. "Then there was no mention of my visit to his home."

"I understood that was settled." He paused a beat. "It is, isn't it? There's nothing more you want to tell me about last night. Nothing else about that kiss I observed."

Jonna felt as if her throat was closing. "No," she said quickly, swallowing hard. "There's nothing."

The doors to the library opened, and Virginia entered with Jonna's tea. The interruption was as timely as Jonna hoped it would be. The minute the maid spent fiddling with the service and pouring her tea was an opportunity for Jonna to compose herself.

"I don't like the idea of you working for another line," Jonna said when she and Decker were alone again. "I wish you had discussed it with me."

Decker pretended to consider her words. "And in exchange?" he asked. "What are you prepared to discuss with me?"

Jonna was silent.

"How about your whereabouts this afternoon and evening? I expected to find you home when I got here. Jack said you left your office this morning."

"That's true," Jonna said. "And I came home and I left again. Didn't Mrs. Davis tell you? I went to the shipyards."

"No, she didn't mention that." A smile edged his mouth, but it didn't reach his eyes. "Was that the story she had agreed to tell for you?"

"I beg your pardon?"

"It's no good being indignant. Not when you're already caught out in the lie." He held up one hand to stop her from digging the hole any deeper. "Mrs. Davis didn't tell me you were at the shipyards because before she had a chance to do so I told her that was where I had been. Our paths should have crossed somewhere today, Jonna. You know very well they didn't."

It was the last thing she'd expected to hear. What business had taken Decker to the shipyards? Had he really been there or was he bluffing, hoping that she would confirm his suspicions? "I visited several different sites," she said. "The Garnet yards. Landon's. All part of the research for outfitting *Huntress*. Perhaps that's how we missed each other."

Decker's gaze didn't waver. His eyes bored into hers. "Were you with Sheridan?"

"No!" Jonna's cup rattled in the saucer as she set it aside. "No," she said more softly. "I didn't see him at all. I wasn't with him." She was struck suddenly by how much she wanted Decker to believe her. "I know what you think you saw last night at Grant's home. Indeed, I don't know how you could help but think the worst of me. I don't regret my decision to tell Grant about our marriage, but I regret that I went there without you. I told you last night that you were right, Decker.

I didn't make that admission lightly, and I haven't changed my mind about it, I didn't go behind your back to meet him today."

There was no mistaking the earnestness in her voice. If she wasn't telling the truth, Decker thought, then at the very least she thought it was important for him to think she was. "I believe you," he said at last. "About Sheridan. What I won't accept is that you were at the shipyards."

Before Jonna could reply, Decker was on his feet. He was going to walk out, she realized. He was going to leave her alone again. Perhaps only for this evening. Perhaps for the rest of her life. Something akin to panic turned her stomach over. She didn't have time to consider what that reaction meant, she only knew she had to do something about it. She stood suddenly. Behind his retreating back she raised her arm to reach out to him. "I wasn't at the shipyards," she said in a rush.

Decker paused, then slowly turned. He'd missed Jonna's outstretched hand but not the way her slender frame seemed to lean toward him or her eyes appealed to him. She did not look so different than she had on *Huntress*'s listing deck, waiting for him to take her by the hand. Then, as now, she hadn't been able to ask for help, but she had left no doubt it was what she wanted.

"You're not going to tell me where you were," he said quietly. "Are you?"

Her mouth was cotton dry. "I can't." She saw him hesitate. For once the calm she associated with him did not seem to be so effortless. "I can't," she repeated hollowly.

Decker was convinced that she believed what she was saying. Wherever she had been, whatever she had done, she was certain she couldn't trust him with it. "Very well," he said. "But know that you're alone by choice, Jonna."

This time she had no words to call him back.

Lying on her side in bed, Jonna watched the flicker of light coming from under Decker's door. The door to their shared dressing room stood open on her side, making it seem that Decker wasn't so very far away this time.

Separate rooms had been a necessity, she reminded herself, but the thought was cold comfort. She had begun applying herself to the problem her marriage presented while still aboard *Huntress*. The demands of running a station for the Underground meant that her escort was sometimes required in the middle of the night. How could she share a bed with Decker under those circumstances?

It had occurred to her that she could pass on the duties of conducting to Mrs. Davis or close her station altogether. Neither of those ideas was palatable. Nor was sleeping alone.

She considered telling Decker about her involvement with the Underground Railroad, but the consequences were enormous if he couldn't keep the trust. It was not that Jonna had anything to fear from Boston's authorities. In many circles, especially those that Grant Sheridan frequented, she would be applauded for her activities. But in the South, where she traded, Remington ships would no longer be in demand. Their holds would be empty or their cargoes left to rot; or, worse yet, fire would destroy a ship in the harbor.

Jonna knew all those things could happen. They had happened to Grant as soon as he became vocal about abolition. She admired him for not backing down or taking the quieter, more secretive approach she had, but she also did not know how his business survived. He had lost two ships to sabotage, one in Charleston, another at sea. In both instances the crews had survived, but later many of the men went elsewhere for jobs. When Jonna questioned him about it, he had been rather philosophical about the loss of the ships and the men, but he hadn't taken it lightly. Ultimately Grant's response had been to change the focus of his trade from points south to the Far East. Occasional business still took his ships to Charleston, but he himself was often on board, almost as if he was daring saboteurs to make trouble while he was present.

Jonna did not think she was as brave as all that. Grant may have found a way for Sheridan Shipping to manage against the odds, but she wasn't sure she could do the same for Remington. Keeping the line running was vital to the welfare of hundreds of people, not just the scores of young women who had passed through her station.

Jonna's eyes were drawn again to the flickering strip of light under Decker's door. It was an enormous trust she would be placing in his hands if she told him what she had been about or what she was about to do. She could lose more than Remington Shipping, she thought. She could lose herself.

Decker sat facing the fireplace, his long legs stretched out in front of him. He had never fully readied himself for bed. His shirt was unbuttoned and his feet were bare, but that was as far as he had gotten. Servants had turned down his bed and laid a nightshirt and dressing gown at the foot of it, but climbing into that bed alone was not appealing.

The papers in his hands rustled as he leafed through them a second time. He sighed, not certain what he was looking for or what he had expected to find. Jonna's ill-advised meeting with Grant had offered Decker a perfect pretext for visiting Sheridan at his offices. Grant was properly suspicious, Decker recalled, but suspicious of all the wrong things. It apparently hadn't occurred to Sheridan that he needed to be less concerned about facing Decker than about leaving him alone.

Sheridan's desk had been locked, but it had presented no challenge to Decker. While Sheridan had been called away briefly to the outer office and then to his warehouse, Decker had rifled the drawers. There was no time to read papers in the office and no possibility that ledgers wouldn't be missed, so he had opted for taking a sampling of correspondence. Less clear in Decker's mind was what he might find or even what he hoped to find. He could acknowledge his judgment about Sheridan was clouded by the man's interest in Jonna. He also knew he couldn't allow that to continue.

If Grant Sheridan was the one person who could help Falconer, then Decker had to find some way to answer his own misgivings.

Stacking the correspondence neatly, Decker placed it upside down on the table beside him. He turned down the lamp until the flame sputtered and was finally extinguished. The fireplace provided his bedchamber's sole illumination. Heat bathed his bare feet and the backs of his hands. He closed his eyes and considered sleeping where he sat. It was not so different than being strapped to a chair at the helm of *Huntress*. It didn't matter that there was no storm visible on the horizon. There was always one brewing when he thought of Jonna Remington.

Behind him the door opened. Decker didn't stir. Had she come to beard the lion in his den or simply to murder him in his sleep? Either was a possibility, and Decker gave no favor to one over the other.

Jonna padded lightly across Decker's room. The floor was cool on her bare feet until she reached the half circle of heat and light in front of the fireplace. She surveyed his quiet, youthful features and wished he had gone to bed before falling asleep. She would have crawled in beside him and laid her head close to his, perhaps even shared his pillow. She would have watched him sleep and drawn a measure of peace from his even breathing and unguarded calm. She might even have risked laying one hand on his chest before she fell asleep herself.

It was out of the question now. There was no room for her.

Jonna glanced at the door. She hadn't closed it in the event she required a quick exit. She resisted going toward it. Heat licked the backs of her legs pleasantly. Crossing Decker's room again seemed like a retreat. It was not in the least appealing even when common sense prompted her.

Instead she knelt beside his outstretched legs and faced the fire. Her shoulder nudged his knee. That small movement stilled Jonna. She waited, wondering if he had felt the intrusion, wondering if he would acknowledge it. In time, when there was no reaction, her head grew heavy. There was no more natural response than to lay her head against his thigh.

Decker looked down at the top of Jonna's head. The deep, rich highlights in her hair surfaced from under the fire's glow. There were shades of coffee and licorice and ebony, and the flames lent it the iridescent luster of a black pearl. He picked up a thick strand and massaged the curling end between his thumb and forefinger. There was no texture so fine as that of a woman's hair.

With some effort he let his hand fall away.

"Don't stop," Jonna said.

Decker's fingers hovered just above the nape of her neck. When he hesitated she raised her head and twisted partway around to see him. Her movement brought his palm against her cheek.

"Please," she said. "I don't want you to stop touching me."

"All right," he said quietly. When he came to his feet he brought her with him. Jonna stood naturally in the circle of his arms, her face lifted toward his. He was not smiling; his blue eyes were intent on hers.

"I won't change my mind," she whispered. "You said from now on it would be my choice. Well, *this* is my choice." Rising on tiptoe, Jonna placed her hands on Decker's shoulders; then she kissed him full on the mouth.

Decker's embrace tightened. Slight pressure at the small of her back brought her flush against him. He was aware of the tiny ripple in her middle as her abdomen contracted with the pull of an indrawn breath. He could make out the outline of her taut breasts, and feel the pleasant abrasiveness of her nipples as they scraped his chest. His hands moved lower, cupping her buttocks. She fit herself in the seat of his palms, her stance widened, and then she was cradling his erection with her thighs.

Jonna's fingers tightened on Decker's shoulders. She held herself steady as the very air around her seemed to shift. She kissed the corner of his mouth, then drew in his lower lip. She teased him with her teeth and tongue, and found herself pleasured by the play. His mouth moved under hers, in response to her overtures. His breath was warm and hinted at the sweetness of peppermint. She would taste of tea, she realized, and wished she had taken sugar with her drink. Decker deserved something more than the tart edge of her tongue.

The shape of her smile was pressed against his lips. He lifted his head and looked at her. The centers of her eyes were dark and wide, and a trace of her secretive little smile was left on her mouth. He didn't ask what she was thinking. He let her fingers thread together behind his neck and pull him close for another kiss.

She held his face still. Her lips were firm on his, her tongue pressed for entry. She felt his slight shudder when she deepened the kiss. Jonna only knew what she had been taught by him, and now she left no doubt that she had paid attention. When his hands tightened on her bottom she rubbed herself intimately against him. Her entire body provided a sweet caress. Decker felt the loss as a wrenching in his gut when she pulled away from him.

Jonna took his hand and led him to the bed. Her fingers slid along the opening of his shirt, and she pushed it off his shoulders. She kissed the warm skin of his chest and let the shirt fall to the floor. Her dressing gown followed almost immediately. Jonna pushed at the waistband of his trousers while he raised the hem of her nightshift. He stepped out of his clothes, and she ducked under hers.

She hardly knew where to look. The room's shadows were not deep enough to hide behind. In spite of her desire she was aware of her nakedness in a self-conscious way. It didn't help that she was very interested in his.

"Oh, Jonna," Decker said softly, his voice edged with quiet amusement. He tipped her chin upward. "Just kiss me. It will make things far simpler than you can imagine."

She did, and discovered he was right. Pushed as though by a force outside themselves, they tumbled onto the bed. Jonna made a small inarticulate sound as Decker's mouth caught her nipple and began to suckle. His teeth and tongue worried the swollen bud. The smallest flicker of sensation in her breasts brought a more heated one in her womb. Between her thighs she was damp.

Her abdomen retracted as Decker's hand passed lightly over it. His fingertips only grazed her, but every one of her nerve endings was responsive to the touch. Sparks of heat spread across the surface of her skin.

Decker now gave attention to her other breast. His tongue flicked the nipple before taking it in a hot suck into his mouth. Jonna's fingers stroked the back of his head and twisted strands of his dark hair. His mouth left her breast and followed the same trail as his fingers. She knew where it would end though he had never done that before. She was surprised at how desperately she wanted him to do it now.

Decker kissed the flat of her belly. His tongue drew a faint, damp line across her pelvic bone. He moved farther down the bed, adjusting her position first, then his. Her knees were raised, her thighs open to him. She watched him bend his head.

The first touch of his lips on her silky, sensitive skin flooded Jonna with heat. Her fingers curled in the bed sheets. His hands slipped under her bottom, and she was raised like an offering to his mouth. Her thighs were bent back and her calves rested over his shoulders. The pressure of this most intimate kiss rocked her. Her neck arched. She closed her eyes.

His tongue darted along the moist folds of her responsive flesh. One moment it was too much, this thing he did to her, in the next it was not enough. Tension pulled her muscles taut. Each breath was drawn in a halting manner as she sipped the air. It was impossible to get enough of it while she was drowning in warm, thick waves of pleasure.

Jonna's inarticulate cry was the first sign of her surrender. Her body's deep shudder was the second. Only at the very end did her fingers uncurl in the sheets and her legs slide to either side of his shoulders.

Decker raised himself up and moved over, supporting himself on his forearms. A log snapped in the fireplace. Sparks lifted and scattered. Shadow and light chased each other across Jonna's face, and for a moment Decker could clearly see her beautifully flushed complexion.

"What else do you want, Jonna?" he asked.

His husky voice was pleasantly abrasive, like sun-soaked grains of sand against her skin. She felt the heavy hardness and heat of him as he settled over her. She knew what she wanted. What she didn't know was if she could say it.

Her hand came out to grasp his shoulder as he started to move away from her. "No," she said quietly, urgently. "I want more."

Decker's smile was small but unmistakably there. "Selfish wench."

She didn't take offense. He made it sound like an endearment. "I want you inside me."

In a moment he was. Filled with him, Jonna let her hands slide over his back. She raised her knees again, cradling him this time and urging him forward. She was lifted to meet his first hard thrust. A spark of pleasure spiraled through her, followed by another, then another dozen.

Jonna moved with him as he moved in her. She did not feel so very selfish as she watched his features become taut with passion and the denial of releasing it. She stroked his arms, his shoulders. His skin was warm. Her fingers could define the muscles across his back. Her thighs caressed his flanks.

She was a single thread of sensation, and she gave herself up to it. She gave herself up to Decker Thorne.

This pleasure was sweeter. She did not come to it alone this time. Decker joined her almost the moment he felt her shudder under him. They shared the vibration and were eventually spent by it.

For a long time neither of them moved. Decker's weight was not entirely uncomfortable. She almost reached for him when he rose from the bed and disappeared into the dressing room.

He poured water from pitcher to basin. Droplets splashed his heated skin. He half expected to hear them sizzle like batter on a hot griddle. There was a mirror above the washstand, and Decker glanced at his reflection. His grin looked decidedly more giddy than rakish. Shaking his head, wryly amused now, he ran one hand through his tousled hair and forced a sober expression.

Jonna was fishing over the side of the bed for her night-shift when Decker returned. He kicked it out of her reach and made no apology for it. "If you want to wear something," he told her, "you can put this on." He opened the drawer of the bedside table and took out the scrimshaw he had given her at Christmas.

Jonna looked at it warily, then favored him with a direct glance.

Decker started to drop it back in the drawer.

"No," she said quickly. Raising a sheet with one hand to cover herself, she held out the other for the ivory pendant. "I'd like to have it back."

It had been his intention to secure it around her neck. Now he let it fall into her open palm. He watched her fingers close over it tightly. Shrugging as if it were of no consequence, Decker lifted the covers Jonna wasn't using to preserve her modesty and climbed into bed. He lay back while she continued to sit there, staring at her clenched fist.

"Jonna?"

She shook her head, not trusting herself to speak. Tears clogged her throat.

Decker raised himself on one elbow to get a better view of her face. She immediately turned away from him. He touched her back and felt the rigid set of her shoulders. "I thought it would please you," he said. "You seemed to like the piece."

"I do," she said on a thread of sound. "It does please me."

There was nothing in her tone to suggest that was true. Decker's hand pushed aside her dark cascade of hair and let it fall forward over her shoulder. He slowly traced a line from the nape of her neck to the base of her spine. "Come here, Jonna."

She hesitated only briefly. Lying down, she turned on her side, facing him, and slipped her fist with the necklace in it under her pillow. Dry-eyed and defiant, she stared at his shadowed features.

Decker shook his head slowly, his faint smile rueful. "I used to think you said whatever came to your mind. I rather admired your straightforward approach. Do you have more secrets now, or is it only that I never really knew you?" When she didn't answer he went on. "What about the necklace upset you? Does it remind you that you meant the ship for Colin? Is that it?"

Jonna's whispered reply was harsh. "How can you think that?"

"It's surprisingly easy."

His simple, truthful reply reminded Jonna that she was responsible for planting that seed. "Yes," she said after a moment. "I suppose it is."

"You're not answering my question."

"I want the necklace," she said. "I even want to wear it. But only if you won't steal it from me again."

Decker started to reach for her, thought better of it, and stopped. He couldn't apologize for something he wasn't sorry for. Given the same circumstances, he would do it again. He couldn't promise her that he wouldn't. "Did it mean so much?" he asked.

Beneath the pillow, her clenched hand began to relax. "I treasured it," she said softly. "And you took it back. I hadn't thought you gave the gift so lightly. I didn't know giving it meant so little to you."

"You know why I took it."

"Do you really think I could have enticed Colin back to

the sea with that scrimshaw? It's a beautiful rendering of *Huntress*, but can you imagine your brother being moved to give up Mercedes, his children, Weybourne Park, or Rosefield because of it?" Though she waited, there was no response from Decker. His silence was expectant, and Jonna filled it with the last thing he expected to hear. "I think you took it from me for another reason."

One of Decker's brows arched. His expression was detached and vaguely skeptical. Inside his chest his heart was hammering. "Oh?" he asked calmly. "And that would be . . . ?"

"Because you wanted to hurt me," she said. "You wanted to get some of your own back after I hurt you." Jonna took a shallow breath and went on before courage abandoned her. "And because you didn't want your brother to know you'd fallen in love with me."

Nothing about Decker's expression changed. His voice was carefully modulated. "Is that right?"

"Yes," she said with more confidence than she felt. "Yes, I think it is. You made it seem as though you were trying to protect Colin from my advances, but perhaps it was just your way of making certain I stayed with you." Jonna's violet eyes narrowed as she tried to discern the slant of Decker's mouth. Was he amused? Astonished? "You could hardly fight your own brother, could you?"

"So you've worked it all out."

His dry tone made her wonder if she had. Perhaps he didn't care anything at all for her and she had just been very, very foolish. "Haven't I?"

Without warning Decker pressed her back against the mattress. He covered her wrists with his hands, pinning her down even though she made no effort to resist him. Her fingers uncurled like flower petals.

"Decker?"

His kiss was deep and unhurried. Jonna felt drugged by it. His weight secured and comforted, and she felt no desire to move or to find any reason that she should.

When he was done with her mouth, he wasn't done. He kissed her downy soft temple, the curve of her cheek, and laid his lips near her ear. His teeth caught the lobe and tugged gently. The soft breath she expelled warmed his cheek. His hands left her wrists and slipped under her head. He held her, his fingers deep in her thick hair, while his mouth returned to hers. This kiss was longer than the first.

The sheet that had covered Jonna's breasts was now at her waist. The slight arch of her body pressed their aching fullness against his chest. At her belly and thighs she could feel how ready he was for her. With no urging on his part, Jonna opened for him.

His hands framed her face. He watched her as he entered her. She was all eyes and a breathy little sigh. His fingers drifted down her neck. Barely touching her skin, they traced a line around her throat, then straight down, stopping at a point just above her heart. He kissed her again, this time only briefly, before his hands drifted lightly over her breasts.

Jonna looked up at him wonderingly. Her right hand folded into a loose fist while her left one touched the place just above her heart. It was her right hand that closed around nothing and her left one that found the ivory pendant.

She didn't ask him how he had done it. She simply accepted that he could. Her arms went around him. "Thank you," she whispered, then brought his head down to hers.

He loved her with his mouth and hands and body. He moved inside her slowly and pressed kisses at the curve of her throat. She rose up to meet him, contracting around him so that she held him with her arms and legs and even more intimately between her thighs. His body rocked her, and she floated back on a single undulating wave of pleasure. Decker was the storm and the sanctuary and Jonna had no other thought but to embrace both things in this man.

Much later Decker lay on his side, watching Jonna sleep. There were no shadows under her eyes, nor any tightness around her mouth. Her features were entirely untroubled. Beneath the blankets one of her hands lay close to his chest, not quite touching but reaching toward him, palm out. Once again he ran his index finger over the heart of her palm. Her fingers curled lightly, then relaxed.

She hadn't asked him for any more confirmation that he loved her. Decker would have told her it was only surprising that it had taken her so long to know the truth. She had been right about most of it. There was really only one point where she had mistaken his resolve.

"I would have fought Colin for you," he said under his breath. He brushed a strand of dark hair away from her cheek. "If it had come to that, I would have fought him."

Decker inched closer to Jonna and fit himself against her softer contours. She murmured something sleepily, then was still. Decker had no difficulty following suit.

Rachael carefully balanced the breakfast tray in one hand while she opened the bedroom door with the other. She stopped on the threshold, immediately bewildered by Jonna's absence, and wondered if she had misunderstood Mrs. Davis. Perhaps her employer had already gone to the harbor. It could mean the tray was for Captain Thorne.

Rachael drew in her lower lip and worried it. Above her dark eyes, her brow was creased. Was her cap on straight? Did she have any stains on her apron? It might be that her gown wouldn't be pressed to his satisfaction. She didn't know what she could expect from the new master of the house, and her heart beat a little erratically when she thought about it.

Others in the house were happy for their employer. Rachael alone had doubts, and her gestures were inadequate to convey them. How many of the others, she wondered, knew the extent of a white master's cruelty? She looked down at her maimed hand. The breakfast tray was shaking, and she required her other hand to steady it. It didn't matter that she tried not to think about what she had been forced to become. The hand that served others served her as a reminder.

Rachael was prepared to back out of the room and return to the kitchen when she noticed the door to the dressing room was open. Was that where Jonna was?

Passing the mirrored dressing table, Rachael bobbed once to scan her reflection. Her cap was straight, and there were no stains on her apron. Her employer would find nothing wrong with her appearance, and if she was forced to make the acquaintance of the captain, at least she would not embarrass herself.

When Rachael entered the dressing room she saw immediately that she had mistaken Jonna's whereabouts. She stood uncertainly on the threshold and looked at the door that led to the adjoining bedchamber. It was several inches ajar, just enough for Rachael to detect movement in the room beyond. She stepped closer and leaned into the opening.

"Rachael?" Jonna sat up when she saw the face pressed to the space between the door and the jamb. "Rachael, is that you?" There was a nod but no other movement. Reaching across Decker's sleeping form, Jonna awkwardly retrieved her dressing gown. She slipped it on, belted it loosely, then motioned for Rachael to come in. She pointed to her sleeping husband and raised one finger to her lips, signaling the young woman to be quiet. It was only after she'd done it that she realized how unnecessary the gesture was. Rachael moved like a wraith around the house at any time, and to Jonna's best recollection, she had never spoken a word.

Jonna moved some things aside on the table. There was only a single serving of everything on the tray that Rachael set down. Jonna assumed it was intended for her since Rachael had entered from her room. "Thank you," Jonna whispered.

Rachael bobbed once in acknowledgment. Almost reluctantly her eyes strayed to the sleeping captain. Decker's back was turned toward her. Only his naked shoulder and a thick head of dark hair were visible.

Jonna recognized the mixture of curiosity and apprehension in Rachael's sidelong glance. She often felt it herself. What was missing from the young woman's look was admiration, but from her angled view of Decker, Jonna supposed there wasn't much to see that could be admired. "Please see that something is prepared for my husband," she said.

Interrupted by Jonna's softly spoken request, Rachael's head jerked back. Her coffee-colored complexion warmed and reddened at having been caught out staring.

"Do you understand?" Jonna asked.

Rachael nodded a quick assent and fled the room, going out the same way she entered.

Watching her go, Jonna was reminded of Delores's parting words. If Rachael understood others as well as she seemed to, then perhaps she could speak. If that were true, why would she choose to remain silent?

Decker stretched lazily, yawned, then rolled over onto his back. Jonna did not notice him immediately. She was staring at the far wall, a small vertical crease between her brows. He did not call attention to himself, but found pleasure in watching her in this unguarded moment.

"I'd pay for your thoughts," he said at last. "But I don't think I can afford them."

Jonna's frown vanished. She looked down at Decker and the expression in her violet eyes softened. "It was a better arrangement for you before you became my husband," she said. "You might have become a very rich man with me as your mistress."

Grinning, he pulled her down beside him. His kiss was thorough. "I am a rich man," he said. He punctuated this statement with a single peck on the lips, then he was reaching for the breakfast tray.

"That's mine," she said. "Rachael is bringing yours directly."

He ignored her completely, sitting up and placing the tray across his lap. "Rachael," he said, uncovering a small bowl of oatmeal. He immediately handed it to Jonna. "I don't remember that name. Is she another one of your good works?"

"Hardly," Jonna said. She accepted the oatmeal and lifted a spoon from the tray. "If there are any good works being done—and I'm not so sure there are—then Mrs. Davis will have to answer for them." She glanced sideways at Decker when he didn't respond. He was looking vaguely pleased with himself for having found the toast and was occupied in slathering it with marmalade. "Hungry?"

He didn't apologize for it. "Starving."

Jonna smiled as he bit off a rather large piece of toast. He appeared to be thoroughly enjoying it. "I thought perhaps we could go to the harbor together this morning."

Decker swallowed. He regarded Jonna frankly. "I'm not certain what I'm expected to do there," he said. "I don't have a ship at my command. There's no run to prepare for, not if you're going to have *Huntress* refitted."

A thread of tension slipped up Jonna's spine. She rubbed the back of her neck, trying to ease it. This conversation could easily become an argument, she realized. It was something she wanted to avoid. "What was your business at the shipyards yesterday?"

"I wanted to talk to one of the builders," he said. "You're not the only one with thoughts about the lines and speed of ships."

"You spoke to Mr. McKinney?"

"I didn't say anything about Mr. McKinney. Your builder isn't the only one at the yards."

Jonna laid her spoon on top of her half-eaten oatmeal. "You were going to go somewhere else with your ideas? Without even discussing them with me?" It appeared that in spite of her intentions they were going to have an argument.

"Where is my place at the Remington yards, Jonna? Where do I belong?"

"At my side," she said. "You're my husband."

"That's our marriage," he told her quietly. "Not your business. Don't confuse the two."

"You told Colin you didn't want any part of my business."

"And I don't." He took another bite of toast. "I approached Sheridan about a position and talked to another builder. I think that's a clear indication that I don't want your business."

"It's an indication that you want to destroy it!" The words echoed before they were blanketed by the heavy, oppressive silence that followed. Jonna's throat closed, and there was a tight ache in her chest. She stared at her hands wondering that they were so steady when she was suddenly so deeply afraid.

Decker moved the tray onto her lap. He raised the covers and slid out of bed. The floor was cold. Neither he nor Jonna had gotten up in the middle of the night to replenish the logs on the fire. As a consequence the hearth was only ashes. He stepped into his trousers and slipped on his shirt.

"Decker!" Jonna's voice was not more than a hoarse whisper as he disappeared in the dressing room. He closed the door behind him soundlessly. She flinched anyway. Pushing the tray aside, Jonna went after him. He was standing in front of his dresser, searching the uppermost drawer for stockings. He ignored her entry completely.

Jonna's violet eyes were luminous. Tears rimmed her lower lashes. One dripped down her cheek. She raised a hand toward him, reaching out tentatively. It hovered in midair a moment before she slowly lowered it again.

"Get away from me, Jonna."

She shuddered at his coldness, but she didn't leave. "Can't you see how frightened I am?" she asked on a mere thread of sound. Her throat ached with the effort to keep more tears at bay. "What if I'm wrong about you? What if you're no different than any other man who's wanted me for what I have and not who I am?" She drew in an uneasy breath. It was almost a dry sob. "For years Jack and your brother have wondered why I kept Grant Sheridan close, but he has always been a safe choice. I know what his interests are, what they've always been. But you're outside my experience. What I don't know is how I'm supposed to think about you."

Still empty-handed, Decker closed the drawer. He turned on Jonna. She was holding the ivory scrimshaw between her thumb and forefinger, rubbing it gently like a worry bead. "There has to be a place for me," he told her quietly. "I can't be a partner in this marriage and nothing outside of it. It may be true that you intend to make modifications to *Huntress* but you took away my command before that. No matter what you say, Jonna, I know it was punishment for some slight you imagined. I won't—"

She stepped forward. Her eyes implored him. "No," she

said. "You're wrong. It wasn't like that. I did it because I wanted you here, with me. I don't know any other way to keep you."

"Is it your intention to fit me with a leash?"

Although the question was quietly posed, Jonna winced. "You're deliberately misunderstanding me." Another tear fell. Her face began to crumple. "I don't know how to make this right!"

Decker gave no indication that he was moved by her distress. "You were the one who wanted separate bedrooms," he reminded her. "That would seem to contradict that you wanted me around."

"You don't understand." She knuckled away tears in both eyes. Her shoulders heaved once. "You c-can't understand."

Decker knew that was only true as long as she didn't tell him the secret that would explain her contradictions. He didn't know if she had ever looked more lonely to him. "Come here, Jonna." He saw her hesitate. Her bottom lip trembled and her eyes were brilliant with the wash of fresh tears. He held out one hand. "Jonna."

She placed her hand in his and stepped into his embrace.

It was this scene that Rachael intruded upon. Habit had taken her back to Jonna's bedchamber. When she realized her mistake she decided to go through the dressing rooms rather than back to the hallway and around to the captain's door. Now she wished she had not taken this shortcut.

Decker stood there, looking over Jonna's head at the doorway. The tray rattled in the young woman's hand, but Jonna didn't hear it above her own quiet sobs. He saw she recognized him. It was more than a flicker across her sloe eyes that gave her away. Her mouth was parted on a soundless gasp, and her knees sagged a fraction.

A small negative shake of his head was enough to keep her

silent. His eyes dropped to the tray and then to her hands. If he had any doubt about her identity it disappeared when he saw the scarred flesh below her right thumb. *She got out of her irons by biting off most of the ball of her hand.* This was the girl he had taken from Michele Moreau's Charleston bawdy house. What else had Graham Denizon told him about her? *She doesn't speak any English and no one here knows her dialect.* How, Decker wondered, was she getting along in Jonna's household?

He motioned her to go into his bedchamber with the tray. Although her surprise had faded, his direction was slow to register with her. He had to gesture a second time. His full attention did not return to Jonna until he heard the girl leave by the door to his room.

Decker looked down at the glossy crown of his wife's hair. Her forehead was pressed against his shoulder. Her tears had made his shirt damp. His lips lightly brushed her hair. He breathed in the fragrance of her, a heady combination of lavender and musk, as he stroked her back. He couldn't help smiling to himself. Jonna had always been able to make him do that. There was no finer piece of work than this woman he'd married.

It didn't matter that she couldn't explain herself. There were things Decker understood without hearing them from her. The constant change of staff in her home, the prevalence of black servants, even the opinion she expressed about abolition, suddenly made sense.

There was only one explanation for the appearance of the young black girl in Jonna's home. This Beacon Hill mansion was a station for the Underground Railroad.

She could deny that she was the conductor, but Decker would never believe it. Mrs. Davis was surely an integral part of what was going on, perhaps other servants as well, but no one could do it without Jonna's approval. Decker considered Jonna's often careless regard for the running of her home. It had never set right with him, not when she delegated comparatively little of the running of her business.

Decker wondered about Jack Quincy's role. Jack was charged with hiring the men at the harbor and at the yards. How many fugitive slaves did Remington Shipping employ because Jonna suggested them? How many times had Decker secreted slaves away on board one of her ships only to have them end up in her home?

Where he thought they had been at cross-purposes, it now seemed they shared a single one.

Decker's attention was drawn to Jonna's tear-stained face as she lifted it. "I don't know how to make this right," she whispered again.

He touched her cheek with his fingertips. "You don't have to make anything right," he said. "You've done nothing wrong. Not a thing."

It seemed he really believed that. She only wished she could share his conviction. Jonna shook her head slowly.

"No," she said. "There must be some way I can show you—"

"Jonna . . ." His tone urged caution.

And she threw it to the wind. "Do you still want *Huntress*?"

Decker didn't have to think. "Yes."

"Then she's yours."

Twelve

From his window Decker watched Jonna walk toward her waiting carriage. Just before she stepped inside she turned to the house and looked up in the direction of his room. She had no reason to suppose that he was standing there, but he thought her expression seemed hopeful. Bright morning sunshine glanced off each of the windows, making virtual mirrors of them. Decker doubted she could see him clearly, yet the smile she offered up was simply radiant.

He should have kept her here, he thought, in his room, in his bed, and made love to her again. He hadn't, not after the enormous generosity of her gift. Loving her just then would have seemed like a payment of sorts for *Huntress*, as if their being together were purely a business arrangement. The last thing Decker wanted to do was reinforce that notion in Jonna's mind. She might have finally concluded that he loved her, but he doubted that she was confident about it or even that she understood what it meant.

What she was, was frightened. On that point she had been clear. What she didn't suspect was that she wasn't alone.

Decker's fingers curled around the earring in his jacket pocket. It had been his talisman since the age of four, a connection to a family he could barely remember. Jonna told him once that he commanded his good fortune, but Decker was never as certain of it as she had been.

He took out the earring and examined it in the heart of his palm. Years of careful, almost reverent, handling had kept the pearl stud lustrous. The engraving was still visible on the gold drop. This earring had led him to Colin and Colin had led him to Jonna. He hadn't commanded his fortune at all, merely followed it.

Decker's fingers closed over the earring. He was returning it to his pocket when the door behind him opened. He let it fall. It slid down the outside of his pocket, not in it, and dropped between the brocade cushion and the arm of the chair beside him.

Rachael hesitated on the threshold when she saw the bed-chamber was still occupied. Her arms tightened protectively on the stack of fresh bed linens she was carrying.

Decker took a step toward her, stopping only when he saw her flinch. He pointed to the linens. "May I take those for you?"

She shook her head vigorously.

He waved her in with a gentle gesture and stepped aside. He watched her, bemused, as she gave him a wide berth on her way to the bed. "Rachael?" he said her name quietly, a question in his tone. Her pause was slight, but visible, and he knew that she heard him even though she didn't look in his direction. "That's what you're called here? Is that right?"

She didn't answer.

Decker went to the foot of the bed and stood. Rachael's movements were rather stiff as she dropped the clean linens and began stripping the old ones. "You understand me, don't you?"

There was another hesitation on her part, but no concrete answer. Not glancing once toward him, she dragged the sheets across the bed and tossed them on the floor.

Decker gave her another moment before he stopped her. Coming around the bed, he laid one hand across her narrow forearm. He felt her tremble, but he had no patience for it. He meant her no harm and given the nature of his previous encounter with her, she had no reason to think he did. "Do you understand me?" he repeated.

Rachael's eyes darted frantically toward the door to the hall, then to the one leading to the dressing room.

"If you think I mean to hurt you, then why come in here at all?"

This time she glanced at the window.

"You thought I'd left already," Decker said. "Is that it?" He realized she must have known that Jonna was gone and had assumed he'd accompanied his wife to the harbor. He let her go, and she immediately stepped outside the circle of his reach. He regarded her curiously. Eventually his eyes dropped to her disfigured hand. "Let me see."

Rachael raised it reluctantly. She shivered when Decker's fingers closed gently around her wrist. Her eyes were wary.

Decker examined her hand. The ball of flesh that had been bitten away had healed well. "Can you move your thumb?"

She wiggled it stiffly, showing him her limited range of motion. Her thumb had a tendency to lie against the underside of her fingers and curl into her palm. When Decker let her go she pulled back her hand quickly, cradling it against her breast as if nursing a fresh injury.

Decker was convinced now that she understood him. He wondered at her command of the language. "Did they teach you English here?" he asked.

She hesitated again but finally nodded.

"You've done well to understand as much as you do. It wasn't so long ago that you escaped the slave ship."

Unclear as to whether some reply was expected of her, Rachael looked away.

"*Salamander.*" Decker saw her suck in her breath, and he knew he had remembered the name of the slaver correctly. Clearly she hadn't forgotten. "You didn't speak then either as

I recall, but no one ever suggested that you couldn't. In fact, I had the impression that no one could understand you. What's happened to your voice, I wonder."

Rachael simply stared at him.

It seemed to Decker there was little point in continuing this one-sided conversation. He pointed to the bed. Before he could direct her to continue with her work, Rachael sat down on the edge of the mattress and began to raise her skirt.

"What are you doing?" The words were clipped and harsh. Decker actually stepped away from the bed. "Put your skirt down."

Bewildered and more than a little frightened, Rachael covered her slim legs again. She sucked in her lower lip, her dark eyes wide as she waited further instruction.

Decker wondered if he could possibly have misunderstood what had just happened. Had she really been prepared to offer herself to him? Where had she learned to expect that from a man? Her large eyes, small, oval face, and delicate frame, gave her a childlike appearance. The fact that she didn't speak only reinforced the suggestion of youth. "How old are you, Rachael?" he asked quietly. "Fifteen? Sixteen?"

She didn't respond.

Decker held up his hands, counting off on his fingers and pointing to her. It occurred to him that she might not know her age, but when he had clicked off seventeen and was on the point of quitting, she stopped him. He wondered if she could possibly be right.

"I've changed my mind," he said. Watching her closely, Decker gestured to the bed again.

She blinked once. Something akin to disappointment registered briefly in her expression, then faded as she became resigned to the inevitable. Rachael began to raise her skirt again, inching it up over her legs. Almost simultaneously she began to lie back.

Decker held up a hand. "Stop. God, I'm sorry, but I had to be sure there was no mistake." She really had been offering herself to him, not willingly, but at what she thought was his command. Had it happened before in this house? Jonna only employed two men. There was a groundskeeper and a carriage driver. They also took care of house maintenance and the heavier duties Mrs. Davis and her female staff could not accomplish. There were few men who came calling. Decker supposed that with the exception of regular deliveries that were made to the house, Jack Quincy was the most frequent visitor.

He would never believe Jack had used his authority in Jonna's home to press his attentions on one of her servants. Decker ran his fingers through his hair. He felt Rachael's eyes on him. She was worried now, fearful that she had displeased him again. He had no idea what to say to calm her.

Decker sighed. "Go on about your business," he said finally. "I'm going to go about mine." He started for the door, then turned. "I'd prefer you don't let on to anyone that you know me. May I have your promise on that?"

Rachael was still sitting on the edge of the bed, her heels hooked on the frame. Hugging her knees, she rocked slowly back and forth, and considered Decker with a wary, sideways glance.

"Your promise, Rachael. It's important." He waited until he saw her nod faintly. "Thank you." Then he left.

Rachael didn't stop rocking until the door had closed behind him. She didn't rise from the bed until his footsteps had receded down the hallway. Her heartbeat assumed its normal rhythm when she followed his progress down the walk in front of the house. He didn't once glance back at the window to see if she was watching him, and she was glad for that. She did not want him to think of her, and in retrospect, she wished he had not been so kind. He deserved better than the trick she had played him and the betrayal she would serve him.

They all did.

Jonna's driver was waiting for Decker when he reached the warehouse. "No trouble?" Decker asked him.

Mr. Poling tipped his chair forward from where he had been leaning it against the wall and came to his feet. "Not unless you count Miss Rem—, I mean Mrs. Thorne herself. She didn't like the notion that I was told to keep an eye on her."

Decker wasn't surprised. "I didn't mean for you to be blatant about it. You could have just kept the carriage nearby."

"I did that," Mr. Poling said. He lifted his hat, scratched his head thoughtfully, then let the brim settle again. "Circled the warehouse a few times, went up and down the wharf—not far, mind you, just enough so my presence wouldn't be obvious—"

"*Obviously* it was."

Mr. Poling shrugged sheepishly. "Suppose so. She must have seen me from her window. Next I knew she was flagging me down on the wharf. Invited me to come in and take myself a seat right here, so that's what I did. She was real pleasant about it, too."

Decker imagined that it meant she was saving her sharpest reprimands for him. "Very well, Mr. Poling. Pick her up directly at six, and no side excursions if I'm not accompanying her." It was hard for Decker to hide his amusement as the older man practically saluted him on the way out.

Jonna was leaning over her desk, studying a blueprint that took up most of the surface. A paperweight held down one curling corner, and two books and a china cup flattened the others. She was teetering slightly to one side as she rested most of her weight on her left leg. It was the only evidence that her twisted ankle was still giving her some discomfort.

Jonna gave the cross section in front of her full attention. Her brow was furrowed in concentration, her mouth flattened. She didn't look up until Decker's frame blocked the natural light from the window and threw a shadow across her work. Her expression didn't change in the least. "I suppose you have some explanation for your behavior," she said.

"I take it you're referring to Mr. Poling. I ran into him downstairs."

"I put him there so you would." She bent her head again and considered the blueprint. "You're in my light."

"My apologies." He stepped aside. His forefinger tapped the edge of the blueprint lightly. "Are those the changes for *Huntress*?"

"No. It's an old clipper design I'm reconsidering." She only glanced at him. "And don't think I can be turned away from your high-handedness with my driver. I'm waiting for an explanation. Preferably a good one."

Completely at his ease, Decker dropped into the chair in front of her desk. There was nothing apologetic about his grin. "Do you know you have a dimple at the corner of your mouth?"

Jonna's mouth flattened further, temporarily deepening the dimple. "Your explanation," she said, refusing to look at him.

"You do," he said, ignoring her. Decker ducked his head and tilted it to one side to get a better view of the feature she was trying to hide. "It's wonderfully maddening. It appears when you're being your most disapproving self." He lifted his head and tipped the chair back on two legs, balancing it precariously as he continued to consider her. "Like now. It makes me want to kiss you."

Jonna's head jerked up. She attempted a sour, deprecating look, but it was difficult to achieve when heat was rushing to her face. "I wish you would be serious," she said.

"I am."

"Oh, very well." Jonna said the words as if they had been dragged out of her. She punctuated them with a small, impatient sigh. Straightening, she came around her desk and stood in front of him. When Decker tipped the chair forward she placed herself squarely in his lap, put her arms around him, and kissed him hard and full on the mouth.

At the moment she felt his surprise melt away in favor of a response, she pulled back, and gave him an arch look, satisfied that he was no longer so irritatingly amused. That smug, reckless smile of his had vanished. She kissed him once more, lightly this time, then stood and put the desk between them. "It's that grin of yours, Decker," she told him. "You goad me with it. You know you do. Sometimes I just want to slap it off your face."

He touched his cheek. His tone was dry. "I like this way better."

"Well, so do I," she said primly. "But I may resort to the other if you don't tell me about Mr. Poling."

Decker leaned forward and rested his forearms on his knees. He answered her now with the seriousness she had always deserved. "You're not going to like it no matter how it's said, so let me simply put it succinctly. You require protection, Jonna. That's all Mr. Poling's presence was meant to provide until I could get here."

"Protection," she said softly. "Oh, Decker, surely not."

"I'm set on this. I don't want to find out that you've narrowly escaped being trampled by a horse or have almost succumbed to smoke and fire in your own warehouse. I'd like to think someone at your side may prevent another incident, but I'll be satisfied with a rescue if it comes to that."

Jonna sat in the leather chair behind her desk. "Is this because I won't tell you where I was last night?" she asked.

"No, but your disappearance made it all the more clear to me that you've never taken the attempts on your life seriously."

"They weren't attempts on my life. They were accidents." Even to her own ears she didn't sound particularly convincing. It was because she was remembering the pair of hands at the small of her back pushing her into freezing Boston Harbor. "At the most they were meant to frighten me. The horse veered away, and I had a lot of time to get out of the warehouse. Anyone might have rescued me from the harbor. It just happened to have been you."

A stillness settled over Decker. He stared at Jonna, his blue eyes boring into hers as he considered what she had just said. "I wasn't there when the horse got away from its owner. And Jeremy Dodd carried you out of the warehouse. The only rescue I made was when you took a tumble off the wharf." He saw her draw in her lower lip, but it was as if her entire body flinched from the truth he was about to toss at her. He swore under his breath. "You were pushed."

Jonna spoke quickly. "There were so many people, Decker. They were all crowding around. I can't be certain what happened."

"I don't believe you." He got to his feet. "You know. You've always known, and you've kept it to yourself, even when I brought my suspicions to your attention. For God's sake, Jonna, why wouldn't you tell anyone?"

"Who is it I should have trusted?" she asked quietly. "You?"

He felt as if she had struck him, and for once he didn't hide behind a careless smile or frost-colored eyes.

"I'm sorry," she said. "But it was true then. It's not true now. Some weeks after it happened I started to tell Jack. There was an interruption, I think. It may even have been the night you were jailed. I've always been glad I never told him."

"You could suspect Jack?" Decker found that hard to believe.

"No."

"But you didn't know who he might tell. Me, for instance."

Jonna nodded hesitantly.

"I see," he said.

"No, I don't think you do. At least not all of it. My reluctance had to do with the very discussion we're having now. I didn't want someone a half-step behind me, Decker. Or living in my pockets. If I had spoken to Jack this business of protecting me would have simply happened sooner. He would have constantly been at my side. I wouldn't have had a moment's peace, and I would have worried him beyond reason. It may have been Grant or Mrs. Davis—or even you—that he set on my heels. It seemed best not to provoke him to do that. You were determined enough without any encouragement from me."

"I'm still determined," he said. "I don't want you hurt."

"And I don't want to *be* hurt. I'm not careless, in spite of what you might think. You can't put me on a ship and carry me off every time you perceive some danger. There must be a compromise, Decker."

"Do you have a suggestion?"

"My secretary is as capable of protecting me as Mr. Poling," she said. "During my work hours he's all that I need."

"Mr. Poling was temporary at best. I was thinking of someone younger."

"Don't suggest yourself," she warned him. "I won't get any work done." Jonna saw his mouth twitch, and she pointed a finger at him. "And not for the reason you're thinking. I'd be plotting ways to kill you if you were constantly underfoot. Even on board *Huntress* you had the good sense not to spend all your time in my cabin."

Decker's eyes dropped to her lips. The dimple was hovering at the corner of her mouth. "What about that young ruffian Dodd?"

"Jeremy?"

"Yes. He proved his worth at the warehouse. Would you accept him?"

Jonna's faint frown betrayed a small measure of her disappointment.

"What's wrong?"

"You might have protested a bit, you know. Offered yourself in spite of my wishes. You came up with his name very quickly. Just because I don't want you underfoot doesn't mean that you shouldn't want to be there."

Decker was laughing as he came around the desk. He pulled her out of her chair effortlessly. "You have a most peculiar mind," he told her.

"Thank you."

"I have no finer aspiration in life than to serve as your footstool."

"And I used to think you had no ambition," she whispered.

He was still laughing as his mouth came down on hers. Decker lifted her, turned, and set her on the edge of the desk. His hands raised her skirt so he could stand more intimately between her legs. His lips moved over hers, touching the corners, running his tongue along the fullness of her lower lip. Her arms were around his neck, and she raised herself up just enough so that he could feel the outlines of her breasts against his chest.

He deepened the kiss. His hands stroked her back, her sides. He wished she wasn't wearing a corset and six petticoats and a pair of lace-edged drawers. He wished he had thought to lock the door or tell her secretary that they weren't to be disturbed. He wished he had just kept her home.

Decker pulled back slowly and stared at the smile tugging at the corners of her mouth. He wasn't proof against that. He kissed her softly. Paused. Kissed her again. Her mouth moved under his dreamily.

She murmured something against his lips. He didn't know what she said, he only knew he liked the sound of it. Her faint hum of pleasure stirred him deeply. His hands lifted away from her waist and framed her face. He touched his forehead to hers. His voice was husky. "I think I'm keeping you from your work."

"Hmmm."

"I know that agitates you."

She nodded.

He kissed her lightly. "I'm going. I'll send Jeremy to take Mr. Poling's post. He'll be here at six to collect you, but don't leave without me."

"All right."

Decker's fingers slid away from her face. "Think about your blueprints," he said.

Bemused, she watched him go. "Now, how am I going to do that?"

Grant Sheridan could see there was a lot of activity on board *Huntress* even before he strode up the gangplank. Men were resetting repaired canvas and scrubbing the hull and decks. Oil was being applied to the rails and the great wheel. The sun and salt damaged wood soaked it up so that it gleamed under the polishing cloths.

No one paid him much attention until he was forced to dodge a bucket of water tossed negligently in his direction. It was his cursing more than his quick sidestep that caused the work to pause.

Mr. Leeds approached. "Can I help you, Mr. Sheridan?"

"I want to see Thorne."

"Mrs. Thorne isn't here," he said, shifting his weight from one leg to the other. "You can find her at—"

"Decker Thorne."

"Oh, you mean the captain." He wasn't intimidated by Grant's black glare. "He's below. Was in the cargo hold a while ago. He might be in his cabin. Do you want me to—"

Grant cut him off, striding away. "I'll find him."

Decker was sitting on the edge of his desk, leafing through his log when Grant came in. "Sheridan." He closed the log and set it aside. He didn't offer his hand.

"I've been thinking about what you said yesterday," Grant said. He opened his coat and reached inside his jacket. He pulled out a sheet torn from a newspaper and waved it in front of Decker. "Did you know about this when we spoke?"

"I don't know about it now," Decker said. "What is it?"

"*The Liberator.*"

"Garrison's abolitionist paper?"

"That's right. It was distributed yesterday. I only had an opportunity to read through it a little while ago."

"And it brought you here?" Decker asked skeptically. "That *is* interesting." He held out his hand. "May I?"

Grant thrust it brusquely in Decker's direction. "He's

been caught," he said, not waiting for Decker to scan the page. "Did you really think I wouldn't find out?"

Decker saw nothing to explain Grant's agitation on the side of the page he was looking at. He turned it over. Everything was made clear. "FALCONER CAPTURED." Beneath the caption in smaller letters was the heading: "Brave liberator of the oppressed is arrested for crimes against property."

Decker read through the article carefully before he gave it back to Grant. He managed to sound credibly unaffected by the news. "You think I knew this before I saw you? I assure you, I didn't. My offer to introduce you and your abolitionist friends to Falconer was made in good faith."

"At a price," Grant said. "Don't forget you wanted something for your efforts."

"I certainly haven't forgotten that. I'm the one out the money."

Grant's flat black eyes regarded Decker narrowly. "I'm thinking now that you never intended to deliver him. Perhaps you were only trying to make a fool of me."

"I never said I knew Falconer, just someone who says he does. That's as close as I'm ever likely to get to him." Decker shrugged. "I suppose it's a moot point. The paper says his name is Matthew Willet. Now everyone knows."

"And you really didn't?" Sheridan was still skeptical.

"I've never heard of Willet. Look, Sheridan, I'm sorry it didn't work out, but I did what I could. The man shielded himself. It's been months since Jonna mentioned that you had an interest in meeting Falconer. It took me time to make any connection at all to him. If I hadn't left for London the outcome may have been different."

"And now there's no money in it for you."

"Exactly."

"Is the money so important?" asked Grant. The question was put forth casually, but his eyes were intent.

"Money is always important."

"But Jonna's rich."

"Yes," Decker said. "She is. But it doesn't follow that what's hers is mine."

Sheridan frowned. "You mean she still holds all the purse strings?"

"That's exactly what I mean."

Laughter rumbled deep in Sheridan's chest. It exploded with a force that reverberated in the small cabin and brought tears to Grant's eyes. "Oh, that's rich," he said, trying to catch his breath. "If you'll pardon the expression." This sent him into a new paroxysm of laughter.

Decker sat on the edge of the desk, his arms crossed in front of him, and waited Grant out. "Right now, Sheridan," he said without inflection, "I can't even afford to have you laugh at my expense."

Grant sobered only marginally. "I did not suspect you were such a wit, Thorne."

Decker's shrug was careless. "I do what I can."

Sheridan smoothed the newspaper account, folded it, and replaced it in his pocket. "Did you know you weren't going to get anything when you married her?"

"I knew."

"But you thought she'd change her mind."

"Let's say I hoped."

Sheridan's smile held no humor. "You should have made a better deal before the marriage."

"I'm not the Yankee you are. Which is why I find myself needing funds now. I won't go to Jonna, so don't advise me in that direction."

"Tell me something, Thorne. Does Jonna know you

were at my office yesterday?"

"Yes."

"I imagine she thought you came to settle the score. I don't think you were entirely convinced that the kiss we shared was completely an innocent one."

"I'm convinced unless you tell me otherwise." Decker regarded Sheridan dispassionately. "Are you telling me that?"

"No, not at all. A congratulatory salute, that's all it was. Had I known then that she had made such a shrewd marriage settlement, my wishes would have been warmer. I've always been impressed with Jonna's business sense." His grin was meant to needle Decker, but he could observe no outward effect. "So what reason did you give for coming to see me yesterday?"

"I told her I was looking for a job."

Sheridan's reaction was immediate. He almost choked on an indrawn breath. "With my line? She believed that?"

"I was convincing," Decker said calmly.

"You must have been." Sheridan's tone stopped just short of being admiring. "Then she doesn't know anything at all about this Falconer business?"

"No. You know what she thinks about Garrison and the others. They're all fanatics in her eyes."

"Yes, she's said that." He paused and added quietly, "I think she sees me in that same light sometimes."

Decker uncrossed his arms. His fingers curled around the edge of his desk. "Do you want to do something about Falconer?" he asked.

One of Sheridan's sand-colored brows kicked up. "What do you mean?"

"I mean the man's going to hang. You read the article. Garrison's probably right about the trial being a mere for-

mality. The outcome is certain, and that's if Whitfield . . .
Whitley . . ."

"Willet," Sheridan interjected.

"Willet makes it to trial," Decker finished. "Don't be surprised if you read a few weeks from now that he's been the victim of a lynching."

Sheridan nodded. "I know how seriously they'll take Falconer's crime. My own line's suffered because of the opinions I've expressed. I don't have the Charleston trade I used to, and I'm not likely to ever get it back."

"Then you'd be willing to mount a rescue?"

"Get Falconer out of jail?"

"That's right. You'd be surprised how easily it can be done." His faint smile was unembarrassed and unapologetic. "I have some experience in things of this nature."

"So the stories about you are true."

"I'm sure some of them are. Are you interested?"

"I want to hear your price."

"Five thousand dollars."

Sheridan didn't visibly react to the amount Decker named. "No," he said firmly. "That's a fortune."

"Then your cause will have a martyr," Decker said. "At no cost to you or any of your friends."

"If it's as easily arranged as you say, there's no reason I can't do the thing myself."

"That's true."

Sheridan had expected Decker to make another offer and ask for less money. When he didn't, Sheridan asked, "What are the risks?"

"Being caught," Decker said. "Swinging at the end of a rope. Those come to mind immediately. Even a successful venture would have consequences. If you're identified with the operation, then your business will suffer more losses. I doubt you'll be able to trade anywhere south of the Mason-Dixon."

"You'll have to deal with the same risks," Sheridan said.

"What will Jonna think about you endangering Remington Shipping?"

"I won't be," said Decker.

"You'll need a ship."

"Not necessarily. But in any event, I have one." He responded to the question in Sheridan's eyes. "*Huntress*. This clipper's mine."

Sheridan was visibly taken aback. "You mean Jonna's allowing you to serve as its master."

"I mean she's given me the ship."

"You're lying. She would never do that."

Decker did not try to convince him. He remained silent and let Sheridan believe whatever he wished.

"I want to think about your offer," Sheridan said finally. "I can't put up five thousand by myself."

"I understand," Decker said. "But I wouldn't wait too long to speak to your friends."

Jonna was waiting for Decker at six o'clock at the entrance to the warehouse. Jeremy Dodd's lanky frame was draped casually over a hitching post a few feet away. His eyes wandered up and down the wharf, taking in the slow but steady traffic. Night was just falling, and his particular interest lay in the young women who were beginning to emerge from the back streets.

"You really can go," Jonna said.

"No, ma'am. I really can't."

"Captain Thorne and Mr. Poling will be here at any minute."

"The Captain was very specific that I should wait for him."

335

Jonna sighed. "Mr. Dodd, who do you think runs Remington Shipping?"

Jeremy didn't hesitate. "You do."

"Then don't you think you should take your orders from me?"

The young man's head swiveled in her direction. His grin was wide. "I figure it this way, ma'am. If I disobey you, I'm only out of a job. If I disobey the cap'n, my life's over. It's not a hard choice."

"I see what you mean." It was an effort to hold back a smile.

Jeremy straightened. "Here's the captain now," he said, pointing across the wharf. "And if I'm not mistaken, there's your carriage."

Jonna looked in the directions in which Jeremy pointed and saw he was correct on both counts. "*Now* you can go."

He gave her a jaunty salute. "Right you are."

He still didn't leave, she noticed, until he had delivered her safely to the interior of the carriage. She wasn't aware she was smiling until Decker asked her about it once they were underway. "It's Jeremy," she said. "He would not be moved from his post. His allegiance to you was both annoying and admirable."

"He's a good man."

"He said you'd take his life if he left me alone."

Decker did not share Jonna's amusement. "I would."

Jonna's smile disappeared abruptly. "You're serious."

"Yes," he said. "I am."

She fell silent. Her eyes drifted from Decker's implacable features to the window. It seemed the stoic brick structures lining the streets were more likely to yield than Decker Thorne. She considered the young women she had pledged to move through her station. How would it be possible without her husband's help? And what would she do if he were unwilling to give it?

"There's something I want to talk to you about."

Decker's voice startled Jonna. He had spoken the very words she had been thinking. "Yes?"

"It's about Rachael."

"Rachael? The girl who works for me?"

"Yes. That one."

Jonna didn't try to mask her surprise, only her wariness. "Have you spoken to Mrs. Davis?"

"No. I think it would be better if you did that."

"What is it?"

Decker hesitated. He hadn't realized how uncomfortable it would be relating the events of the morning to Jonna. "Rachael came in to change the linens after you'd gone. I think she expected me to be gone as well. I attempted to have a conversation with her, but with no success."

"She doesn't speak, Decker. I'm sure your efforts made her uncomfortable."

He didn't disagree. "I suppose I became impatient with her. I pointed to the bed. I only meant to indicate she should go on about her business."

Jonna felt her insides clenching. She wondered if she could choose not to hear any more. "And did she?"

"She sat on the bed and lifted her skirt. She seemed to think I wanted her to—"

Jonna raised a hand, cutting him off. It was every bit as unpleasant as she had expected. "Perhaps you misunderstood."

"I thought that. Hoped for it, actually. But there was no misunderstanding." He wasn't going to share that he had made sure of it. Jonna didn't need to know everything. "Rachael's been ill used, Jonna. She's been given reason to expect that when a man points to a bed she's supposed to lie on it."

"I'll make certain she knows she's safe with us," Jonna said. "I won't speak to Mrs. Davis about this yet except to have her reassign Rachael's duties. That won't be a problem." Her eyes slid away from his for a moment. "Why didn't you tell me earlier?"

"I was going to," he said. It was an honest reply, still, he didn't know if he'd be believed. "But we argued about your protection. I didn't think about Rachael again until I was at the ship. I thought it could wait until now."

Jonna nodded.

"Don't you want to ask me anything else?" he said after a long silence.

At first Jonna didn't understand; then she saw the uncertainty in his eyes. She suddenly realized he hadn't known what he could expect from her. "I'm not going to ask you if you accepted Rachael's offer, or even if you were tempted by it." Jonna's smile was as soft as her reply. "I'm trying very hard not to live down to your expectations, Captain Thorne."

Decker let the warmth in her violet eyes wash over him. He moved from the seat opposite her to the place at her side. She slipped her arm through his and leaned against him. It was a comfortable place, she thought, at the side of this man. The hood of her plum cloak slipped back, and Jonna felt Decker's cheek touch her hair. The tenderness of the gesture brought tears to her eyes. Her heart swelled.

"Jonna?" Decker was struck by her very stillness. Quiet did not come easily to her, and it had been several minutes since she had moved. He lifted his head to get a better view of her face. The carriage lantern cast a warm orange glow over her complexion. Under the light, traces of tears were visible on her cheeks. She had made no attempt to brush them away, yet she wouldn't have wanted to call attention to them. Jonna wouldn't want him to have seen them now, but it was no longer her choice.

Decker rested his head against her soft crown of hair, and Jonna slept on in the shelter of his shoulder and under the crook of his chin.

Mrs. Davis poked her head into the kitchen and pointed to Rachael. "Mrs. Thorne would like you to help her get ready for dinner," she said. "Go on. She was almost asleep on her feet when she got here. Lay out a fresh gown for her and dress her hair. That should be enough to revive her."

Rachael adjusted her cap and smoothed her apron. She waited for the housekeeper's approving nod before she left.

Jonna was sitting at her dressing table when Rachael entered. She followed the girl's movements in the mirror. "I'd like to wear the wine silk this evening. Do you know the one I mean?" When Rachael looked uncertain Jonna drew the outline of the heart-shaped bodice against her chest. "It has jet beading along the neckline." She saw Rachael's expression clear. "Will you get that for me?" She pointed to the gown she had been wearing, which was lying over the back of a chair. "And take that one for laundering."

While Rachael disappeared into the dressing room Jonna finished plucking pins from her hair. She ran her fingers through the length of it, separating the strands. The strap of her chemise slipped over her shoulder and Jonna let it lie there. She rubbed her temples. The nap in the carriage had left her more tired than refreshed.

Rachael laid the wine silk gown carefully at the foot of Jonna's bed. She walked over to the dressing table, but she didn't pick up a brush. Instead she slipped her hands under Jonna's and began to massage gently. The pressure of her fingertips eased the tension behind Jonna's eyes and in her neck. She sighed gratefully.

"You can't imagine how I'll miss this when you're gone," she said. The fingers on her scalp paused only briefly, but Jonna felt it. She caught Rachael's reflection in the mirror. "Mrs. Davis says you've performed well at all your duties. It's time to find a placement for you."

Rachael's eyes clouded. She touched her throat.

"I don't think it matters that you can't speak. It's never interfered here. You've always been able to make yourself understood." Jonna noticed that Rachael was not particularly pleased with the compliment. "No decision's been made yet," she said. "I don't have any place in mind. You mustn't worry that I'll send you anywhere where you'll be hurt. Captain Thorne thinks you've experienced your fill of that already."

Heat rose in Rachael's cheeks. Her coffee-colored complexion masked her blush, but she couldn't hide her distress. She shook her head vigorously.

"He told me what happened this morning," Jonna said gently. "He doesn't know anything about you, Rachael, nothing about your background or how you came here on the Railroad. He thinks you're a freeborn black because I've told him that's all I hire."

Jonna was watching Rachael closely. Though the young woman's fingers were still working against her scalp, Rachael's distress was only marginally contained. "None of us know what you may have suffered," Jonna went on. "But in this house I want you to be safe. No one has the right to make you lift your skirts or give yourself in any way against your will. Do you understand what I'm saying?"

Rachael's fingers stilled. With visible effort she managed to nod slowly.

"While you remain in my home I want you to come to me if there's ever a problem. I'm going to ask Mrs. Davis to reassign your duties. I wanted you to know that it's not because I'm unhappy with your work. Captain Thorne wants to avoid any possibility that he's misunderstood again."

Jonna handed Rachael the brush. "He's not angry with you, Rachael. Only concerned. He offers his protection as well." She closed her eyes as Rachael made the first pass through her long hair. Tension seeped out of her with each stroke.

Rachael hastily knuckled away a tear that clung stubbornly to her lashes. She opened her mouth to speak, then her gaze fell on the disfigured ball of her hand and she closed it again. So much worse could happen to her if she said anything. Anything at all.

Jonna looked up as Rachael set down the brush. "Thank you," she said. "I feel much better. Will you help me with my gown?"

Rachael picked up the silk carefully, fanning out the material across her arm for Jonna's inspection. The color shimmered and shifted like burgundy swirling in a wineglass. Thousands of jet beads were sewn along the neckline. They sparkled darkly against Jonna's pale skin as Rachael fastened the gown at her back.

Jonna turned this way and that, studying her reflection in the cheval glass. "It's no good, is it? I don't do justice to this gown."

Out of the line of her sight, Rachael simply stared at her in disbelief. She entered Jonna's field of vision and pointed to the dressing table again. Her silent command brooked no refusal. In short order she began to work her deft magic on Jonna's hair. Using jet combs to lift the heavy fall at the back and a beaded headband to make a crown in the front,

Rachael's efforts accented Jonna's slender throat and naturally regal bearing.

"Oh my," Jonna said as she stared at her reflection. The effect was quite extraordinary. "Oh my." Above her head, she saw Rachael was beaming. "You have every right to be pleased with yourself," Jonna told her. "You've made a silk purse."

Turning on her stool, Jonna looked straight into the younger woman's dark expressive eyes. "What do you know about Falconer?"

"You're very quiet," Decker said. They had finished dinner nearly an hour earlier and retired to the music room. Jonna lost interest in playing quickly, and Decker didn't press. "You didn't say much during dinner either."

"I didn't think you noticed."

"It registered," he said. "But it was such a pleasure simply staring at you, I didn't remark on it."

"That's an extravagant compliment."

"It's the truth. You're beautiful, Jonna."

She looked away immediately, uncomfortable. "I told Rachael she'd managed to make a silk purse this evening."

"And by implication named yourself a sow's ear." Decker shook his head. "You have a remarkably twisted perception of yourself. What is it you see when you look in the mirror?"

"Decker," she said warningly. "Let's change the subject, shall we?" She didn't give him an opportunity to have a say one way or the other. "I spoke to Rachael about what happened this morning. I think she was afraid you were angry with her. I assured her that wasn't the case. She knows she has our protection as long as she's in this house."

"And how long will that be?" Decker asked. He wondered how Jonna intended to conduct her underground station with either him or Jeremy Dodd so close at hand. Perhaps that was what her silence had been about. She had to be considering the problem as well. He didn't like complicating her efforts, but he couldn't do otherwise. She had to trust him with what she was doing before he could help her.

"How long?" she repeated. "I don't know. She's welcome to stay here, of course, but you've often remarked on how these girls come and go. She may decide she doesn't like her new duties and apply elsewhere."

"It wouldn't be easy for her, not when she doesn't speak."

"No, you're right. She wouldn't find it easy. Perhaps I should ask Mrs. Davis to give it some thought. Rachael may appreciate knowing she has some choices."

Decker's eyes were caught again by the jet beading along the neckline of Jonna's gown. He followed the bodice as it cut across her bare shoulders. She was wearing the ivory piece he'd given her. It wasn't the right accent for the gown. He didn't mention it because he knew she didn't care and because he rather liked the idea that she wore his gift around her throat.

"You're staring again," Jonna said.

A smile played around his lips. "Am I?"

"You know you are." She stood and crossed in front of him to the fireplace. Sweeping her dress back, she poked at the fire to make it give up a little more heat. It wasn't until she was returning to her chair that Decker's hand snaked out and captured her. He brought her down firmly on his lap.

"You needn't look so pleased with yourself," she told him, looping her arms around his neck. "I was hoping you'd do this."

"And I was hoping you'd let me." Her gown shimmered as it settled around him. Decker bent his head and lightly kissed the curve of her neck. She arched her throat and offered herself up to his mouth. The heat of his lips circled her skin like a brand.

The centers of Decker's eyes darkened as he studied her face. Her lips parted on a breathy little sigh. He only had to look at her, she thought, for her to feel his touch. His eyes had dropped to her lips, and she could feel the heat of his mouth. When he looked at her hair it was as if his fingers were sifting through it.

Jonna's kiss whispered across his mouth. His hands slipped along her midriff and up her rib cage. They passed lightly over her breasts. She murmured something against his lips and they went back. She felt her flesh swell in response to the caress, and she leaned into him.

Mrs. Davis had to clear her throat twice to be heard above the roar in their ears. Jonna and Decker looked up simultaneously in the direction of the parted doors, both of them a little dazed. Jonna's instinct was to remove herself from Decker's lap, but he held her. She knew a small measure of relief that his hands were no longer cupping her breasts.

"Mr. Quincy's come calling," Mrs. Davis said. She moved to block Jack's entry, but he had a good view over the top of her head. The housekeeper's lips were pursed disapprovingly.

Jack's voice boomed. "And I've brought someone with me. Go on with you, Dorthea." He grinned wickedly as she blushed at his familiarity. "Step one way or the other. In or out."

"It's all right, Mrs. Davis," Decker said.

The housekeeper raised her eyes heavenward, but she moved to one side.

Jonna's whisper was harsh, and she accomplished it without moving her lips. "You have no idea who he has with him."

"You're right. I don't." He wasn't at all perturbed. "Who's with you, Jack?"

Jack walked into the room. He tipped his hat in a gentlemanly greeting to Jonna, not at all discomfited by finding her on Decker's lap. He jerked his thumb behind him to indicate the shadowy figure still in the hallway. "He just arrived from Charleston on *Remington Siren*. He was inquiring at the harbor after you, Decker, so I brought him here."

Decker's eyes narrowed as he strained to see past Jack. Jonna's attention was also riveted in that direction.

Graham Denison stepped into the room. "Evenin', Decker," he drawled softly. "I wonder if I might have a word with you."

Thirteen

Graham sat in one of the library's brocade wing chairs, but his body leaned stiffly toward the fire. He gratefully accepted the tumbler of whiskey that Decker thrust in his hand. The first large swallow went down smoothly and warmly. "Winter," he murmured. "Another peculiar Yankee notion."

Decker said nothing. Cold alone did not explain his friend's pale as salt complexion or the tense way he held his body, almost as if he were protecting himself from the very heat he craved.

Graham took another swallow, a smaller one this time. He glanced at Decker and wasn't at all surprised to find the other man watching him closely. "Tell me about the very lovely lady in the other room," he said. "You were remiss in making introductions. I imagine the oversight was intentional."

"It was, but not because I was afraid she'd succumb to your singular charm. You didn't look as if you could stand much longer."

Graham's small, self-mocking smile became more of a grimace. "You noticed that, did you?" He inched himself back in the chair so that only his long legs were extended toward the fire. His boots, usually polished to a sheen that would reflect the flames, were dull with dust. It had taken a great deal of strength to hide his injury from Jack Quincy, and he wasn't even certain how effective his efforts had been. There seemed no point in making the same effort for Decker. Still, he wasn't ready to reveal the extent of the problem. One of his dark brows lifted archly, and his smooth drawl came forth. "You still haven't told me about the lady," he said. "Would she be Miss Remington?"

"She would be Mrs. Thorne," Decker said.

Graham's flinty, blue-gray eyes sparked appreciatively at the hint of possessiveness in Decker's tone. "Congratulations. Mr. Quincy never breathed a word of your good fortune."

"I doubt he was certain what to make of you," he said. "Frankly, I'm not sure myself." Decker picked up the crystal decanter of whiskey from the serving tray and topped off Graham's glass. He sat in the opposite wing chair and placed the decanter on the floor beside him. Sipping his own drink, he regarded Graham over the rim of his glass. "Should I send someone for a doctor?" Decker expected Graham to deny there was any need, or to put him off. The first indication of how serious the problem was came when Graham simply acquiesced.

Decker rose to his feet immediately and disappeared in the hallway. He was gone less than a minute. "Mr. Quincy had already advised Jonna that a physician might be necessary. She sent for Dr. Hardy. He should be here within the hour. A room is being prepared for you. Do you want to go there now?"

Embarrassed that his weak condition was so obvious, Graham summoned a small amount of color to erase the pallor in his cheeks. It lasted only a moment. "Didn't mean to put you out," he said. "I didn't know about you and Miss Remington."

"Don't concern yourself," Decker said. "And don't waste your energy with apologies. You can't appreciate how little of a problem this is for Jonna. I'd rather hear what you're doing in Boston and who the hell it is they have in a Charleston jail."

Graham knocked back another mouthful of whiskey. It was not the anesthetic he hoped it would be. "You know about Matt Willet, then."

"Just learned of it today. Grant Sheridan took great pleasure in telling me. This was after I offered to arrange for him to meet Falconer. He thought I was trying to make a fool of him."

One of Graham's dark brows raised. "And weren't you?"

Decker permitted himself a small, sly smile. "A fool's born, not made."

Graham chuckled softly. "No love lost there, I see."

"None."

"Too bad. It doesn't seem right somehow, not with the two of you working for the same cause. Do you know, if I hadn't been able to find you, I was going to look up Sheridan. I wasn't sure where else I might apply for help."

"Boston's a sympathetic city," Decker said. "You could have gone almost anywhere."

"But not without considerable explanation. Sheridan's views are well known. He seemed a better alternative than simply choosing blindly. I thought he might offer some protection or introduce me to some friends who would."

"I think he would have done that for you," Decker said. "But only if you had refrained from using my name as a way of ingratiating yourself. Doing so wouldn't have moved him to help you."

"I take it this has something to do with the fact that Jonna Remington is not Mrs. Sheridan."

Decker nodded. "That's part of it. Sheridan knew my brother Colin. They didn't see eye to eye much, especially where Jonna's future was concerned. After Colin established himself in London and I came here, Sheridan just shifted his animosity." Decker put his glass on the end table beside him.

Withdrawing his pocket watch, he glanced at the time. "By my reckoning," he said, "you have forty minutes before the doctor arrives, perhaps even less before Jonna's curiosity gets the better of her and she invites herself in here. I won't turn her out, Graham, and you won't be able to. What you need to say in confidence needs to be said now."

Graham had wedged his upper body between the back and the wing of the chair. His right elbow rested firmly against his ribs, applying steady pressure to the small puncture wound in his side. His jacket, shirt, and vest hid the bandage which was wrapped around his middle. In spite of the layers of clothing, Graham could sense that the bandage was becoming damp. He hoped it was sweat breaking from his fevered body. He was very much afraid it was blood.

"Matthew Willet is one of my Carolina neighbors," Graham said without inflection. "He owns a few thousand acres of prime cotton and tobacco land, and calls his place Spring Hill. I've never known him to free a slave or to ever mention that he was considering it. That would be true of Willet's father and grandfather, too. His family helped settle the colony, and they've used slaves ever since indentured servitude went out of fashion. That's a fairly long acquaintance with the institution. I don't think there's a more unlikely candidate to take Falconer's identity than Matt Willet."

"And yet he's the one in jail."

Graham waved his hand holding the drink dismissively. "Not for long. He'll be cleared."

"If he's not lynched first."

"Willet's not some dirt farmer or shop owner trying to do right by his conscience. A man like that would be strung up in no time. Willet's daddy and granddaddy will see that he has protection. He won't be incarcerated long." Graham's reserved smile was wry. "After all, he's innocent."

That was true enough, Decker thought. But it didn't explain anything. "So why is Willet in jail?"

"He had the misfortune to be in Michele Moreau's establishment the evening it was visited by the authorities. Apparently they had some information that Michele's whorehouse was being used as a station on the Underground. They searched the premises and found the closet in the attic."

"Empty?" Decker asked.

Graham shook his head. "There wasn't enough warning to get them all out. We were fortunate to only have to account for three. The two women were moved downstairs, but the man, a runaway from Georgia, stayed behind. I only know what Michele told me. She accompanied the authorities on their search, protesting her innocence all the time, while I was shown to one of the bedrooms. Apparently they dragged Seth out of the closet and on threat of ending his life right there, forced him to tell them how he had come to be at Michele's."

Graham finished his drink. He wanted another, but he didn't ask for more. The whiskey was only making him drunk, not numb. "I'm told he gave a good performance. His lies were convincing. They couldn't imagine that he would dare to give them anything less than the truth. He exceeded their best hopes. Seth gave them Falconer."

"Did someone tell him to do that?"

"No. It just happened. It was part of Michele's hasty plan that Seth should name someone in her house as his contact on the Railroad, but she never said he should identify the man as Falconer. She told me later that it simply spilled out of him. She was as shocked to hear him say it as the men who were escorting him."

Decker was envisioning the search of Michele's second-floor bedrooms. There would have been outraged patrons and indignant whores, and a cacophony of sputtering, squealing, and swearing. He almost wished he could have witnessed it. "I take it you were fully occupied when they came to your room."

"Cathy," Graham said with a certain fondness. "She made it look that way." The whore straddled him just moments before the door opened. When the sheriff poked his head inside, she arched provocatively and never stopped the slow undulation of her hips. Seth was given only a moment to see the same sight, but he didn't mistake the look that crossed Graham's face for passion. Unlike the sheriff, Seth recognized it as pain.

"When he didn't identify me, they moved on. All hell finally broke loose when they came to Willet's room. Not only did Seth identify Matt and call him Falconer, but he was caught in bed with two of Michele's whores. Young, *black* whores."

Decker's brow furrowed momentarily; then his features cleared and his quirky half-smile showed his appreciation. "The women who had been hiding in the attic," he said.

Graham nodded. "That's right. Michele stripped them down, made them up, and put them in that drunken sonofabitch's room. I suspect the first he knew they were there was when the screaming started. By all accounts he was three sheets to the wind. The sheriff recognized Willet, of course, just the same as he recognized me, but with Seth saying Willet was Falconer, and there being two lovely blackbirds in his bed, something had to be done. They couldn't lay any charges at Michele. She produced papers showing she had purchased both girls at auction and they were legally hers. As for Seth being in her attic, she swore she didn't know how Willet had managed it, but she accused him, quite effectively as it turned out, of doing it all on his own. If there was an accomplice, then it was one of her whores, she told them, and good luck to them in discovering which one it was."

Decker had no difficulty imagining Michele's arrogant, self-righteous anger. She would have been perfectly believable, careful not to overplay her hand. He wondered if she had used a few of the Gallic expressions he had taught her. She seemed to have an affinity for French swear words, if no appreciation for the language. "So Willet was taken away."

"They didn't have much choice," Graham said. "It seemed odd to them that Willet would come to a whorehouse to bed those girls when he could have had any that he wanted on his own plantation. In their mind the behavior was so unusual that it lent credence to Seth's accusations."

"And Seth?"

"As far as I know he was returned to his owner in Georgia."

"The girls?"

"Still with Michele. I had arranged for Seth to use the Railroad by way of Michele's because of the girls. Michele would not release them until they had an escort north. They both came from the same slaver."

"*Salamander?*" Decker asked.

"No. Another reptilian ship." He paused, thinking. "I believe Michele told me it was *Chameleon*. In any event, the girls don't speak any English. They couldn't have made it far without help, even with papers of manumission. When it became clear that I would have to leave Charleston myself, I considered bringing them. Michele talked me out of it."

Decker shook his head slowly. There was no mistaking the regret in Graham's voice. He was still thinking he could have done otherwise. "Thank God she did, and thank God you listened."

Graham ignored that. "Michele bought the girls with my money. There was no other purpose for the purchase except to free them. Michele was right to demand an escort for them; I just should have planned it better."

Decker didn't argue. The sickly pallor of Graham's face only seemed to underscore his determination. Decker's eyes dropped surreptitiously to his pocket watch again. It was his opinion that the doctor couldn't arrive too soon. "I'll arrange for the girls' transportation the next time I'm in Charleston. It won't be difficult at all, not if they have papers. They won't have to stay in the hold, and I already know they'll be welcome here."

"I confess I was hoping you'd make that offer. I was going to ask if your wife would be agreeable. I recall that you said she hires freeborn blacks. This situation is different, but the young women *are* free."

Decker almost smiled. Graham would enjoy hearing his story about Jonna's secret Underground station, but it could wait until Graham himself was a more appreciative audience. Right now he looked as if it was all he could do to hold himself in the chair. "Is that why you're here?" asked Decker. "To ask me if I'd help those girls?"

Graham's unyielding blue-gray eyes had lost a large measure of their sharpness. "I'm responsible for them," he said.

Decker waited. As an explanation, it did not go nearly far enough. It might account for Graham Denizon's presence in his home, but not in Boston. There was some more pressing reason Graham had had for leaving Charleston.

Graham didn't respond to his friend's silence. He was patient in his own right. "Do you think that my room might be ready?" he asked.

The question moved Decker to his feet immediately. "I'm sure it is. Come, I'll take you there." It was less of a suggestion than a command, but Decker didn't apologize for it. He watched Graham's awkward rise from the chair and realized he had probably left it too late already. Graham's balance was unsteady at best, and the whiskey he'd taken hadn't helped. Decker held out his arm, but Graham ignored it.

"I'll be fine," he said. Then he dropped like a stone.

Falling to one knee beside Graham, Decker barked out to Jack. He wasn't at all surprised when the man responded quickly, or that Jonna was only a few steps behind him. He didn't think they were listening at the door, but they hadn't been far beyond it. "Jack, help me get Graham upstairs. Take his feet. I'll get under his shoulders. Jonna, what room—"

"My parents'," she said. "It's really the most comfortable."

Decker nodded. "Ready, Jack?" He did a three-count, and they lifted Graham between them. He had a long, lithe frame, but it was well muscled and unconsciousness made him a dead weight. Decker expected it. Jack staggered a bit. "Careful," Decker said. "Don't drop—"

Jonna's gasp cut him off. One hand immediately rose to cover her mouth, the other pointed to Graham. Where his jacket had fallen open a dark red blossom of blood was visible on his vest.

Jack looked over his shoulder to see what she was pointing at. "Damn if I knew that was the problem," he said under his breath.

Decker didn't comment though the injury startled him, too. "Let's take him up there now, Jack. Jonna, will you hold the door?"

She preceded them into the hallway and up the stairs. Once they had Graham in his room, she quickly turned down the bed and rang for help. She waited outside while Jack and Decker stripped Graham out of his clothes. When Rachael and Amanda arrived she kept them in the hall and passed to Rachael Graham's soiled clothes, then sent Amanda off for hot water, towels, and bandages. "And bring the doctor here as soon as he arrives," she called after them as they hurried away.

Jonna stepped inside the room again. Jack was standing at the foot of the bed, his hands behind his back as he surveyed the scene, while Decker was sitting in a chair he'd moved closer to Graham's side. Jonna went to Decker and laid one hand lightly on his shoulder. Graham lay very still, his breathing labored. Against his dark hair, his face was nearly bloodless. Even his lips were pale. There was a small flower of blood seeping through the sheet that covered him.

"Jack says his name is Graham Denison," Jonna said. She hesitated, then went on, unsure if she should breach the subject at all. "We have a contract with some Denisons in Charleston. Is he—"

"Yes," Decker said. "He's one of them."

"But Jack's never met him before tonight. We've been doing business with that family for years."

"Graham's grandfather is the one Jack knows. And there's a younger brother."

"How is it you know him?"

Decker didn't answer immediately. He glanced at Jack first, his eyes darting once toward the door. "Would you mind?"

Jack grinned at the less than subtle hint. "I'll be outside if you need me."

When they were alone, Decker looked up at Jonna. She had drawn in her lower lip and was worrying it gently. "I met him in Charleston at the home of Michele Moreau," he said. "She invites gentlemen to play cards there from time to time. Graham is a frequent guest."

"And you?"

"Just filling in at the table for someone else."

Jonna's hand fell away from his shoulder and folded in a loose fist at her side. "It's a brothel, isn't it? That's why you sent Jack out. You knew he'd recognize the name and give it away."

Decker started to explain, but the door opened and Jack poked his head through. "Dr. Hardy's here." Decker nodded in acknowledgment and stood. "We can talk about it later, Jonna."

"I don't think I want to." Her voice was barely audible.

He kissed her lightly on the mouth. Her lips were cool and dry, and she didn't respond. "Don't assume you know what it means," he told her. "Don't rush to judgment." He placed his palm against her cheek and lifted her chin slightly. She respected him enough to look at him and listen. Now, if only she would trust him. "And don't think the worst of me."

Jonna stared at him. It had been a very long time since she had thought the worst of him. Not that he would have any reason to believe it, she realized. She had never told him differently, and she had often acted in ways that fostered that impression. She wasn't at all certain what she thought about him frequenting a brothel. She had always known there were women in his life, even if she chose not to think about them.

Decker let his hand slide away from her face. She hadn't said a word, yet he believed he had captured her promise. He hoped so.

Hardy's entrance into the room separated them. Jonna stepped back from the bed and took the chair with her to give the doctor space. While he was examining his patient, Amanda arrived with hot water and linens. Jonna took the basin and directed Amanda to put the bandages and towels on the chair. When the girl continued to hover uncertainly near the fireplace, Jonna sent her away. The less that was known about the nature of Graham's injury, the better.

Dr. Hardy did not see many gunshot wounds in his practice. He was familiar with gout, influenza, and setting broken bones. He treated migraines and fevers and stomach ailments. His patients were more likely to fall through the ice in the Charles River than come to him with a lead ball in their flesh.

Hardy turned Graham over just far enough to look for an exit wound. The puckered hole was there, surrounded by dried blood and loose skin. He nodded to himself, satisfied. It meant he wouldn't have to probe for the ball. He doubted this patient would survive that kind of imprecise exploration.

The physician looked from Decker to Jonna. "Which of you is going to help me?"

"I am." They spoke simultaneously, and nothing in their tones suggested that either of them would back down.

"Very well," Hardy said. "There's something for both of you. Jonna, bring the water here. Decker, you hold his legs down in the event he starts to thrash."

They worked silently for the better part of thirty minutes. The wound had to be thoroughly cleaned and sutured. The doctor found bits of thread in the puncture from the shirt Graham had been wearing when he was shot. He drew them out with tweezers and each gentle extraction started the bleeding again. He applied more alcohol after the flesh had been stitched; then Jonna helped him wrap Graham with a fresh bandage.

"He needs to rest," Hardy said solemnly as he collected his things. "The ball didn't hit any vital organs. There was evidence of healing, but the injury was aggravated again. The bruising around the hole suggests he was hit hard there. Probably by a club, perhaps just a fist, but the blow couldn't have been more on target. Serve him liquids today and tomorrow,

357

food as he can tolerate it after that. I'll stop back in a few days unless you come for me before then."

Nodding, Jonna took in all the doctor's directions. "Thank you, Dr. Hardy. I appreciate your efforts on this man's behalf."

"Oh, you'll get my bill, Jonna," he said good-naturedly.

She smiled and added softly, "I'd also appreciate it if you keep this to yourself. If it should come to anyone's attention that you were here this evening, I'd rather you'd say it had something to do with me."

"I can't think why anyone would want to know," he said. "Or why I would tell them. Just the same, you can rest assured that I won't say anything out of turn." He dug in his black leather case and pulled out a small amber bottle. He handed it to Jonna. "Take this tonic in the morning with your tea."

Jonna examined the bottle. The maker claimed on the label that just a teaspoon a day would relieve headache, toothache, nausea, constipation, fatigue, muscle cramps, and insomnia. "But I don't have any of these ailments," she said.

Decker grinned. "I think the doctor's saying that if you want to be the reason that he's here, then you've got to let him treat you."

"Oh." She looked up in time to see Hardy and her husband exchange amused, indulgent glances. Her mouth flattened in annoyance. She was not entirely witless. "Thank you, Dr. Hardy," she said, this time dismissing him. "Jack will escort you to the door."

"Prickly, aren't you?" Decker said after the physician had gone. "Don't apologize for it. It's one of your most delightful traits."

Quite unable to help herself, Jonna prickled again. "I had

no intention of apologizing."

Decker kissed her without warning.

"What was that for?"

"For having the good sense to have a dimple at the corner of your mouth."

Further annoyed that she had risen so easily to his bait, Jonna's dimple deepened as she compressed her lips. He simply smiled at her. It was no good even pretending to be aggravated with him, she thought. She placed the bottle of tonic on the bedside table. "Will you want to stay with him?" she asked.

Decker was instantly serious. "A while longer," he said. "Could you arrange with Mrs. Davis to have someone with him at all times?"

"Of course. I'll see to it right now. I have to talk to Jack as well."

"All right."

Jonna watched him as he turned back to the bed and gave his full attention to the man lying there. Was it friendship that kept Decker here? she wondered. Or just his humanity? A full minute later, Jonna left soundlessly.

It was after midnight when Decker returned to his room. Jonna was sitting up in bed, a book cradled in her hands. She closed it and put it aside as he crossed the space separating them. Her face lifted most naturally for his kiss. He hadn't known what to expect when he opened the door. Jonna could easily have been in her own room, asleep in her own bed, and he would have felt the full measure of disappointment he was guarding himself against.

"How is he?" she asked quietly.

Decker began to get ready for bed, unbuttoning his jacket. He tossed it over a chair. "He seems to have fallen into a natural sleep. His breathing was coming easier when I left him with Amanda."

Jonna watched him disappear into the dressing room. "Did you know he had been shot?"

"No," he called back. He pulled his shirt free of his trousers. "I suspected illness, not injury. I didn't know it was a pistol wound until his jacket fell open."

"So he didn't tell you anything about it."

"Not a thing." Decker finished undressing, washed quickly with the cool water in the basin, and returned to Jonna. He was tying the loose drawstring of his drawers as he walked in.

Jonna reached for the bedside lamp to turn it down. She stopped when she noticed that Decker was no longer moving toward the bed. She glanced over her shoulder at him. He was simply no longer moving. His entire attention was fixed on the small table that complemented the sitting area of the bedchamber. "What is it?" she asked. There was nothing on the table but a brass lamp and a porcelain figurine. Neither of those items was worthy of Decker's intense concentration.

"There were some papers on that table," he said, walking toward it. "Were you reading them?"

"If I had been, I would have returned them." Jonna bent her head to see if they had fallen under the nearby chair. They weren't there.

Decker paused beside the table. He tapped the polished surface lightly, thinking. Had he taken them out of here? To the library, perhaps? He tried to remember if he had placed Sheridan's papers with his sketches for *Huntress*. The papers could easily be at the ship.

Jonna's voice came to him as if from a distance. He shook off his reverie and looked at her. "Did you say something?"

"I asked what the papers were. Obviously you think

they're important. Might you have taken them to the harbor this morning?"

"I carried some sketches inside my jacket," he said. "I may have put everything together." He remembered reading them in this room when Jonna joined him last night. And this morning, before he could look at them again, Rachael had come in. Had he simply taken them in a hurry, without thinking, when he left? The more he considered it, the more likely it seemed. Rachael certainly had no use for the papers, nor had anyone else in the household. How many of Jonna's servants could even read?

Decker ran a hand through his hair. His drawn brow cleared a little. "They must be at the ship," he said. "I'll find them in the morning."

Jonna raised the covers as he climbed into bed. Belatedly she realized he hadn't told her what the papers were, nor had he identified their importance. As she stretched out beside him, rubbing her feet against his legs to warm them, this lack of answers didn't bother her at all. She turned away long enough to extinguish the lamp. His arm slipped across her waist.

"I'm sorry about Mr. Denison," she whispered.

"So am I." He paused. "Thank you for taking him in, Jonna. It was generous of you."

She wished he hadn't said it quite that way. "You make it sound as if it were my decision alone."

"Wasn't it?"

"No. That is, I didn't mean it to be . . . it shouldn't have been. This is your home as well." She had never told him that before, she realized. He probably felt as much a guest here as Graham Denison did. "I want this to be your home."

Decker didn't say anything. He couldn't speak. He felt her take his hand and thread her fingers between his. She squeezed gently and edged closer. The room had taken on the silence of a confessional.

"I never loved your brother," Jonna said. "Not the way you think I did. He was a good friend and mentor. There was a time when I imagined that he might love me, but it was just that—my imagination. I was sixteen then, coming out of a year of mourning my father. For the first six months I was numb with grief. Papa had prepared me for years to run the line, but I was still too young when the time came. Perhaps if I had been Papa's son . . ." Her voice trailed off. Several moments passed before she spoke again. "Colin and Jack held my hand through that first year. Sometimes figuratively, sometimes in fact. I suppose it was inevitable that I would begin to think Colin's affections might be engaged. It was just a schoolgirl vanity. I never thought the same of Jack."

Jonna felt Decker's thumb pass across the back of her hand. There was enough light for her to see that his eyes were intent on hers. She had his full attention. "When Colin took to the sea again I was disappointed, but not surprised. It had always been his mission to find you and Greydon. He could hardly do that in Boston Harbor."

"Colin *does* love you," Decker said.

Her smile was soft, a trifle wistful. "I know. And I know the nature of that love. It's the same I feel for him. Brother to sister. Friend to friend. Student to teacher. I was afraid to see him at Rosefield. It had been so long since we exchanged anything but letters. I wondered if I had mistaken my feelings or his. He had a brother now. He had you, Decker. I didn't know if there was a place for me any longer."

"You were jealous," he said softly, slowly. There was something akin to wonderment in his tone. "Of me."

"I was . . . jealous." It was not so easy to admit, but it was the truth. "I know that you thought my affections ran more deeply and that you didn't entirely trust Colin. I played on your uncertainty, even when I knew that nothing had changed between Colin and me."

"You were getting a little of your own back."

Jonna hesitated. "That was part of it."

Decker said nothing. He simply waited and placed no expectation on the silence. She would tell him or she wouldn't.

Jonna's throat was tight, her mouth dry. When she spoke her voice was husky. "I let you believe some things that weren't true," she said. "About *Huntress*. I never intended that Colin should have it. It wasn't built for him at all."

"But you let me think it was."

"I've just said that, haven't I?" Her expression was earnest now. "And it was your notion in the first place. It had never occurred to me until you presented it. I merely went along. I had no expectation that you would force a marriage to keep *Huntress* and me out of Colin's hands."

"I thought you were of the opinion last night that I married you for love."

"Well . . . yes." Her tone was uncertain. "But I didn't know that then. And I'm not sure I know it now. It's not as if you've told me so."

He didn't tell her now either. "You gave me *Huntress*."

"Yes," she whispered. His head had moved closer to hers. She could feel his warm breath on her cheek.

"Even though you built the ship for someone else."

"Yes."

He waited again. He didn't know the answer to the question he wouldn't ask.

"I built it for a man I've never met," she said finally. "I built it for Falconer."

Rachael stared down at the sleeping man. She touched his

forehead with the back of her maimed hand, and for a moment forgot why she had done it as she studied the contrast between their skins. His was warm and faintly damp. Hers was cool and dry. His was pale as milk; hers like coffee.

She backed away from the bed and bumped into the chair behind her. She sat down slowly. It wasn't entirely a surprise that this man was here. After all, he was acquainted with Captain Thorne. Yet his coming here seemed out of the ordinary. Rachael had never expected to see him again once she left Michele Moreau's brothel. But then, she reflected, she hadn't expected to see the captain either.

In fact, she had prayed she wouldn't.

The mantel clock behind her struck once. Her patient didn't stir. She was expected to remain with this man until she was relieved in four hours. By rights Amanda should have still been in attendance, but she'd begged this favor from Rachael just after the captain left. Rachael hadn't been able to refuse. Amanda had helped her out on many occasions. This was but a small repayment of kindness.

Or it had been until Rachael had seen clearly who she was attending. Now other decisions had to be made. There was little choice involved. Her direction had been set when she was first placed on the slaver *Salamander*.

Rachael did not expect to be noticed leaving the house, and she wasn't. There were no other pedestrians on the street at this late hour. The air was brisk as she walked down the hill. It blew under her woolen cape and parted it so that she had to hold the material in a tight fist to keep it closed. She walked with her head down, in part to keep the icy air off her face, in part so that she might not be recognized.

There was some traffic as she turned the corner at the bottom of the street, and for a moment her shrouded figure was illuminated by a lamp. She did not see whether the drivers of the wagons and carriages took any notice of her. She didn't look at them.

When she started out she wasn't at all sure that she could find her destination unaided. It was not so often that she left the Remington house with Mrs. Davis or one of the other servants. Neither had she much experience with the Boston streets when she had been in service elsewhere. There was more surprise than satisfaction when she found herself at the proper doorstep.

Rachael didn't knock, but extracted a key from her apron pocket instead. She let herself in quietly. The foyer was dark, and there were no lights coming from under any of the doors in the hallway. Rachael drew some comfort from the servants being in their quarters. Her presence would be difficult to explain. They would want to know why the runaway had returned.

She drew a calming breath and waited for her eyes to adjust and her heartbeat to slow before mounting the staircase.

His suite began at the first door off the landing. Again, she didn't knock. Unless he had someone with him he wouldn't lock the door. She almost hoped he had found someone to take her place.

The handle turned. Tonight, at least, he had no one in his bed.

Sheridan sat up abruptly. "Who's there?" It was a rough demand, one he fully expected to be answered. His eyes narrowed as he stared at the door. He heard it click closed and could make out the darker shape against it, but not the intruder's identity.

"It's me," Rachael said quietly.

Grant threw off the covers. His nightshirt gave him a ghostly appearance as he crossed the room to her. He placed his hands on her shoulders. She had brought some of the cold night air in with her. He guided her to the fireplace and let her warm herself at the dying embers. Kneeling in front of the hearth he began to build a fire.

His thoughtfulness touched her. She had not expected this kindness. When the fire was blazing she took off her cape. Under one arm she held some papers. She handed them to him.

"What are these?" Grant asked, rising to his feet. He thumbed through them quickly once, then more slowly the second time. It was quite clear what they were. He didn't bother asking that question again. "Where did you get them?"

She hadn't yet determined what she would say to that. If she told him she had come upon them in a common room, like the library or one of the parlors, it might not be so readily apparent who was interested in them. Her hesitation cost her. Grant's free hand snaked out and caught her by the throat. He applied no pressure, merely held her captive, but the threat was there. The pad of his thumb moved lightly across her windpipe.

"I found them in Captain Thorne's room," she said.

Grant studied her. Her eyes were as wide and dark as a fawn's. Her delicate features were set in stillness. "Tell me, is it fear that makes your voice so appealingly husky?" he asked. "Or the fact that it gets so little use at Jonna's."

Was she supposed to answer? she wondered. Did he expect her to say she feared him?

Grant's hand slipped away. "Never mind." He sifted through the papers again. "How did you know to bring these here?"

Had she made a mistake? "Aren't they yours?" she asked.

"They are. But that begs the question. How did you know they were mine?"

She pointed to the letterhead on the uppermost paper he held. "It says Sheridan Shipping. Some of the others are marked the same way."

"It does indeed," Grant said softly. His regard was frank, curious. "When did you learn to read?"

Until now she had kept it from him. Even on his visits to Mrs. Davis in Jonna's absence, she hadn't told him about the housekeeper's lessons. It had been easy to keep that secret then. There had been so little time for him to talk to her on those occasions. Her situation forced them to keep any exchange to a few words. It had been his idea that she shouldn't speak. He told her more confidences would be shared with someone who couldn't give them up.

There were times when he came to the house that he didn't see her at all. He may have suspected that she busied herself elsewhere in the mansion when she knew he was about, but he couldn't prove it. And he couldn't ask after her. Knowing that she could frustrate him was one of her guilty pleasures.

"I've been learning at Miss Remington's," she said. Intuitively she understood that she should not refer to Jonna as Mrs. Thorne. "I have been since I arrived."

"Jonna's teaching you?" His tone was harsh, incredulous.

She shook her head quickly. "No, Mrs. Davis. She teaches all the girls."

"But it's Jonna's idea."

"I suppose." She almost recoiled from his black look. "Yes, she approves of it. She makes certain Mrs. Davis has time in the evening for the lessons. She asks for nothing while we're engaged. Anything she needs, she gets for herself. Anything that needs to be done, waits, or Miss Remington does it alone."

"How very accommodating."

She pretended she hadn't heard the sneer in his voice. "Yes," Rachel said. "She is."

Grant's eyes narrowed. Was he imagining her quiet defiance, or was it really there? There was nothing about her posture that was challenging, quite the opposite. Her eyes were turned away from him; her arms hung loosely at her sides. Even her fingers were extended. No clenched fists here.

He put the papers on the mantel and reached for her crippled hand. She didn't recoil from his touch, but he felt her tremble. He held her hand in his larger one and raised it. Firelight burnished her dark skin. "It seems there should have been another way," he said.

Rachael said nothing. There was no real regret in his voice, no sorrow, just the quiet conviction that he had acted as he had because it was the only recourse open to him.

Grant stroked her hand gently, not at all repelled by the disfigurement. It was proof of her sacrifice, proof that she would surrender herself to him. He led her toward the bed. Sitting down on the edge of the mattress, he released her. He watched her as she began to disrobe.

"What do you think of your new master?" he asked. His eyes followed her fingers as she removed her apron and began to unfasten her bodice. "Have you been of service to him?"

His question provoked a pause in her fingers, but she didn't answer it.

"Perhaps he finds himself satisfied with Jonna," Grant went on. It was hard to imagine that being the case. Jonna Remington had never revealed herself to be a particularly responsive woman. "Do they share a bed?"

"They have separate bedchambers." She pushed her gown over her hips and let it fall to the floor. Grant touched her wrists, and she came to stand between his outstretched legs. "They're joined by a dressing room. I can't say if they share a bed." It was a lie. She had changed the sheets. She *knew*.

Grant's eyes were almost as black at the outer edges as they were at the center. They roamed over Rachael's slim neck and narrow shoulders. He pushed the neckline of her chemise over her arms. For a moment the high curve of her small breasts kept it in place, then it fell. She withdrew her arms. Grant stared at her breasts. He let his hands slide over them, rubbing her sensitive nipples with his thumbs. They were already hard. His right palm moved to rest just above her heart. He captured the frantic beat under his large hand.

"Why did you come here tonight?" he asked. "Was it to bring me those papers?"

She nodded, and leaned into him. She was a slight weight against him, and he supported her easily.

"Was it *only* to bring them here?"

There had been another reason. She thought about the man sleeping in the guest wing of the Remington house and about the man sleeping with Jonna Remington. But she knew what Grant wanted her to say. He actually made it simple for her to tell him what he wanted to hear and to delay the betrayal. "No," she said, as he took her breast in his mouth. "Not the only reason."

"Falconer?" Decker repeated. Nothing that he knew about her involvement with the Underground Railroad had prepared him for this. "You actually built *Huntress* for him?" He pulled his hand away from hers and sat up. "I think you'd better explain yourself."

Jonna sat up as well. She crossed her legs in front of her, tailor-fashion, and drew a pillow to her chest. Her position blocked Decker from reaching the oil lamp. She had no wish to bear his scrutiny and no desire to witness his amusement. "I *will* explain," she said, "but you mustn't rush me. It's not so simple a thing as you might think."

He chuckled softly. "Jonna, the very last thing I expect is that it will be simple. Just find a place to start and go from there."

"Do you remember our conversation about the abolitionists?" she asked him. "It was months ago. It's all right if you—"

Decker held up a hand and stopped her. "I remember," he said. "We were in your dining room. You were of the opinion that the publisher of *The Liberator* was a lunatic."

"A fanatic," she corrected. "I'm still of that opinion. But most of what I told you then was something less than I believe. I've never attended meetings at Faneuil Hall. Grant's fervor on the subject always unsettled me. I took a different tack and acted on my principles in a quieter manner. Or perhaps it's that I'm really just a coward, Decker. I know how Remington Shipping would suffer if I spoke out. I watched it happen to Grant. His Charleston and Baltimore trade is only a fraction of what it was five years ago. No matter what I've been able to accomplish, my actions may reflect more selfishness than nobility."

She is so very earnest, he thought. He caught a smile tugging at the corners of his mouth and tamped it down.

"I'm not such a good person, Decker. You shouldn't think that I am."

"All right," he said solemnly. "But what is it that you've done?"

"These past three years I've been a conductor on the Railroad," she said in a rush. "I know you have no strong opinion about abolition. I used to be critical that you took no position on it, or for that matter about anything much at all. Now I think you're simply more honest than I've been. There's no pretense about you."

Decker shifted slightly, made more than a little uncomfortable by this observation. "I'm not certain that's entirely true," he said carefully. "You could—"

Jonna didn't let him finish. "You've never tried to change my opinion of you," she said. "You've simply been here, haven't you? Day after day . . . for years now. In and out of my life, knowing there were times I didn't notice at all, and knowing there were times you came to my attention for all the wrong reasons. I never fully considered the kind of man who could do that, but now I realize it's one who's so comfortable with himself that he doesn't require the good opinion of others to define him."

Decker tried to shift the subject from himself. "I thought you were going to tell me about Falconer," he said.

"I was . . . I am." Jonna pushed the pillow away from her. She reached forward and laid her hand on Decker's thigh. "It's just that it doesn't matter very much anymore. I built *Huntress* to carry men and women from slavery to freedom. I designed her with that single purpose in mind and named her to fit the purpose. I thought that only Falconer could take her helm, or perhaps that only he would want to, but I think you're a man of similar compassion and conscience."

Decker shook his head. "Jonna, you said yourself that I have no strong opinion about abolition."

She leaned forward. Her voice was quiet with intensity. "But you have a passion for freedom. You risked your own once for Mercedes. I asked if it meant so little to you. You told me you did it because it meant so much."

"So I did," he said. He had forgotten it until now. "Perhaps you're wrong about me. I may only have been trying to impress you."

Jonna shook her head. "I won't believe it. I think it was as honest an answer as any other of yours. And I don't think you

371

feel any differently about freedom when we're talking Tess or Amanda or Delores or Rachael or—"

"I take your point," he said gently, before she went through an entire litany of names. "And no, I don't."

"*Huntress* is your ship now, Decker. I would never take it back. But I'm wondering if you might use her from time to time for the purpose for which she was built?"

He was quiet a moment; then he nodded.

Jonna threw her arms around him. "I'm not wrong, am I?" she demanded. She planted kisses on his cheeks, his mouth, his jaw. "You *are* the right man."

"I don't know if I'm the right man," he said. His arms circled her waist. "But I *am* Falconer."

Fourteen

It was still dark outside when Jonna woke. She raised herself on one elbow and studied Decker's sleeping profile. His features were relaxed. The lines at the corners of his eyes had softened. His breathing was steady. His thick, dark hair was tousled, and a lock of it fell forward over his smooth brow. Gently, so as not to disturb him, she pushed it back. Then her hand lingered a moment, her fingers trailing lightly over his temple, his cheek, and finally his jaw.

He was really quite a beautiful man. Had she told him that? Or was it only one of the things she had meant to say as he was making love to her? So many thoughts had remained half-formed and unspoken as his body covered hers. Jonna felt a measure of heat surface and spread upward from her breasts to her face as she remembered the things she *had* been able to tell him. Darkness had made her bold.

Love made her reckless.

Smiling, Jonna sat up carefully and moved to the edge of the bed. There was no reason that both of them should be up so early. She padded quietly into the dressing room and rang for help. Half an hour later, when sunlight was just beginning to break through the drapes, Jonna was sitting shoulder deep in a steaming hip bath.

She leaned back against the rim. The nape of her neck was cushioned by a folded towel. Her arms rested lightly on the curve of the tub and her fingertips dabbled in the water. She thought about picking up the soap and the cloth lying on the chair at her side. It seemed a monumental task. Instead she closed her eyes.

The water lapped at her sensitive skin. Heat seeped into her flesh. It was not difficult to imagine that she was still joined to him. There was a lingering sense of fullness between her thighs and a warm, pleasant ache in her breasts. Jonna pressed the faintly swollen line of her lips together. She could still feel his mouth on hers, taste him on the edge of her tongue.

Falconer.

It mattered so little. Even now it surprised her how unimportant it was that Decker Thorne was the man known as Falconer. She had come to admire him apart from that secret self, just as he had hoped she would. His patience is truly remarkable, Jonna thought. She would not have been half so restrained.

Explanations had come in fits and starts throughout the night. She had wanted to hear what he had to say, but she had wanted to love him more. In the end her curiosities, both intellectual and carnal, were satisfied.

Jonna's eyes opened as she heard Decker stir in the other room. She waited, wondering if he would call out for her. When he didn't, she realized he had merely turned over in his sleep. She smiled to herself, the shape of her mouth a trifle smug. It was a rather heady notion that she might have exhausted him.

Sitting up, Jonna reached for the bar of scented soap. Water dripped from her hand onto the washcloth. As she picked it up, it attached itself to some papers that were lying under it. The papers loosened almost immediately, and Jonna had to react quickly to keep them from falling into her bath. She let the soap and cloth drop, making a grab for the papers instead. Two sheets fluttered to the floor but several others clung to her damp fingers.

More annoyed than curious, Jonna placed them back on the chair. Hadn't Rachael seen them when she'd set the soap and washcloth down? But then the girl had been almost asleep on her feet, Jonna reminded herself. Rachael shouldn't have been sent to prepare the bath in the first place, not after night duty with their injured guest. Her eagerness to please should not be taken advantage of, Jonna thought, and she made a mental note to speak to Mrs. Davis about lightening the young woman's duties.

Sighing, Jonna leaned over the tub and picked up the sheets on the floor. She was on the point of putting them on the chair with the others when the heading of one caught her eye. Sheridan Shipping. She frowned. How on earth had this come to be here?

Jonna glanced over it quickly, then the one under it. Neither was a particularly important piece of information. One was a schedule, the other a correspondence to a Charleston supplier. She set them down, took up the others, and skimmed the contents.

Grant Sheridan rose from his bed. Slipping on his dressing gown, he walked to the window and drew back the drapes. Sunlight bathed his hard features as he looked out onto the street. There was no chance that he would see Rachael there. She would have left hours ago, under cover of night, fleeing his home as quietly as she had come upon it. Still, he knew it was why he stood there.

She had been exceptionally accommodating last night. The memory of her in his bed stirred his body. If he had heard her get up to leave he would have stopped her and taken her again. Perhaps she had known that given the chance he would have proved he wasn't finished with her. It would account, in part, for her quiet exit from his bed.

As willing as she had been to make herself available to him in any manner he chose, Grant had never been less certain of her, or of his hold over her. It was not so easy to define the change in Rachael, but he felt it, not in what she gave him, but in what she held back. Perhaps it was some newfound confidence that he detected. She had learned to read, after all, and that was not something he could take away from her.

He cursed softly and shrugged his powerfully built shoulders. He let the drapes drop back into place and rang for his manservant. The measure of anger that he felt was not directed at Rachael, but at Jonna. If Rachael was really possessed of a new confidence, then Jonna Remington was at the root of it. His mouth curved in a derisive smile. He would not think of her as Jonna Thorne. The name would never suit, and he would not accustom himself to it. Why should he? he wondered, when Jonna was going to be Mrs. Sheridan. It only required Decker's removal. Because of Rachael's timely help, he was one step close to that end.

Grant went to the fireplace to retrieve the papers Rachael had carried with her. Had she understood what she held in her hands, or had she merely delivered them to show good faith? Or, as he had begun to suspect last night, had she brought them as an excuse to be with him? It was a pleasant irony, Grant thought, that he could reward Rachael's loyalty by keeping her as his mistress while punishing Jonna.

Surveying the mantel, Grant's small, satisfied smile faded. His brows drew together. The papers were no longer where he had placed them. He looked over his shoulder at the table in the sitting area and then at the one at bedside. Both were bare of the documents. Turning on his heel, he knelt on the floor and looked under the chairs. He poked at the fireplace for some evidence that they had been swept inside by a draft. It would have been a consolation to know they were destroyed by the fire. That outcome was better than having them returned to Decker Thorne's hands, or worse, to Jonna's.

It was on that point that Grant had questioned Rachael several times. Did she know if Jonna had seen the documents? How could she be certain her employer hadn't? Had she overheard Decker discussing them with Jonna?

Grant had been satisfied by Rachael's answers. Although there were no guarantees, it was likely that she had removed them from Decker's room before even he had had a chance to study them. Much harder for Grant to accept was the fact that Decker had them in the first place. There had been only one opportunity for the man to place his hands on them—the occasion of his visit to Grant's office.

It was of little satisfaction to Grant that he had been suspicious of Decker's offer to acquaint him with Falconer. Obviously it had been a sham to gain entry to his office. Grant remembered being called out briefly. It was hard to believe Decker had made such a thorough job of rifling the contents of his files.

Not that everything he had taken was important. Quite the opposite was true. The fact that the documents were so diverse, and in the majority without consequence, supplied Grant with the clearest indication that Decker's search was not for a single specific item. The looting was random, done by a thief who lifted valuables indiscriminately and hoped he would find one or two priceless gems among the glass beads.

The gems were there, Grant thought. He had seen them for himself last night. He had been careful not to make too much of the documents when Rachael gave them over, but later, when he questioned her, he realized he might have aroused her suspicions. Or perhaps she knew more than she let on from the very beginning. She could read now, he reminded himself. If she had read the headings, then she may have read the content. Was that it? he wondered. Did she understand what she had seen?

Grant slowly sat down in one of the large armchairs. Rachael had returned the documents to him, but it seemed that she had also taken them back. Had it been her purpose all along? He stared at the glowing embers in the fireplace, his dark eyes vaguely unfocused as his thoughts tumbled and collided.

"Rachael," he murmured softly. "What dangerous game is this?"

Jonna stood framed in the doorway of the dressing room. She was wrapped in a towel that had been hastily drawn across her middle. The corner tucked between her breasts was already starting to slip its mooring. Her shoulders were damp, and water ran in thin rivulets down her arms and legs. Droplets fell on the hardwood floor with no apparent rhythm. Her hair was haphazardly secured with two tortoiseshell combs. Curling tendrils fanned her forehead and the curve of her neck.

She looked quite delicious.

Decker's sleepy-eyed gaze grew a little sharper. He noticed the deeply disapproving dimple at the corner of her mouth at the same time he became aware that she was holding something in her hands.

Jonna held up the papers so he could see them more clearly. The Sheridan Shipping letterhead was a bold, black beacon. "Are these the papers you were looking for last night?"

Decker sat up. Dragging a sheet around his hips, he hitched it carelessly and skirted the corner of the bed. "Where did you find them?"

Jonna pulled them back when he reached for them. "I was going to ask you the same thing."

He ignored her retort. There was marginally more impatience in his tone when he had to repeat his question. "Where did you find them?"

She blinked, struck by his irritation. "I found them in the dressing room. They were lying on a chair in there, no doubt precisely where you left them."

"That's not where I put them." He was certain of that.

"Then perhaps Rachael moved them when she was tidying up. Does it matter? It begs the question of how they came to be in your possession."

"I took them from Sheridan's office."

"Did Grant give them to you?"

"No." He said it without hesitation and saw the last bit of hope in Jonna's eyes disappear. "I took them without his permission."

"Then you stole them."

"Yes."

Jonna wondered that she wasn't more disappointed in him. Did she love him so much she was willing to excuse behavior that was outside the law? She stared at his extended hand. Perhaps, she thought, it was that she loved him enough to entertain an explanation. After a moment she placed the papers in his open palm. "To what purpose?" she asked. "What did you hope to find?"

"I'm not sure."

She looked at him oddly, and her voice softened. "You're not sure? That doesn't sound like you at all."

He shrugged. "I thought there might be something. . . ." Decker glanced at the papers briefly then back at her. "I'd hoped there'd be something I could use to keep him away from you."

Jonna's brows shot up. "To keep him away . . . You intended to blackmail him?"

He shook his head. "I want him out of your life."

"He *is* out of my life."

"That's not what I witnessed the first night we were back here," Decker said. His expression dared her to contradict him. "I know what I saw, Jonna. Sheridan was pressuring you to accept his embrace. You had your own reasons for not admitting it then, but that doesn't change the fact of it. He still wants you. Our marriage makes no difference to him."

"You can't know that," she whispered.

Decker's eyes held hers. "I know it better than anyone," he said. "In his place I would feel the same."

Jonna shook her head slowly. "No," she said gently. "You wouldn't. You would still love me. That's no part of what Grant feels or what he's ever felt for me. It's the right of ownership that moves him, nothing else. You wouldn't know anything about that. What have you ever wanted that you couldn't carry?"

The center of Decker's eyes darkened as he stared at her. The look of quiet amusement was absent from his own expression. Without warning, still holding the papers, he lifted her. "*Huntress* aside?" he asked.

Jonna's arms circled his neck. Her heart skipped a beat, and her violet eyes gleamed. The ship had been for Falconer's work, not for Decker's pleasure or gain. "*Huntress* aside," she whispered. "Has there ever been anything else?"

"Not a damn thing." He took her to bed. Sheridan's stolen documents were discarded and forgotten as passion flared.

Jonna was water slick and warm from her bath. Her body moved against his without resistance. The towel opened and her legs parted. She took him inside her almost immediately, and she was damp and warm there as well. Experiencing little in the way of conscious thought, Jonna was not embarrassed by her eagerness any more than Decker was ashamed by his arousal.

She stretched under him, arching her back. Her taut breasts were lifted. His lips closed over one nipple, and the gentle tug of his teeth tore a cry from her throat. There was no part of her that wasn't sensitive to his touch. He was joined to her deeply, fully. Her fingers threaded through his hair. Her thighs gripped him as he rocked her back. She contracted around him as he began to withdraw, and then he thrust forward again, harder this time so that she felt his penetration at the tip of her womb.

"Yes," she said. "Like that . . . just . . . like . . . that."

His hands pinned her wrists. She reveled in the rough embrace, in the surging hunger that drove him more furiously into her and against her. His lips crushed hers and she parted her mouth under his. Her teeth caught his lower lip and she tugged. A moment later her tongue licked the same spot.

He raised his head. The muscles in his arms and back bunched. She was watching him. Her violet eyes were luminous and her mouth was parted damply. She simply stared at him and slowly, deliberately, tightened the wet walls that secured him to her. It was his undoing.

Jonna felt the warm liquid rush of his seed spilling into her. He stretched over her, taut, and pressed into her again, the thrust more shallow this time as the contraction of pleasure controlled him. His hands slipped off her wrists and her arms closed around him. She held him that way until his body was still.

Decker eased out of her, but he did not move away. His eyes grazed her features. He thought it was the suggestion of a smile that touched her mouth, but he couldn't be sure. He had never known such a driving need to be joined to her. His voice was hushed and husky. "Did I hurt you?"

Jonna shook her head. "I'm not so very delicate."

Yes, she was. But he didn't tell her so. He remembered how sweet, how very small she felt under him. He drew a finger across the fragile line of her collarbone. The light scent of lavender teased his senses. His hands had swallowed the fine bones of her wrists, and her slender body had been rocked by his unyielding strength.

Decker smiled. He touched the gold chain at her throat, then traced the line of it until his fingertip rested against the scrimshaw. He held it a moment, thinking of the ship, of her elegant lines and proud bearing, and then of this woman, who was not so different a beauty from the one she'd created.

His hand drifted lower, over her breast, down the length of her flat belly. She sucked in a breath as his fingers dipped between her thighs. "You haven't had your pleasure," he said softly. His hand cupped her mons. "Did you think I'd forgotten?"

Jonna knew what would happen as soon as he touched her. Her hips moved, and she arched against the heel of his hand. The slight pressure was all she needed to slip over the edge. She clutched his shoulders and shuddered against him, her body flush to his. His fingers did not stop the intimate caress until the last vestige of tense pleasure had been skimmed from her body.

Jonna closed her eyes. All sense of weightlessness had left her, and now a lethargy stole over her limbs, a satisfying weakness invaded her muscles. She considered that she might never move again and would find it quite agreeable not to do so.

Decker kissed her temple. Her pulse beat gently against his lips. "I love you, Jonna Thorne."

She smiled sleepily. Perhaps she would not go to work at all today, she thought.

★ ★ ★ ★ ★

"How are you feeling?" Decker waved Graham's attendant out of the room as he spoke to his guest. Amanda bobbed once and hurried away, taking a breakfast tray with her. "You look marginally less close to death this morning than you did last night."

It was an exaggeration but not much of one. Graham found he had it in him to smile, albeit weakly. "If you say so."

Decker grunted softly. "I do." He took up the chair abandoned by Amanda and stretched out his legs toward the bed, regarding his friend consideringly. "The doctor was optimistic about your recovery."

"Would you tell me otherwise?"

Decker thought about it a moment. "Yes, I probably would. You'd want to know, wouldn't you?"

Graham nodded. His eyes darted toward the door, almost as if he were expecting an intrusion.

"Jonna's still sleeping," Decker said. "Otherwise you'd be right to look for her on my heels. I told her about Falconer last night. And a little bit about you." His blue eyes filled with quiet humor "She's accepted the truth about me, but she's reserving judgment on your account."

Graham did not smile. In light of Jonna's kindness, he felt churlish for raising the question, but it had to be asked and answered. "Are you certain you can trust her, Decker?"

"With my life," he said. "And yours."

Graham shifted his position slightly. The small movement brought a searing pain up his side, starting at the point of his wound. "It may come to that." He caught his breath, then forced himself to relax. "I've been betrayed once," he said. "So have many others on the Underground. I don't like to think it can happen again."

Decker understood what Graham hadn't shared last

night—the real purpose of his visit north. "You came to warn me."

Graham nodded once. "I was shot helping the slave Seth and six others move across the Georgia line into South Carolina. One man was killed. I was the only other one hit. Seth stayed with me and the rest scattered. God knows he would have been better to take his chances running alone. They were on our trail for three miles before we lost them at Sidling Creek."

"They?"

Graham shrugged and immediately regretted the movement. He grimaced. He allowed Decker to fix the pillows at his back and make him more comfortable against the headboard. "I assume there was more than one. A small band of bounty hunters is usually formed to bring back runaways. I know there were two or three hounds following us."

"I'm surprised you got away at all. How did you run with that gunshot wound?"

"I was riding, posing as a bounty hunter taking slaves back to Carolina. If we had been approached I would have told them that story and gotten away with it," His grin was rueful. "No one asked though. Just fired off a few shots from a distance and let all hell break loose."

"Were you set up?"

"I've given it a lot of thought," Graham said. "I believe it was no more than a chance encounter. But what happened later, at Michele's, that was not by chance. She was visited by the authorities because they *expected* to find runaways there. There were other stations on the same line of the Underground similarly visited this past month. Almost as if someone has been following one of the Railroad lines north."

"But how could anyone learn every station along a line? It's impossible. No one knows. Not you. Not me." He stopped as a thought occurred to him. "Only the people who use it know . . . the runaways."

Before he'd even said the words, Graham saw that Decker understood. "I know," Graham said. "It's hard to believe. I've tried to think of another explanation that would account for the arrests and captures, but it defies me."

"Betrayal by the people we're trying to help?" asked Decker. "It defies logic."

"Not really," Graham said. "Michele told me what they did to Seth to get him to talk. He held out and chose to tell lies over the truth. There may be others who experienced worse. It's always been a risk."

"But you think Falconer has been compromised."

"Yes . . . perhaps. There's no way to be certain. It's just that an entire route of the Underground collapsed like a row of dominoes. When the raid at Michele's occurred I realized I could be witnessing the end of another line. You're the primary connection to Michele's station, Decker. Most of the runaways she's kept leave by a Remington ship . . . always the one you're on."

Decker swore softly. He stood up and strode to the window. The rolling, loose-limbed walk was gone. Tension pulled his body into a single angular line. He couldn't shake the feeling of foreboding. Quite without realizing what he was about, he opened his jacket to reach for his good-luck piece.

The earring was gone.

Only by its absence did Decker become consciously aware of his search for it. Stillness settled over him. Outside the window a cold breeze lifted the branches of a pine tree. A small, brown swallow fluttered upward from the boughs before diving for the deeper shelter of a neighbor's porch. A carriage rolled along the street, and someone hurried down the sidewalk. Beyond this room life was proceeding at its determined pace. Decker's senses were heightened to it because for the briefest moment he knew his own heart had stopped.

He drew a breath slowly, forcing a calm he didn't feel. When he turned toward the bed he saw that Graham was watching him.

"What is it?" Graham asked.

Decker's smile was wry, but he said nothing. It was not often that he felt foolish, yet that was precisely the reaction that washed over him now. He would find the earring in one of his other jackets. Or it would appear in the laundry, and some maid, fearing for her position, would return it quickly to Mrs. Davis, just as Tess had done before. Belatedly he realized that Graham was still expecting a response from him.

Decker couldn't talk about his lost talisman. It was a petty, selfish consideration in light of Graham's news. He spoke instead of the thing that had driven him to his feet in the first place. "It's my wife," he said quietly. "She's a conductor on the Underground."

A spark briefly lightened Graham's flinty stare. "You're not serious."

"I wish I weren't. I only found out recently. Apparently she's had this station open for three years."

"For as long as you've been Falconer. There's an irony."

Decker acknowledged the truth of that. "We never suspected each other."

"But she knows about you now?"

"The important things. She knows I've used her ships to hide runaways and transport them to New York and Boston. She knows it's why I wanted *Huntress*." Decker sat on the arm of the chair. "You'll find this incredible, Graham, but she had that clipper built for the purpose of running slaves north. There will be no faster ship on the water until she designs and builds it. I hadn't thought anything could stop her . . . until now. Your news is not welcome."

"At least you don't have to worry that she'll be arrested and face a trial. The conductors below the Mason-Dixon line don't have that assurance. Some of them will be hanged for their part in the Underground. If your identity as Falconer is revealed, you'll never be able to take a ship into any Southern port."

"No ship on the Remington line will be able to enter them either. Not without risk of being burned or looted." Decker laid an arm across the back of the chair. His fingers beat a light tattoo as he considered the full consequences. "It doesn't matter whether it's Jonna or me who's found out. The result is potentially the same. Remington Shipping will have no trade in the South."

"Would it bankrupt the line?" Graham asked.

Decker almost smiled. Graham was thinking like a Yankee trader now. "It could. Jonna worries about it, but she's seen Sheridan face the same problem and survive it financially. Without Southern trade, though, there's no access to the runaways and no way for Remington ships to carry them. No matter what noises Jonna makes about finances, I believe that ultimately her concern is for those she helps. She knows she can't do it if the line goes under." Decker was seized by an unfamiliar restlessness. He stood and moved to the fireplace.

Graham watched his friend cross the room. His stride was deliberate, his destination, aimless. It was like watching a wild animal pace the length of its cage. "Double jeopardy," Graham said quietly.

Decker had been staring at the floor. He looked up. "What's that?"

"Double jeopardy," Graham repeated. "Two times the danger. An accusation leveled at either one of you has the same effect on the Remington Line. If you weren't married

. . ." He stopped because he had no right to say what he was thinking. He had already overstepped himself.

"If we weren't married," Decker continued for him, "Jonna could plead ignorance of my use of her ships. God knows, until last night, she was. The only thing she knew about Falconer was what Sheridan told her. And his information came from what he read in Garrison's *The Liberator.*"

"She could deny involvement," Graham said. "But it doesn't necessarily follow that she'd be believed."

Decker merely cocked an eyebrow. "You don't know my wife."

Graham's soft chuckle ended in a wince. "Tell me."

"She has a reputation for straightforwardness. She doesn't mince words, and she doesn't suffer fools. Jonna Remington is known for dealing fairly with people. Her word is as good as a contract for most merchants. She speaks her mind to the point of tactlessness, and no one's ever accused her of subtlety. Her stated position on abolition has always been a moderate one. She's never given a hint that her true position is otherwise. If I stood accused of transporting runaways on one of her ships, and I was only her employee, she could deny knowledge and no one would doubt her. With me as her husband, no one will believe her." Decker's slight smile was wry. "No one would credit her marrying without knowing everything about her husband. Not when she kept Grant Sheridan at arm's length for the better part of five years."

Graham grinned himself. He looked forward to making her acquaintance. "She's quite something, isn't she?"

"Quite," Decker said softly.

Graham's eyes rose to the portrait above the mantel. "Her parents?"

Decker glanced at it. "Yes. Charlotte Reid and John Remington."

Graham was thoughtful as he studied the painting. "It may be that I've alarmed you for no good reason," he said, pulling his eyes away. He had met Jonna only briefly, yet he didn't think he was being fanciful when he judged she was possessed of strong features from both her parents. "I cannot be certain that there is any more risk to you than there ever was." At some pain to himself, Graham shrugged and added with rhetorical carelessness, "After all, other than Jonna and me, who in Boston knows you're Falconer?"

Decker felt as if he'd been struck. *Rachael.* He stared at Graham, almost without seeing him. "There's just one—"

The door handle was twisted, interrupting him. Decker briefly put a finger to his lips and turned on his heel as Jonna walked serenely into the room. She was wearing a silk plum gown that shimmered as she moved. She stopped long enough to look from her husband to her guest. The hem of her gown swayed softly about her ankles. The silence in the bedchamber seemed abrupt and expectant. Jonna was certain she had heard voices before she entered.

"You were talking about me, weren't you?" she accused without malice. "Was he being kind, Mr. Denison? Or were you being entertained with the vast catalog of all my shortcomings?" Jonna set down the tray she was carrying at Graham's bedside. Besides a small bowl of broth and a cup of tea, it held a bottle of laudanum and the stolen documents from Sheridan's office. "I was on my way here when I met Virginia in the hall. She was charged with ladling this liquid down your throat. I confess, she appeared rather undone by the prospect. Rumor among the servants is that you've already given Amanda and Rachael a difficult time with the same task."

Graham looked past Jonna's shoulder to Decker. His blue-gray eyes made an eloquent, though silent, plea for help.

Decker merely held up his hands.

Jonna followed the direction of Graham's gaze. When she caught her husband's eyes over her shoulder, she smiled. "You'll get no assistance from that quarter, Mr. Denison. He's been in much the same position as you. In this very room, now that I think on it. I suspect he's well on his way to being amused by your distress."

Graham noticed that Decker was indeed grinning behind his wife's back, though perhaps not for the reasons that Jonna was inclined to believe. Graham suspected it had something to do with the trim figure and curved bottom she presented as she bent over him.

Jonna held out a spoonful of laudanum. She merely raised one eyebrow when Graham closed his mouth mutinously.

"Oh—" The spoon was jammed in his mouth as soon as he opened it. He swallowed. "Very well," he finished lamely.

Jonna had the grace and good sense not to appear too triumphant. "I appreciate that you have no wish to be drugged, but there's no reason to experience every nuance of pain. You're quite pale, Mr. Denison."

"Graham."

"Graham, then. And I'm Jonna." She held out her hand and blinked in surprise when he gallantly kissed the back of it. "Oh, my," she said, sinking into the chair behind her. She looked over her shoulder at Decker. "Did you see that? Your friend is charming. I don't recall that you were ever so charming in your sickbed." Decker only grinned at her, and she turned her attention back to her guest. The sparkle in her eyes faded, and the dimple at the corner of her mouth made a brief appearance. "I've heard that charming works best on snakes," she said flatly. "Cobras, specifically. I'd be grateful if you didn't try it on me. You're not here on sufferance. You're here because my husband says you're a man worth knowing and helping."

Graham realized Decker hadn't misled him about Jonna. She did not mince words. "I take it you have reservations."

"I trust Decker," she said. "But, yes, I like to arrive at my own opinion."

"Jonna," Decker said, his tone cautioning.

"It's all right," Graham said. Her eyes were an unusual shade of blue, he saw, almost violet. But this observation was an afterthought. The first thing he noticed was that they could pin him back against the headboard with the same directness as his grandmother's. "What do you want to know?"

"Decker tells me you frequent an establishment owned by a Miss Moreau."

"That's true enough," Graham drawled. He glanced at Decker who could only shake his head. Apparently Jonna's thinking was as much a mystery to her husband as it was to Graham. "It's a brothel."

Jonna's mouth flattened. "Thank you for that clarification," she said dryly. "I understand you often play cards there."

"Guilty."

"So you're a gambler."

"That's right."

"And intemperate?"

"I've been pie-faced on more than one occasion."

"Employed?"

"Only in the sense that my family owns a plantation."

"But what do you do?"

"Nothing if I can help it."

A smile tugged at the corners of Jonna's mouth. "Are you a wastrel, sir?"

Graham considered the word. "Why, yes," he said finally.

"I believe I am. Though I prefer the phrase self-indulgent."

Jonna nodded, unsurprised. She shifted in her chair and looked back at Decker. "I believe you're quite right about him. He's a man worth knowing and richly deserving of our help, though there's no accounting for his character. What sort of man cares so little for his reputation that he behaves irresponsibly in public and hides his noble acts?" She raised a single brow and eyed Decker with significant intent. Then her expression softened. "He must be a man like you," she said.

Decker *and* Graham experienced a temporary heat in their cheeks. It was Graham who found his voice first, but then he didn't have the force of Jonna's eyes on him just then. He cleared his throat. "I'm flattered that you make the compar—"

She turned on him. "I'm not a flatterer," she said. "I told you that I would like to arrive at my own opinion, and I have. Decker will tell you that once done, I'm not easily swayed. I'm steady that way. Intractable, some would say."

"*I* would say that," Decker said.

Jonna smiled. "Who knows about you, Graham?" she asked. Had he been as careful as Decker, she wondered, to keep his inner self a secret from others?

"You," he said. "Your husband. Miss Moreau. There are others who know me as part of the Underground but can't put a name to my face or place me at Beau Rivage."

"Beautiful Shore. Is that the name of your plantation?"

"Not mine," he corrected. "My family's. My brother makes certain I don't assume too much in the way of responsibility." He felt her eyes on him again, studying him thoughtfully. Had she detected the faint note of bitterness in his voice, or had she imagined it was only his careless regard for family matters. Jonna Thorne might reconsider that he acted in any way nobly if she thought his behavior was motivated by revenge. Great change, he reflected, was not always prompted by a high-minded, heroic code. Sometimes it only required a profound act of selfishness.

Graham yawned with more intensity than was strictly necessary to make his point. "The laudanum," he explained. "I'm afraid I'm . . ."

Jonna rose and helped him ease back on the bed. She could see that the effort cost him. The laudanum had only taken the edge off his pain. "The doctor said you were injured twice," she told him. "Once when you were shot, and again, later, when your wound was only beginning to heal. What happened on the second occasion?"

Decker was also interested in Graham's explanation. He moved away from the fireplace to the foot of the bed.

"There's not much to it, I'm afraid," his friend said somewhat wryly. "I passed the time playing cards on my voyage to Boston. I should have remembered from my school days with you Yankees that you take no more kindly to cheating than my Carolina brethren. I, being a paying passenger and all, found myself dodging a fist in my gut instead of another pistol ball."

"You were fortunate they didn't keelhaul you," Jonna said. "Really, Graham, if you're going to be a dissolute gambler, you should hone your skills. It's reckless to be caught cheating." She glanced at Decker, then back at Graham. "As reckless as my husband's taking things that don't belong to him."

Decker ignored Graham's interested look. For the first time he saw the documents lying on the tray at Graham's bedside. He addressed Jonna. "I take it you brought those in here for a reason."

"I didn't think you'd want them misplaced again," she

said. "Amanda came in to straighten your room."

Decker had a sudden vision of the papers fluttering to the foot of his bed while Jonna had occupied his full attention. "Thank you," he said. "I've yet to have an opportunity to study them."

Jonna made a small shrug. "I have. There's nothing there really suited to your purpose, Decker. Some contracts. Correspondence. That sort of thing. I confess to a bit of guilt at even looking over the lot of it—Grant is still Remington's competition, after all—but the most interesting thing from my perspective was his African trade. I hadn't realized Grant had expanded in that direction, or that he had ships to spare for it. It's something to consider, isn't it? I mean, in the event that Remington Shipping loses its Southern business connections."

She frowned, suddenly aware of Decker's keen interest. Graham's was only a fraction less intense, but then, she reflected, he had had a good dose of laudanum. "What is it?" she asked. "What's wrong?"

"What do you mean that Sheridan has African trade?" asked Decker.

"He has contacts in certain ports. Monrovia. Accra. Calabar. Given his views, it makes sense that he would develop a trade there. He doesn't hold with the European colonization of Africa. I suspect he's trying to get a foothold on the continent by establishing trade."

"But he's never mentioned it to you?"

Jonna shook her head. "Not once, though it's not entirely odd. I imagine his secretiveness was meant to discourage competition. The accounts indicate it's quite a profitable route."

"What sort of cargo?"

"You didn't get a complete record. I have no idea of the

nature of his trade. Bananas, coffee, and cocoa, most likely. He only has two ships serving the route. *Salamander* and *Chameleon*. I've never seen them, so that suggests their home port is somewhere other than Boston. Rio de Janeiro, perhaps. Havana. Charlotte Amalie in the Tortugas."

"Charleston." Both men spoke simultaneously.

Startled by their vehemence, Jonna actually took a step away from the bed. She looked from one to the other. There was a misunderstanding here, most obviously on their part. "That can't be right," she said. "Grant Sheridan has very little trade in and out of Charleston. When he does, he goes there himself, to conduct business and protect his ship."

Decker ignored her. He rounded the bed and went for the papers on the table. Graham had already pushed himself upright and was reaching for them at the same time. He got them first, divided them in half, and handed the partial stack to Decker.

"Whatever are you two about?" She did not like the bewildering sensation that raised the hair on the back of her neck. Neither man tried to hide the urgency he was feeling. And it seemed to her that Graham Denison was not looking so tired as he had a few minutes ago. He hadn't repeated that single yawn. Jonna thought she could easily be persuaded that his tiredness was mere subterfuge. He simply hadn't wanted her to develop her line of questioning. "You may as well tell me," she said. "I'll find out—"

"Here it is." Decker pulled one paper free of the others. He snapped it in his hand. "*Salamander. Chameleon.* This is a contract with the masters of those ships. Signed by Sheridan himself."

"Of course Grant would sign it," Jonna said. "They're his clippers."

Graham held up the document in his left hand. "Proof of that." He handed the paper to Decker. "It's a registration for a clipper built here in Boston. *Fixed Star.* Look at the back of it."

Decker turned it over. It was why he had missed it the first time he had leafed through the documents. *Fixed Star* had been sold to the Ivory Coast Trading Company and reregistered as *Salamander.* "But there's no proof that this company belongs to Sheridan."

"Yes, there is," Jonna said. She held out her hand for the documents in Graham's possession. "May I?"

"Gladly." He passed them to her.

"It's an offhanded reference," she said. "In one of the letters. It didn't mean anything to me when I first saw it, but if it's proof you want . . . here it is. The letter is for Grant in care of the Ivory Coast Trading Company. The address is his office on Malvern Street. Does that help?" She gave it to Decker.

He didn't glance at it. Instead he tossed all the papers to Graham and took Jonna in his arms. "You, madam, are a wonder."

She stared up at him. "You needn't sound so surprised," she said with some asperity. "It's not flattering."

Decker heard Graham chuckling softly, but then he was kissing Jonna and he was only aware of the roar in his own ears. Her lips parted under his, and her arms went around his neck. Standing on tiptoe, she pressed her body flush to his.

"My," Graham said appreciatively. "She *is* straightforward."

Decker and Jonna smiled in unison. It broke the seal on their kiss but not the promise in their eyes. Decker set her away from him gently. "You'll turn her head with that sort of compliment, Graham."

Jonna poked him in the ribs with her elbow.

"What was that for?" he asked.

"For just being a little too full of yourself. It seems two people in this room know something I don't. Which isn't precisely fair, since I apparently told you whatever it is you know."

"That sort of logic is fairly dizzying," Graham said dryly.

"Or perhaps it's the laudanum."

Jonna gave him a sour look. "I'm perfectly aware that the laudanum has had no—"

Graham held up one hand, cutting her off. His brows were drawn together, and he was staring at her mouth. "Are you aware you have a dimple"—he touched one corner of his lips—"right here?"

"Fascinating, isn't it?" Decker observed.

If it would not have been such an infantile gesture, Jonna would have stamped her feet. Instead she smoothed the folds of her plum silk gown and quietly sat down. Taking a page from Decker's book, she fell silent.

Conscious of a fault, Decker and Graham exchanged regretful glances. Decker sat on the wide arm of Jonna's chair, one leg stretched to the side. "You won't like it," he said. "I know you've always held Sheridan in esteem for his principles."

"What has that to do with anything?" she asked.

"*Salamander* and *Chameleon* are slavers."

Jonna's lips parted, but there was no sound. She didn't look at Decker but at Graham. When he nodded in confirmation Jonna bent her head and stared at her lap. Tears welled in her eyes. Nothing had prepared her for this, yet she didn't doubt she was hearing the truth. Slaver. The word did not distinguish between the ships and the men who dealt in the trade. It was used to describe both.

"I understand you were engaged to him at one time," Graham said.

Usually this would have brought an immediate denial from Jonna. Now she simply shrugged.

"Whiskey won't wash down a betrayal," he said quietly, more to himself than to her.

Jonna's violet eyes lifted suddenly and she glimpsed the pain in his. Graham Denison knew something about betrayal. It explained the flint in his eye and the steel in his voice that no drawl would ever soften. His expression was quickly shuttered, his smile reserved. "I wasn't thinking of having a drink," she said.

"Revenge is no antidote either." Graham saw her eyes flash briefly.

"I was considering how to make him answer for his crimes," she said. "If that's vengeful on my part, then so be it. Importing slaves is illegal—everywhere in this country."

"True," Decker said. "But it's largely overlooked. Southern authorities won't prosecute."

"We're in Boston, not Charleston, and I'm not the only person he's fooled." She waved her hand in an impatient, angry gesture. "All his talk of Garrison, *The Liberator*. Those meetings at Faneuil Hall. His principled stand on abolition." Jonna had to catch her breath. She stared at her hands. They were actually shaking. "All of it was lies."

Decker looked down at her bent head. Her thick hair was secured in a twist by two silver combs. He had an urge to touch the vulnerable nape of her neck. "I suppose none of us is what we seem."

"Don't defend him," Jonna said sharply. "His deceptions have hurt people. My God, Decker." She turned to look at him, her face lifted, eyes awash with unshed tears. "He wanted to meet Falconer. Can you imagine he had any reason at all except to expose you?"

Decker couldn't think of one. He laid his hand lightly on Jonna's shoulder. He had come precariously close to setting a trap for himself, he realized. He counted himself as one of those Grant Sheridan had fooled. Decker had never intended to reveal himself to Sheridan as Falconer, but even admitting that, he knew the man was dangerous. Decker was only realizing now precisely how dangerous. "He doesn't know anything about Falconer," he said calmly. "And he doesn't know anything about you. I believe you're right, Jonna. We should look at legal means to lay open Sheridan's slaving business." He pointed to the documents he had stolen. "I wonder if I should return those?"

"You will not," Jonna said firmly. "I won't allow you. They're evidence. We'll turn them over to my lawyer and listen to his advice. If it's sound, we'll take it. In any event, it's unlikely that Grant's missed them. They're not the sort of papers he'd go searching for without good reason—and we must not give him one."

She was peripherally aware that Graham was studying her as if she were an insect in a jar. Jonna turned on him and gave him an arch look. "Well?" she asked.

"Fascinating," he whispered.

Above Jonna's head, Decker grinned. "I know, isn't it?"

A tentative knock on the door covered Jonna's derisive snort. "Yes?"

Mrs. Davis stepped inside. Her anxious glance went to each of the bedchamber's occupants. "I'm sorry to disturb you, Mrs. Thorne. Captain. I hope you're resting comfortably, Mr. Denison."

"Yes, thank you," Graham said.

In spite of her mild irritation, Jonna's smile was gentle. "The reason you're here, Mrs. Davis?"

The housekeeper patted her apron down. "It's about Rachael," she said. "I don't know quite what to think of it. She's gone off to Faneuil Hall with Mr. Sheridan."

Fifteen

Mrs. Davis was not prepared for the volley of questions that followed her announcement or the fact they came simultaneously.

"Faneuil Hall?" Jonna asked. "Are you quite sure?"

"How long ago?" Decker said.

"Who's Rachael?" asked Graham.

As if struck by this barrage, the housekeeper actually took a small step backward. Her eyes darted from one to the other as she answered each query. "Mr. Sheridan was very specific about their destination," she said. "It was not even thirty minutes ago. Rachael is the youngest maid among my staff."

Jonna's frown was thoughtful. "Did Mr. Sheridan arrive here with the intention of taking Rachael?"

Mrs. Davis considered that a moment. "I suppose he did," she said. "At first I naturally thought he came here to see you or the captain, but he didn't inquire after you at all. I imagine he thought you'd both gone to the harbor, and I never had a chance to tell him differently. The poor girl looked quite bewildered by his request—as I was myself—but she went along with it." The lines in the housekeeper's careworn face deepened. She was aware now that she had acted precipitously by allowing Rachael to leave. "I should have come here immediately," she said regretfully. "It's just that Mr. Sheridan said he'd discussed this with you."

"We had," Jonna acknowledged. "But it was soon after Rachael's arrival, and I was adamant that she wasn't to be displayed to his abolitionist friends."

Graham's attention shifted to Decker. "This girl's a Negress?"

Decker nodded. He could not convey the depth of his concern without alarming Jonna. "That's right," he said. "And we know now that Grant Sheridan *has* no abolitionist friends."

"I can't make any sense of this," Jonna said. She looked up at her husband. "Whatever could Grant be thinking?"

"I'm sure I don't know," he said dryly. "And I doubt that it matters. I'll be happy to retrieve her."

"Would you? I'd be grateful."

Decker touched her cheek. "Of course."

Graham's flint-colored eyes narrowed as he studied Decker's face. There had been a moment when he'd caught something more than his friend's carefully shuttered expression. "I wouldn't mind taggin' along," he drawled. "Perhaps some company wouldn't come amiss."

Turning back to Graham, Jonna didn't see the exchange that passed between the two men. In that moment Decker was able to communicate that there was some danger in retrieving Rachael, even though he could not explain the nature of it. "Absolutely not," she said firmly. "You need to rest."

"Jonna's right," Decker added. "And anyway, I'd prefer that you stay here with her."

Jonna glanced at him oddly. "Don't you mean that you'd prefer *I* stay here with *him?* I mean, I'm not the one bedbound."

Decker smiled. "Yes, that's what I meant."

Graham's slight nod was imperceptible to the housekeeper and Jonna, but not to Decker who was looking for an affirmation.

Bending, Decker gave Jonna a brief kiss on the lips. "I won't be long." He glanced once more at Graham, but said nothing. The housekeeper stepped aside to let him pass. She was on the point of making an apology when Decker simply escorted her gently out the door.

Jonna smiled as she heard him reassuring Mrs. Davis that no regrets were necessary. She waited until his voice faded before she gave her full attention to Graham. "I confess," she said softly. "It's a relief Grant has no idea that Decker is Falconer. I could not have let him go otherwise."

"I understand," Graham said. He added offhandedly, "It would change everything if Mr. Sheridan knew."

"Yes," she said. "Yes, it would. And in light of what we know now about Grant, it would be tantamount to Decker walking into a trap."

"That's what I was thinking."

Jonna was seized by an unfamiliar restlessness. She stood and walked to the window.

"Can you see him?" Graham asked.

"What?" She was startled out of her reverie. "Oh, no. Not from here. He will probably ride rather than take the carriage. He'll leave by the back." She hesitated. Her faint smile was wistful. "I hadn't even realized I was looking for him until you asked. Isn't that odd?"

Graham had no idea if it were odd or not. He only knew that he would not mind being the object of Jonna's concern. "Decker's fortunate to have you looking out for him."

Jonna turned slowly back to Graham. "I was only looking for my husband," she said. "Not looking *out* for him. Is there some reason I should be doing the latter?"

"I misspoke. I didn't mean to give you cause for concern."

She was silent a moment, unconvinced. "I suppose I'm having second thoughts," she said at last. "I should have gone with him."

Graham knew that was the very thing Decker had wanted

to avoid. "I can't think of any reason for that."

"I know Grant's moods," she said. "Decker doesn't—though I suspect he understands Grant's character better than I do. There was no regard there even before Decker knew Grant was a slaver. I shouldn't be at all surprised if there is a fight."

At the very least, Graham thought.

Jonna sighed. "I'm not used to helplessness. It's rather what I'm feeling now."

"I understand perfectly."

Jonna was at once sympathetic. Her features softened with concern. "Yes, of course you do. There's really no point in my going on, is there?" She moved to Graham's bedside and touched the bowl of broth on the tray. "This is still warm. Will you have some? Or would you like it hotter? I can ring for more."

"No, that will be fine." Afraid she might want to spoon-feed him, Graham held out his hand for the bowl. "Please, won't you sit down? You'll give me a crimp in my neck if I have to stare up at you." Jonna returned to the chair, but Graham could see that it was an effort for her to stay in it. "Tell me about this Rachael," he said. "Why did Mr. Sheridan choose her?"

"I suppose because she presents such a vulnerable figure. Grant was much taken with her the first time he saw her here. Looking back on it now, I imagine he saw her as someone who could further affirm his position as a social reformer. I told him she was a freeborn black, but I remember that it made little difference to him. He still thought there was some statement he could make using Rachael. I was offended that he would want to exploit her."

"And is she a freeborn black?"

"No," Jonna said. "It's what I had to tell Grant, of course, but Rachael's a passenger on the Underground."

"I see," Graham said slowly. But he didn't, not yet. "What makes her particularly vulnerable? Her age? I believe Mrs. Davis mentioned she's the youngest of the staff."

"It's not her youth," Jonna said. "At least not entirely. She does appear to be younger than her years. The best we can determine is that she's about seventeen."

"She doesn't know?"

"That's hard to say. Sometimes it's difficult to communicate with her, though I've begun to suspect that's her choice. Certainly she understands what's said to her, but she doesn't speak at all. Mrs. Davis is teaching her to read, and it's been an arduous journey for both of them. Rachael's very eager to please on many accounts, but in other ways she is rather stubborn."

"Why doesn't she speak?"

"I couldn't say. Doctor Hardy examined her when she first came—it was necessary because of her hand—but he could find no physical reason for her silence. It may be that she simply chooses not to speak. One of the other servants told me recently that Rachael sometimes talks in her sleep." A chill washed over Jonna. Her beautifully drawn brows creased as she frowned. "But I asked her about that," she said softly, more to herself than to her company. "And she simply looked at me blankly."

"Pardon?" Graham said. "You asked her about what?"

"I asked her what she knew about Falconer. That's the name Delores told me Rachael spoke in her sleep. It seemed terribly unlikely, but I asked Rachael anyway. She gave no hint that she understood me, and I felt very foolish for questioning her." Jonna's face cleared suddenly. "She couldn't know Falconer, could she? It's so very odd to remember that he and Decker are one and the same. Decker would have told me about Rachael, don't you think? I mean, if they were acquainted, he would have recognized her."

Graham nodded slowly. There was some piece he hadn't quite grasped, something Jonna had said that was just beyond his fingertips. It came upon him so suddenly he didn't think about hiding the urgency. "What was it you said about the girl's hand?"

Jonna blinked, startled. "I'm not certain that I did."

"The doctor," Graham said. "You mentioned the doctor was necessary because of her hand."

"Yes, that's right. She had an injury that had only been partially attended to."

"What sort of injury?"

"A dog bite, I suspect. That's what we gathered from her. I thought it probably happened sometime during her run North."

"The ball of her hand?" asked Graham. He pointed to his own. "Just here?"

Jonna nodded.

"A small girl. Delicate, really. Large eyes. Skin like coffee."

"Well, yes. How did you—" She stopped. "Oh, you remember her from last night. She was one of the servants who stayed with you."

He shook his head. "There was no one here like that. Not that I saw. I remember someone named . . ."

"Amanda?"

"Yes. Amanda. She's the only one who attended me."

"Then perhaps you slept while Rachael was here. I know she was on duty last evening."

"It doesn't matter," Graham said. "It's not where I know her from. She was among the last group that Decker transported out of Charleston. I never knew her name, but I don't doubt it was Rachael. She escaped a slave ship—*Salamander*—and found her way to Michele Moreau's. She didn't speak English, Jonna, but she could speak. No one understood her tongue, so she was mostly quiet."

"There must be a mistake, then. Rachael understands English well enough. She always has. How much could she have learned if she had only just arrived on these shores? And why wouldn't she talk now? You must admit it makes no sense."

"It makes no sense to *us*. I'm not convinced there's not some sense to it."

"The logic of it fails me. We must be talking about different girls."

"This girl supposedly bit her hand to slide free of her shackles."

"No," Jonna said, shaking her head. "Dr. Hardy was quite clear about it being a dog bite. I think he would know the difference."

"But I don't know that I would have," Graham said. "Or that anyone else would have. What if she communicated one thing to the others who were at Michele's, when something else entirely had happened?"

"To what purpose?"

"To give credence to her tale when she appeared from nowhere. To keep others from questioning her too thoroughly. It's clever when you think about it. She pretends to understand little of the language until all danger has passed, but once she's separated from the others and placed in a station on the Underground, she gradually shakes off her identity as an escapee from a slaver and takes on one that better fits her here in the North. She doesn't speak and people assume that she can't."

"But why?"

"Here's what I know about people who don't talk much," he drawled softly. "They hear everything. And mostly it's because they're paid so little attention."

"What am I not understanding here?" Jonna asked. "Will you please speak plainly?"

Graham ignored her as he started to climb out of bed. Beads of perspiration immediately dotted his upper lip.

Jonna came to her feet and blocked his path. "What do you think you're—"

"Faneuil Hall," he said. "I believe I have a need to see the place again for myself. It's been a few years since I visited." He caught her suspicious glance. "Harvard graduate."

"Oh." Then she realized she had been momentarily set off course. Graham had neatly maneuvered around her. His pained expression notwithstanding, he was moving rather better than she would have expected. "You shouldn't be up at all. Dr. Hardy said bed rest. You'll reopen your wound and bleed to death."

He shrugged. "Where are my clothes?"

"In the laundry, I'm sure. I gave them to Rachael myself."

Graham was not deterred. He went to the armoire and examined the contents. "Something in here will do."

"I fail to see what—" She stopped because it was obvious to her that he would not be swayed. "Then I shall accompany you. Someone will have to be there to catch you when you—" Jonna hurried across the room to support Graham's arm as his knees began to buckle. "There, do you see? You aren't going anywhere." She took the clothes he'd collected from the armoire, dropped them on a chair, and led him back to bed.

Graham swore under his breath as he sat back on the mattress. Later, he thought, when her guard was lowered, he would take his leave. Decker would never forgive him for putting Jonna in danger. "Perhaps you're right," he said softly, turning gingerly on his side. Jonna pulled the covers up to his shoulders. "I've mistaken the matter."

"I'm certain of it," she said. "Rest now. I'll have a word with my housekeeper. She's had my confidence from the beginning, and I trust her opinion. I'm convinced you and I are not speaking of the same girl, but Mrs. Davis may have reason to think otherwise."

Graham closed his eyes.

Jonna waited a few minutes until Graham's even breathing signaled his surrender to sleep. He was in no way fit enough to follow Decker, and she had known the quickest way to defeat him was to insist on accompanying him. He wouldn't tolerate that. Jonna let herself out of the bed-chamber quietly, remaining in the hallway a few moments to be certain he didn't stir.

Then she went in search of Mrs. Davis. "Please have the carriage brought around," she said when she found her. "I'm going out for a little while. Oh, and perhaps it would be best if there were frequent checks on Mr. Denison. He's taken it into his head that there's some reason he should follow Captain Thorne."

Mrs. Davis did not attempt to conceal her distress. "Why should he do that? Is there something wrong?"

"Not at all," Jonna said soothingly.

The housekeeper allowed herself to be consoled. "It's no problem," she said. "I'll look after him myself."

"Thank you." Jonna turned away to get her bonnet and pelisse. She stopped when Mrs. Davis called to her. "Yes?" One of the housekeeper's hands was extended. She held something between her fingertips. "What's that?"

"I believe it belongs to the captain," Mrs. Davis said. She dropped it into Jonna's outstretched palm. "Rachael gave it to me. She found it somewhere. The laundry, most likely. I couldn't get the sense of what she was trying to tell me."

"It's Decker's. Odd, he didn't mention that it was missing. I wonder if he knows he doesn't have it." She turned the earring over and ran her finger lightly over the teardrop of pure gold. The delicately engraved ER winked at her. Elizabeth Regina. A queen's gift worth a king's ransom. She was holding history in her hand. Jonna was not particularly superstitious but she didn't like to think that Decker was without his talisman. "I'll make certain he gets it. Thank you, Mrs. Davis."

Beaming, the housekeeper went to arrange for Jonna's carriage.

Decker's soft groan was muffled as he opened his eyes. There was nothing to see. The space he was in was dark and cramped. He was lying on his side, his knees drawn closely to his chest. His ankles and wrists were bound. There was a handkerchief stuffed in his mouth, and another length of material ran around his head, securing it. He tested his range of movement. Without freeing himself, the most he was capable of was a slight roll to the front or back. Neither was a particularly satisfying position.

He'd known it could come to this, but he'd thought that knowing gave him enough of an advantage. Behind the gag, Decker's smile was wry. Well, it wasn't the first mistake he'd ever made. What he had to do was make certain it wasn't the last.

He tested his leeway with movement again, this time head to toe. By inching along, first in one direction, then in the other, he was able to determine that he hadn't much in the way of room to maneuver. It was not a pine box that held him, but it might as well have been. The trunk that his unconscious body had been shoved into was surely intended as a substitute coffin.

He wondered that he hadn't been killed. Perhaps he was valuable as a hostage now and was meant to be served up as a corpse at some later time. That line of thinking deserved some consideration, but not just now.

Decker's deft fingers began to twist in the ropes that held him. He had deliberately chosen not to carry a pistol. He didn't entirely regret his decision. The pistol might have prevented him from ending up in this trunk, but if it had failed, it certainly wouldn't have helped him out of it. What Decker carried in his boot was better. A scrimshaw knife was the sort of tool a man wanted in a tight place.

"Did she say where she was going?" Graham demanded.

Mrs. Davis's chin came up. "You're supposed to be resting, Mr. Denison. Mrs. Thorne was specific about that."

"I'm sure she was. She doesn't want me in her way any more than I want her in mine." Graham was wearing clothes that belonged to Decker. The fit was better than what he could find in the late John Remington's armoire. "Did she say where—"

"Only out. It's not my place to question her. And it's not yours either."

"It is when she's walking into a viper's nest."

Some of the starch went out of the housekeeper's spine. "What?"

He ignored her as he buttoned his charcoal gray jacket. "Are there any pistols to be had, Mrs. Davis?"

"Certainly not. Mr. Remington didn't hold with—"

"Can you at least direct me to Mr. Sheridan's home from here?"

"But Mrs. Thorne said—"

"The directions," he snapped. "I can find Faneuil Hall myself, but I doubt that's where this will end."

Mrs. Davis's fingers curled spasmodically at her sides. "Very well," she said, heaving a short sigh. "I have no liking for vipers' nests."

"Neither do I, Mrs. Davis." Graham smiled thinly. "Neither do I."

She gave him the directions and the easiest route to the harbor as well. "I could send someone for a hack for you. Jonna's already taken the carriage."

"No, just a mount." Graham didn't know how well he could ride, but walking any great distance was out of the question. "Will you see to that?"

"Of course." She bowed her head slightly. "This way."

Decker found the going slow. The bonds were tight and poor circulation eventually made his fingers clumsy. He ached to stretch out, but there was nowhere to go. He wondered how Rachael had fared. Was she trapped in a separate trunk or had Sheridan simply killed her and left her behind? She'd been halfway dead when Decker had come upon her.

As Decker suspected there had been no meeting at Faneuil Hall that morning. Nor was any scheduled for later in the day. It had simply been a convenient ruse to take Rachael from Jonna's home. The why of it still eluded Decker. He had his suspicions that Grant Sheridan was somehow behind the betrayals all along the Underground Railroad and that Rachael was one of his informants, but until he was able to get out of the trunk, suspicions were all he had.

After leaving Faneuil Hall, Decker had gone to the harbor. When he couldn't find Grant there, he went to his home. He was shown to the drawing room and expected to wait there until his presence could be announced. That was not

Decker's way. Soon after the butler left Decker began his own exploration. He came upon Rachael in one of the bedrooms. She was lying on the marble apron of the fireplace, moaning softly. There was swelling around one of her eyes, and purplish bruises darkened her cheek and jaw. Her lower lip was split, and a trickle of blood was beginning to dry under her nose.

Sheridan was not in the room. Decker made sure of that before he knelt beside the injured girl. It was only after he held Rachael in his arms that anger made him lose his edge. He gave the young woman full marks for trying to warn him, but he had only seen fear in her eyes. He hadn't understood that her fear had been for him.

The blow to his head had knocked him out immediately. One moment he had been staring at Rachael's battered face, holding her fragile frame in his arms, and the next he had seen nothing but a blaze of white light. Sheridan's strike was enough to blind him with the hot, soaring flare of a thousand imaginary stars.

He had known nothing then. He didn't remember being bound and packed and moved, yet all those things had happened. Decker had realized shortly upon waking that he was no longer in Sheridan's home. He was familiar enough with the rise and fall of the sea to know he was aboard a ship now. Whatever vessel it was, she had not left the harbor.

Decker heard voices occasionally but none that he recognized. He wondered if Sheridan was somewhere around, perhaps even sitting on top of the trunk. With a single blow, Sheridan had removed a rival and captured Falconer. What was less clear to Decker was whether Sheridan knew the extent of his success.

He continued to twist his wrists in the ropes, considering what truths Grant had forced from Rachael with blows of his fists.

★ ★ ★ ★ ★

Graham took hope from the carriage he saw standing in front of Sheridan's home. He dismounted, secured the mare, then spoke to the carriage's driver. "Are you with Mrs. Thorne?"

"That's right."

"She's inside?"

The man nodded. He pointed to Graham's mount. "That's one of her mares. You must be the fellow that showed up last night." He tipped his hat and scratched his head, clearly bewildered. "Thought you were injured. Gut wound, they said."

"Flesh wound," Graham said. "They were wrong."

The driver grinned. "Apparently so." His eyes drifted up the walk. "Here comes Mrs. Thorne now."

Jonna's stride covered the ground quickly. She met Graham's flinty stare fearlessly. "What are you doing here?"

"I suspect the same thing you are."

"Well, it's all been for nothing. No one's here."

"But you came out of the house. You must have talked to someone."

Jonna sighed. It seemed there was no deterring him. He had no sense of his own condition. Decker would certainly be unhappy with her for leaving Graham. "I spoke to the butler. He says that Decker came earlier, but left without waiting for Grant. He doesn't know Rachael."

"And Sheridan?"

"Apparently he's leaving Boston. His trunks and bags have already been taken to the harbor."

"Which ship?"

"*Watersprite.* She's a sloop, not one of his merchants. Grant uses it on occasion for short trips to Philadelphia and Baltimore."

"Do you think Decker's gone there?"

"I have no idea. But it's where I'm going." Jonna opened the door to the carriage. "You may as well come with me," she told Graham. "It will do you less harm than riding."

"I'd rather follow," he said. "I'm not convinced that showing up together is a sound idea."

"Which is precisely why I left you behind." She gave instructions to her driver, climbed into the carriage, and snapped the door shut.

Shaking his head, his eyes appreciative, Graham watched her go. She was a piece of work, he thought. Lucky, lucky Decker.

There was more activity on the ship. Decker felt the vibration of the crew's movements as they went about the business of making ready to sail. He knew he was topside now, not in the cargo hold, and he didn't know what to make of that situation. If he freed himself from his bonds and called attention to his imprisonment in the trunk, did it follow that he would be rescued? There was the distinct possibility the crew knew very well what Sheridan was about. The trunk may have been left in the open to assure there could be no escape.

Decker eased the scrimshaw knife out of his boot. Holding it in his bound hands was awkward. It took several attempts to manage a fairly secure grip that would give him the leverage to saw at the ropes.

Jonna's bonnet was flattened by the wind as she strode up the short gangway. *Watersprite*'s sails were still furled, but the small crew was working with purpose and vigor. "Is Mr. Sheridan here?" she asked of the first man who paused in his task.

"Below, Miss Remington. Shall I escort you?"

She did not bother to correct him about her name. "I'll find him myself." Jonna crossed the deck swiftly. Her wide skirts were compressed by the narrow passage that led below. The ship's rolling motion became more pronounced as soon as she was without points of reference. Her stomach lurched almost immediately.

Grant was sipping a brandy in his cabin when she walked in unannounced. Jonna was keenly aware that he was in no way startled by her presence. It was as if he had been expecting her. In the next moment, he confirmed it.

"You've taken rather longer than I would have thought," he said calmly. "Please, won't you sit down?" He stood himself and offered up the large leather chair that was behind his desk. "How long ago did you receive my message?"

Jonna waved aside his courteous gesture. "What message? I haven't received anything from you."

Grant's sandy-colored brows were drawn together momentarily. "I sent someone to your office with it."

"I've been at home all morning."

"That explains it then. He must have missed you." Grant shrugged. "It's unimportant now. You're here."

"Don't you want to know why?"

"I can't think that it matters one way or the other."

Jonna unfastened the ribbons of her bonnet and took it off. She did it deliberately, calculating that Grant would believe she had lowered her guard. Apparently he had planned to draw her here. That knowledge heightened her awareness of the danger she was in. "Where is Rachael?" she asked.

Grant took a sip of his brandy. "Would you like a drink? No? I suppose you think it's too early. That's a shame really. It would relax you. You're rather tense, I've noticed. Why is that, Jonna?"

Jonna had come to notice a few things herself. Grant was not quite as steady on his feet as he might have wished to appear. Although he certainly wasn't inebriated, he was well into his cups. His dark brown eyes were slightly unfocused as they gazed past her. His normally rigid, at-attention posture was unnaturally loose. "Please, Grant. I want to find Rachael. You had no right to take her from my home this morning. You know how I feel about putting her on display with your friends."

"Then you'll be happy to know it didn't happen. There was no meeting this morning. I had the wrong day. I made my apologies to Rachael and offered to take her back. She led me to believe she wanted to walk. I realized she's never had much opportunity to explore the city so I let her. Perhaps I should have done otherwise, but there you have it. I was in rather a hurry myself, what with needing to get here."

Jonna thought there was little about his story that she could believe, but she was fascinated by his facility for spinning lies. "I know there was no meeting, Grant. I went to Faneuil Hall myself."

Grant finished his drink and poured another. "I regret I've caused so much inconvenience," he said deeply. "I assure you it wasn't my intention."

"Where is my husband?" Jonna asked.

"I'm sure I don't know. Have you misplaced him?"

Jonna reached for the desk to steady herself as the ship lurched. Her eyes widened as she realized *Watersprite* was making sail. Dropping her bonnet, she sprinted for the door. She was unceremoniously hauled back by Grant. His powerful arm snaked around her middle, and he balanced her easily against his hip.

"Are you certain you won't have that drink now?" he asked softly.

★ ★ ★ ★ ★

Graham found Jack Quincy aboard *Huntress*. Jack stopped his conversation with several of the crew when Graham motioned to join him at the taffrail.

"Can't say that I expected to see you today." Squinting, Jack eyed Graham's pale face. "And now that I get a good look at you, damn if I think it's a good idea for you to be here. Does Jonna know?"

"She knows," Graham said. "She's the reason I've come."

"Oh?"

"I'll explain it all to you once we're underway."

"Underway? *Huntress* isn't going anywhere."

Graham leaned against the taffrail for support. He needed his strength to stand upright, not argue. "Are you familiar with *Watersprite*?"

"Aye. Grant Sheridan's sloop."

"Fifteen minutes ago it left this harbor with Jonna on board."

"Decker?"

"I don't know where he is." *Or if he's even alive.* Graham kept this last to himself. "You have no reason to trust me," Graham said. "You don't even know me. But you saw last night that Decker has me in his confidence. I hope that counts for something with you. He charged me with keeping his wife safe and unless you help me now, I will fail him." He paused. "And I will fail her."

Jack Quincy did not need to hear any more. "Look lively, lads," he bellowed. "We're going to chase down a water sprite."

"What can you possibly hope to gain?" Jonna asked. Grant had let her go once she'd acknowledged there was no escape, but she continued to hover near the door with him only a few steps away. The rise and fall of the sloop was making her stomach roil. She wondered how long he would insist she remain in the cabin if she was sick at his feet.

"Gain?" he asked. "What have I ever wanted but for you to be my wife?"

"That's out of the question. I'm married, Grant. And if I weren't it would still be out of the question. I don't love you. More to the point, you don't love me. You never have." Jonna wondered about Graham Denison. Had he seen her board the sloop? Was he on deck even now? Jonna was conscious of her eyes straying toward the door. She forced herself to redirect her gaze. She would have no advantage if Grant believed she expected to be rescued at any moment. "It's always been about Remington Shipping," she went on. "Though I fail to see why. You've taken great pains to assure me that your own line is doing well."

"Oh, and it is," he said. "Within certain limits. But I have no particular liking for those limits. They would not be so confining if you would design ships for me, Jonna. With a few more clippers like *Huntress* there would be no competition."

"That's not going to happen."

"Are you certain of that?"

"Quite certain."

"So it doesn't matter to you that I know you've been operating a station on the Underground?"

Jonna's mouth flattened. "No, Grant, it doesn't."

His glance narrowed as he regarded her over the rim of his glass. "You don't seem surprised."

"I'm only surprised that you took so long to threaten me with it." Jonna's stomach lurched again. She shifted her weight as the deck beneath her shifted. *Watersprite* is misnamed, she thought. The sloop did not glide over the waves or cut through them cleanly. "May we go topside?" Jonna asked. "I'm going to be sick."

Grant regarded her a moment longer, trying to make out the truth of her words. In the end he handed her a basin.

Jonna clutched it to her middle and bent her head. When she was certain she had Grant's full attention, she flung it at him. It caught him on his cheekbone, just below his left eye. His head snapped back and he staggered a step sideways. Jonna ducked the arm that reached out to grab her and ran out of the cabin. She gathered her skirts protectively close to her as she mounted the stairs. Behind her, Grant's feet pounded the deck and echoed in the passage.

Jonna fairly exploded topside. She looked around frantically for something else she might use as a weapon, all too aware that the six-man crew had stopped their activities and that Graham Denison was nowhere around.

Grant stepped on deck without Jonna's same sense of urgency. He rubbed his cheek with his forefinger. When he dropped his hand the red mark where Jonna had struck him remained.

Jonna quickly retreated until the backs of her thighs were pressed against a solid wooden object. Set off balance, she sat down suddenly. She looked down cautiously, afraid she was actually sitting on the ship's rail. It was a relief to discover that one of Grant's trunks was serving as a seat. She had no hope of survival if she landed overboard.

Grant motioned the crew back to work. The very ease with which they returned to it warned Jonna that she could expect no assistance from them. She wondered what price the men had set for their part in her abduction.

Jonna fixed her eyes on a point on the horizon and stared stonily.

"Did you expect there might be some help for you here?"

asked Grant. "Your husband perhaps? My crew?"

She said nothing.

"Decker stole from me, Jonna. Did you know that? He came to my office and took things that belonged to me. I don't know why I was surprised when he finally showed his true nature. I warned you about him from the beginning."

"Where is he?"

Grant's gaze didn't waver. He shrugged his massive shoulders. "I thought we would be married in Charleston," he said. "Does that suit you?"

Jonna decided she had had enough. "You've had far more to drink than I suspected. Don't force your hand with me, Grant, and I'll be charitable about forcing my hand with you. I know about your slaving business. I know your position on abolition is not nearly the same as your practice. I would say we're even, you and I. You can hurt my business in the South by revealing my connection to the Underground. But I can destroy your reputation in the North by revealing your duplicity. Who do you think will be damaged the most?"

"Come here, Jonna. I want to show you something."

It was not the brisk air, but the silky tone of Grant's voice that made Jonna shiver. She stayed her ground.

"Very well," he said. Grant crossed the space separating them in three long strides and hauled Jonna to her feet by her elbow. He gestured to several crewmen who had been watching the exchange. They moved quickly from their appointed tasks to this new one. Without further orders from Grant they picked up the trunk Jonna had been sitting on as well as the one behind it.

Jonna tried to pull her elbow away from Grant's grasp. His fingers merely tightened. "What is it I'm supposed to see?" she asked. Rising panic made her voice sharp. She watched the men, two with each trunk, grunt with the effort to lift them. They set them down on the sloop's narrow rail. The balance of each was precarious at best. With the constant pitch of the sloop, Jonna didn't know that either could possibly remain there long.

She raised her face to Grant. "Is this it? You want me to watch your trunks fall overboard?"

"Those trunks hold some valuable cargo," Grant said. "Precious, you might say. One of them contains a young woman I found in a Charleston brothel and set up for a time in my home in Boston. I see I've shocked you. You're wondering how it's possible that you never saw Rachael there. Keep in mind, Jonna, you were never as interested in my household staff as I was in the odd comings and goings of yours."

"You're a thorough bastard, Grant. Rachael's hardly more than a girl."

"In age only," he said. "She always knew what she was about. When the time came for me to require her services in another manner entirely, she was willing enough."

A wave of nausea washed over Jonna, but it was not from the motion of the sloop this time. It was Grant's nearness that provoked the sensation. She breathed deeply, forcing calm.

"I sent her back to Charleston," he said. "And she moved north on the Underground. I had no notion of who might be caught by the net we threw out. Imagine my surprise when she landed herself in your home. I could hardly credit that you would risk Remington Shipping for such a thing."

"But if she's done everything for you, then why is she in that trunk?"

"Because I'm very much afraid she's turned on me. Rather like you, Jonna. It requires some punishment, wouldn't you say?"

Jonna fixed her gaze again, this time on a dark object in the distance. "Surely you don't intend to pitch her trunk overboard."

"That depends. I may choose to toss your husband instead."

It was Grant's hold on her elbow that kept Jonna upright. Her heart hammered, and the blood draining from her face seemed to settle in her feet. She wavered but didn't fall. "Decker!" In her mind she had screamed his name. What came out was only a hoarse whisper.

Grant's narrow smile was without humor, although he was finally enjoying himself. "That's right," he said softly. "I could be persuaded from making you a widow, but then I would require your promise to divorce. I don't know that you would give it, and if you did, I'm not sure I could be convinced that you'd honor it."

"Put them down," she pleaded. "For God's sake, Grant. You can have whatever you want. My business. My designs. I won't say anything about *Salamander* or *Chameleon*."

"Very affecting, but also unnecessary. My mind's set on this. I've given it a great deal of thought, Jonna, and I believe the only way I can assure your cooperation and your silence is to prove that I will do anything to gain it." He gestured to the trunks. For a moment they both teetered as the men holding them thought he meant for them to be dropped. He stopped them with a sharp shake of his head. Losing both trunks now would change his bargaining position. "I'm going to let Jonna choose," he said. "Jonna? The trunk on the right or the left?"

They are both empty, she thought. They have to be. Grant Sheridan could not be so cruel or obsessed. "I won't," she said. Her stomach spun again, and she sought the object in the distance that had been her focus earlier. It was at a different point than before, no longer on the line of the horizon, but nearer now, and with a shape and clean, sharp lines that she could distinguish.

Huntress.

She only needed time. Jonna raised her face to Grant. "You can't make me choose. I won't do it."

"You must. If it would make it simpler for you, pretend I'm bluffing. You can always console yourself later that you didn't really believe me. It will ease your own guilt." He waited a long moment. "Well, Jonna? If I make the choice you can be assured it will be your husband who drops in the Atlantic. If you decide, your chances are even that he might be spared."

Jonna felt strangely light-headed. "I can't," she said weakly.

"They're still alive, Jonna. I made certain of it. Whoever falls, will drown."

She shook her head slowly. Her mouth opened, but no sound was uttered. She couldn't do what he was asking. It could all be a ruse on his part, but she couldn't assume that. If he was telling the truth, how could she live with herself if she made the choice?

"Why don't I tell you that your husband's in the one on the right," he said. "Does that make it easier for you?"

Jonna closed her eyes. Her knees sagged briefly. Grant yanked her up and steadied her.

"You can save your husband," he said. "You only have to give Rachael over to her grave."

"Please," she whispered. "Anything you want. Anything."

"I want this. It will make everything that follows so much easier if you have this moment in your memory."

"Go to hell!"

Grant pointed directly at the trunk on the right. "All right, men. Let him go."

Jonna screamed. She yanked free of Grant and ran to the

rail. One of the men who had released the trunk grabbed her by the waist to keep her from going over the side. "It's floating!" she cried. She looked back at Grant. "It's floating!"

He was unmoved. "Not for long. It's not watertight. Give it time."

Jonna's frantic eyes turned to the water. Beside her the other trunk was being lowered to the deck. She paid it no attention as the one in the water began to sink. Tears filled her eyes. "Stop it, Grant! Cast a net for it! I swear I'll kill you myself if you let it go!"

"It's too late, Jonna." His voice was actually gentle. He nodded once to the man who held her, and she was released. Grant placed an arm lightly around her waist and drew her back from the rail. "You don't really want to watch, do you? Come below with me. Rachael will be needing your help."

Jonna's legs moved in the direction he guided her. She looked over her shoulder once, not to her husband's icy grave, but to the trunk from which Rachael's battered body was being removed. The last tenuous thread of hope was cut. She managed to hold the rising bile back until they reached Grant's cabin.

"Take this," Grant said, handing her a tumbler of whiskey. He directed one of the men who brought Rachael in to empty the basin in which Jonna had retched. "Rinse your mouth and spit. The next mouthful you can swallow."

Dazed, Jonna went through the motions without question. The whiskey settled solidly in her stomach. The effect was at once burning and comforting. She faced the bed where Rachael lay. The young woman was huddled in a fetal position. Her eyes were tightly closed, and her entire body shook with cold. Jonna arranged the blankets over Rachael while Grant dismissed the crewmen.

"I'll need some hot tea or broth," Jonna said. "She's freezing."

"Later."

Jonna got up. Without asking permission and careless of the consequences, she poured Rachael a glass of whiskey. She cradled Rachael's head while the girl sipped the liquid. Jonna encouraged her efforts. Her voice was soothing, yet somehow detached, and Jonna recognized that she had no feeling left in her. She was perfectly, blissfully numb.

"Jonna?"

"I have nothing to say to you, Grant. Leave us. I'll take care of Rachael by myself." She might have said more, but she was yanked roughly to her feet and thrown sideways into the leather chair. Jonna stared up at Grant, no expression on her face as he bent over her. He braced himself on the arms of the chair, effectively trapping her.

"Have a care how you talk to me," he said with soft menace. "I can do to your face what I did to hers and with even less regret. And if you find that you care so little for yourself, keep in mind there is always someone close to you I can hurt." He straightened slowly. "You should have turned to me, Jonna. I gave you so many opportunities to come to me for guidance and support. There was that time you fell in the harbor. Why did you never come to me about that? Was it because Decker saved you then?"

Jonna could only stare at him.

"You never once asked for help after you were injured on the wharf. And the fire? I thought you would come to me then. You almost did, but Thorne was there and he took you away. It always seemed that you valued the counsel and protection of others. Colin. Jack. Decker Thorne. Why was that, Jonna?"

Her voice came as though from a great distance. "You arranged all those things?"

"You were so self-sufficient. You wanted for nothing. It was only meant to get your attention and bring it around to me."

"I might have been killed," she whispered.

"No, I was careful. There was never any chance of that."

"Decker was beaten for asking questions about what happened on the wharf. He was put in jail. Was that your doing, too?"

"He had to be stopped. I don't apologize for it."

It was difficult to breathe with him so close. She gave him her shoulder and averted her face. "Get away from me."

There was a moment of silence in which Grant Sheridan didn't move; then a voice from the doorway drawled, "I'd do what the lady suggests, Mr. Sheridan."

For very different reasons, Jonna and Grant remained perfectly still. On the bed, Rachael pushed herself up. Her one good eye opened, and she stared into the sloop's dark passageway. "Falconer."

It was the second time in her life a prayer had been answered by this man.

Sixteen

Grant raised himself up slowly. He stared at the man on the threshold for a long moment before his eyes moved past him and refocused on the shadowy figure behind him. "It can't be," he said softly. "It can't—"

Graham Denison stepped more fully into the room. Decker Thorne was on his heels. The steady tattoo of water dripping on the teak floor reminded everyone in the cabin that Decker had cheated death.

Jonna began to lift herself out of the chair, but Grant blocked her. She gave a heave worthy of a longshoreman and shoved him out of the way. Even Graham had to sidestep her to avoid being pushed aside. She gave a happy cry as she threw herself into Decker's arms.

"I'm wet," he said, grinning. He clutched her hard.

"I don't care." Her body was close enough to his to wring another spoonful of water from his sodden jacket. Cupping his face in her hands, she kissed him full on the mouth. "How did you . . . what happened . . . were you really . . . ?" The questions were delivered breathlessly, separated by the sweetly hurried kisses she placed along his jaw. "I thought I would never . . . did they . . . you should get out of those . . ."

Very gently, but firmly, Decker separated himself from his wife. He put her behind him by taking a single step forward and shielding her with his shoulder and arm. "*Huntress* has captured your sloop," he told Grant. "I imagine if you hadn't been so intent on terrorizing my wife and Rachael, you would have felt the change in the ship's pitch. They're rigging the tow lines now, and then we're returning to Boston. You'll have some charges to answer there."

Grant didn't blink. He leaned back on his desk, resting one hip on the edge. His casual posture indicated indifference. His eyes did not. "Charges? You should explain yourself."

It was Jonna who answered. "You tried to murder my husband."

"Because two of my clumsy crew dropped a trunk overboard? You make it sound as if it were intentional. I assure you, I didn't know that anything was in it save my own belongings."

Jonna started to step around Decker, but he restrained her with his arm. "We'll let a jury decide the truth of the matter," Decker said calmly. "There's also Rachael's condition to be considered. Unless it's your contention that she was injured by someone else's fists."

Grant's attention shifted to Rachael. She was sitting up on the bunk, a blanket pulled around her hunched shoulders. She hadn't looked at him once since Decker and his companion walked into the cabin. Although he was certain she was following every word of the exchange, her focus was entirely on the stranger, and her face, for all that it was bruised and battered, had an expression that could only be called adoring.

Grant's arms had been crossed in front of him. Now they fell to his sides and rested lightly on the desktop. He looked back at Decker. "We separated after leaving Faneuil Hall. I realized that I should have escorted her back to Jonna's, so I had my driver return. My worst fears were realized when we came upon her in an alley. Apparently she was accosted there. I took her to my home as it was closer."

Decker's expression remained neutral, but his voice had a

certain edge to it now. "And let her lie on the floor in one of your bedrooms."

"I don't know anything about that," Grant said. "She must have gotten out of bed on her own. I know I certainly put her in one."

"You abducted me," Jonna said.

Grant frowned. His eyes were sympathetic as they alighted on Jonna. It was almost as if he felt sorry for her. "Is that the story you're going to tell to soften your own guilt? I've always thought of you as more honest than that, Jonna. My crew will testify that you came aboard quite willingly and that your intention to leave your husband was clear." Grant tapped a forefinger lightly on the polished desk. "That's certainly how I remember it. As my trip could not be delayed, and you refused to leave, there was really no other option but to take you along. I can't say how sympathetic Boston nabobs will be to your adulterous manners. I believe they will be less inclined to forgive you than me."

Made speechless by Grant's twisted, facile explanation, Jonna simply blinked in astonishment. If he could toss off these lies on the spur of the moment, she had no doubt he would be extremely effective with time to prepare a defense. She looked sideways at Decker. He seemed unaffected by Grant's revelations.

"*Salamander* and *Chameleon*," Decker said.

"What about them?"

"They're slavers."

"Really?"

"And they're yours."

Grant shook his head. "I can't say what purpose those ships have been put to since I sold them, but I am interested in how you've come by this information. Is it possible you've returned to your old thieving ways, Captain Thorne?"

Graham Denison had had enough. His drawl was soft, and his voice was without any real menace. Somehow that made him seem more dangerous. "I say we just kill him."

Sheridan swiveled slightly and faced Graham. "Who the hell are you?"

It was not Graham who answered. Rachael's whisper was husky with emotion. "He's Falconer," she said.

Jonna cast a startled look at Decker. She had heard Rachael say that name earlier, with the same hushed reverence. When Decker walked into the room behind Graham, Jonna assumed she knew which of the men Rachael was referring to. Decker's complete calm helped Jonna mask her own confusion.

"Falconer?" Grant asked. He had convinced himself that he had misunderstood Rachael earlier. "Is this true, Thorne?"

Decker shrugged. "I told you I would help you make his acquaintance."

"But the paper," Sheridan said. "*The Liberator* reported—"

Graham nodded. "You must be talking about Matt Willet. I'm sure everyone in Charleston has come to realize they were mistaken about poor Matt. He's no more likely a candidate to carry the Falconer name than say . . . oh, I am." Graham indicated Rachael with his hand, but he never took his eyes from Sheridan. "But you have this young woman to tell you it's a name I sometimes answer to. More usually I'm known as Graham Denison." His flint-colored eyes shifted just once to Decker. "I don't mind killing him," he said. "Unless you want to?"

Decker pretended to consider it. Finally he said, "I'm still hopeful we can resolve this in court."

Graham's indifferent shrug caused him a moment's sharp pain. He sucked in his breath and managed to make it seem that he was only impatient with Decker's line of reasoning. "It's your decision, of course." He pointed to Rachael. "But I believe she'd be grateful if we killed him."

Grant was wary, but not cowed. "I told you what happened to her," he said.

"You've hurt her," Jonna said quietly. "In ways I'm only beginning to understand. You used her to expose stations on the Underground. You used her to betray people who were trying to help her. Tell us what really happened to your hand, Rachael."

Rachael's head bent. She stared at her crippled hand. She was quiet for so long that Grant began to hope she would say nothing while the others despaired of her speaking. "He held me down," she said at last. There was no emotion in her voice, but tears slipped free of her lowered lashes and slid over her cheeks. "He held me down while they greased my hand with meat drippings. The dog they brought in was half-starved. It had to look real, he told me. It had to seem I was so hungry for freedom I would mutilate myself to get it. I screamed and screamed. . . ." Her voice trailed away. She didn't look up, but she could feel their attention on her. "He told me not to worry. There would be people who would help me, he said. I should only remember their names and their faces and where it was that they took me in. And if I came across one named Falconer I should remember everything and tell him all of it." Now when she fell silent her dark eyes lifted to Graham. "And I have remembered, but I've never said a word. Not to anyone."

Graham nodded. "I know you didn't. There were others he sent out, and they weren't as strong as you."

"If I had never passed through Miss Remington's home,

he wouldn't have seen me there and he wouldn't know about her station on the Underground. I wouldn't have told him. I never told him about any of the others. He couldn't have made me tell."

"I believe you," Graham said gently.

Rachael used one corner of the blanket around her shoulders to dry her tears. Feeling was absent from her voice as she spoke. "I think you should kill him."

Grant's dark eyes narrowed. His gaze seemed to pull Rachael's attention to him, but she didn't flinch. "Slut," he said softly under his breath. Satisfied to see her eyes darken with a mixture of pain and anger, Grant turned to Decker. "Let's have done with this, shall we? You have a story. I have a different one. We can produce any number of witnesses to support each of us. Is there really any point in pursuing this when Remington Shipping will be ruined?"

Decker placed a light restraining hand on Jonna's wrist. "You're not making a convincing case to save yourself," he said. "It seems that killing you would be a more satisfactory solution than making your lies public."

"You don't believe me about *Chameleon* and *Salamander*, do you?" Grant said easily. "I assure you the sale of those ships was done several years ago. I have papers to prove it. It's unfortunate that you didn't steal those when you rifled my files." A thought struck Grant. "You know, I may have something right here that would show you . . ." He reached for the desk drawer that was closest to him. Before it was opened more than two inches Grant cried out from the unexpectedly sharp pain in the back of his hand. At first he didn't understand it. In spite of where the pain was located he thought his fingers had been slammed in the drawer. That would have made sense. What did not make sense was the knife that appeared from nowhere and was now lodged deeply in the flesh between his thumb and forefinger. Dazed, he lost the opportunity to pull it out. Decker did that.

Holding the finely honed scrimshaw blade against the corded muscles of Sheridan's throat, Decker finished opening the desk drawer. He did not glance down, but felt his way around the space. "I see," he said softly. "You do have something in here." He pulled out a pistol. The weapon's polished maple butt was smooth and cool to the touch. He held it out to Graham. "Is it primed?"

Graham checked it. "Primed and ready." He tested the weight of it in his hand then raised his arm. "And aimed."

Nodding, Decker took his knife away from Grant's neck. He used it to extend his gesture toward the cabin door. "Although killing you sounds just fine to me, I like the idea of you facing a jury instead. Remington Shipping will survive, I'm sure. Certainly Jonna's not frightened by your threats. And as for Mr. Denison, now that he's safely north of Mason-Dixon, he's prepared for the public to know he's Falconer. I suggest you step lively topside, Grant. Jack Quincy and the rest of *Huntress*'s crew are probably anxious to discover what's happened down here. They need to see that we have you well in hand and that Jonna's perfectly safe."

"I'll go first," Jonna offered. She stepped into the passageway and waited just long enough to be sure that Grant was following.

Graham kept the pistol leveled at Grant and went after him. Decker paused beside Rachael. He hunkered down and touched her wrist. "Stay here until we have him safely on deck and secured on *Huntress*. I'll come back for you then. It will only be a few minutes."

She looked at him in some confusion.

"Do you understand?" he asked.

But Rachael's confusion had nothing to do with Decker's

statement. Her concern was larger than herself. "That's all?" she asked. Disbelief edged her husky voice. "You're not going to kill him?"

"No," Decker said. He could hear footsteps receding quietly in the passageway. He did not want to be far behind. Sheridan didn't know that Graham was holding himself upright by sheer force of will, and Decker didn't want him to find out. "We're not going to kill him."

"But I—"

Decker had no more time to explain himself. "You're safe now. I'll be back right away." He held out his scrimshaw knife and laid it in her open palm. "Here, take this. No one will hurt you." He stood and hurried out the door.

Jonna smiled widely as she stepped on deck and saw Jack Quincy on board *Huntress*. Members of the clipper's crew had subdued Grant's men, and now they were sitting side by side at the sloop's rail, connected by a rope that looped through their bound hands. The tow lines had already been rigged, and the clipper dwarfed the sloop, forcing her to ride in the wake.

Jeremy Dodd took Jonna's elbow and escorted her to one side as Grant stepped out of the hold. "Are you all right?" he asked.

She nodded. "Fine." She turned to watch Grant. He was remarkably unaffected by the capture. His ship, his crew—all confined, yet he acted as if it were of no account. Was it really possible that he would be believed? she wondered. She remembered how easily the lies came to him. People were never eager to believe they had been duped. Grant's friends in the abolitionist movement might rally to his defense rather than admit they had been deceived by him. Was he counting on that?

It was as if Grant knew the path of her thoughts. He gave

her an arch look, his handsome features unmarred by worry. "It's not over, Jonna. Not in any way. You know I don't give up."

Jonna gave him no reaction. She had to believe that he was wrong and that it *was* over, else she would be moved to kill him herself.

Graham Denison heard only part of the exchange as he came topside. Frowning, he motioned to Jeremy. "Do you know how to use this?" he asked, indicating the pistol.

"Aye," Dodd said. "I'm good with it, too."

"Then take it and keep it aimed just like this."

Jeremy and Jonna came forward at the same time. Jeremy took the weapon, and Jonna took Graham's arm. Her touch was all he had been waiting for. He leaned on her heavily, finally acknowledging the depth of his pain and the extent of his weakness. Jonna pulled his arm around her shoulder, and when one of her crew offered her assistance she shook her head. This was a weight she wanted to bear. This man had saved her life. More than that, he had saved Decker. "Thank you," she whispered.

A moment later Decker appeared. He surveyed the situation and held up a hand in Jack's direction to indicate that all was ready. "Bring her alongside *Huntress*," he told his crew. "Mr. Sheridan is going to be a guest on a Remington clipper."

Men went to work immediately on both ships. The slack in the towline disappeared as the sloop was hauled in close to the clipper. Jonna's insides roiled as the deck pitched sharply under her feet. Grinning weakly at Decker who was watching her closely, she managed to hold her balance and the contents of her stomach. She shook her head as he started to approach, so he stopped in his tracks, considered her a moment, then went back to helping steady the sloop.

Graham saw the quick exchange between them. Not a word was spoken, but everything had been communicated. "Does Decker always do what you want?" he asked Jonna.

Jonna gave him a sideways glance. "Hardly ever. Is that what you thought just happened?"

"Well, it looked as if—" He stopped, caught by the flurry of movement from the hold. He held up his free hand, palm out. "No! No, don't—"

Following the direction of his gaze, Jonna cried out the same alarm. "Decker! Stop—"

Rachael had nothing to fear from Decker. He was too far away from her to halt her mad run at Grant Sheridan. He yelled a warning, but realized that even that was going to come too late. At the first shout Grant had turned toward Graham and Jonna and made himself an even more vulnerable target. He only saw Rachael's approach out of the corner of his eye. The knife Rachael held in her fist glinted once before it was buried deep in his shoulder.

Grunting with the sharpness of pain and the impact of Rachael who had run full tilt into him, Grant stumbled sideways. He tried to throw Rachael off, but she clasped her legs around his thighs and held on. One of her arms locked around his neck. She withdrew the blade and plunged it in again, this time solidly in his back.

Her bruised face was not contorted in rage. There was no fierce anger in her dark eyes. Her features were strained as the limits of her strength were tested, but it was only that, nothing more. It was as if she had made peace with her hatred and was acting accordingly. Emotion was no longer guiding her. She had arrived at the conclusion that killing Grant Sheridan was a rational solution.

Grant fell to his knees as the blade was lifted for a third assault. Decker's arm stayed Rachael's hand this time. Only the tip of the knife caught Grant, but it sliced his skin cleanly. Almost immediately a thin thread of blood appeared at the base of Grant's ear and wound around to his throat. Decker's hand closed over Rachael's wrist. He squeezed hard and her fingers opened convulsively. The knife dropped and slid out of reach on the next roll of the sloop. Jeremy bent down, careful to keep his pistol aimed, and picked it up.

Decker hauled Rachael off Grant. She offered no resistance when he passed her to one of the crew, but she would not be led away. She watched without emotion as Decker knelt beside Grant and rolled him onto his back. No one spoke. There was the sound of water slapping against the hulls of the ships, and there was the sound of Grant's labored breathing. It seemed to her that one was no louder than the other.

Grant's eyes were open, and for a moment they focused on Rachael, faintly accusing and yet somehow sad, as though she had disappointed him. If she had had the knife in her hand just then, she would have driven it into his heart.

Decker saw a shudder pass through Grant as he drew his next breath. A trickle of blood appeared at one corner of his mouth. Decker's eyes lifted to Jonna, then to Graham. He made a small negative shake of his head.

Rachael saw the movement as did everyone else who was watching. She was the only one who came forward. Her touch was gentle on Decker's shoulder. He hesitated, gauging her intent. What he glimpsed in her eyes caused him to move away. She took his place at Grant's side and, lifting his head, cradled it in her lap. She stroked his hair with her crippled hand and murmured his name softly. From a distance it almost sounded as if she were singing to him. A siren's song. A song of the sea.

Grant Sheridan, dead by her hand, died in her arms.

★ ★ ★ ★ ★

For a long time no one moved or spoke. Tears welled in Jonna's eyes, but she couldn't have said for whom she cried. A sob caught in her throat. She held it back, shivering just once. Decker went to her side and took her hand. Without being asked, Graham eased himself away so Jonna could accept her husband's embrace. He fixed his stare on Rachael. She was no longer looking into Grant's sightless eyes, but gazing out to the near endless expanse of water off the starboard side. Jeremy Dodd lowered his weapon slowly, realizing at last that he had no use for it. On board *Huntress* the crew stood at the rail, looking down on the strange tableau, still and silent.

Decker felt Jonna slip something into his hand. His fingers closed around it. The shape was so familiar to him that he didn't have to look at it or ask what it was. "I thought I lost it," he whispered against her forehead. "Where did you—"

She raised her face. "Rachael found it."

Decker slipped it into the pocket of his coat. He looked past the crown of Jonna's hair to where Rachael was kneeling. Her detached, faraway gaze riveted his attention.

He couldn't move Jonna aside fast enough. Rachael was up and running for the rail. It was Graham who stepped in her path and held out his arms to stop her. "Don't—" Breath was driven out of his lungs as Rachael's flailing hands found the center of his wound. He felt her small body climb over his fallen one. She was driven by her single-minded determination to reach the sloop's rail. He grabbed a handful of her petticoats. The material was torn out of his hands as she threw herself overboard.

Jeremy threw out a lifeline.

"It won't work," Decker said. "She has to want to take it."

He marked the position of Rachael's body as it slipped beneath the water. Peeling off his coat, he tossed it to Jonna. Then, for the second time in the space of an hour, he was plunging into the Atlantic Ocean.

Epilogue

Decker stood at the bedchamber window. A pale slip of moonlight touched his features. It edged his profile, marking the character in his face with its cool blue color. It touched the strong line of his nose and emphasized the muscle working in his jaw. There was a faint slant to his frame as he leaned toward the window, a yearning that had physical expression. His arms hung loosely at his sides, but only one hand was open. The other was closed around a pearl set in a crown of gold and the smooth golden raindrop that was suspended from it.

Lying on her side in their bed, Jonna watched him. Decker didn't look in her direction. He thought she was still sleeping. She would have been if he hadn't left the bed. The heavy blankets had offered a warm and comfortable shelter when he was sharing space under them. She did not think he had been gone long before she was aware of his absence.

Jonna didn't stir. Her body felt deliciously heavy in the aftermath of their lovemaking. It was not difficult to imagine that she was under him again, his mouth on hers, his fingers in her hair. He had been tender and fierce by turns, kissing her breasts, having a nipple with the damp edge of his tongue, then drawing the swollen bud into the hot suck of his mouth. His fingers trailed lightly over her skin while he watched her, fascinated, as though he had just discovered how exquisitely sensitive the inner curve of her elbow was or how responsive she could be to the sweeping touch of his thumb on her thigh.

It had not all been done to her. Her need to tease and prolong the sweet torment was as great as Decker's. With her mouth near his ear she had whispered her intentions, then had taken her time honoring that promise. She kissed his jaw, his mouth, the base of his throat; and when he was under her, she pinned back his wrists and straddled him, letting her hair fall forward so only the curling ends caressed his chest.

She had released his wrists then and brought his hands to her breasts. She held them there for a moment, letting him feel the swell of her flesh beneath his palms, watching his eyes darken and the faintly amused line of his mouth disappear. She pushed his hands lower, arching slowly as his palms covered her ribs, her waist, cupped her hips, and finally rested on her thighs.

She was the one who smiled now. A slightly wicked smile. A reminder of a certain promise. She let his hands fall away as she leaned forward. Her teeth caught one of his nipples and worried it gently. His entire body tensed beneath her, and where she cradled him between her thighs she felt him surge powerfully. She was hot and damp and ready for him, but she did not take him inside her. Not yet. Not that way.

She placed teasing, tasting kisses down his chest as she moved lower. The force of his heartbeat vibrated against her lips. Her fingers rested on his hips and then between his thighs. She cupped him with her hands before she took him in her mouth.

Decker expelled a breath he didn't know he'd been holding. The next breath he drew was caught in his throat. He raised himself up on his elbows, and the sight of her exquisite mouth engaged in this most intimate caress was almost too much. Flames could not lick at his skin with more soaring intensity than Jonna's tongue. There were no bonds that could hold him more securely than the sweet suck of her mouth.

A soft groan was torn from his throat. He said her name

once, then again, as if he couldn't help himself, as if her name were part of a litany and the saying of it would cleanse his soul.

He touched her hair. It slipped through his fingers like a dark waterfall as she slowly raised her head. She held the rigid length of him in her hands and laid her mouth over him just once. The light kiss gave her the warm, salty taste of him on the tip of her tongue.

He drew her up and as she was turned and covered by his body she was keenly aware of her own. She sensed the smooth lines of her legs next to the muscled hardness of his. There was the contrast of his rough fingertips against the silky skin of her inner thigh. Her body had to yield to accommodate his. It was the curve of her breasts that flattened when their bodies came flush together, her thighs that opened when he pressed his entry.

He held himself still inside her and let her know the same delicious torment of restraint that he felt. "You did that to me," he whispered against her mouth.

Perhaps she should not have looked quite so pleased. But then he wouldn't have punished her with the slow, deep kiss the way he had. When it was over he was moving in her and the rhythm was like the kiss they had just shared, slow and deep, but unlike its echo because the intensity and power swelled with each thrust and the sensation radiating outward was just as sweetly hot as it was at the center.

What she felt where they were joined she also felt in her fingertips, along the length of her legs, and at the back of her throat where his name stirred on a soft expulsion of air. A wave of pleasure rolled under her, arching her throat, lifting her breasts and belly, and finally raising her hips as she rode the crest. She shuddered and felt the change in his rhythm almost immediately. Her fingers skimmed his back and pressed whitely into his taut buttocks. She contracted around him and his body went as rigid as the length of him between her thighs.

Afterward he held her. His breath was warm against her cheek, his fingers sifted her hair. They didn't talk. In time, she slept.

Now Jonna sat up slowly. She knew Decker must have sensed her movement, but he didn't turn. Her linen shift fell softly past her thighs and calves as she rose from the bed, and her bare feet were virtually soundless on the hardwood floor. She came up behind him, sliding her arms around his naked chest. She laid her cheek against his back.

He closed his eyes and placed one hand over hers. He stroked the back of her hand. Her nearness settled his heart.

"Was it another dream?" she asked him.

"Yes."

Jonna did not so much hear him as feel the answer. His skin was warm against her cheek. She kissed him. "You could have wakened me," she said quietly.

"I know."

"I wish you would."

He knew that, too. "Perhaps the next time."

Jonna let him go. She stepped around Decker, placing herself between him and the window. "It's been two weeks since the last one. There may not be another."

He touched her cheek with the back of his hand. Her eyes were wide, luminous. "Maybe not."

"I was there, Decker. I saw what you did."

"What I *tried* to do."

"Yes," she said firmly. "What you *tried* to do. There was no failure in your attempt. She wanted to die. You knew when you dove in the water that Rachael wouldn't thank you for saving her life. I think you have to live with that before you can sleep with it."

Cool, blue moonlight touched his faint smile. He looked at the heirloom earring before he laid it on the windowsill. "Is that right?"

"Yes." She laid her hands on his chest as his arms went around her waist, his fingers threading together at the small of her back. "Decker?"

"Hmmm?" He felt her hesitation and tried to imagine the subject that would give Jonna pause or force her to choose her words carefully. "What is it?"

"These dreams of yours . . . I think . . ."

"Yes?"

"Before Rachael there were others. Not dreams, I mean, but real people—flesh and blood—and you couldn't save them either. Your mother and father. You were there when the highwaymen murdered them. And Mère and Jimmy Grooms . . . you saw them hanged." Her voice trailed away. She stared at his implacable features, the eyes that were as cool as moonshine, the smile that was an enigmatic wonder.

She had found the heart of it, Decker thought. His heart. These last six weeks his dreams had been filled with disturbing images. It was not only Rachael he searched for beneath the icy water, but his mother and Mère, his father and Jimmy. He would come within inches of their outstretched fingers, but never connect. He imagined he could hear them call his name, and the sound of it was clear, as though it traveled over the water rather than through it.

"But you saved Mercedes, Decker. And Colin. And since then, dozens of others whose names you haven't always known." She touched his mouth with her forefinger. "You saved me."

He shook his head. Her finger drifted over his chin, along his jaw, and came to rest at the base of his neck. "You're wrong," he said.

"No, I'm not. You saved me. From Grant and from myself." Jonna raised herself on tiptoe. Her mouth brushed his. "I need you, Captain Thorne. You can't imagine quite how much."

Decker kissed her. Her lips opened under his, and a full minute later when he drew back, they were damp and still sweetly parted. "I wouldn't mind hearing," he said.

She smiled at that. "I need to argue with you, and I need to laugh with you."

He did not mind at all that she mentioned arguing first.

Jonna ignored his amused grin. "And I need to see that wicked grin of yours when I look up from whatever I'm doing and find you watching me."

"Wicked?"

It was wicked now, she thought. But not obviously so. Decker was never obvious about it. That was what always sent a shiver through her. She never knew for sure. "I need to see you when I wake up and before I go to sleep."

"Oh, Jonna." He bent his head and touched his forehead to hers.

"And that's the very least of it, Decker. More than anything, I need to love you." She cupped his face. His mouth was only a hairbreadth from hers. "Let me comfort you," she whispered. "When the nightmares come, let me in."

Decker lifted her. He didn't carry her back to bed, but sat instead in the large wing chair. Her arms circled his neck, and her head rested on his shoulder. For several minutes the only sounds in the bedchamber came from the fireplace and the mantel clock.

"Do you think she loved him?" Jonna asked. "Rachael, I

mean. Do you think she loved Grant?"

"I don't know."

"I see her face sometimes. Just as it was while she held him in her arms. Her grief was so profound . . . I thought perhaps that she might have loved him at one time."

Decker remembered Rachael's face, too, but he thought about it differently. "If she loved him, then it was for the person he might have been, not the person he was." He stroked Jonna's hair. "She wanted us to kill him. I didn't understand then, but afterward, when it was too late, I realized that's what she had been trying to tell me. It was her plan all along, I think. Sheridan knew about the papers I took from his office. Neither you nor I told him. He could only have known about them from Rachael. She showed them to Grant to get a reaction and took them away for the same reason. She was like a child throwing a stone into a pond. She started the ripple without understanding that she couldn't control or direct it. Events got away from her very quickly after that. When she saw Graham in this house—the man she thought was Falconer—she only knew she needed to act. I don't believe she thought it through any more than that."

"She never betrayed us," Jonna said. "I don't believe she ever would have."

Decker's fingers continued to sift through Jonna's silky hair. He watched her lashes lower by slow degrees. There was a sleepy flush on her cheeks. "There's something I've been meaning to tell you," he said quietly.

"About Rachael?"

"No, not about Rachael. About you."

With kittenlike charm, she rubbed her cheek against his chest. "Hmmm?"

"You're married to a very rich man," he said.

She smiled deeply, but did not raise her eyes. "Because

you have me in your arms?" she asked.

"There's that," he agreed. "But you should know that Colin set aside something for me a few years back."

One of Jonna's brows lifted. She gave him an arch look. "Something?" she asked. "You mean a trust?"

"I mean Rosefield."

She blinked. Her mouth opened, but no words came out. She allowed Decker to put a finger under her chin and close her jaw. Jonna's hands slipped from around Decker's neck. "You might have said something," she said after a moment.

Decker shrugged. "I don't have the title. It hardly seemed worth mentioning without that. Colin's still the earl."

Jonna knew very well why he had never told her. "I suppose I deserve this little surprise," she said. "Though I'd have thought Colin or Mercedes would have given up your secret."

"They almost did. I asked them not to. It's not as if I have any interest in living at Rosefield. Colin's managers take care of the estate. I told Colin when he settled it on me that if we ever found Greydon I would cede it to him."

"And now that you have a rich wife you don't need that extra bit of baggage."

He grinned. "Precisely."

"Still," she said under her breath. "You might have hinted."

Decker's low laughter rumbled in his chest. He touched Jonna's cheek and kissed her lightly on the forehead.

Jonna settled back in his arms to snuggle against the warm breadth of his chest. "Did Graham know?" she asked.

"No. It wasn't a secret just from you. I never told anyone."

That softened her a bit. "I'm going to miss him," she said. "He was a good friend to us. Did you realize he was going to tell everyone he was Falconer?"

Decker shook his head. "Not until the words came out of

his mouth. I suppose Rachael's mistake gave him the idea. The first time she heard Falconer named was when Graham and I were trying to get her out of Charleston. We walked into the room where she was being held at the same time. Someone said Falconer. Neither Graham nor I acknowledged the name, but Rachael thought they were talking about Graham."

"A natural mistake," Jonna said. "He cuts a very dashing figure."

"You think so?"

Jonna lifted her head and smiled enigmatically. Decker erased it with a thorough kiss. "Oh, my," she said softly.

Decker went on as if there had been no interruption. "When Rachael made the same mistake on board the sloop, I think Graham saw an opportunity and seized it. It certainly set Sheridan off balance."

It had, Jonna remembered. "It could have ended there," she said. And it probably should have. Grant's murder and Rachael's suicide meant that no one knew of Graham's claim to the Falconer name. "He didn't have to tell the authorities that he was Falconer. I know some explanation was required for what happened that morning, but I don't know that he had to give that one."

"It was the most expedient."

Jonna didn't argue that point. She knew Decker was not speaking for himself as much as he was relating Graham's opinion. "He should have consulted us before he said anything. He took so much on his own shoulders with that admission. All of the responsibility. All of the blame."

"All of the heroics," Decker said dryly.

A small smile lifted the corners of Jonna's mouth as she recalled how much Graham had despised that consequence of his deception. The Boston papers, including Garrison's *The*

Liberator had filled columns with Falconer's exploits. Grant Sheridan's murder and the revelation that he was a slaver carried the front pages from Augusta, Maine, to Atlanta, Georgia. The emphasis of the reporting depended on geography. Northern accounts vindicated Rachael. In the South, she was vilified.

In all the stories Falconer lost his anonymity.

"Graham gave up so much," Jonna said quietly. "When he linked his name with Falconer he surrendered his family . . . his home. Do you think he considered all of that when he did it?"

"I think he considered it," Decker said. "And I think he weighed it against what could be gained if you and I were not implicated with the Underground. We're still free to act, even if he's not. That was what he wanted. Remington Shipping hasn't come under any particular scrutiny and *Huntress* will be able to move easily in and out of Southern ports. Our involvement with Sheridan was explained away by your long business and personal association with him."

Jonna's eyes lifted to Decker's. "Didn't you find that strange?" she asked.

"What?"

"Well, that no one really questioned me. I said I didn't know Grant was a slaver, and everyone believed me. I said I'd had no dealing with Falconer, and they believed that as well."

Decker grinned. "It was all in the way you said it," he told her. "I believed you myself."

"Really?" She considered that. "I never thought of myself as a particularly skillful liar."

"You're not." Decker touched her lips with his forefinger. "But that morning you were inspired . . . and convincing."

Jonna kissed the tip of his finger before she drew his hand away from her lips. She held it in both of hers, caressing the heart of it with her thumb. "I was frightened," she whispered, looking down at the hand in hers. "But not half so frightened as I would have been if you hadn't been there. When I saw that trunk go over the side, when I saw it start to sink—"

"I had already cut the ropes," Decker reminded her. He knew how much it pained her to think of him trapped in the trunk. She felt her own helplessness and imagined his terror. "I was almost free by then."

"Yes, but if Graham hadn't been on *Huntress*, if he hadn't been watching through the eyeglass, if he hadn't seen Grant's men drop the trunk overboard . . ." A small shudder went through her, and she closed her eyes momentarily. "It could have been—"

"It wasn't," he said gently. "It wasn't. They fished me out. I was wet and bruised and none the worse for it. Escaping a trunk is not so hard as you might believe. Jimmy Grooms had the way of it, and I learned a thing or two from him." He didn't tell Jonna that his part had always been to pick the pockets of the crowd while their attention was riveted on Jimmy making his escape. She wouldn't want to know that Grant Sheridan had provided him with his first opportunity to try Jimmy's techniques.

Jonna tried to imagine what it had been like for the men aboard *Huntress* when the trunk was opened and Decker stepped out. With the exception of Graham and Jack Quincy, she visualized them all as slack-jawed and wide-eyed, whistling in amazement just under the collective breath they released.

"I regret that we couldn't spend more time with Graham," she said. Of necessity, she and Decker had had to distance themselves from the man who was now called Falconer. They had successfully hidden the fact that Graham had ever been a guest in their home and it had not been difficult to make people believe their paths had only crossed with his because of Grant Sheridan—and for very different reasons. In the newspaper accounts it was reasoned out that Falconer's pursuit of the slaver had the timely and fortunate consequence of preventing Jonna's abduction. No one who knew the larger truth was prepared to come forward with it.

Decker's hand closed over Jonna's. He gave it a small squeeze. "I believe Graham regretted the same. He said as much last night."

"When you saw him off?"

Decker nodded. It had been a late departure. *Remington Siren*, bound for the China Seas, left Boston Harbor after nightfall. She carried a rich cargo and no passengers. The crew, with the exception of one new man, were used to the rigors of a long ocean voyage and knew what to expect. Graham Denison had only said that he was willing to learn. "He thanked you again."

"Thanked me?" That he should have done so startled Jonna. "For what? Putting him to work aboard *Siren*?"

"For helping him disappear."

Jonna sat up a little straighter. She looked hard at Decker. "Disappear? What do you mean? You never—" She stopped suddenly because she saw the answer revealed in Decker's eyes. He had known all along what it meant when Graham had expressed an interest in Remington Shipping. "I can't believe I was so naive," she said. "I thought Graham meant to learn the business the same way you did and Colin before you. It seemed a logical assumption since he can't return to Beau Rivage."

"Logical, perhaps. But wrong. He'll stay with *Siren* for a while. Maybe as far as Panama. Maybe all the way to Shanghai. But he won't be coming back to Boston. Not anytime soon. He had no peace here as Falconer. He had invitations to speak at abolition meetings the entire time he was recovering from his injuries. And once they knew he was healed the requests for his time tripled. He was asked to luncheons and dinners and teas, and he wanted none of it. Garrison wanted him to write about his experiences, a publisher contacted him about a book. Staying in Boston would have meant giving up something of himself that he wasn't prepared to surrender. I don't blame him for wanting to disappear."

"Neither do I," Jonna said softly. "But it doesn't mean I won't miss him." She burrowed more deeply against Decker. Her toes wriggled between his thigh and the arm of the chair.

"Cold?" he asked.

"A little."

"I can do something about the fire."

"No," she said. "I like it just like this. Next to you." She delved a little more deeply with her feet, pressing her toes into the warmth between the cushion of the chair and the arm. Her head lay against Decker's chest again. "This is very—"

Decker looked at Jonna's face. "What is it?"

Her frown deepened as she wiggled her toes. "Something just bit me." She gave a little yelp as it happened again and jumped off Decker's hap. "Something in that cushion bit me."

Grinning at her accusatory tone, Decker obligingly let himself be hauled to his feet so she could investigate. How like Jonna, he thought, not to be afraid of the thing that bit her, but to go right after it herself.

"Ah-ha!" she said triumphantly. She straightened and spun to face him, her fist closed around the object. "You really should be more careful, Decker." Jonna opened her fingers to reveal what she had found. In the heart of her palm she held a pearl stud in a crown setting. Dangling from it was an engraved raindrop of pure gold. "How many times can you expect to lose this and have it found again?"

Decker's brows drew together. He stared at the earring, but he didn't take it out of her hand. "It was in the cushion?" he asked.

Watching him, Jonna's smile became a bit uncertain. "You just saw me take it out of there."

He didn't say anything. Turning on his heel, he strode to the window. On the sill was the earring he had set there just before he took Jonna in his arms. He stared at it.

"Decker?" Jonna hesitated, wondering what kept him so still. When he didn't respond, she approached him slowly and laid a hand on his arm. "What is it?" Her eyes shifted from his sharply engraved features and the muscle working faintly in his jaw. She followed the line of his gaze. "That's not possible," she whispered. But she was seeing the earring on the sill and she was feeling the one clutched in her hand, so it had to be possible. But it couldn't.

Decker reached for the earring on the windowsill at the same time Jonna's fingers opened. He put his open palm beside hers, and they stared at the exquisite, perfectly identical pair. "This is the one you gave me on board Grant's sloop," he said. "The one you're holding is the one I thought I lost."

"How can you know that?"

"Because when you found it in the cushion I remembered how it came to be there. I was standing beside the chair, in the act of putting it in my pocket, when Rachael came into the room to change the linens. I must have missed the pocket and dropped it onto the chair instead."

Jonna was staring hard at the earring in his hand. "But Mrs. Davis gave me that one. She said Rachael found it in the laundry."

"She may have," Decker said. "But not in *my* clothes."

"Then whose? It's not as if there's been anyone else—'" A tremor seized Jonna's hand as the answer was borne home to her. Her fingers tightened spasmodically around the earring. She looked at Decker and knew she was seeing a mirror of her own awed expression. "The night he came here," she said softly. "His clothes . . . they were bloody and . . . and I gave them to Rachael to take away. She must have found it later and—"

"We can't know she got it that way."

"There's no other explanation. How else could Rachael have come by it?"

Decker didn't want to think it, let alone say it. "Sheridan."

"No. You don't believe that. You can't. Grant was older than you, Decker. He couldn't have been your brother."

"Graham might not be either. Possession of the earring isn't proof by itself. It might have been stolen. Graham has a family, remember? Grandparents, parents, a younger brother. He never mentioned that he was missing this, did he?"

"No, but—"

"Surely he would have valued it. Rachael must have come by it some other way."

Jonna shook her head firmly. "No. She gave it to Mrs. Davis because it didn't belong to her. It was Graham's, Decker. You allowed yourself to believe it for a moment. I saw it in your face. Now you're trying to talk yourself out of it. Why don't you want to believe again?"

Decker looked down at the earring in his palm for a long moment, then back at Jonna. "Because twelve hours ago I let him leave Boston Harbor," he said quietly. "I let him go, knowing that he wants to disappear."

Jonna's own smile was gentle. She placed one hand flat on his chest and lifted her face to his. "*Huntress* was built for the

455

chase," she said. Her violet eyes were bright now. She knew what could be done. "And you command her. What she can outrun, she can also capture. Twelve hours is nothing, Decker. You're Falconer. You can catch the *Siren*."

He had never held anything so dear as Jonna's absolute belief in him. Decker's arms circled her waist. He bent his head. "I already have," he whispered against her mouth. "I already have."